BOOK ONE OF AURAGOLE'S JOURNEY

auragole
of the
mountains

shirley latessa

A Waverly Press Book

Waverly Press
www.shirleylatessa.com

acknowledgments

I would like to thank all those who
have helped make this book possible:
Rebecca Schacht, Susan Handman,
Jeffrey Ward, Gabrielle Ortiz,
Gina Latessa, Yael Gani,
Jane Lincoln Taylor, Doug Safranek.

dedication

This book is dedicated to all
the young women and men who have
graduated or will graduate from
the Waldorf Schools worldwide.

Northern Desolation

Wild Woods

Mattelmead
City

Little Thoren

MATTELMEAD

Ancient
Woods

Thoren River

THORENSPHERE

Thoren
City

GLOVALE

S O R R E N H E I G H T S

Woeful
Peaks

North Gate

Noonbarr River

ISOFED

South Gate

WILDENFARR-
LOW-DESERT

Isofed River

Deep Forest

W e s t e r n   S e a

N

Southern Desolation

| 0 Miles | 100 | 200 | 300 |

| 0 Kilometers | 200 | 300 |

Northern
Valley

VALLEY of the AGAVI

Gandlese
Mountains

NOONBARR

Lake Mimbi

East Gate

Isofed River

Auragole's Valley

to the Easternlands →

Roaring River

Gandlese
Mountains

Bitter Sea

© 2003 Jeffrey L. Ward

Do not seek answers that cannot

be given to you,

because you would not be able to live them.

Live the questions now.

Perhaps you will then gradually,

without noticing it, some distant day,

live into the answer.

— RAINER MARIA RILKE

N

prologue

MEEKELORR, LYING NEAR a stream in the Easternlands with a small troop of his soldiers sleeping nearby, woke suddenly from a strange dream. He sat up, pushing away both the blankets and the grogginess. He wanted to think about the dream, to fix it in his mind so he could tell it to Pohl.

A young man was standing over a grave. Three other graves were nearby. Then, as happens in dreams, the young man was walking in the mountain forest heading somewhere with great determination. In the dream his friend Pohl had shaken him awake and then pointed to the boy. "Be aware and be wary, Meekelorr, that boy's destiny is woven into yours."

"I see him," Meekelorr assured Pohl. "The boy seems simple, pleasant enough, hardly a threat."

"You are shortsighted, friend. That boy is like a sleepwalker. He doesn't know what it is he is moving toward, yet he will be a determining player in the world events that are nearly upon us."

"He will aid us?"

"That," Pohl said, "or destroy us; then there will be little hope left for this world."

Meekelorr, fully awake now, reached over and shook his friend Pohl, who was snoring peacefully next to him.

The older man sat up quickly and grabbed his sword.

"Whoa, Pohl, no danger. But I must tell you this dream while I can recall it."

LORENWILE, PERFORMING IN a café in the capital city of Mattelmead on the northern coast of the Westernlands, almost faltered in mid-song. He was See-singing a song of battle for his audience, many of whom were officers in the army of Ormahn of Mattelmead, when an image interjected itself between him and the images he was singing. He recovered quickly and finished his performance.

Later, in his dressing room, Lorenwile thought about what he had seen. A boy standing at a grave, then moving through the woods in search of. . .what? What was his goal? But the boy had something to do with him. Could he be the one? If so, then Lorenwile would have to travel again. But not yet, not quite so soon.

Well, these are the days we have been waiting for, he thought with satisfaction. Everything that he did from now on he would have to do with quiet calculation.

Lorenwile rose from his makeup table, looked critically in the mirror at his appearance, once again polished his jeweled pendant, put on his easy-go-lucky grin, and strode out the door on his way to a late supper with members of Ormahn's court.

BINTA KNOCKED ON the door to the Lady Claregole's chambers. It was unusual for her to do so, since it was past midnight in the Valley of the Agavi in the Gandlese Mountains, and all in that peaceful hidden valley were asleep. But Binta felt that what she had to report to the Lady could not wait.

"What is it? What troubles you, Binta?" The Lady Claregole drew her night shawl around her shoulders and stepped back to allow her help-friend in.

"Oh, Lady, a far-seeing, a far-seeing!" she repeated over and over again.

The Lady drew the older woman to a chair near the fire. Though summer was not yet at an end, it was chilly at night in the mountains.

"Sit, my heart-friend." When she had arranged a coverlet around the old woman's legs, the Lady Claregole sat opposite her. "Now, tell me your far-seeing."

The woman shook her head and said, "Never, Lady, never in all my long life has my sight gone beyond our own valley or the nearby mountains, nor beyond our own people." Binta *tsked* in obvious wonder. "That is why I did not wait until morning to speak to you."

The Lady Claregole sat patiently while her help-friend composed herself.

"Lady," Binta finally began, "you and your brother have father-kin outside our own people."

The Lady Claregole's eyes widened. "Truly?" she said, but not in disbelief.

"Truly," Binta responded. "He is great-nephew to your father, Lady. And this young man, hardly more than a boy, begins now a journey in search of your father. Alas, futile from the start." Binta once again shook her head. Then her face brightened. "But, dear Lady, I think his footsteps will bring him here to our valley; though, as he is not one of us, I cannot say for certain."

The Lady nodded. "Thank you, Binta. This is curious news indeed. I will tell my brother in the morning." She stopped speaking, for Binta's brow had furrowed, her eyes closed, and her hands moved in the air. "What are you seeing, heart-friend?"

"Something else, something else. . ."

Claregole sat back in her chair and waited.

"He, he. . .forgive me, Lady, but I cannot see his heart. He is not Agavian. But this I do see and know, he has some part to play in the Last Battle."

Claregole rose from her chair. "Then it will be in our life-time." She smiled at the older woman. "So, all the signs are read correctly—and here is yet another one. Come, Binta, I will see you to your room," and she helped her out of the chair.

"Wait," Binta said, as they moved through the door. She stood in the hall of the Great Mansion, her eyes shut tight, her hands again making strange gestures in the air. "There is more—a strangeness I can barely fathom."

She opened her eyes, and the two women resumed moving toward Binta's room. "I cannot see whether he will aid us or bring us harm," and Binta shook her head in confusion.

"Ah, my dear heart-friend, that too is because he is not Agavian." She hugged the woman. "Sleep, dear Binta. You have done well," and Claregole left Binta at her door.

A few moments later, lying in her own bed, the Lady Claregole pondered the odd news that Binta had brought her.

THE STARMASTER, SITTING over his calculations in his cottage in the Sorren Heights, stopped and stared at his own writings. Then, with Beya, the she-wolf that was his companion, he stepped out of the cottage and walked up the short path to the small plateau at the top of the hill, where he could see without obstruction the dome of the heavens. It was August. The night was cloudless and ablaze with stars. He stared for a long time, patting Beya, who sat next to him contentedly.

"So, Beya, the time has come. The boy is leaving his valley. Somewhere here in the Westernlands the Nethergod waits and prepares. And the boy begins his own journey."

The wolf looked up at her friend.

"What the outcome will be is not known." The Starmaster

turned to descend the path back to the cabin. "You see, Beya," he said as if she could comprehend, "the stars no longer compel. The boy is free to pick up his task, turn away from it, or turn it into a terrible evil. Such is freedom in our times, friend. Such are our times."

THE ONE SOME in humanity called the Nethergod stood staring out the window of his manor house. He looked past the manicured lawns and into the trees on their far side. He was seeing the woods there, but also another forest where a young man, hardly more than a boy, was preparing to leave his home.

So, he thought, watching the innocent scene in his mind's eye, the boy is about to begin his journey. Good. Good. We will let him wander for the time being. When the times are propitious for us, we shall cast our net and see if we cannot gather up this little fish.

first friends

PART ONE OF AURAGOLE'S JOURNEY
AURAGOLE OF THE MOUNTAINS

N

preface

HE WAS STANDING on a flat plain, the grass like silk and soft as down. Twelve mountains encircled him, their perfect peaks reaching up to a flaxen-colored sky.

Beautiful, beautiful, he thought, lifting up his arms in a joyous gesture.

"Auragole."

"Auragole, gold, golden, hear. . ."

He turned round and round, seeking the source of the words that the wind carried like dandelion puffs toward him. His name caressed his face, and what else? Gold. Hear what?

"What, what?" he cried to the purple and ruby mountains. Music.

"Sing to me," he called with longing.

The thought—he could almost see it, almost hear it—fluttered between the peaks like a bird singing.

"Auragole."

"Yes."

"See, child of humanity."

"What?" he begged.

Sunless light turned the sky into a chalice, pouring amber-colored wine down the sides of the mountains into the valley. He knelt, his face upturned to taste the wine; then he flung himself on his back to gaze with pure delight at the radiant sky that filled his eyes with its sweetness.

"*Auragole.*"

He turned his head to watch the sound dance over the grass.

"East," it said, "west."

"Yes?" he asked. "What?"

"*Auragole.*"

"Yes," he answered, sitting up.

"Auragole."

"Yes."

This time the call brought him out of the dream into half consciousness. He stood up. The downy grass slowly disappeared and joy ran out of him like rain down a tree trunk. A hard earthen floor was under his sandaled feet. A familiar sorrow began to creep into the hollow of his bones. He struggled first to hang on to the dream, wanting desperately to lose himself there where the mountains and the sky enclosed him in their nurturing embrace.

"Not back here," he whispered.

But the dream faded.

Though it was dark he knew he was in his mother's room. It was too cold. The fire had gone out and he cursed himself. The August nights had been unusually chilly this year. It was as if autumn was sending its message ahead of it on a wind that came roaring out of the north. Auragole had meant to stay awake, but too many nights of sleeplessness had taken their toll and he had fallen into a deep slumber in the rocking chair.

He moved to the window and pulled back the heavy curtains. It was still dark. Thick clouds covered the stars. It would rain soon.

"Auragole."

He dropped the curtains and hurried to his mother's bed.

"It's cold," she whispered in a voice as thin as a cobweb.

"I'll light the fire," he said, and started toward the hearth.

"Wait," her voice was barely audible. "No time." Her hand reached out and grasped his sleeve.

Stricken, he knelt down at her bedside; the hope he hadn't known was there, crumbling like dried earth about his knees. He couldn't see her face, drawn and wasted now. Only her long, shiny, black hair had remained unchanged as the illness had taken more and more hold of her body. He took her hand.

"A favor, son. Please. . ."

"Mother, anything, what?"

"A deed for me, a last deed."

"Anything." And he willed the tears to halt behind the painful sting of his eyes.

A chorus of sounds fluttered eerily through the moist night as he listened attentively to his mother's final request, holding her bony hand next to his dry cheek.

N

chapter one

AURAGOLE FINISHED SHOVELING the dirt on his mother's grave in the pouring rain, then stood there with water sliding down his long black hair, down his face, mingling with his tears. Tomorrow, before leaving, he would plant the purple irinus on her grave as he and his mother had for his father, Goloss, two years earlier, and six months before that for Spehn, who lay next to his wife—their tiny stillborn daughter encircled in her mother's arms. Four graves. Now he was the only one left of their small community.

After his father died, it seemed as if the will to live had gone out of Itina. Yet how often his parents had quarreled—usually about him, about how he was being raised, about what he should be taught. Auragole hated their fighting. He tried his best to please them both. But it was difficult. Often he would slip out of the house when the arguments began, go down to the creek, and throw pebbles into the stream. When Spehn was alive, he sometimes joined him. Spehn, dear Spehn—he had been Auragole's salvation when the conflicting demands of his parents had created confusion in him.

Standing at his mother's grave, Auragole wanted to say some words—some words of comfort, of forgiveness, of farewell—but no words came to him. He turned from the graves and walked back to the cottage. It was cold. The fire had nearly gone out. Placing several logs on the embers, he stood before the struggling flames drying off. No need now to be sparing of the wood. Tomorrow he would turn the animals loose—what else could he do?—and then head east.

He looked around at what had been his home for nearly eighteen years. Would he ever come back? He doubted it. Hadn't he always wanted, as long as he could remember, to leave this place—at least for a time—and go out into the great world to find adventure? He had never spoken of these desires—not even to Spehn. After all, his family had run from that world, where, they had told him time and again, there was only war and chaos. They had journeyed far into these deserted mountains to find, finally, their valley and with it, shelter and peace. It often made him ashamed that he was not content with what his family had found for themselves and, they thought, for him. But, oh, how he longed for adventures, like those in the stories he had heard—mostly from his mother, but also from Spehn—and like the ones in the poems his mother had recited for him and made him learn by heart, and the songs Spehn had sung to him and taught him. As a child, he knew he would have to wait until he was sixteen. It was then his father planned to take him back to the Easternlands to find for him a wife, and perhaps others to join their community. But before Auragole turned sixteen, his father became ill. Unexpectedly, Spehn had died after a short illness, and six months later, his father. It was then that Auragole realized he would never leave his valley—at least not while his mother was alive. And so, heart aching, he had given up his dreams, had farmed and hunted, and had helped his mother maintain their small holding.

And now. . .she, too, was gone. Did she know when she laid that final task on him, that she was also setting him free?

Auragole helped himself to what was left of the stew simmering in the pot over the fire and sat and ate it all with little appetite. It was habit. One never wasted food.

After he finished his meal, Auragole assembled the things he would take with him on his journey: clothes, his extra pair of boots, food, medicinal herbs, the sword Spehn had given him as he lay dying, the bow he had made with his father, along with the arrows he himself had made, the best knife in the house— the one that had belonged to Goloss—some cooking and eating utensils, and the small harp his father and Spehn had made for him. He thought about taking the few books that were his mother's treasure, that had been part of his daily lessons, but decided to leave them. They were heavy, and after all, he knew each by heart. If only he had a horse, but the wild horse he and his father had captured after a week's tracking was dead now two years. And with his father and Spehn both gone, he had not been able to capture another one.

After packing, after the rains had stopped, Auragole stood in the doorway of the cottage, gazing out at the familiar view. Mountains were much feared by the people of both east and west, especially the wild Gandlese range that divided the Easternlands from the Westernlands. It was believed by most people, Auragole had been told, that unearthly beasts had come to dwell there after the Golden Century. That was five hundred years ago, during the first years of the continuous wars that had destroyed the countries in both the east and west. But Auragole had never seen any strange, unearthly creature, and his father had laughed at the superstitions of the Easterners.

The clouds hung now like shrouds over the mountains that surrounded his valley, but Auragole knew the shape and color of each. When the mists hid the mountains as they did now, he had often thought—even as a child—that they, at least, had been given a chance to escape for a time from their eternal vigil.

WALKING THROUGH THE mountain forest toward the east that first day, Auragole was filled with an indescribable and unaccustomed strangeness. For the first time in his life, the future, which had been as dependable as the seasons, was unreadable. It filled him with uncertainty but also with excitement. He was free—free, perhaps in a way his father had never meant by the word he so loved. Free, the way a wild animal might feel if it were able to form thoughts.

When he camped that night, he could not fall asleep. He felt, alongside his still-strong sense of loss, a great longing for this new, unreadable future. And it was due to his mother that he was heading toward it. He lay near the fire thinking of her. She had been a stern woman, a demanding woman, often angry with him.

But he had not wanted her to die.

And she had not wanted to live.

Before she closed her eyes for the last time, she had extracted a promise from him. And he meant to keep it. She had begged him to go back to the Easternlands, to her birth land of Stahlowill, there to seek out her uncle, and ask him for. . . But she had not lived long enough to tell him what he was to ask of his great-uncle. Eagalorr was the only member of Itina's family who had been alive when she left over twenty years ago. Auragole doubted he was still alive after so many years and so much war. But Auragole had promised her that he would seek him. And wasn't he going where he had always wanted to go, toward a world of people, toward a world of adventure?

N

chapter two

SYLVANE WAS BEING stalked, and it filled her with fear. She was in these endless and unfamiliar mountain woods trying to find the eldenmyrr flower to make a healing broth for her foster sister, Glenelle, and had wandered too far from their campsite. But she had been concerned for Glenelle's health, and had been intently watching the ground, looking among the stones and shadows for the shy flowers with their small white petals. It was foolish to walk here with so little concern, but the vast Gandlese Mountains were, they had been told, uninhabited.

And then she had heard the sounds.

With mounting alarm, she thought that it must be some strange, unearthly Gandlesean creature that was following her, and she began to run, quickly losing her bearings. She had heard terrible stories about these unnatural beasts back east in her settlement. That was why few people ever ventured into this mountain range. Only traveling with the caravans that came from east to west a few times a year was safe.

But maybe it wasn't a beast. Maybe her pursuer was one of those fierce, dreaded warriors known as Guttlubbers. But how could that be? Surely, those terrible killer soldiers were not here in the Gandlese. They were all over the Easternlands, she had been told. Her foster father had seen them, had even fought with them. They dressed in uniforms of gray and white. Like wraiths, Sylvane had imagined them. Still, it was only rumor that the Guttlubbers had a hideout in the Gandlese. No one had actually traveled there to corroborate the story.

No, this creature following her must be some sort of Gandlesean beast, for if it were a killer soldier, wouldn't he have struck by now?

Not very comforted, she tried desperately to lose the beast. But no matter which way she turned, whatever hiding place she found, when she came out of it, she could still hear the thing behind her. Yet it never showed itself, had not yet attacked. Sylvane's nerves were so frayed she needed to scream. But she was afraid to scream. How much longer could she run?

Why doesn't it do something, anything?

She continued to run, as fast as she could, barefoot, thoroughly losing herself amid the tall, unfamiliar trees and brush. All sense of direction left her. When she came, for the third time, to the old elm log that lay like a bridge between two maples, her frustration overwhelmed her. Sylvane sat down, and did what she hardly ever did—she cried.

What happened next completely bewildered her. From a clump of bushes behind her she heard a sweet male voice singing. It was so unexpected and yet so comforting that after her initial amazement, she gave up weeping and listened, momentarily forgetting her fear.

Go now, my child, into silver dreams.
Glide with the fish beneath golden streams.
Fly with the birds in blue-black skies.

Soar with the sun when it starts to rise.
Sleep well, my child, and have no fear,
I am here.

A thousand miles,
a thousand tears,
a thousand hopes,
a thousand fears.
Far we have come,
far you will roam.
Only my love
will call you home.
Only my love
to be your nest.
Come to my arms, child,
here find rest.

Child, be the wind in the high Gandlese.
Lie on the grass and take your ease.
Float on a lake of snow-white foam.
Then take my hand, I'll bring you home.
Sleep well, my child, and have no fear,
I am here.

A thousand miles,
a thousand tears,
a thousand hopes,
a thousand fears.
Far we have come,
far you will roam.
Only my love
will call you home.
Only my love
to be your nest.

Come to my arms, child,
here find rest.

Relief flooded through her. It was human. Thank the stars, it was human and not some ravenous beast. Nothing to fear. She stood up suddenly. Nothing to fear? Where she came from, humans, outside those of one's own settlement, were more to be feared than animals, unearthly or not. And what if this was a Guttlubber?

A tall young man with long black hair stepped out of the trees—a hunting bow held loosely in his hand, a short sword at his hip, a pack on his back, and a harp slung over his shoulder. Sylvane jumped up from the log with a loud intake of breath and once again ran as fast as she was able.

"Wait, please," he called. "Why are you running from me?"

But Sylvane, terrified, didn't wait. She flew on and on, with her pursuer loping behind her, calling, "Wait! Please wait!" until, moments later, she suddenly fell to the ground, a large splinter embedded in her foot.

In a moment he was hovering over her.

"Please," his words were barely above a whisper, "don't be frightened." And then he knelt next to her, took her foot in his hand, and carefully looked at its bottom. "It's a splinter. Shall I take it out for you?" His gaze never left her face.

Sylvane swallowed her fear and nodded. The young man stood up, placed his bow on the ground, removed his backpack and small harp, and set them next to his bow.

Well, he's not dressed in gray and white, Sylvane noted with relief, just brown trousers and shirt, a nicely woven vest, and a black wool cape. He's probably not a Guttlubber.

He was quite tall, half a head taller than her foster brother, Glenorr. He had handsome features, not quite a man's yet. She guessed he was eighteen or nineteen, close to her own age. One could see that in a few years he would be broad of chest and shoulder. His eyes looked coal black in the late-afternoon light and he watched her with barely a blink.

"Don't stare!" Sylvane said, surprising herself with her own temerity.

He blushed. "Forgive me, I'm forgetting my manners. But you see, I've never seen a *young* woman before. You are very pleasing."

That startled her even more. She was lost and vulnerable. Sylvane stood up, prepared to flee again, but the weight on her injured heel made her gasp.

"Wait!" he said. "What have I done? Why do you run from me?"

His voice sounded so troubled, so forlorn, that Sylvane sat down once more, cautious but curious.

"Why have you been chasing me?" she asked, her words chiding. She sat down and took her aching foot into her hand. It was red around the wound.

"Not chasing," he said, "following."

He knelt down, removed a small tool and some salve from his pack and, putting her foot on his lap, quickly worked the large sliver out. Then he put salve on the wound.

"Why were you following me?" Sylvane asked.

"I don't know. I meant no harm. It's just that I hadn't thought to see another human in these woods. You'd best put your boots on, even if it hurts. The woods are no place for bare feet."

"I was hot," Sylvane said, but pulled the boots from around her neck where she had worn them tied like a shawl by their laces. It hurt to put the boots on, but she was determined not to show it. "Why didn't you just come out and show yourself?"

"I don't know. . . Seeing you was. . .was unexpected."

He's definitely peculiar, Sylvane decided, as she tied the laces on her boots.

The young man sat back on his heels and watched her.

"You're staring again!"

"I'm sorry. I don't mean to be rude. I apologize." He lowered his eyes but only for a moment. "You don't look at all like my mother."

"What is that supposed to mean?" Sylvane's inflection rose slightly. "Why should I look like your mother?"

The young man scrutinized her again, then answered her, his voice sounding strained. "I've never seen a woman. . .other than my mother."

"Really?" She struggled to look imperious.

"My family lived on a small farm, four days from here. It's quite isolated, and my mother was the only woman there." Head cocked, he gazed at her short brown hair.

She ran her fingers through her hair, trying to bring some order to the unruly curls.

"My mother had long, straight black hair, like mine, which she wore in two braids tied around her head." He twisted his hands in the air to show her. "And she was as tall as I am, and ample. Your hair is short and brown like a squirrel's and full of ringlets. And I never thought women could be so short and small of bone."

Frankly, she didn't like being assessed so. "Young man," her tone was arch, though she was again thoroughly alarmed, "you cannot go around speaking to women like that. To speak so is odd, and if you had not been so helpful I would certainly run away again. Everyone knows women come in all sizes and with all colors of hair."

He blushed. She watched his inner struggle. "I do know that. I know that," he said, "from story and song, but I've never seen it for myself. If I'm not showing you my best manners, then I apologize." His fingers brushed across his forehead.

He's obviously sorry for upsetting me, she thought. Seeing his confusion, her heart went out to him and once again she lost her fear. "Now it's I who am rude. Thank you for removing my sliver."

"You are very welcome."

She held out her hand, which he took, then quickly dropped.

"What are you called?" she asked.

"Auragole, son of Goloss and Itina."

She waited for him to go on, but he was silent, watching her intently. It was disconcerting. "Did you say you come from these mountains?" she finally asked.

"Yes."

"But I thought no one lived in these mountains!"

"I am the last." There was a catch in his voice. "My mother died seven days ago. Come autumn it will be two years since my father died of the wasting disease, and six months before that our friend, Spehn, died of a fever. I am all that is left of our community," and his face filled with sadness. "My father was from the Easternlands and escaped to the Gandlese from the wars. He dreamt of a new community that would arise in these mountains. He came away from the country of Stahlowill with nearly forty souls. But because of the terrible tales his companions had heard about the Gandlese, many of those who had followed him were afraid to go so far into the mountains. They remained in the eastern foothills."

Only Spehn and Spehn's wife had followed his parents, he told her. The two couples had driven their cattle and donkeys, had carried their seeds and their tools farther than the others had dared.

"Our valley in the Gandlese is the only home I've known." Auragole's black eyes softened and he swallowed hard. Then he stopped and waited.

So Sylvane said, "Go on."

"Well, Spehn's wife died in childbirth not long after I was born and their child died too." Auragole's words came out haltingly. "Since my mother bore no other child, my father's dream also died."

"Sad. . .but that seems to be the way of dreams, doesn't it?"

"I don't know anything about that," he answered, after a moment's thought. "I know that Goloss planned to go east with me when I was sixteen to find. . ." and he blushed, ". . .a wife for me and hopefully find others to join our community. But his illness prevented it."

"Were you happy in your valley?" She thought it sounded idyllic.

Auragole sat staring at the ground and rubbing absently at his forehead. Sylvane thought that he was not going to answer her. But just as she was about to speak, he said, "It was a life without adventure, you see, and a life without people."

For her part, Sylvane thought him very lucky indeed to have been away from people who fought constantly, and over everything.

Auragole stood up and put the salve and tool back into his pack.

"I'm sorry about your family," Sylvane said. "Still, you are one of the lucky ones. Your family escaped from terrible turmoil. You are fortunate indeed to have had a quiet childhood."

"Perhaps that is so." He stood a few feet from her, watching her again. "May I ask your name?"

"It's Sylvane."

"How is it that you are all alone in these mountains?"

Sylvane looked out at the endless trees and shuddered, suddenly remembering that she was lost. "I'm not alone; at least I wasn't before you started chasing me all over these woods."

He apologized once again.

She was angry, but her anger wasn't really directed at him. "I'm being rude again. Sorry."

She told him that she and her foster sister, Glenelle, and her foster brother, Glenorr, the twins, had started out on a caravan. The caravan had left the Easternlands on its way to the country of Mattelmead in the Westernlands.

"But now we're traveling by ourselves." She thought it best

not to tell him that they had been put off the caravan.

Auragole came back to where Sylvane was sitting and crouched down in front of her.

"My father and I saw a caravan from a distance once when we were out hunting—before my father became ill. It was heading north. My father thought it might be heading to a long winding valley in the northern mountains that leads down into the Westernlands."

"Yes, yes, the Northern Valley," Sylvane said excitedly. "That's the route of the caravans."

"But why go to the west? Isn't the west also war-torn? So my father was told before he left the Easternlands."

"But that was long ago, and much has changed since your father left the east."

"Ah. I saw one other caravan, also heading north. That was after my father died and I was out hunting alone."

"Why didn't you contact them?"

"My father warned me to be careful of the caravans. He said they could bring death and the destruction of our community. He didn't trust other human beings much. Nor did Spehn."

"And you, are you afraid of humans?"

"I don't know any." He pointed to the pile of flowers she had dropped. "You've been gathering eldenmyrr. For what purpose?"

"It's for my foster sister, Glenelle. The trip has been hard on her. Her health is. . ." Sylvane didn't meet his eyes. "Her health is. . .fragile so we couldn't keep up with the pace of the caravan. That's why we left it." At least half of her statement was true. She turned back to him. "I want to make her some eldenmyrr tea. It will strengthen her."

"My mother too used eldenmyrr as a strengthening tea." Auragole stared at her until she colored and looked away. Rising, he asked, "Where are your friends?"

"That's just it," she said. "I don't know. Your chasing me about in the forest has made me lose my way." Sylvane knew she was being cruel, that her accusation was only half true. She had probably wandered too far before he began to follow her.

"Then we must find them." He offered her his hand.

"How?" Sylvane took his hand and stood up. "One place looks much like another in these endless mountains—around and around and up and down. . ." She stared out at the dark forest and shook her head.

"We'll follow the trail you made. It will lead us to them."

"Really?" she said, and threw her arms about him in thanks. Reddening, he pulled away, and picked up his backpack, harp, and bow. Sylvane gathered up the spilled flowers.

"Because of your injured foot, we'll move slowly," he said, and led the way into the trees.

They walked in silence for a time. "I'm sorry about your mother," she finally said. "I had two mothers taken from me by death."

He gave her a look so filled with sympathy that she lost her heart. Like a butterfly it fluttered wildly, then flew out of her. . . like that. She didn't question it.

As they walked, Auragole studied the ground intently.

"What are you looking for?"

"For signs of your footsteps." He pointed now and then to a broken twig, an overturned stone, trampled leaves, a footprint in the moist soil.

Sylvane gave herself over to his guidance with no more worry.

As they walked, the sun moved lower through the trees, slanting its light and casting long, eerie shadows.

"To where are you traveling, Auragole?"

"I'm going to the Easternlands, to the north, to my parents' country. Have you ever been to Stahlowill?"

"No. I've never heard of it. But the Easternlands is very large. They say it stretches a thousand miles from the Gandlese to the Eastern Ocean. And I don't know how long it is, north to south. So Stahlowill must be far from Mape. Mape is in the south near the Bitter Sea. Have you heard of it?"

He shook his head. "Stahlowill is a hilly land, though I understand much of the Easternlands is flat as a cake."

"Very flat—not like this." She looked around.

"I can't imagine it." He smiled.

Sylvane realized that it was the first time he had smiled since she met him. He has a lovely smile, she thought, and her heart gave another little flutter. "If flat land is strange to you, mountains are confusing to me. One gets turned around so easily."

"I hope to find my mother's uncle in Stahlowill," Auragole said after they had walked a time in silence. "It was my mother's dying request. He was a teacher at a school there when my parents left. If he is still alive, he would be the only kin I have left. But he must be quite old now."

"How old are you?" Sylvane asked.

"Come end of September I will be eighteen. And you?"

"I was eighteen last June. And the twins are twenty-one. So there's no one left at your farm now?"

"No one. A few days ago, I turned our animals loose, boarded up the cottage and barn, packed what I could carry, and left."

"Will you go back there?"

"I don't know."

And then they were at the camp. He had, to Sylvane's relief, found it in less than an hour.

N

chapter three

IT WAS THERE that Auragole first saw Glenelle. He stopped at the sight of her and the moment froze, then cracked open. Auragole could not hold on to the contents of his soul. Feelings he was unable to name flew out of him like trapped birds suddenly set free. Glenelle's skin, next to the darkness of her blue cloak, looked translucent. Her long golden hair lay all around her face like a pillow made from strands of the sun. She was like the heroines in the stories his mother had told him—heroines he had seen only in his imagination. Her face was fine-featured, with high cheekbones and soft, well-shaped lips. He stood unable to move, so shaken was he by the sight of Glenelle lying next to a shallow stream.

Auragole exhaled deeply and turned to see Sylvane watching him with an unnameable expression on her face. She sighed, gave him a half smile, and said, "She is lovely, isn't she?"

The quivering of his breath was his only response.

Without warning, an arm flew around Auragole's throat and a knife pressed dangerously against his ribs.

"Don't move or you're dead!"

Auragole had been so intent on the sleeping girl that he hadn't heard anyone approach.

"It's all right, Glen." Sylvane's words were sharp. "He's a friend."

"How do you know? How do you know he's not a Guttlubber?" There was a dangerous edge to the man's voice. The knife did not leave Auragole's side.

"Am I such a fool that I cannot tell who's a friend or who's a foe?" Sylvane sounded furious. "Of course, he's not a Guttlubber. Look at his clothes. Step back, Glen. Let him be."

Auragole had not moved. But he could feel the temper rise up hot.

"Tell him to drop his things," Glenorr demanded, "and to turn around slowly." Carefully, he removed his arm from around Auragole's throat and the knife from his ribs. Holding it ready, Glenorr warily backed away.

Auragole did not need Sylvane to repeat Glenorr's message. Curiosity warred with anger in his face. But he held his tongue and slowly dropped his pack, his bow, his sword, and his harp to the ground. He turned to face a young man with blond, neck-length hair that hung in waves. He was broader in the chest and shoulders than Auragole, but not as tall. He looked amazingly like his sister, but where her face looked sweet and serene in sleep, his looked hard and cold. And his jaw was tense. Auragole had no doubt that the man could use the knife he was holding. He remembered then what Spehn had told him about the untrustworthiness of the human race.

". . .*People are not often the way they are in the stories we have told you, nor are there many living who are filled with the virtues and qualities your mother has tried to instill in you. . .*"

"Speak," Glenorr ordered Auragole. "Who are you?" His knife was pointed at him, and he had crouched down ready to spring.

Auragole said in a tight voice, "I am called Auragole, son of Goloss." He glared at Glenorr. "And I am from these mountains."

Sylvane's words were a torrent rushing out as she explained how they had met and how Auragole had led her back to the camp, and some of what he had told her about his life.

Glenorr's eyes never left Auragole's face as she spoke. But finally he seemed satisfied. "That's all right then," he said, and put the knife back in his belt with no apology, and held out his hand. His eyes, which had been cold as a glacier only a moment before, now looked like a clear summer sky.

Auragole's anger melted away. He took the young man's proffered hand. They're from the east, Auragole told himself. It's natural for them to be cautious with strangers. He would have to learn to accept such wariness, even to emulate it if he was going to survive when he arrived in the Easternlands.

"Come look at what I've found." Glenorr's face lit up with pleasure.

Sylvane pulled Auragole by the sleeve. Glenorr led them to a heap of stones piled under a yellow-tinged beech. His mood had completely altered and the previous tension he had exhibited seemed forgotten. "I've been categorizing these stones and rocks. I've never seen the likes of them in all the Easternlands."

Auragole didn't understand. He looked first at Glenorr and then at Sylvane.

"I shall have to take them with me, of course," Glenorr went on. "It's possible that they are unknown in the Westernlands. I've been so busy, I didn't know the day had gotten away. If I had realized how long you were gone, Sylvie, I would have come looking for you myself. Did you find the eldenmyrr?"

"Yes."

"That's good." Then he seated himself next to his finds, leaned against the smooth gray bark of the beech, and began writing in a large, well-worn book that he had withdrawn from under his cloak. Instantly he was absorbed in his work.

Sylvane pulled Auragole away from Glenorr and over to the campfire, which had nearly gone out. Auragole didn't know what to think. He was very confused about this, his first meeting with people outside his small community. As a consequence, he kept silent and helped Sylvane gather twigs to rekindle the fire.

"Glenorr's been collecting stones and plants all the way from Lake Mimbi," she told him, as they moved about the edges of the clearing. "I don't know how much more our poor donkey can carry. Glenorr's very clever. He hopes to go to the Academy for Nature and Categorizing in Mattelmead. It's been a dream of his ever since the first stories about Mattelmead came to our settlement. He wants to study in Mattelmead City with real teachers."

"Why, if you're going to the Westernlands, have you come almost directly south from Lake Mimbi? The route the caravans use is west from Mimbi and then north."

"Directly south? Have we?" Sylvane paled. "Glen," she called, "we've been traveling south, instead of heading west before turning north. Didn't I say so?"

"Well, it's a lucky thing," he called back. "These stones are a real discovery," and Glenorr bent over them with no concern for their plight.

"Were none of you taught how to travel by the position of the stars?" Auragole asked, perplexed. "Or how to follow the movement of the sun?"

"We don't know anything about the stars," Sylvane said.

"But. . .but then how do you find your way?"

"We know, of course, the way the sun travels," Sylvane said, "but here in the mountain forests it's not easy to see the sun. The days are often cloudy and there are no roads, only goat trails. We must have misjudged." She stood, hands on hips, staring at Glenorr, a forlorn look on her face. "We were given maps, but they are difficult to follow, especially here in the mountains."

Then from the stream came a soft moan. Sylvane instantly turned her attention on the sleeping girl. "Come," she said to Auragole, "and meet Ellie." She took him by the sleeve and led him to her.

"She's so beautiful. . ." he said, trying to retrieve the birds his soul had once again loosed.

Glenelle's eyes were closed, her arm flung over her brow to protect her eyes from the afternoon light. The sleeve of her blouse had fallen away, leaving her arm bare.

Auragole swallowed as he admired its curve. "How white her skin is."

"She's pale because she's been ill," Sylvane said. "I'd better put the eldenmyrr on to brew."

She left him sitting on his heels watching Glenelle and hurried to where their supplies were.

Auragole watched Glenelle as he had often watched sunsets as a boy, her loveliness filling him with an unspeakable joy.

The sleeping girl moaned again. Auragole stood up, uncertain what to do.

"I can't anymore," Glenelle said, in her half sleep.

Sylvane came quickly back and shook Glenelle gently by the shoulder. "Wake up, Ellie."

"They won't let me go," Glenelle whispered.

"Yes they will. Wake up."

Glenelle's eyelids fluttered.

"Sit up, Ellie." Sylvane pulled her to a sitting position.

Startled, Glenelle's eyes flew open.

"We have company," Sylvane said, almost shouting.

"Company?"

"Yes, yes." Sylvane turned to Auragole. "Say something to her."

"Hello," he said, his voice hoarse. He looked beseechingly at Sylvane.

"Tell her your name."

He cleared his throat. "My name is Auragole and I met Sylvane in the woods." He didn't know what else to say.

It was enough. Glenelle looked at him, awake now.

"Auragole, what a nice name." Glenelle's eyes met Auragole's.

He saw that they were as blue as Glenorr's. But where Glenorr's had greeted him with ice, Glenelle's were the blazing blue flames of fever.

"Sylvie, it's so chilly here," Glenelle said, though it was midday and August warm.

"I'll build up the fire," Auragole said, and was quickly on his feet. He turned from Glenelle, pulling himself away from the strangeness he was feeling, relieved to be doing something. He gathered sticks and branches in the shadows of the trees and soon the fire he and Sylvane had kindled was blazing.

Sylvane helped Glenelle to the fire. She sat there, wrapped in her cloak and blanket, trembling. Sylvane put the pot of healing herbs on to brew as Auragole fed sticks to the fire. As the heat increased, Glenelle ceased her shivering.

Finally, his task completed, Auragole sat down across from the two women and stared once again at Glenelle. As if Glenelle felt his gaze, she turned her head from watching the slow progress of leaves floating on the stream to rest her eyes on Auragole's. He began to feel the blood rise to his face.

"Won't you stay for supper?" Glenelle invited him in a voice just above a whisper. It was a lovely voice, he thought—soft, yet musical, like water slipping over stones.

"Certainly he'll stay for supper," Sylvane said, "and camp here tonight, too."

"I'll stay if you let me contribute something," Auragole said, and stumbled to his feet. He had to get away, if only for a few minutes. "I'll catch some fish. Will that do?" And when Glenelle clapped her hands in delight, he unpacked his net, and disappeared around a curve, heading up the stream.

That evening, at the meal, Auragole asked the Easterners for news from the Easternlands. He was eager to know anything and everything they could tell him. "Everything I know about the east is from my parents and that information is twenty years old."

"It's probably worse now than when your parents lived there," Glenorr said, tossing twigs into the fire. "Nearly five hundred years of wars and battles, and no peace in sight. At least not in the Easternlands," he added. "There's no law in the Easternlands."

Sylvane, hugging her knees, picked up the narrative. "They say that there are lands beyond the Eastern Ocean, but it's been centuries since anyone has heard from them. No one sails the great seas any longer, and only a few hardy souls on the Grand Continent travel the lakes or rivers. Terrible monsters live in the waters," she told Auragole. When she asked him if he had ever seen any strange creatures in the rivers or lakes in the Gandlese, he shook his head.

"Well," she told him, "no one who has ventured out onto the sea has ever returned. And I know for a certainty that there are weird and fierce creatures in the rivers, for I've seen them myself."

In the Easternlands, Glenorr told Auragole, the once rigidly guarded borders of past kingdoms were long gone, and gone too were the great towns and cities of the Golden Century. All learning, commerce, all culture had disappeared. Only the settlements survived—small farming communities held together by strong leaders.

"Yes, I have heard of settlements. My father told me of them," Auragole said.

These communities, Glenorr told him, fought endlessly among themselves with weapons of a bygone time, for gone too was much practical and almost all technical knowledge.

"It's just as well," Sylvane said, "for if we had had the weapons of our forefathers, perhaps all of humanity would be gone by now."

"That's stupid!" Glenorr said. "We have lost all technical knowledge that might have saved our civilization. Nothing is as terrible as the loss of our science and our technology."

"How about all the loss of life?" Sylvane retorted.

"Don't start that old argument, you two," Glenelle murmured from where she sat huddled in her cloak and blankets.

Glenorr ignored Sylvane and directed his words at Auragole. "In the Easternlands, settlements not only fight each other but they also battle marauding bands of landless persons wanting settlements of their own. Sylvane, Glenelle, and myself are from a settlement in Mape, in the south."

"Why are you are going to the Westernlands?"

Glenorr drew his knees up and looked thoughtful.

"The father of the twins, Ardur," Sylvane answered, "is leader in our settlement. . ."

"Conditions are bad there now, very bad," Glenorr said.

Sylvane told Auragole that only a year before, Ardur's wife, the twins' mother, had been killed in a raid on the settlement.

Glenorr's face looked angry in the firelight. Auragole felt a sudden kinship with this man who had lost a beloved parent.

Ardur had taken it hard, Sylvane went on. For twenty-eight years Henny had been his companion and his solace. And good, dear Henny had been mother to Sylvane since she was three, when her own parents had been killed. Sylvane was one of the fortunate ones, for usually children of the dead were put out of settlements to fend for themselves. "There is little enough food for one's own family, how stretch it to include those who cannot yet work?" But Henny took her in and Sylvane would always be in her loving debt and in the debt of her family.

Glenorr told Auragole that Ardur had feared he could not hold off against the increasing attacks on his settlement. So, he had decided to save his two youngest children by sending them with a caravan to Mattelmead, a country that welcomed those who came with skills or wealth.

42

"Are there no longer wars in the west?" Auragole asked. "I know nothing about the west," he added, "only that caravans come from the east and head there."

It was Glenelle who picked up the account. "Oh yes, war there too," she said, with a small sigh, "but it's not as terrible as in the east, or so those who have returned have reported, nor has it been going on as long."

"There are six countries in the west with established borders," Sylvane said.

"Seven," Glenorr said. "That doesn't mean too much—well, something. But it doesn't mean peace. That would take a strong leader."

"Without strong leaders no one pays much attention to the borders dividing country from country." That from Glenelle.

"One strong leader," Glenorr said, "that's what's necessary."

"Our father thinks the west has a good chance now to pull itself out of all those centuries of war," Glenelle said.

"How. . .why now?" Auragole asked.

"Because of the country of Mattelmead and its king, Ormahn," Sylvane said, with a smile of pleasure.

"You see, Auragole, a king has arisen there who is both strong and well loved by the people," Glenelle told him. "You know what a king is, don't you?"

"Yes." He knew about kings from the stories his mother and Spehn had told him, and from the history he'd been taught, and from song. "But I thought there were no more kings anywhere on the Grand Continent—only warlords."

"In your father's time that would have been correct," Glenorr said, "but there is a king now. King Ormahn of Mattelmead is like the great kings of the past. He has built a new and shining city, near the Western Sea, also called Mattelmead." Glenorr became very animated as he told Auragole about King Ormahn. "It is said, even in the east, that if Ormahn can stay alive and in power, if he can quell all the petty disputes within his own borders, then he might attempt to conquer his weaker neighbors. . ."

". . .and unite the west into one great, peaceful kingdom." Sylvane finished Glenorr's thought.

"Who knows," Glenorr said, "perhaps he has begun the conquest already."

Auragole thought about such a wonder with longing. "The west is unknown to me, though I have heard many tales of the east."

"Forget about the east. There's no chance for peace there. But the west. . ." Glenorr let the thought hang there, a smile lighting up his face. "Everything rests on the west and Mattelmead. But it's not just war and the conquering of countries that make Ormahn great. He's doing something beyond the making of war. He's establishing universities and centers of medicine in Mattelmead City." Auragole heard the excitement in Glenorr's voice. "Ormahn has welcomed learned men from everywhere, including the east, to come and study or to teach. Now listen to this, Auragole, for this is truly astonishing. It is said that there is work for all who want it, so that no one need go hungry."

Auragole was amazed. How he wished his father and Spehn could have known that there was new hope for the Grand Continent, perhaps for the whole world.

"But most important," Glenorr said, "they are finding new cures for illnesses." His eyes rested for a moment on his sister, and then he went on. "With a king like Ormahn, it could turn out to be the Golden Century all over again, only better. If he conquers the west, he can conquer the east. Then, at last, there will be peace for the whole Grand Continent and an age of enlightenment and order could begin again."

Glenorr told Auragole how he and the two women had been taken by two of their older brothers to the western town of Jantuli to await the twice-yearly caravan that crosses the Gandlese and the Westernlands as far as the coastal country of Mattelmead.

"It's a journey of nearly two thousand miles and many months' duration," Glenorr told Auragole. "It's a very expensive trip, because the caravan leaders must pay off the warlords whose territories they pass through on their way to Mattelmead."

The high price had been purchased with the jewels that Ardur had taken in a battle from a leader of another settlement many years ago. These jewels, fashioned in the Golden Century, had been Henny's treasure and she had looked beautiful when she wore them, to the pride of her husband. The bargain for the journey had been struck. A wagon, a mule, a donkey, and supplies had been purchased for them and they had set out with guides, armed guards, and about one hundred fifty others who had been able to put together the high fare. Here Glenorr paused.

Auragole was utterly confused. "Then why did you leave the caravan?"

Glenelle looked mournfully at Auragole and was about to speak, but Sylvane jumped in. "We don't need them. We're better off alone. We'll find our own way." Quickly she rose and began clearing away the supper utensils.

"But you've traveled in the wrong direction. . ." Auragole said.

"Have we?" Glenelle asked. She smiled that sad smile of hers and looked at Auragole. "Perhaps you can help us, Aurie. You seem to know your way in these woods."

He swallowed hard. "I was born here, you see. I'd be glad to help—in any way I can."

"If it wouldn't cause you inconvenience, perhaps you would stay with us a few days. You see, I have spells." The last Glenelle said quietly.

"Ellie!" Sylvane and Glenorr said, simultaneously.

"I have spells," Glenelle persisted, her voice growing stronger, "and when I have them I rant and rave and am, so they say, quite frightening."

"Truly?" Auragole said.

Sylvane glared at Glenelle.

"Truly. And I say frightening things and make wild predictions."

"Glenelle, that will do!" Glenorr's voice was angry.

But Glenelle rose shakily to her feet. "Enough, Glenorr! Enough hiding. We thought we were alone in these mountains, hundreds and hundreds of miles of deserted mountains. But look, Sylvane has found Auragole. And I know he is a good man." She smiled winningly at Auragole. "We need help to put us on a right path toward Mattelmead. We know so little about traveling in mountains." She turned to her brother. "Why shouldn't we tell him that I have an illness?" Glenelle sat down again.

Glenorr's face looked thoughtful. "You're right, Ellie." He turned to Auragole. "My sister has a sickness. That's why we were put off the caravan. That's one of the reasons we are so anxious to get to Mattelmead, where Ellie can be cured. The illness, when it comes upon her, makes Glenelle do and say strange things. Most people are superstitious, really ignorant, and so those traveling with the caravan were frightened. Needlessly," he said, looking at his sister with affection. "Could Ellie do harm to anyone?" He didn't wait for an answer. "So the leaders put us off the caravan. They were illiterate and stupid. They wouldn't even give us the wagon and mule we had paid for. They put us off with only our donkey, some maps, a few utensils, and a little food."

"It's just as well we're on our own," Sylvane said. "Ellie gets exhausted after these. . .these spells, and she has to rest. So we stayed a few days at Lake Mimbi after the caravan left, and then started on our way. The wrong way it seems."

"Somehow I can't seem to regain my strength," Glenelle said. Her smile was once again tinged with melancholy.

"Now that Sylvane's found the eldenmyrr flower, you'll be ready to run in a few days," Glenorr said, stroking her shoulder.

"I wanted to ask Auragole if he would stay until my strength

46

comes back. A few days only, and then help us get started in the right direction."

"I'll stay," Auragole said, his words tumbling out. "Gladly. I should like to help. Tomorrow I'll look over your supplies and study your maps."

"And maybe he'll sing for us," Sylvane said.

Glenelle clapped her hands in delight. "Oh, Aurie, do you sing?"

"Yes," he said, and looked baffled. "Do you not?"

"No, none of us sing."

"Do none of you play instruments?"

They shook their heads. "No, none of us play," Glenelle said. "Do you?"

"Yes, I have a small harp Spehn and my father made. We all sang, my mother and father, even Spehn—though Spehn preferred tale-telling and my mother loved to speak poems. I learned from them all. My father preferred to listen, but he had a very nice singing voice." Auragole grinned a little sheepishly and shrugged. "I thought all humans sang and played."

"Ah, Aurie, what a wonderful childhood you must have had," Sylvane said. "Most humans, at least in the east, do not sing or play. But," and her face brightened, "Ellie is a wonderful tale-teller. Perhaps while you stay with us for these next few days she will tell you tales and you can sing for us, and tell us your stories."

Auragole readily agreed.

They sat speaking for a while longer. Glenelle asked Auragole why he was traveling east, and he once again told his story.

Auragole went to sleep that night feeling an inexplicable sense of wonderment.

N

chapter four

"YOU CANNOT GO a week on these supplies," Auragole told Sylvane the next morning.

"I know," she said.

"What did you intend to do? How can you travel so ill-prepared? Did they not give you enough food, the leaders of the caravan?"

"Yes, they gave us food," she said, "but only for a month. And we've been in these woods almost three weeks. I was hoping the forest would be filled with fruit, with nuts and herbs."

"Does Glenorr know that your supplies are low?"

It was hard to explain about individuals like Glenorr to one who had not lived among people, but Sylvane did her best. "Glen is a thinker; therefore his mind is often busy with important things. I try not to bother him with unimportant things."

Auragole's eyes widened. "But surely eating or not eating is important."

"Certainly it's important," she said, "but it's not for people like Glen to worry about. His father sent me with the twins to help look after them. Glen needs his mind for more-difficult things." It was her responsibility to get the twins to the west safely. How, Sylvane wasn't certain, but that much she felt she owed her foster family.

"Is thinking separate from living?" Auragole asked, looking over at Glenorr who was sitting under the beech with his note-book, absorbed in his writing, surrounded by stones. "I. . .I don't understand."

Sylvane had no answer, so she asked, "What can we do about our supplies?"

Auragole watched Glenorr for a while longer. She hoped he wasn't going to say anything to him. Finally, he turned to Sylvane and said, "When I went fishing yesterday, I saw a small grove of pear trees. We can pick them and dry them. We can also catch and smoke fish. We can gather herbs for soups and teas."

"Good, good!" Sylvane was delighted.

At that moment Glenelle came up to them where they were standing near the stream. "Good morning, you two." Glenelle sat down on a large flat rock and stretched languidly. "Isn't it a lovely morning—warm as midsummer. The stream looks so inviting. . . I'm going to bathe just around that bend."

"You look. . .look much improved today," Auragole said.

"I am improved. In another day or two I shall be able to travel." She lifted her chin and smiled. "You must be bringing me luck, Auragole of the Gandlese Mountains."

"I. . .I think it's the eldenmyrr."

"Aurie is going to help us build up our supplies, Ellie." Sylvane told her about his suggestions.

"Good," Glenelle said. "I'll help."

"You'll rest," Sylvane said. "We want you healthy for our trip."

Later that day, Sylvane sat with Auragole while he pored over the maps they had been given by the leaders of the caravan.

"Before my father left Stahlowill, he was given a map of the Gandlese by my mother's uncle. But also my father made maps and taught me how to make and read them. I think he loved mapmaking very much, for he charted an area of many miles around our valley. According to your maps, you should have continued west from Lake Mimbi for four or five days," he told her. "Then you should have turned north. After a little more than two weeks or so, you would have come to the Northern Valley in the high mountains. That long and twisting valley would have led you out of the mountains and down into the foothills of the Westernlands."

"I understand what you are saying, Aurie, but I can't make any sense out of scribblings on paper."

"I'll teach you. I'll stay until. . .," he cleared his throat, ". . . until Glenelle is well enough to travel; then I'll go as far as Lake Mimbi with you. I'll teach you to read the maps."

Sylvane gave him a hug. He blushed but didn't pull away.

For seven days, as Glenelle's strength grew, they picked pears and apples and caught fish, which they dried or smoked. Auragole found many places where the eldenmyrr flowers grew and they picked these and dried them along with many other herbs that Auragole knew were good for eating or for medicine. Glenorr was fascinated with the new herbs and the ways in which they could be used. He wrote everything down in his notebook in a tiny hand. Both he and Glenelle occasionally joined them in their work. Sylvane knew that Glenorr could be a hard worker, and so could Glenelle. But she was firm with her foster sister, making her stop at the first sign of fatigue.

In the evenings around the fire, Auragole asked questions about the Easternlands. And they answered him as best they could. He drank in all their tales, his face mirroring his thoughts, his dark eyes intent on whichever one of them was speaking. Sylvane watched Auragole with pleasure. He questioned them minutely about the battles they had been in.

He seemed fascinated by those stories, particularly if there was an act of heroism or danger contained in them.

"I am good with a bow and arrow, and with a sword. My father and Spehn taught me well, though I have never fought against humans. But I have used my skills to hunt, sometimes quite large game."

Some nights Auragole would sing in what Sylvane thought was a wonderfully sweet voice, or he would recite one of the poems his mother had taught him, or tell them a story. On other evenings, it would be Glenelle who would tell the story. Sylvane noted with some poignancy how Auragole's face fairly shone with joy and with longing when Ellie recited. If only she, too, had some small gift to offer, but Sylvane could neither sing nor tell tales. Therefore, she was not surprised that Auragole had given his heart to Glenelle and not to her. Sylvane had long ago buried jealousy. It seemed natural that Glenelle should elicit love—it had always been that way. A few years earlier, another whom Sylvane had cared for, had loved not her but Glenelle. Nothing had come of it for either woman. The young man had died, his love unspent, in a raid on their settlement.

How wonderful Auragole's life sounded to Sylvane. The singing and the harp-playing, the poetry-reciting and tale-telling. It sounded idyllic. The birth of a calf was an event, or the catch on a hunting expedition, even a drought. No wars, no battles, no skirmishes. Lonely, yes, but what was that set against the peaceful childhood that Auragole had been given by his mother and father? How she admired stubborn Goloss, who had marched his small band of travelers deeper and deeper into the dreaded Gandlese to get away from the horrors and madness in the east. She loved to hear Auragole tell about his life. But especially she loved to hear him sing.

One night, he sang them what he called the Prince Riddle Song.

There is a riddle
here in my song.
The tale is short
but the melody long.

I sing of a prince
not born of a king.
He wears neither crown
nor does he wear ring.

He has no silk cape.
He has no silk shirt.
Will this prince heal
or will this prince hurt?

Who is his father?
Who is his mother?
Some say he has
neither one nor the other.

Is he one cursed
or is he one blessed?
Will he bring strife
or will he bring rest?

Will he bring peace
or will he bring war?
Seek you the answer?
Then search for the door.

Some call him wise.
Some call him fool.
Where is his kingdom?
Whom does he rule?

Where is the door?
Where is the gate?
Where is the young prince?
Why does he wait?

So here is my riddle.
One you can ponder
whether at home
or whether you wander.

Will he bring love
or will he bring hate?
Would you an answer?
Look for the gate.

Yet where is the door?
And where is the gate?
And where is the young prince
for whom we all wait?

So here is my riddle
and here is my song.
The tale has been short
but the melody's long.

I sing of a prince
not born of a king
who wears neither crown
nor does he wear ring.

"Lovely, really lovely," Glenelle said.

Auragole blushed and rubbed his forehead. "What do you think it means? If it's a riddle song, it should have a meaning."

"Perhaps it's about Ormahn of Mattelmead," Glenorr suggested.

"Or about his son, who would certainly be called a prince," Sylvane said.

"What does it matter?" Glenelle said. "A song is a song, meant for the pleasure of the listener. Why worry or even wonder about it?"

"I. . .I thought perhaps it was a puzzle that one was meant to figure out," Auragole said. "My mother sang it to me when I was very little and then she simply stopped singing it. I'm not sure, but I think it was the first song she ever sang to me. I remember wondering about it and trying to imagine who this prince might be. When I asked her, she said all riddle songs have meaning, and that someday I would perhaps find the answer. But then I was very young so it might have been something one says to placate a curious child."

"Mothers are like that," Sylvane said. And for a moment she looked sad. But then she smiled. "Well, if your mother is correct, perhaps you'll find out one day."

"Perhaps. It doesn't really matter. You're right, Glenelle. It's a song. If it gives pleasure, that should be enough."

One day Auragole asked Sylvane if she thought she had a task.

"What do you mean, a task? Do you have a task?"

"I don't know. . .but I feel that there's something that I should be doing, out there in the world, some deed like the heroes in the stories, some. . ." He reddened.

"That's all well and good, Aurie. But it's hard to do more in this world than survive." Then she saw the crestfallen look on his face. She had said the wrong thing, had not understood him. "Glenorr has a task." She was suddenly animated. "He wants to be a scientist. He wants to go to the Academy for Nature and Categorizing in Mattelmead. So your looking for your task makes perfect sense," she assured him.

He still looked skeptical. "Do you think so?"

"I do."

54

"Perhaps I will find it when I find my uncle. . .if I find my uncle. . . Do I seem. . .seem foolish?"

"No. I think it is wonderful to want to do something more than just survive. Most people, because of the wars, only think about how they are going to get through the day and find the next meal. But I think it is very important to have a task. I have one," she said, her face brightening with sudden realization. "My task is to see my foster brother and sister safely to Mattelmead and see them well-established there."

One night, after the evening meal was over, Auragole asked them who the Guttlubbers were.

"Dreadful men," Sylvane said. "An organization of murderers. Bands of killer soldiers."

"They roam throughout the Easternlands wreaking havoc on people," Glenorr told him. "Wherever they hear that there is a settlement or village that has strong leaders and law and order, they sweep down on it and attempt to destroy it."

"They kill without mercy," Sylvane told him, with a shudder. "They have uniforms of gray wool, with white tunics over them, as if they were innocent—like the brides of the past. But they aren't innocent. They are corrupters and destroyers."

"It's a strange name, Guttlubbers," Auragole said. "Does it mean anything?"

"I've heard it said that it refers to the way they kill, leaving the guts of their victims strewn all about." Glenelle grimaced in distaste.

"Horrible," Auragole said, with a shake of his head.

SOMEWHERE IN THE middle of the night before they left for Lake Mimbi, Sylvane felt a hand on her shoulders, shaking her. She sat bolt upright, her heart pounding.

"What is it?" she asked. Auragole was bending over her.

"Shhh," he said. "Keep your voice low."

"What's the matter?"

Auragole pointed past the low-burning fire. She couldn't see anything.

"Stand up slowly."

She did, and then she saw them, or saw their eyes reflecting the fire. "Oh, my stars," and she inhaled deeply. She saw four, or was it five, pairs of glowing eyes several yards away on the other side of the fire.

"We have to build up the fire."

"Right. There's a pile of twigs and branches nearby." Luckily it was on their side of the fire.

"I'll do it. You wake the others. But don't let them cry out. If the wolves attack, better to be awake than asleep."

Sylvane looked at him, her eyes large.

"What weapons do you have?" He didn't wait for an answer. "Get them." He gathered the wood and began slowly to add twigs to the fire.

Sylvane crept over to where Glenorr was sleeping and shook him awake. She flung her hand over his mouth as soon as he opened his eyes. "Wolves," she said. "Get your sword." Glenorr didn't have to be told twice.

She woke Glenelle. When Glenelle heard there were wolves, she crept to where her bag rested against a nearby tree and retrieved her bow and arrows, then moved cautiously toward the fire.

When the three were standing near Auragole, he said, "I hope they don't wait us out. There isn't too much wood left."

"What about in the trees behind us?" Sylvane asked.

"Best to stay near the fire," Auragole said.

"How many are out there?" Glenorr asked.

"I counted five. But there could be more."

Sylvane bit her lip. "What do we do?"

"We wait," Auragole said. He held his bow and an arrow loose in his hand, and glanced at their weapons. "Two bows, two swords. That should be sufficient. Sylvane, you feed the

56

fire. Keep it going as long as you can. And don't get too far from your sword."

"Right," she whispered.

Auragole strung his bow and held it ready. Glenelle did the same. Glenorr gripped his sword and watched. As she fed the fire, Sylvane kept glancing at the wolves, who were pacing slowly back and forth. How long before dawn, she wondered? How long before they would attack?

About an hour passed and she finally whispered, "I'm almost out of sticks and wood."

"Then pick up your sword."

It was the largest wolf that attacked first. Glenelle shot it between the eyes before it had covered much ground. The second wolf took Auragole's arrow in the throat a few feet from the fire. The other three wolves turned and slunk away.

The four of them stood their ground, back to back, as they watched the woods around them. A half hour later dawn announced itself, sending a trail of pink down the valley between the mountains to the east.

"Thank the King." Sylvane sank to the ground and wept.

Glenorr pounded Auragole on the back. "Good shot, man! Good, good shot."

Glenelle walked toward the body of the wolf she had killed.

"Wait, Ellie," her brother called to her. "Let's make sure they're both dead," and he walked up to the wolf Glenelle had shot and drove his sword through its heart. He pulled it out and walked over to the wolf Auragole had killed and did the same.

Glenelle stood looking down at the wolf she had killed. Sylvane rose and walked over to her foster sister. Glenelle's eyes were bright and feverish. That was not a good sign. She saw Auragole watching Glenelle. "Come away, Ellie. The beast is dead."

Glenelle allowed Sylvie to take her arm and lead her back to her blankets. "Sleep, dear sister. It's been a strenuous night. No need to be up early. Everything is fine now. You and Aurie have saved us. We're all safe and Auragole is going to help us now."

When the sun was a bit higher, casting beams of light through the peaks, Auragole and Sylvane gathered wood and built up the fire once again. They didn't speak. But Sylvane was happy to be in his presence. When they had enough wood, they returned to their blankets and slept.

N

chapter five

LATE THAT MORNING, they started on their journey north toward Lake Mimbi.

As they packed up, Auragole said to Sylvie, "I don't see how we're going to manage all these supplies and Glenorr's stones too."

"I simply can't leave these stones here," Glenorr called over to them. "They may never have been categorized before. I must deliver them to the academy in Mattelmead."

It wasn't Auragole's place to argue with Glenorr, even though he knew they carried too much in their backpacks, because Glenorr's finds were tied to the donkey. Auragole had agreed to help them only as far as Lake Mimbi. It was not his right to tell these travelers what to do. So he shouldered an extra load, as did Sylvane and Glenorr. Only Glenelle was spared. Still, Auragole thought she carried more than was good for her slight frame and fragile health.

The donkey, laden with Glenorr's stones and plants, was

often difficult. Once he broke loose and they spent the better part of the morning trying to catch him. Their progress was slow. Glenelle never complained, and Auragole admired her for it. But Sylvane kept watch over her foster sister and when Glenelle's strength showed signs of failing, Sylvane made them stop for the day. While the two women set up camp and started the fire, Glenorr looked eagerly for new stones and plants. So it was left to Auragole to hunt for small game or fish for their supper.

"We'll try to keep much of the food we smoked and dried for your trip after we separate," Auragole told Sylvane. "I can hunt and fish for myself later." But one glance at Glenelle and he began again to worry about how the group would fare once he left them.

One night, as they sat together after their evening meal, Glenelle asked, "What is it that your uncle teaches in Stahlowill?" It had turned cool after a warm and humid day. A breeze blew out of the west and it felt good to sit around the fire.

How to explain something Auragole himself hardly understood? "My parents rarely spoke about their families—I think it pained them—for most of them had died in the wars. At the time my parents left Stahlowill there was only this one uncle on my mother's side who was still alive. Not until after my father died did she speak about him. She told me my uncle was a teacher who taught tales about the old Gods at a school there. This would have angered my father, had he been alive to hear her. My father believed the stories about the Gods were made up, and that their so-called existence had been disproved centuries ago in the Golden Century."

"Your father was right," Glenorr said, with a laugh. "Swords, no one believes in the Gods anymore. A school to teach tales about the Gods? How remarkable. And of what use to the world?"

"Did your mother believe in the Gods, Aurie?" Sylvane asked him.

Glenorr made a chortling sound, and Auragole looked first at him and then turned to answer Sylvane. "I'm not sure," he said to her. "She spoke to me of many things, but of the Gods only twice, that time after my father died, and one time before he died—when I was a very young child wanting to know the origin of things. She spoke about invisible Beings who had created the earth and then had gone away and left human beings to fend for themselves. This caused a terrible quarrel between my parents."

"I don't see how it is possible to teach anything about the Gods," Glenelle said. "All the books about them were destroyed in the war years. On the other hand, there are many tales about them that people have handed down from generation to generation, and some of them are charming and quaint." Her eyes lit up. "I know you love the old stories about heroes doing brave deeds, Auragole, for I've watched your face as I have told them. But as for myself, I love best the stories about the Gods. They're so. . .so magical."

"She tells them well," Sylvane said, and nodded her approval. "Pity the written works have all been destroyed."

"That isn't all that was destroyed in the wars," Glenorr said. "Everything human beings had created out of their own genius was destroyed too. But in Mattelmead, because of King Ormahn, it will all be found again."

"Do you believe in the Gods?" Sylvane asked Auragole.

His fingers stroked his forehead in a gesture that was now becoming familiar to her. "I don't know anything about them. So how can I believe in them?"

"Smart man," Glenorr said.

"I call him shortsighted, like you, Glen," Sylvane said. "Why can't there be invisible Beings who created humans and the earth? The wind is invisible and yet we believe in it. We had to come from somewhere."

61

"The wind. . ."

"Don't start that old disagreement, you two," Glenelle said.

"Do you believe in the Gods?" Auragole asked Sylvane.

"I say it's possible. People believed in them for many, many ages, all the way up to the Golden Century."

"Then men became smart and began studying the earth," Glenorr said. "All stories about Gods are ultimately great foolishness. Most people with sense today don't bother about the Gods."

"Many people still believe in the Gods, Glenorr, and you know it," Sylvane said.

"Dear girl," Glenorr said, "Gods are an invention of ancient peoples, who lived thousands of years ago. Whatever world phenomena they couldn't understand they attributed to some God or other. But science changed all that in the Golden Century, when people discovered the laws underlying nature. Laws, not invisible Beings. But some people are too stubborn to believe the evidence of their senses." He crossed his arms in front of his chest, and went on as if he were talking to a child. "There are laws in nature, sweet child, that have nothing to do with Gods. In Mattelmead they are rediscovering these laws."

Auragole listened in fascination as the two argued.

"If there are laws in nature, Glen, who put them there—a cabbage or a potato?" Sylvane asked, her temper rising.

"Why do I bother talking to you?" he said. "You haven't a thought in your head worth keeping."

"Stop it, you two," Glenelle said, but her tone was mild.

"Do you see why I'm anxious to get to the academy in Mattelmead?" Glenorr said, turning to Auragole. "I need people to talk to, people who use their brains." He glared at Sylvane. He was on his feet then. He bent down, scooped up his blanket, and moved to the other side of their campfire.

"Thoughts aren't everything," Sylvane called loudly after his retreating back. "I still believe in the Gods, no matter what you say!"

"Belief is not logical!" Glenorr shouted back. "It's subjective! You can't prove it!"

"It doesn't matter," Glenelle said. "Why keep at this same argument? Some things are unknowable. We can no longer find out about the Gods. All the documents concerning the Gods are gone. If the Gods do exist, they don't show themselves to humans now as the tales tell us they did in the past. If they exist, they are no longer bothering about us. Still, there are many stories that have been handed down. I could tell you some of those if you like, Aurie."

"I'd like that very much," he answered. "I confess, I have been curious about them."

"Tell him about the King God," Sylvane suggested. "The King God is the best-known." Sylvane turned to Auragole, with a rather defiant smile. "And there are those on our Deep Earth, I have heard, who still worship him, despite Glenorr's logic."

From where he lay, Glenorr made a derisive, snorting noise.

"Good," Glenelle answered. "Tomorrow night I'll tell Aurie a story about the King who is, according to the tales about him, the creator of all earthly things."

When Auragole lay in his blankets that night, his thoughts drifted back to an event when he was seven years old.

For more than a week, the summer heat had brooded over their valley like a hen on an egg. Auragole lay awake trying to sleep in his low-ceilinged room, but it was too hot. After a time he rose quietly, wrapped himself in his cloak, tucked his knife in his belt, and let himself out the window. He was headed for the river half a mile away even though he was forbidden to do so because there was danger from roving bands of wolves. But he was hot and irritable and therefore willing to face both the wolves and the beating he was sure to get in the morning if he did not arrive home before the others awakened. As he silently moved past his parents' window, he heard them quarreling. These quarrels between his father and mother always made him

63

uneasy. Since he was once again the subject of their arguing, he stayed and listened.

"But I had to tell the boy something!" His mother's voice was shrill and angry. "He asks so many questions. Does the boy have to be ignorant to be. . ."

"You didn't have to tell him about the Gods," his father said in a loud voice.

"But he's a bright boy and curious, and he wanted to know the source of all things, as children should. He asked how the mountains came to be, how the seeds know when to grow, in what way humans are different from animals. He asked me if he is an animal. Did you want me to tell him that he is an animal, Goloss?" She flung the words at him.

"But you didn't have to tell him about the Gods!" Auragole could hear the rage in his father's voice and it frightened him. "We agreed to that before he was born."

"Will you hold me forever to a youthful promise?"

"Yes," his father shouted, "forever! Will you ruin everything I have dreamed of for the boy?"

"Your dreams! It's always your dreams! You cannot hide all truth from him." His mother was crying. His mother never cried. He could hear both frustration and fury in her words. "And you cannot feud forever with the Gods."

Auragole had been appalled at hearing his mother weep. He felt that he had caused her tears. Why was his father so angry? His mother had said so little to him, only that the Gods had created the Deep Earth and humankind, and then had gone away. He couldn't understand his father's rage, nor could he understand what his mother had done that was so terrible. It was he who was to blame.

"He is to be a beginning," his father said. "He is to be tied to no one. He needs no Gods and few men. It is from Gods and men that all troubles flow. We made promises to each other."

"But we were young and angry then. Must that anger rule the

*rest of our lives?" His mother was pleading with his father now.
"Is it right to raise a child so ignorantly?"*

*"He must never know the bonds imposed by Gods. . .or
human beings," and now it was his father who pleaded. "He
must grow up to be a truly free man."*

*The argument went on until, his head whirling, Auragole
crept back to bed, his visit to the river forgotten.*

For years after that night his mother was silent on the subject.
Shrugging her shoulders when Auragole questioned her or not
meeting his eyes, she would say, "Take your questions to your
father."

But Auragole knew better.

*"Gods," his friend Spehn explained, "are tales made up by
people to explain world wonders. They are silly tales, suitable for
small children, about Beings with magical powers, sometimes
invisible, who can create moon and sun, rocks and trees, men
and women."*

*"Tell me some of the tales," Auragole begged him more than
once.*

*"I've forgotten them," Spehn said. "They are all nonsense.
Learn from nature about nature. She is a good teacher."*

Auragole spoke to his father about the Gods only once. He
was in his eleventh year. They were out hunting. A few times a
year they traveled, sometimes far, into the wooded mountains
after large game. It was a happy time for Auragole because his
father, usually a taciturn man, would talk freely. Around the
campfire at night he would tell Auragole tales from his youth. It
was on those special occasions that Goloss spoke about his
brothers and sisters who had all died in the wars.

*They had made camp near a lively stream. The day had been
a fruitful one. The next day, with their packs and their donkey
laden, they were to start the two-day journey home. They had
finished their soup of meat and herbs, and were contentedly
sipping the strong senta tea. His father had told him about his*

own father and was now lost in some pleasant memory. Auragole hadn't planned it, but the words were out of his mouth before he even thought them.

"Why do you hate the Gods?"

His father looked up at Auragole without expression, but his blue eyes became dark. "What Gods?" he finally asked.

"I don't know," Auragole said. "Any God."

"There are no Gods. There is the earth, the plants, the animals, and humans. That's all."

"But how did we come to be, the earth and humanity?" Auragole suddenly felt brave and so he pursued it.

Suddenly Goloss's hand flew out and struck Auragole hard across the cheek. Auragole was too stunned to cry out. He had taken many a beating for the foolish and willful things children do, but this was the first time his father had struck him across the face.

"I want you to remember that blow forever. There are no Gods. I didn't raise you so you could grow up foolish. There is nothing greater for a human being than freedom. But not if you suddenly become illogical and seek after childish answers to your questions."

His father looked away from him, and Auragole was glad, for tears were stinging his eyes. "In time, men will find answers to the questions you ask, Auragole—as they once sought them in the Golden Century." Goloss's voice was low and husky. "And they will seek them on the earth and not in magic rites or invisible beings." He moved away from Auragole then, wrapped himself in his cloak, and lay down near the dwindling fire.

But Auragole lay sleepless, that night etched now forever on his memory.

THEY HAD PLANNED to camp three days at Lake Mimbi to rest and repack, then to separate and go their different ways. Auragole felt heavyhearted as they made camp there that first night. Even the talkative Sylvane was unusually quiet. Auragole noted that Glenorr, who could usually distract himself with searching for new stones or plants, was morose. He fidgeted with his notebook and then he went to sleep. Glenelle, exhausted by the day's walk, went to sleep immediately after dinner.

Sylvane sat perched on a rock near the fire, her long skirts tucked under her legs, studying the maps that Auragole had tried to teach her to read. What a dear friend she had become, Auragole thought, feeling a great fondness for the spunky woman he had come to rely on. If he had had a sister, she most certainly would have been like Sylvane. He watched her pursed lips and was uneasy. He had taught her to fish with pole and net, as his father had taught him. He had made her a pole and would give her his spare net. If there were streams all the way west, then they shouldn't starve. He planned to give them all the food they had dried, and all the food he had brought from home. He could hunt and fish on his way east.

But would they find their way out of these mountains? They had made one bad error. They knew nothing about reading direction from the stars or from the growth of certain plants. And Sylvane, try as she might, had little aptitude for map-reading, much to Auragole's dismay. And what would they do if they ran into wild animals, or if one or the other were injured? Auragole picked up his harp and began strumming on it while gazing across the dark lake to where the tall snowcapped mountains of the north waited. He could barely make them out in the moonlight. The three Easterners would have to travel through them. Could they manage to carry their supplies and Glenorr's ever-increasing finds? He looked at the sleeping Glenelle, then sighed audibly. Sylvane rose and came to sit down next to him. She tried to smile, but it was a poor attempt.

"No need to worry, Aurie. We'll manage very well. Glen is an excellent swordsman. I'm not bad myself, if need be. You saw Glenelle's skill with a bow. We can take care of ourselves."

It was an extravagant declaration, he was sure. But that was the way Sylvane was. She had an unconquerable spirit. Here she sat in a wild forest, miles from other humans, ready to lead her small party out of the mountains. Auragole said nothing, just turned to stare at Glenelle, her sleeping face ghostly in the moonlight.

Sylvane's voice lost its playfulness. "I'll take good care of her. She'll be better soon." Sylvane folded up her maps and put them carefully into her pack. "Don't look so troubled, Aurie. I couldn't in good conscience ask you to postpone your trip east and to come to Mattelmead with us. . ."

Auragole watched her and listened.

"Did your mother ask you to go east to find your uncle immediately? Or is it possible to do. . .to go somewhere else first?" She jumped up, then hurried to the other side of the fire and curled up in her blankets.

Auragole sat a long time near the fire weighing what Sylvane had said. It was true. He hadn't promised to go east immediately. He could, if he chose, go west with his new friends—for didn't they need him? Would they be able to find their way through the most difficult part of the mountains without him? Brave as they were, they were not skilled travelers. He thought about seeing the new king and his heart leapt with excitement. Would not his father have approved of Ormahn, the savior king—the one who intended to end war for all times?

Ellie moaned in her sleep. She looked so pale and vulnerable. Firelight flickered across her troubled face. In Mattelmead there were doctors who would cure her illness. Auragole felt dissolved in tenderness for her. Was this love? And if it was, must he lose it so soon to go hunting for an old man who was probably dead? Would he ever find another who could stir his heart as Ellie had?

And suddenly he was thinking about his father and their last conversation on the night that Goloss died.

His father had called him into his room and had sent his mother away. It had been difficult for Goloss to talk, but he put all his will behind his final words.

"It would have been different," he whispered hoarsely, *"if Spehn's wife had lived and borne children and if your mother had had others. A community would have grown here in peace and freedom, but that was not meant to be. They are jealous of humans."* Goloss stopped speaking and for a moment Auragole thought the end had come, for his eyes closed. But Goloss opened them again. *"You will have to go out into the world, at least for a time. Have I prepared you for war, for cruelty?"* Again he stopped. *"I must warn you,"* he whispered, and Auragole put his ear close to his father's mouth, *"as I warned you about the Gods."*

"About what, father?"

"About love." He looked at Auragole and Auragole could see yellow flames burning deep in his father's sunken eyes. *"If you seek it, you will find illusion. Forget what you have heard in song and story."*

"But. . ." Auragole started to interrupt.

"Let me speak, Auragole, for I cannot fight the blackness much longer. Everyone will speak to you of love and sing its praises. The thief will tell you he loves you as he takes your goods. The king will tell you he loves you as he takes your freedom. The priest will tell you he loves you as he takes your will. And the woman will tell you she loves you as she takes your manhood. They will all lie. They will all entrap you in the name of love. Don't be fooled. Don't succumb to their illusions. There is no such thing as love. Accept what rises in the blood but don't call it love. Admit what lives in the instincts but don't call it love. The people of the Easternlands killed or were killed with slogans of love on their lips." He gasped. *"Don't succumb and you will be free, free."* Then the flaming eyes saw no more.

chapter six

IT WAS VERY late. The moon was high, illuminating the still, cool lake. Suddenly Auragole was wrenched awake by the sound of eerie laughter. Sylvane was at his side in an instant. Auragole held his knife in hand. "What is it?" Auragole asked her.

Glenorr came up to them then.

"Shhh," Sylvane warned them both and pointed to a rocky promontory some distance away that jutted out high over the murky lake. Glenelle was standing on its edge, her head thrown back, her face distorted, laughing uncontrollably.

"Glenelle's illness," Glenorr said, standing near the water, agony in his voice.

Auragole stared up at Glenelle's face, unable to believe what he was seeing. Her face, usually so serene, so lovely, was now horribly contorted."Quiet!" Sylvane admonished Glenorr. "We have to get her off that rock. She could fall into the lake and she doesn't know how to swim. We mustn't frighten her."

"Ha, ha, ha! You will die!" A harsh, guttural, unrecognizable voice came from Glenelle. "You will die in the snow—you and all your companions."

The sound and the words chilled Auragole.

"You will die! The snows will bury you! You will never leave these mountains, never!" The ugly, unfamiliar voice grew in intensity until it was shouting, "Cold, cold, white, ice!"

Suddenly it was Glenelle shrieking in terror as she fell into the water.

"Oh, my stars!" Sylvane began to tug at her skirt, but in an instant Auragole had stripped to the waist and had plunged into the icy water. He swam with long, hard strokes to the spot where he had seen Glenelle go under. She didn't come up. He dove under the dark surface. He had calculated correctly. In seconds he had brushed up against her. Auragole grabbed her and brought her up into the air. But Glenelle struggled with him. She tore at his hair, scratched his face, and tried to kick. They both went under the water again. He almost lost hold of her, but he grasped her by her hair and pulled her into the air. Still she kept fighting. So he slapped her a ringing blow across the cheek. Ellie looked at him then as if she were seeing him for the first time, called him by name, and then went limp. Auragole, swimming slowly, pulled her to shore.

Glenorr and Sylvane met him there. Glen took Glenelle from Auragole's arms and Sylvie wrapped her in her blue cloak, and they put her down on the grass. She lay there, eyes closed, coughing the water out of her lungs. Auragole turned her on her stomach and pressed on her back until the coughing stopped.

"Take off her wet things," Auragole said, and shivering, bent down, picked up his own shirt, and walked back to the campfire to dry off. He put some wood on the low-burning embers, then sat close to the fire, drying off, and trying to understand what he had just seen and heard.

"Thank you, Aurie, thank you for saving my sister's life." Glenorr sat down close to Auragole. "I owe you for that." He was trembling visibly in the flickering light. "If you hadn't been here, Sylvie and I would have both plunged into the water. We would surely have drowned since neither of us can swim."

Suddenly, Glenorr's face turned red with anger; his jaw jutted out. "If ever I meet the leader of that caravan, I'll kill him," and he cursed the man roundly, then wrapped his arms around his knees and began to rock ever so slightly. When he spoke again, it was filled with the caring he felt for his sister. "Ellie deserves something better—you see that, Auragole. She should be surrounded by softness and elegance and beauty, not by the terrors and ugliness of war, or the harshness of these endless mountains." He gestured halfheartedly at the night. "She's a sensitive soul—who would deny that?—and she's lived through some terrible experiences. Her mind snaps now and then and she speaks her fears."

Auragole rubbed his temples as if he could rub understanding into his mind. "Then her words mean nothing?"

"How could her words mean anything? Can the future be known? Not logical, not logical at all. The simple truth is she realizes that we must get over some very difficult mountains and she's frightened. This is the form her fears take. In Mattelmead, there are extraordinary doctors who can cure sicknesses of the mind. Surely you can understand what that means, Auragole? In their laboratories, where they seek new cures, they say they are making medicines that have never existed before, not even in the Golden Century. So you see, our one hope is to get through these difficult mountains and into the west and then to Mattelmead. It's Ellie's only chance." He gave Auragole a searching look.

There was such an ache in his heart that Auragole thought it would burst. He made his decision at that moment. He would go with them to Mattelmead. He wanted more than anything to free Glenelle from her sickness, to get her to doctors who would rid her face of the ugliness he had seen there and rid her heart of its fears. What mattered the chaos within his breast? What man of virtue and quality, on seeing such a need, would turn away? What man would fear his own overwhelming feelings? He would do the right thing. He was sure his mother would approve—even if it meant delaying his own task.

Sylvane came up to the fire with Glenelle's wet clothes. "She's sleeping now. She told me that someone had pushed her into the water. That is why she fought you so hard. She thought someone was trying to drown her until your slap caused her to open her eyes. She stopped fighting when she saw it was you."

"You see what I mean?" Glenorr said.

Auragole put on his shirt and cloak. "We'd better carry her to the fire," he said to Glenorr.

Looking at the troubled, pale young woman now lying near the flames, Auragole asked, "Will she be all right tonight?"

"Yes," Sylvane said. "She'll sleep now. The water revived her. She's herself again. Strange, though, what she said."

"It was only fear speaking, Sylvie," Glenorr said. His tone brooked no argument. "Let's get some sleep. We all need it."

They returned to their blankets. Auragole was wide awake. The image of Ellie on the rock, the unrecognizable sound of her voice went round and round in his mind. He felt sick with worry. What would have happened had he not been there? Would the three of them be dead by now? The thought was intolerable. He sat up and saw Sylvie moving quietly toward him. She put a finger to her lips before he could speak.

"I want to talk to you, but I don't want Glen to hear." She motioned for him to follow her, walking away without waiting for his response.

Auragole got up and followed her, barefoot, into the trees and out of earshot of the two who were asleep. "What's the matter?"

"It's not sickness, not some madness of the mind—what Ellie has." She shook her head.

The trees were heavy with darkness. Moonlight scarcely filtered down through the tangle of elm leaves above them.

"What is it then?" Auragole touched her arm and felt his own hand tremble.

"Ellie falls unconscious and Beings take hold of her."

"Beings!"

"Shhh!"

He lowered his voice. "What do you mean by Beings?"

"Invisible Beings from an invisible world. Gods." Sylvane shuddered and went on, "Only I think the ones that take hold of Ellie are evil."

"You mean like the ones in Ellie's stories?" Auragole sounded skeptical.

"You don't believe me?" There was disappointment in her voice.

"I don't know," he answered. "I'm sorry, Sylvie, but I don't know anything about invisible Beings."

"I understand." And then she frowned. "If you mention any of this to Glen, he'll tell you it's nonsense, that it's human beings who are responsible for good and evil, and that Glenelle has a sickness, a madness, because of events in her life. But it's not true."

"But how does one know what is true, Sylvie?" Auragole was thoroughly confused by what he had heard that night. Sylvane's explanation struck him as absurd, but then Glen's seemed almost as strange. He felt lost in it all. He asked her to explain further.

"Ellie has a weakness." Sylvane spoke slowly, as if by sheer conviction she could help him see the truth. "I don't know why, but now and then an evil Being enters her and it says terrible things. You heard that voice. It's not Ellie's voice—surely you heard that it was not Ellie's voice?"

Auragole nodded.

"It wants to frighten us," Sylvane went on. "I think it wants to prevent us from getting to Mattelmead, from finding a king like Ormahn. Perhaps the evil one that gets inside Glenelle doesn't want Glen to go to the academy. Glen could become a great scientist." She looked back over at the fire. "Ellie doesn't remember what she says after. . .after these spells."

"She doesn't? Do you. . .did you tell her?"

"No. Why frighten her needlessly? It's horrible, what she said. Dying in the snow."

"Do you believe it?"

"I don't know." Sylvane suddenly looked small, vulnerable, and forlorn. It tore at his heart.

Auragole put a hand on her shoulder. "Don't be so troubled, Sylvie. I've decided to come with you to Mattelmead. You're right, my mother didn't say I had to go east immediately. I'll see to it that Ellie. . .that all of you get to Mattelmead. I promise you that. I can go east after that."

"Oh, Aurie." Her eyes filled with tears. "Once again you are giving us back our lives. Are you sure? I mean you so wanted to find your uncle."

"I am sure."

Sylvane hugged him tightly and, for the first time, he hugged her back with affection. Then she ran back to the campfire and left him standing in the trees.

As he tried to fall asleep, he thought about his decision.

"*. . .I'll see to it that Ellie. . .that all of you get to Mattelmead. I promise you that. I can go east after that.*"

And then he remembered something Spehn had told him a long time ago about promises, something he had never forgotten.

"*A promise can be a cruel master, Auragole, and yet we must live under its yoke if we are to be truly human.*" Then Spehn had looked at him and sighed. "*You know nothing of people, Aurie.*"

Auragole grinned at the old man. "*I know the best of people.*"

They had been fishing down by the stream not far from the cottage.

"*Don't make light of it, Aurie,*" he said. "*Human beings can be worse than animals, for they will say one thing and do another,*" *will smile and compliment you while they steal your pack or take your life. People are not often the way they are in the stories we have told you, nor are there many living who are filled with the virtues and qualities your mother has tried to instill in you. Most humans have not been taught to keep their word as you have been taught. Most people are selfish, have little concern for another's needs, or even value another's life. Nothing holds people together now—not laws, not friendship, not kinship. They have become worse than animals who must follow the demands of their instincts."* Spehn pulled a fish out of the water, unhooked it, and put it in the basket. *"Ah well."* He smiled at Auragole then. *"That is something you will one day learn for yourself, when your father takes you east to find . . . "* He paused then, his face thoughtful. *"I hope the lessons aren't too hard."*

But surely, Auragole thought, as he drifted into sleep, these new friends of his were not the people Spehn meant. Surely these were honest people and true. No, there could be no correlation between what Spehn had said and the promise he had just made to his new friends. Surely not.

N

chapter seven

THEY SET OFF five days later from Lake Mimbi with Auragole leading the way. They encountered few difficulties until they turned north seven days later. Then the going became increasingly hazardous. Sylvane kept a close eye on Glenelle as they wound through narrow valleys and gorges, climbing steadily higher, heading for the snowcapped mountains and to the high Northern Valley that would lead them down into the foothills of the Westernlands.

Though it was only the first week in September, summer was gone in these taller wooded mountains. Autumn leaves were raining down, landing on them as well as on the forest floor. Their crunching sounds and those of the pine needles made a mournful accompaniment. The weather was becoming colder. Often there was frost on the ground in the morning. When Glenelle's strength seemed up to it, Auragole insisted they travel long distances each day. He must be worried about getting to the Northern Valley and through it before the snows come,

Sylvane thought.

Each evening Sylvane watched Auragole study the maps the Easterners had been given.

"What are you looking for?" she asked him.

"My father had maps—some he had made himself. But his maps didn't extend as far south and west as this one. I was just wondering if there was a more hospitable way down into the western foothills."

But Sylvane told him that the Northern Valley was the way the caravans always went. They traveled due west, passed along the southern shore of Lake Mimbi, and eventually turned north, just as the maps she gave him showed. "Maybe Glen knows," she said, and watched as Auragole approached her foster brother.

"It's possible that there are valleys or passes through the mountains farther south, but no one from the east uses them," Glenorr said. "I can tell you that only the Northern Valley is considered a safe route. It winds down from these mountains and descends into the country of Noonbarr in the Westernlands. Noonbarr is a sparsely settled country with large, self-sufficient farming communities, far larger than the settlements back east. Each is run by its own warlord. Caravans pay off the warlords so they can pass through Noonbarr unimpeded. And with the amount of armed men on the caravans, most warlords would rather take the money than fight. The north of Thorensphere, to Noonbarr's west, is also sparsely populated. Money and arms speak there as well."

"I see," Auragole said, and put the map back into the pocket inside his cloak.

As they walked through the cold mountains, Sylvane thought often of the words Glenelle had uttered as she stood on that rock. None of the others had mentioned it again. But try as she might to dispel it, Sylvane felt a cloud of anxiety hovering over them as they hurried north. Sylvane imagined, from the increased pace of their march, that Auragole thought about it too. She wondered if Glenorr did. If Glenelle remembered anything of what she had predicted, she never mentioned it.

They seldom conversed as they traveled in these higher mountains. Their supplies and equipment were heavy. Glenorr collected less and less as the days passed by. He was as tired as the rest of them, and went to sleep immediately after supper. Auragole seldom hunted. He said there would be time for hunting after they were in the Northern Valley or beyond it, so they ate frugally of their supplies. Now was the time to conserve their energy. So with little urging they all went to sleep immediately after dinner. There were no more late nights around the fire exchanging life stories, listening to songs or tales.

On the tenth day away from Lake Mimbi, they stopped their day's march somewhat early, for they had come to a good camping spot, a clearing surrounded by maples, still golden in the aging sunlight. A ridge lay to the north, and just at the edge of the clearing and south, a narrow stream ran rapidly downhill.

This is a pretty glade, Sylvane thought. Her mood lightened as they made camp.

Supper was over. They were sipping senta tea and chatting idly. Shockingly a voice broke in. "Well, lads and lassies, I suggest you stay very still."

Startled, they looked up, and there above them on a spur of rock stood a red-haired, red-bearded young man. In his hands was a bow with an arrow pointed at them.

"I need food," he said, a wisp of cloud curling behind him in the vastness of sky.

He looks like a legendary hero out of one of Ellie's stories, Sylvane thought, then wondered if he might be a Guttlubber and shuddered.

To Glenelle, the stranger said, "You, pretty lady, hand up some of those biscuits and some of that fish, and then, one by one, hand up your weapons."

Glenelle turned first to Glenorr, then to Auragole.

In a low voice, Auragole instructed, "Do as he says, Ellie." His eyes were fixed on the man's bow and arrow.

"You're a smart lad," the man said, and then collapsed.

Auragole, running and stumbling up a narrow path fit only for goats, was the first to reach him. Sylvane was close at his heels.

"Look," Auragole said to her, pointing to a cave opening hidden from their campsite by some leafy bushes.

He scooped up the man's bow and arrow and gave them to her. Then with a curt command to Glenorr, who had joined them, the two lifted the man and carried him down to the fire. Glenorr made a quick search of the stranger. He found only a single knife stuck in the man's belt beneath his cloak. Glenorr tucked it into his own belt below his cloak. The man's left leg was wrapped in dirty bandages. Glenelle, feeling it gingerly, speculated that it was broken.

With Glenelle and Glenorr guarding the intruder, Auragole and Sylvane returned to the promontory to inspect the small cave. They found a blanket, arrows, a pot, a cup, one fork, a backpack containing a change of clothes, a water container, but no food. And, to Sylvane's relief, no white-and-gray uniform.

When they returned to level ground, Glenorr came over to them. His eyes were cold, that ice-blue Sylvane so abhorred. "He could be a Guttlubber, but since you say there was no uniform, I suspect he's a thief."

Sylvane's heart began to beat rapidly at the impact of Glen's words. She walked over to where the red-haired man was lying. He groaned.

"Of course he could have buried his uniform if he got cut off from his comrades," Glen said.

Kneeling, Glenelle put her hand on the stranger's head. "He's feverish, perhaps from hunger. He may not be either a Guttlubber or a thief, just starving."

"That's right, Glen. He's probably just hungry," Sylvane said, as she looked at the unconscious figure. He was of medium height, wide in the chest, with large, powerful arms. Yet underneath his red beard, his face looked gray and his cheeks hollow.

Auragole was staring at the man, a puzzled look in his eyes. When he caught Sylvane watching him, he grinned crookedly. "I've never seen red hair before," he said. "Is it common among the people of the east?"

"Not so common," Sylvane laughed, "but not so strange, either."

Glenelle instructed Sylvane to make the healing eldenmyrr tea and she hurried to comply.

"Wait!" Glenorr grabbed Sylvane's arm, but she shook free. He turned to his sister. "You offer help to a Guttlubber, or worse, a thief?"

Glenelle didn't answer Glenorr. Her mouth was set, and Sylvane was familiar with both her stubbornness and her warm heart. With Auragole's help, Glenelle changed the man's bandage.

"He must have set his ankle himself," Auragole said, with obvious admiration. "I broke my ankle when I was ten, falling from a tree. Spehn set it and the pain was terrible."

After they changed the bandages, the two women bathed the man's face and neck until they could feel the fever subside beneath their fingers. Every now and then Sylvane would glance up to see Glenorr watching them with a cold, dark expression. Glenelle pointedly ignored him. When the eldenmyrr leaves had steeped long enough in the hot water, Sylvane brought the tea in the clay cup they had found in the cave. She looked down at the stranger.

"He's a handsome one," she said. "What do we do with him?"

"You know very well what we do with him. In our settlement, Guttlubbers and thieves are hanged." Glenorr said it quietly, but Sylvane felt a shiver run down her spine. It was true. Of course, she had never seen a Guttlubber near her settlement, but she knew that anyone caught sneaking into their settlement to steal their supplies—whatever the reason—was hanged just outside their walls as a warning to others. It was no different in other settlements.

Auragole stared at Glenorr, a shocked expression on his face. "Would you hang a hungry, feverish man?"

"A man who steals, dies. It's the law of our settlement."

Auragole's mouth opened slightly.

Glenelle's lips tightened, but she said nothing to her brother. Defiantly, she turned to Sylvane and asked her to hold the man's head. Sylvane knelt down, lifted the man's head to her lap, and held him while Glenelle attempted to feed him spoonfuls of eldenmyrr tea. His eyelids flickered and he swallowed.

Glenorr watched the two women. And Auragole watched Glenorr. Sylvane could taste the coldness of Glenorr's stare as if it were snow on her tongue. After a few moments, Glenorr turned and walked the several yards to the stream. He picked up pebble after pebble lying in or near the water, looking, no doubt, for something new. For a time he seemed absorbed in his work. Sylvane felt relieved, but wasn't convinced that the crisis had passed. She knew Glenorr too well.

Some moments later, the young man's eyes opened. They were light brown, flecked with gold. He grinned at Glenelle. "Now that's as pretty a face as I've seen in a long time."

"I think he's recovering," Glenelle said, and stood up.

The man tried to sit. "You'd better prop me up. I'm weak as a reed."

Sylvane rose as Auragole put the man's pack under his head. The man grinned at her as she came into his vision. "Well, hello there." He looked up at Auragole. "A veritable feast for the eyes, two beauties."

Sylvane blushed but lifted her head a little higher.

"I think he can take a bit of food now," Glenelle said.

"Those are sweet words, indeed," and he ate a few bites of

fish, then fell into a quiet sleep.

The women covered him with his blanket, then they walked to where Glenorr was sitting, sorting through stones and rocks in the rapidly failing light. Auragole followed them.

"We need to talk, Glen." Glenelle's voice was firm as she stood in front of him, her blond hair billowing behind her, her thin shoulders erect, making her look taller than she was.

Auragole and Sylvane stood behind her. Glenorr gazed up at Glenelle. The dying sun was setting in his eyes. They looked red and malevolent. "What's there to talk about? Our law says Guttlubbers and thieves die." His voice was low, impersonal.

Sylvane could sense, rather than see, Auragole trembling beside her. She didn't know if it was from fear or rage.

"We're not in our settlement now, Glen," his sister reminded him in a voice as hard as his own. "That law doesn't apply here."

Sylvane sighed with relief. It must have been audible, because Auragole reached out and touched her arm.

"We must keep our laws until we reach Mattelmead." Glenorr's voice rose; the coldness was turning to passion, which was the way with Glenorr. "If a man gives up his laws, he will soon be reduced to the animals from which he comes. The ability to make laws and follow them is what distinguishes us from the beasts."

An idea suddenly occurred to Sylvane. "What do you think we should do, Aurie?" She turned toward him. "What are the laws in your settlement?"

Auragole's face was a war of confusion. His words shook as they came out. "We should wait until morning and talk to the man. Perhaps then we can judge the man and not the deed."

"One judges the action and not the man, for his actions make him who he is." Glenorr stood up slowly, dropped the stones he had been holding, dusted off the mud from his hands, and slowly drew out his sword.

All the other weapons lay near the fire.

Auragole, without hesitation, moved toward him, stepping in front of Glenelle.

Furious, Sylvane rushed past them both, but Glenorr brandished his sword in her face and looked angry and ugly.

"I think waiting until morning makes good sense," Sylvane said. "Peace, Glenorr, waiting harms no one."

"And I say kill the intruder now before his strength returns and he becomes dangerous."

"No!" Glenelle shouted, her blazing eyes confronting Glenorr's as she rushed to stand next to Sylvane.

"Stop it!" Auragole's words pierced the dusk like an arrow. "Stop it!" He moved around the two women and faced Glenorr.

Glenorr turned to aim his sword at Auragole's heart.

Auragole stopped only inches from it. He lowered his voice but there was fierceness in it. "There will be no talk of death tonight or in the morning. If this man is harmed, if there is any attempt to kill him, I am finished with all of you. You can go west without me." His breath came out in short gasps. "Can you be mad? I know nothing of your laws and rules and care to know nothing. But I do know that a man's life is not a trivial thing to be ended because of a few biscuits."

Glenelle and Sylvane looked from Auragole to Glenorr. Glenorr's face was white with anger. But Auragole did not relent. Something changed in Auragole's expression. He raised his hand and pointed at Glenorr. "Can you, with all your ability to categorize, Glen, with all your thinking power, can you lead Glenelle and Sylvane safely through these mountains?"

Before Glenorr could respond, Sylvane rushed over to Glenorr and took his arm, ignoring the sword in it. "This will wait till morning," she said. "Come, let's clean up and go to sleep."

"We will place a watch on the thief tonight," Glenorr said.

It was agreed that each of them should take a two-hour watch. First, Glenorr, then Auragole, followed by Sylvane, and in the early hours of morning, Glenelle. Glenorr returned his sword to its sheath, turned his back on them, sat down near the fire, and began to write in his notebook.

Sylvane did not sleep during Glenorr's watch, nor, she observed, did Auragole. But all remained quiet.

chapter eight

AURAGOLE AWOKE TO sounds of laughter. The sun was slipping above the horizon between the mountains. Ellie and the injured man were engrossed in conversation. He was sitting up, munching biscuits and dried fish and telling a story in a rich, deep voice.

"No, I almost got caught, but I bit the man's leg and he let go, and I ran as fast as a fox with a hound after him," he said with a grin, and Glenelle rocked with laughter. As he saw Sylvane and Auragole approach, he waved his hand at them. "I'm in your hands, dear captors, and I am indebted to you for my life." Auragole looked at Ellie. Her face was flushed. Something in his stomach twisted into a tight knot.

"This charming man has been telling me the funniest stories," she said. "I haven't laughed so hard in months."

"Is that so?" her brother said, coming up behind Auragole and Sylvane.

Hands on his hips, Glenorr stared down at the man, and

Auragole knew that the judgment had begun.

"Are you a Guttlubber?" Glen asked.

The man looked at Glenorr with obvious astonishment. But something in Glenorr's eyes must have made him wary, because he answered soberly. "I am not."

"Do you deny that you are a thief?"

"I don't deny it, lad. Among other things, I have been a thief."

"I knew it!" Glenorr said, with a smirk of satisfaction.

"In these times one does what the situation demands," the acknowledged thief retorted. "I was hungry and injured. How did I know you were friendly? I was hardly in a position to take that chance."

Auragole asked the man his name.

"Donnadorr." He gave Auragole a thoughtful look. "Are you the leader?"

There was only a moment's hesitation before Auragole told him yes. No one challenged his words. No one.

"I'm from the east, from anywhere my luck finds me, anywhere I can get a little work or a little diversion." He grinned at Glenelle.

"Did you belong to a thieving band that raided settlements?" Glenorr's tone was cold.

"Ah, my friend, nothing so horrible." The words were light as Donnadorr went on, but Auragole saw his eyes narrow as he regarded Glenorr. "I know many who like killing, but I do not. I have little taste for the violent life. I find no joy in inflicting pain, though many do. Don't misunderstand me, I've killed— who hasn't?—but only in defense of my life. I've lived with people in the north and in the south. I have friends all over the Easternlands, but also enemies. I've stolen when I had to, but never needlessly, never for the joy of it. I don't remember my parents. I've never had a home. I've lived by my wits and my brawn. But now, injured, weak, and weaponless," he grinned at the two women, "I find myself in your good hands."

Glenelle and Sylvane smiled back at him, obviously satisfied with what they had heard. But Glenorr looked stern and determined. Auragole watched him with growing concern.

"Where are you heading?" Sylvane asked Donnadorr.

"To the west, of course," he answered, "to Mattelmead to offer my services to the splendid King Ormahn. I couldn't afford the fare of a caravan, so I set off alone."

"We're going there too," Sylvane said. "This is fortunate."

"Now if I had known that, my pretty, I would not have tried to steal your food. I would have asked politely if I could join your party." He roared with laughter, and the women laughed with him.

Glenorr motioned Auragole to follow him. When they were far enough away from the others, he said, "A fine situation we have on our hands. He's clever and he's won the girls over. We should have finished him last night. Now what do you suggest we do?" Glenorr smiled mirthlessly.

Auragole didn't answer him, but his heart was pounding. He turned and walked back to the campfire, took his ration of food, and sat down.

"I stepped into a hole." Donnadorr said this to Auragole. "It was foolish to misstep so, but I was tired and not watchful. I've been here over a week."

"Without food?" Sylvane asked.

"I've had a little, and there was fresh water from that stream. I've been unable to catch much fish, unfortunately. Still, I'm lucky. You came my way."

Sylvane smiled again at his answer.

"Well, lad," Donnadorr turned to Auragole, "what's it to be? Am I to be treated as a thief or as a misguided friend?"

Auragole looked at the young man. He liked his face. Yet he had known too few people to judge quickly.

Glenorr came and stood in front of the man. "Do you know

what the law is for thieves?"

"Where, lad?"

"In the settlements back east."

"I do, and I'm grateful we're not in the east but in these beautiful unsettled mountains."

"We carry our laws with us," Glenorr said.

"I see." Donnadorr still smiled, but his light-flecked eyes narrowed slightly and his hands clenched as he looked up at Glenorr. Auragole saw the quick appraisal he gave him. "So, then, it's my death you want?"

"No, Glen!" Sylvane and Glenelle said simultaneously.

Auragole stood up. "There will be no talk of killing here!" The words exploded out of him. "That's my decision. You're in my mountains, therefore the laws of my settlement prevail." As if from the mild breeze that had just blown through the camp, the thought had come. Auragole glared at Glenorr as if asking him to defy him.

Donnadorr drew himself up shakily to his feet and said his words to Auragole, though Auragole knew they were meant for Glenorr. "I'm glad to hear that, for I have to tell you, injured or not, weaponless or not, I am a hard man to kill."

Glenelle moved to stand between her brother and Donnadorr.

The next words out of Auragole's mouth surprised even him. "Glenorr," he said as he threw the remains of his food wastefully into the fire, and turned to face him, "we can't go off and leave an injured man. We'll remain at this campsite until Donnadorr's ankle is healed. That way he can accompany us to the Westernlands. We could use an extra pair of hands—since we have no use of the donkey."

"You would risk snow in the Northern Valley?" Glenorr asked, his mouth a rigid line.

"For a man's life, yes."

"Even though we are late as it is?"

"That part is not my fault," Auragole said evenly. "You traveled in the wrong direction."

The two glowered at each other. Glenorr's hand moved inside his cloak. "You would risk rising one morning to find all our supplies gone?"

"The man will not betray us. We have saved his life."

Glenorr began to laugh. There was little warmth in it. "You're a fool who knows little of human nature. But you saved my sister's life. I owe you." And Glen walked away.

The confrontation was over. Auragole had won, and now, somewhat stunned by the outcome, he was undisputed leader of their little caravan. Pride and exhilaration struggled with fear and uncertainty. It was up to him now to guide these strangers safely across these mountains. Could he do it?

THEY STAYED TEN days in that clearing until Donnadorr's ankle had almost healed. Day after day, Auragole went out in search of fruit or nut trees but found little. He and Sylvane fished in the stream in their clearing and were, to their relief, successful. Glenorr and Glenelle gathered autumn herbs, and they made broth with some and dried the rest. Donnadorr wanted to work along with them, but Auragole insisted he stay off his ankle. Sylvane tried not to worry about snow in the high mountains or about Glenelle's prediction. Donnadorr was now part of their troop, and that was comforting. After all, there's strength in numbers, she thought.

Glenorr spent his free time gathering samples of stones. His new finds seemed to cheer him. He rarely spoke to Donnadorr, but he was mockingly courteous with Auragole. Sylvane didn't know if Auragole was aware of the sarcasm. He had begun to school his expressions. He seemed quieter, caught up in some inner dialogue or conflict of his own. She often saw him watching Donnadorr.

Why not? Sylvane thought. Ellie and I are obviously taken

with him. Don does make us laugh. He tells marvelously funny stories, and he's always cheerful. Laughter can heal. Laughter can take one's cares away for a time. She loved Donnadorr for that. Oh, not in the way she loved Auragole. That way was not so easily taken apart. Love is not cloth with warp and woof and threads to be pulled at, but something with layers that weaves itself deeply into the soul. But she adored Donnadorr for the joy he brought them. It lightened their load and made their waiting time together sweet.

Every night while they remained at that camp, Donnadorr and Glenelle vied for best tale. And Sylvane enjoyed hearing them. Auragole, though their light banter seemed to baffle him, listened with obvious pleasure to these new stories. Donnadorr's tales were either funny or filled with mystery. Often they were stories of unearthly Beings who had once descended from the Creative World to the Deep Earth to fight and to love as humans did. Others were romantic tales; others incomprehensible tales of how the earth had been created. There were tales of the King God and of the Prince God, of one called the Defender, and of other Gods worshipped before and during the Golden Century. Though Auragole too knew many tales, he told none while they waited for Donnadorr's leg to heal.

He sees in Don a rival, Sylvane surmised, and doesn't know what to do about it.

Donnadorr also sang—and obviously loved it. His was a full, deep voice. And to Sylvane's relief, it wasn't long before he and Auragole were singing together. Auragole's voice was lighter and higher than Donnadorr's, but his tone was as pure as water in a brook. The two taught each other songs. Soon they were doing harmonies. Donnadorr carved a flute of reeds and taught Auragole to play it. Auragole taught Donnadorr to play the harp. The campsite rang out with music and story. It was the joy of singing that was the cause of peace between the two men. Even Glenorr came closer to the fire to listen when they sang.

Those were halcyon days—indeed, as innocent and carefree as Sylvane had ever known.

ONE COLD LATE September morning, ten days after they had come upon Donnadorr, the travelers resumed their journey. It was nearing the time of the autumn equinox. It should take about two weeks to get to the Northern Valley, Auragole told his companions, once again consulting the map that Sylvane had given him. Donnadorr's ankle had not completely healed, but the weather had grown perceptibly colder and a grayness had come that refused to depart. Auragole, though he did not say so, feared that it might already be too late to get to and through the Northern Valley before the snows blocked their way. The mountains they were heading toward were very high and their peaks were covered in snow.

The elation of leadership was long gone, leaving a trail of worry in its track. But who other, Auragole wondered, could find the way through the mountains? Not even Donnadorr was as expert as he in reading the signs that kept them heading in the right direction. So Auragole was the acknowledged leader—and what else was there to do but move ahead?

The farther north they traveled, the more difficult the going became. The path was almost always steep and often narrow, fit only for goats. The wind blew incessantly. There were fewer trees now. It took longer to gather wood for the fire each night. There was little game and fewer streams to fish, so they ate frugally of their meager supplies. Auragole told them that if they could get to the Northern Valley on the provisions they carried, he was sure they would find food as they moved into lower ground.

It was Donnadorr, Auragole knew, who kept the group's spirits up, singing when the path seemed impossible. He told humorous stories in a boisterous voice as they walked, making the mountains echo with laughter. Only Auragole seemed bothered by the unpromising weather, and therefore took only a modicum of pleasure in Don's tales. Why hadn't they left Donnadorr some food, and gone on their way? He knew the answer—it had been his own willfulness, his irritation at Glenorr, his desire to be the accepted leader of the group. It seemed important then that he have some talent that the others did not have. He could sing and he could recite. But Don seemed better at both. All he had of worth was his skill as guide, his knowledge of mountain travel. One night he dreamt they had killed Donnadorr that first day. Only it wasn't Glenorr who had wielded the knife, it was Auragole!

Each night, as they camped, Donnadorr carefully unwrapped the bandage on his ankle. It was swollen and Auragole knew that despite Don's cheerfulness, it hurt him. But Auragole said nothing, nor did he slacken their pace.

As the days passed, as their difficulties in traveling increased, Auragole could barely bring himself to speak. The more silent Auragole became, the more Donnadorr joked and told stories, or sang as they walked. Auragole could feel his own resentment growing. It was easy for Don to sing. He wasn't worried about snow in the Northern Valley. Don's cheerfulness only made Auragole more taciturn. Was the man unaware of what difficulties they were facing—and all because of him? When Glenelle's strength was low, it was Donnadorr who took part of her load. All this Auragole saw but said nothing. He had heard about jealousy in stories and songs as a child. It was an ignoble emotion, but he felt it all the same, and he could not rid himself of it. Nor did he try very hard.

ON THE FIFTH day of their march north, trouble found them. Since sunup, they had been moving along a narrow, dry riverbed—a far easier walk than the goat paths they had been following. The mountains rose steeply on either side. Auragole, who had been out front, dropped back to talk to Donnadorr, who was walking beside Sylvane.

"Something's out there," he told Donnadorr in a low voice.

"I know." Donnadorr nodded, his hand gripping his bow. "What do you think it is?"

"Some animals, I suspect."

"Not too hungry, I hope."

"Keep your sword ready," Auragole told Sylvane. "I'm going to warn the others."

Sylvane watched him speak first to Glenelle and then to Glenorr. Glenorr and Sylvane pulled out their swords; the other three readied their bows. They marched on, listening for anything unusual in the small sounds around and above them. Sylvane could hear nothing out of the ordinary. Auragole was just ahead of her, and when she saw his back stiffen, she listened harder, looked harder, but heard and saw nothing.

It seemed as if hours passed, but Sylvane's sense of time was all askew, embedded as it was in fear. Fear seemed so thick around her that she had to repress the desire to whack at it, at anything. She had heard so many stories, not only of wild animals but also of weird creatures in the Gandlese, that her mind envisioned grotesque picture after grotesque picture. She couldn't pull her inner eye away from its gruesome gallery. The troop stayed close together, their eyes scanning the high hills on either side of them. They were vulnerable, and Sylvane knew that Auragole knew it too. It had been his choice, this path. But really, how else to go? They couldn't walk along the sheer face of the mountain.

When it happened, it was fierce and over quickly. Four wild dogs suddenly leapt out at them, coming from a ledge about ten feet above them. Two were killed in midair, one by Glenelle and one by Donnadorr. Auragole shot the third after it landed and was running toward Sylvane. Glenorr dropped his sword and killed the fourth with his knife as it jumped on him. His shoulder was grazed, but his heavy cloak had prevented serious injury.

The next moment remained frozen in Sylvane's memory. She

was standing, her back against a wall of rock, her sword outstretched, the blood drained from her face. Donnadorr was surveying the scene with a grim look on his face. Glenorr, biting his lip, was looking at his torn cloak. But Glenelle, poor Ellie, was standing over the dog she had just killed, her hand on the protruding arrow, her foot on its grotesque, death-distorted face. Her head was thrown back and on her face was a look of pure ecstasy. But it was not her face. And there was Auragole staring at Glenelle, his face white with sweat and uncertainty.

The dogs, they decided later, must either have been lost or turned loose by some caravan heading west. Left alone in these mountains, they had become wild. Hunger had made them attack. Foolishly perhaps, Sylvane wept for the dogs, but then she had a fondness for animals. Glenelle said nothing that night, but her eyes were unusually bright and her cheeks were deeply flushed.

N

chapter nine

IT WAS PAST noon. They were three or four days away from the Northern Valley when the snows came—gently at first.

"Let's hope it's just a light fall," Auragole said, and insisted they keep going.

But snow dropped down with a steady insistence. After an hour, the air was so dense they could barely see ahead of them.

"We'll have to find shelter," Auragole called out to them.

They had been walking along a valley with the mountain wall to their left and west. The snow was blowing from the north, the direction they were heading in.

"What's up there?" Glenorr called.

"Where?" Auragole shouted, above the noise of the wind.

"Up about thirty or forty feet," Glenorr shouted back, pointing. "It might be a cave."

Auragole looked up but saw nothing but snow. Then the wind shifted for a moment and he saw what seemed like a large opening in the rock. "It could be," he said. "I'll see if I can find a path. Stay close together, and follow me." He moved ahead of them into a sheet of snow. The others followed, holding hands, until Auragole had located the narrow path. "Wait here," he instructed, and began to climb.

When Auragole returned, he said, "Glen was right. There is a cave up there. I've looked inside. From the little I could see, I would say that it's empty of animals. It should be more than adequate to keep us out of the snow. Hang on to each other and follow me. Watch your footing."

Because the snow blinded him, the donkey followed docilely up the path. With relief, the five stumbled into the darkness of the cave.

"Hellooo," Donnadorr called out, and an echo resounded, filling the cave with his voice.

"Great stars!" Sylvane said, and grabbed Auragole's arm.

They lit a small fire with the emergency wood the donkey carried and saw that they were in a large cavern. They could barely see the ceiling. Auragole took a torch, and followed by Glenorr and Sylvane, they examined the cave. At its north end was an opening leading into a tunnel.

"It might go all the way through this series of mountains," Glenorr said.

"Hard to say," Auragole answered. "Caves are tricky."

They returned to the others.

"It's a possible exit," was all Auragole told them.

"There's about four hours of daylight left," Donnadorr said. "It looks like we'll have to spend the night." He turned to Auragole. "Is my judgment correct, dear lad?"

"Yes," Auragole answered, rather testily, and began to set up camp. He hated being called "dear lad."

The snow came down all that day. As he watched it morosely, Auragole knew that it could be one of those mountain storms that go on for days, perhaps for weeks in these northern mountains. The group spoke little. Donnadorr sang quietly to himself—mournful, sad melodies. Auragole could not draw his thoughts away from the Northern Valley. In his mind he could see it feet-deep in snow and remembered the words that Glenelle had spoken at Lake Mimbi. But surely that was only Ellie's sickness speaking. Surely the future could not be known.

That night Glenelle had another spell.

A low wailing woke Auragole. He grabbed his knife and sat up. The snows had stopped and the light from the full moon streamed into the cave. And then he saw Glenelle. She was standing in the ashes of the extinguished fire with her arms clasped about her. She had taken off her cloak and dress and was standing in her petticoat in the freezing air of the cave.

"No, no, no!" her voice moaned.

Auragole moved silently to where Sylvane was sleeping. He shook her, then put his hand over her mouth so she wouldn't call out. She looked at him, a startled expression on her sleepy face. Auragole pointed to Glenelle standing in the ashes, her eyes closed.

"Listen," Auragole whispered.

"Don't tell me," Glenelle's voice pleaded.

"Fire, fire!" A different voice issued from her mouth with a mocking laugh.

"What is it?" Donnadorr called softly from Auragole's right.

"Shhh!" Auragole said.

Donnadorr came up beside them. "What is it?" he asked again, this time in a whisper.

Glenelle was holding herself and rocking back and forth.

"Fire!" the ugly voice hissed. "There will be fire all around you and you won't escape—none of you. Fire brings death!"

"How? Where?" Glenelle begged, in her own voice.

"I will tell you how and I will tell you where. It will come in a mist of red, then a large, green. . ."

"Glenelle! Wake up!" A harsh command echoed through the cave. Glenorr rushed over to her and shook her hard.

98

Glenelle opened her eyes. "Oh, Glen! Oh, Glen!" she said, moving into his arms. "It's horrible!" She was shaking violently.

Sylvane hurried to her. "Get her clothes," she called to Auragole.

He found them, and Glenorr and Sylvane helped her dress. Donnadorr and Auragole relit the fire.

"What is it? What's the matter with her?" Donnadorr asked Auragole, as they piled on some of their precious twigs.

The twins sat on the far side of the burgeoning fire, Glenorr's arms tightly around Glenelle. Sylvane prepared some of their dwindling supply of eldenmyrr tea for brewing.

"Ellie's madness."

"Madness?" Donnadorr said, looking across the fire at the trembling woman.

Auragole then told him, first what Glenorr had told him and then what Sylvane had said. "So judge for yourself."

"No need to judge, dear lad, only to help. The cause is less important than the cure. Now we must redouble our efforts to get to Mattelmead. Surely there a cure will be found."

"I remember. . .this time I remember the. . ." Glenelle looked first at Glenorr, then at the rest of them. She couldn't go on.

"The dream?" Sylvane said.

"It wasn't a dream." Glenelle shook her head. "It wasn't. It was more real than any dream."

"Of course it was a dream," Glenorr said, stroking her hair.

"What do you remember, Ellie?" Auragole asked her.

"I was in some horrible, hot land. Around me were hills. They were desolate and barren. As far as the eye could see, there was nothing growing. Even the light seemed tinted brown. A few feet ahead and a little above me, a lady was sitting on a jagged rock. She looked like she was part of the rock—or as if she had grown out of it. Her face was white. . ." Glenelle started to tremble again.

"Stop it, Ellie!" Her brother's voice was hoarse with concern.

"You're making yourself ill again."

"Let me finish!" she said. "The lady's face was white, but the rest of her was covered in a winding cloth. I wanted to run but I couldn't move. Her eyes held me fast. She told me there would be a fire and none of us would escape alive." Glenelle's voice quivered uncontrollably.

"Ellie! Let it be!" Her brother shook her.

"No!" she shouted, and broke free of his arms. Rising, she moved a few feet away from them. She stood there, swaying back and forth. "I looked off to my left and on the horizon I could see the fire. It was coming toward me. And behind it a green, a green. . ." She faltered.

"A green what, Ellie?" Sylvane's words were a cry.

"I don't know. I don't know. Glen brought me back." She began to cry. "I was filled with fear, filled with fear."

"It was only a dream, Ellie." Glenorr came over to her and took her in his arms. His voice was gentle now and filled with caring. "Dreams have no reality. Our fears and worries take strange shape in our sleeping minds, that's all."

"I knew a man who had prophetic dreams," Donnadorr said softly.

"Truly?" Sylvane turned to him.

"Truly my love," he said, and then he laughed. "What Ellie needs is some tea to warm her, a hearty fire, and a cheerful song. We could all use some tea."

So they added more of their dwindling supply of twigs to the fire, and Sylvane served Ellie the eldenmyrr tea, and brewed some senta tea for the others. While they sipped it, Donnadorr sang funny songs. When Glenelle smiled at some silly lyric about a farmer, his wife, and an impossible hen, Don said, "I think we can all sleep now."

But Auragole couldn't sleep. He lay awake a long time thinking about Ellie's dream. Finally he rolled over and saw Donnadorr sitting up, staring at the dying fire. Don's face in the light looked unusually pensive.

Auragole sat up then.

"Can't sleep, lad?" Don turned his head to look at Auragole.

"Not yet."

"Worried?"

"Tell me about your man with the prophetic dreams."

"Ah, him." Donnadorr absentmindedly stroked his red beard. "He dreamt of his own death and died."

They both sat silently watching the fire. Finally each lay down. Auragole fell at last into a restless sleep.

By morning it was snowing again. And it continued to come down all that day.

THEY SPENT FOUR days in the cave, three without fire, and with cold, meager rations. They huddled together for warmth and slept more than was good in the cold.

Everyone watched Auragole, waiting for some decision. He was the man of the mountains and their leader. What does he think we should do? Sylvane wondered, but asked nothing. Nor did any of the others.

On the morning of the fifth day, Auragole finally said, "I think we should find out if that tunnel leads to another exit farther north." He spoke without enthusiasm.

"But what if it leads nowhere?" Sylvane said.

"Then we'll be no worse off than we are now," he said, with a hint of irritation. "We'll mark the way, so we'll be able to retrace our steps, should it prove necessary."

The others stared at him.

"It's better if we're up and moving," Auragole said. "Let's go."

"Right you are, lad," Donnadorr said.

So they packed up their supplies and entered the tunnel.

It was high, about ten feet, but narrow—in some places only a few feet wide. They walked in single file. Auragole led, carrying only one lit torch, saving the others. Glenelle walked behind him and Sylvane behind her. Glenorr, leading the donkey, came after Sylvane, and Donnadorr walked in the rear making marks with his knife to help them find their way back, should it be necessary. At first he tried to teach them a marching song, but their hearts weren't in it.

Sylvane had never been in a mountain tunnel before. She hated it. How heavy, how nearly unbearable the weight of the mountain above and around her seemed. The dampness seeped into her bones. She swallowed again and again so as not to scream. She knew, as did the others, that should they find another exit, there would still be the snow to contend with unless this passageway went clear through the mountains into another climate. Little chance of that. After a while she stopped thinking.

Despite the rest they'd had in the cave, everyone seemed exhausted. It was cold and their rations were skimpy. Glenelle had been silent since her spell, and Sylvane kept a close watch on her. Though her strength seemed ample enough for her back-pack, her eyes were sunken and her face drawn. Sylvane's heart ached when she looked at her.

The tunnel climbed steadily. Sylvane wondered if that was bad or good. Auragole said nothing.

"It's warmer in the tunnel," she said once, trying to keep her voice light. But didn't that mean that they weren't near another exit? Twice they came to a fork in the tunnel. Auragole chose the way to go, but on what basis, Sylvane had no idea. Dutifully, Donnadorr notched the entrance to the tunnel they had left. Often they heard scurrying sounds, but they never saw anything.

How long they walked before Auragole called a halt for food and a rest, Sylvane couldn't tell. They ate. They rested. And then they walked again, stopped again, ate again, and tried to sleep.

Auragole woke them in what Sylvane assumed was the morning.

Though how he knew was a puzzle. Perhaps he didn't. Perhaps he surmised it.

After a small, cold meal, they resumed their journey.

One morning—was it their second or their third?—after they had been walking for perhaps two hours, Sylvane became aware of an odor that shouldn't have been there. She called out, "What's that strange smell?"

"Fire!" Glenelle said, her voice barely audible.

"More like burning candles," Donnadorr said.

"Let's go back," Glenelle pleaded.

Glenelle's dream-vision was vivid in Sylvane's mind.

Auragole spoke sharply. "There's nothing to go back to, only snow and. . ." He didn't finish his sentence.

"But the fire. . ." Glenelle's voice cracked.

"Put that dream out of your mind!" Glenorr said, louder than was necessary. "It smells like candles. That's all."

"If there are candles, someone put them there," Auragole said. "Perhaps we'll find help."

"Someone or some *thing* put the candles there," Donnadorr said.

"What kind of *thing*?" Glenorr's tone was mocking.

"Perhaps the Elemental Beings who live in caves. They don't like the children of humanity. They think us fools."

"Elemental Beings belong to your folktales and not to reality. Your ignorance and your fears make you foolish."

"To know the enemy is not the same as to fear the enemy," Donnadorr answered, with a smile. But there was no mirth in his tone.

Sylvane drew closer to Donnadorr.

"We go on," Auragole said. "There might be help ahead."

"Oh, Aurie," Glenelle said.

"Forward we go. You're the leader, dear lad," Donnadorr said, and took Glenelle's hand.

With their swords drawn, they cautiously moved ahead. The

air became warmer and the smell of burning wax was stronger. There was a yellow glow up ahead.

"I think we've come to the end of this tunnel and that light is probably coming from another cavern." Auragole motioned to Donnadorr to follow him and told the others to wait. The two moved silently toward the shimmering golden haze until they stood at the large opening. Swords drawn, they entered it.

"Gods and stars!" Donnadorr exclaimed, in a voice filled with amazement. His words echoed loudly back to the others.

The two dropped their swords to their sides and walked out of sight as the other three rushed to join them.

"Extraordinary!" Glenorr said, pulling the donkey and following the two into the large rocky room lit by what seemed like hundreds of candles. Glenelle and Sylvane were at his heels.

The new cavern was as large as the original one they had found several days before. But this was as unlike the first as a mansion is to a hut. From the floor to the ceiling were natural shelves of rock and on the shelves were large glass jars, each about the size of a man. Stuffed into these jars were books and scrolls. On the floor, scattered about, were stones and large rocks and more books and scrolls. There were hundreds of lit candles on all of the shelves throwing grotesque shadows about the cave. There was a smell of decay heavy in the room and it mingled with the burning wax and another unidentifiable odor.

Sylvane shuddered without knowing why.

Glenorr, on the other hand, was ecstatic. "A library! Earth and metal, it's a real library!" His words ricocheted about them. "I thought they had all been destroyed!" He began picking up one book after another, one scroll after another. Some fell apart the minute he touched them. "There are books here from the Golden Century and scrolls from before that. What a find! What a find!" His voice shook with emotion and Sylvane could see the tears in his eyes. "*The New Science*," he read, "and look at this one, *Wild Life of the Bergathian Forest*. That's near our home!"

"Why is this library here under a mountain in the deserted Gandlese?" Sylvane asked, feeling very uneasy. She picked up a book whose cover was made of leather inlaid with precious jewels. Its pages fell apart as she opened it.

"Well, lads and lassies," Donnadorr said, "I've seen a good many sights in my travels, but this beats all. Thousands of books in the middle of a mountain in the middle of nowhere. The Gods protect us," he added.

"What do you think, Aurie?" Sylvane asked, staring at all the lit candles.

"I think we should look around," he answered, but his mouth was a tight line and she knew he was uneasy.

"I've never heard of putting books in preserving jars," Glenelle said, looking at the glass containers on their shelves.

They took off their packs, laid down their weapons, and turned the donkey loose, then spread out around the cave picking up books and scrolls. Many of the scrolls were in languages no one recognized; even the letters were unfamiliar. Many were so old they disintegrated as they were picked up.

"*A Guide to the Making of Weaponry*," Glenorr read out loud with mounting excitement. "*A Manual for the Making of Horseless Carriages; Rock Layers: A Guide to the Ages of the Earth*. These are all from the Golden Century. Do you realize that some wise people, fearing the wars, must have hidden books here in this remote cave? How marvelous! How extraordinary! Swords, if we could get these books to Ormahn, he could revive some of the knowledge that has been lost in these centuries of war. What a reception we would get in Mattelmead then. All doors would open to us, perhaps even the doors to the palace."

Glenorr sat down near a pile of books and began reading title after title, shaking his head in wonder, laughing as tears rolled down his face. "It's astounding! It's amazing! We mustn't rush out of here. What a discovery! I must have time to look these books over. I'll leave my rocks. We'll take as many books as we can. But which ones? We'll get rid of everything we are carrying that's extraneous. We have to take these treasures and news of this cave to Mattelmead."

"Some of these books have jewels embedded in them," Donnadorr said, his eyes sparkling. "Now that would be worth taking to Mattelmead. Forget the books, lad. Get the jewels. We could buy a dozen palaces with the likes of some of these," he said, waving a jewel-encrusted book at them. He promptly sat down and started to dig out the jewels with his knife.

"Knowledge is a greater treasure than jewels, you mindless thief," Glenorr shouted from across the cave.

"You take those books from here and you'll be a thief yourself, my fine scholarly lad," Donnadorr retorted.

"Peace, peace," Glenelle said. "Let each take what he desires and leave the others to do the same."

"Take them where?" Sylvane heard Auragole mutter to himself. He looked up to see her watching him. He gave her a half smile and then said, "Come, let's see if we can find another exit. It will be bad for us if we've come to a dead end and have to retrace our steps. Our food supplies are very low."

Sylvane nodded and followed him around the cave, stepping behind great rock outcroppings. They finally saw it. It was remarkably well hidden in an unlit corner, a large tunnel, much wider and much higher than the one they had traveled through.

"Aurie's found another passageway," Sylvane fairly sang out in relief.

"Good job, lad," Donnadorr called. "Gather your treasures, friends."

"No rush," Glenorr said.

Before they could begin another argument, Auragole hissed at them, "Hush!"

Sylvane heard it too. "Hoofbeats!" she said. And coming our way, she thought in alarm, remembering their swords among their belongings at the other end of the cave.

"Hide!" Auragole shouted, and grabbing Sylvane's hand, pulled her away from the newfound cave entrance.

Everyone scattered, hiding behind rocks or stacks of books. Auragole pulled Sylvane behind a boulder. Just in time!

The man came riding in at extraordinary speed, galloped halfway into the cave, then spun his large gray horse around and came to a halt. He sat erect, a figure in gray, waiting.

Then Sylvane heard the sound and turned in terror toward the tunnel. A screech, high and horrible, cracked like a whip into the cave. She saw, to her dismay, first fire, then the beast itself plunging through the opening. A river of flames flooded from his mouth and nostrils.

"Oh, dear Gods," Sylvane said, and clung to Auragole, whose body had gone rigid. "It's like something out of the old legends."

It seemed indeed a beast out of the legendary fear of the people of the Grand Continent, or one of those awful new beasts that were said to inhabit these mountains since the end of the Golden Century. It was five times as large as the horse, with a long heavy tail that it dragged on the ground behind it. It had green metallic scales, and its body shone and reflected all the candlelight around it. Had the earth itself spawned this impossible creature? Sylvane shook in fear.

The beast shrieked as it entered the cave, one long, piercing howl of anger, and headed for the man on the horse.

The man sat motionless astride his animal, his unsheathed sword glowing golden as if light from the sun lay lodged in its blade. He waited with extraordinary calmness. Then he shouted, "Charge," and the great gray horse leapt into movement, running directly at the monster. Just as the scaly beast breathed its fire breath, the man veered his horse and thrust his sword with incredible force into the side of the monster's neck. It glanced off and fell at the horse's feet. Now the monster roared, and to Sylvane it felt as if the earth itself roared. The beast moved swiftly. With a quick swipe of its paw, it knocked the man off his horse.

The man lay on the ground struggling for breath. The beast paused, looked at him, and from deep inside its shimmering long throat a thin sound came forth. It was like laughter—eerie, ugly, human laughter. The man sat up cautiously and reached slowly for his sword only a few feet away.

With a flick of his paw, the beast knocked the sword out of the man's reach. The man rose, unarmed, and faced him. The animal, it seemed to Sylvane, glared at him as if waiting for the man to cower in fear. But there was no sign of fear in the man's face.

Suddenly, Auragole wrenched himself away from Sylvane's grip and bounded out of their hiding place into open space.

Sylvane jumped up, thinking to go after him.

"No, Sylvie," he hissed. She ducked down again behind the boulder, and peered out in total dread.

Auragole cupped his hands to his mouth. "Ho there, you ugly brute," he yelled. "You ugly, green, cowardly beast."

The animal was enormous, yet it turned with remarkable agility and charged at Auragole. Sylvane noticed the rock in Auragole's hand just as he threw it. It flew in the air and hit the beast squarely between the eyes. To her horror she saw fire flame from the beast's mouth. And then her view was blocked as the thing sprang toward Auragole. But at a shout, it veered and charged the man who, in the diversion Auragole had created, had remounted his horse. He held his sword in readiness.

Sylvane, without care for her own survival, ran to where Auragole's body lay crumpled like an abandoned rag doll. Fear was wrapped around her like a huge cloak, fear that this young man whom she couldn't help but love was dead.

valley of
the agavi

PART TWO OF AURAGOLE'S JOURNEY
AURAGOLE OF THE MOUNTAINS

N

preface

AURAGOLE WAS RUNNING, *filled with fear, through a dark tunnel. He could barely see the pinpoint of light that he knew he must reach. It called to him, telling him that he was safe, but he didn't believe it because of the fear.*

The arm was too tight around his chest, the leather too hard beneath him. He tried to tell them that the motion was going to make him sick again, but he had no voice.

He was standing outside a large gate made of gold with finials of crystal that glowed so brightly he could not look at them. He stared up at the heavens. The sky was a soft yellow. He searched for the sun but saw none, nor did he see a cloud. It was restful to gaze thus at the heavens. He would wait forever at the gate, staring up at the pale, amber, peaceful vastness.

"Aurie, Aurie, please answer. Don't leave us!"

The ground was solid under his back. It held him down, would not let him go. He begged it to let him go.

He could not look at the tree without turning away time and again. It dazzled. He could feel the roots beneath the ground grow as he walked toward it. Its jeweled branches reached into the yellow heaven and disappeared out of sight. Suddenly there was a figure before it so resplendent, so luminous, so drenched in light that he cast down his eyes for fear of losing himself in its shining. He stopped, but the Being moved toward him. Trembling, Auragole fell to his knees and closed his eyes against the wonder and the bright radiance.

When the figure reached him, it touched his head, and Auragole opened his eyes. He saw, through the differentiating light, rubies where the figure had trod. They were like drops of blood, so filled with life were they. Again the Being touched Auragole's head and peace flowed through him. He lifted Auragole up and Auragole stood gazing into a face so sweet that he began to cry for sheer happiness. Auragole could look at him now. He never wanted to look away.

The Sweet One beckoned Auragole to follow him, and Auragole followed him. Another Being came after. Auragole caught sight of him out of the corner of his eye. He was white flame, yet like himself somehow. Auragole did not question it, for his eyes and his heart were consumed by the first figure, so beautiful, moving with stately grace ahead of him.

He led Auragole to a silken lake of deepest blue. He summoned him with a delicate movement of his hand, and Auragole ran to stand beside him at lake's edge.

"Aurie, please don't go," the voice was tearful. "Stay with us."

Hands snatched at him, pulling him away. He tried to fight them, tried to get back to the Beautiful One and the Mother Lake. He kicked and fought and screamed, "No!" But he had no voice.

There was nothing but dark sky now and it was whirling about him in a frantic dance. The movement was pain. He wasn't afraid now, merely filled with a sorrow he couldn't contain. It poured out of him into the blackness, drowning all the stars and sun and moon, flowing out as far as the sky was large. He was the whole dark universe and it and the pain were all inside him.

"It is the beast's poison that has caused this. I have no remedy with me." Auragole heard the voice from the periphery of the universe. "We must hurry."

Auragole rolled back into himself until he was a tiny point in the middle of his forehead. "I don't want any remedy!" he screamed, but his lips didn't move. He gave up trying to make them understand and floated back out into the darkness, this time pulled by a voice and an arm of golden shimmer.

He was standing again on the shore of the radiant lake. The Sweet One stood before him containing his shining. The Other, the Flaming One, waited at his left.

"Too soon, my child," the Beautiful One said. His voice was all around Auragole, gentle as mist.

Auragole shook his head and tried to speak. "You are not on the Deep Earth," he cried. "Why should I return there?"

"I am on the Deep Earth."

"But how, when you are here?"

"Only a memory of me lingers here."

Auragole did not understand. He wanted desperately to stay with the Sweet One. "No one remembers you on the earth, not even I. Let me stay here, for here I can see you. Here I can know you as I have in ages past."

The Sweet One, the Beautiful One shook his head. "You knew me before, child, with powers that were not as yet your own. We met as my gift to you. But in these terrible and crucial world days you can know me through your own efforts. And it will be your gift to me. You are now able, in your inner isolation, in your deepest solitude, to find me, though all deny me. Step by step, you can find me with your most human quality. Find me with what is most yourself, then you will never lose me again."

"I don't understand. What is most myself?"

He touched Auragole's face, and light and quiet rest drifted through him. If Auragole had tears, then he was crying, for he understood him—but only for a moment, and then forgot again.

Auragole looked out at the blue lake. The Sweet One was gone. The Other stood aflame beside him, waiting. "I must go back," Auragole told him without words.

They were pouring something into his throat. He stopped struggling.

The white Flaming One took him by the hand and guided him through the darkness.

"I must go back," Auragole said.

chapter ten

"YOU DRIVE YOURSELF too hard, my friend," Pohl said to the tall man sitting opposite him. Pohl leaned toward him across the intricately carved desk, fashioned so beautifully by the Agavians—as was all the furniture in the Last School. "As soon as we arrive from the Easternlands, you take off on Sunflight to that cave again where you engage in a senseless battle with that nemesis of yours. . ."

"Not senseless, Pohl." Meekelorr rose from his chair with a natural grace, and began to pace about the large room, stopping at one point to look at the painted design on the ceiling with great concentration.

No doubt Meekelorr did not like the way this conversation was going, but Pohl refused to be put off by Meekelorr's seeming detachment. If Pohl, a doctor as well as a friend, didn't speak, who would?

"Sit, sit, Meekelorr, don't move about this place like a skittish colt." Perhaps the Lady Claregole would talk some sense into the man if he could not, but even that was uncertain. Her own burdens were great now and she knew that if Meekelorr drove himself to the edge it was because of need.

Pohl knew that too.

Still, Pohl thought, if he gets ill or careless or breaks down, perhaps everything will be lost for us. So Pohl pursued the conversation. "In addition to *that* battle, which you nearly lost, you travel back to the school with the injured boy and his companions, sleeping hardly at all those four days, and then you spend two sleepless days and nights riding in pursuit of the moonleaf. . ."

". . .which I found."

". . .which you found, and two sleepless days and nights riding back. . ."

"Time was running out." Meekelorr's eyes finally met Pohl's.

"I grant you it was nearly hopeless without the moonleaf. I'm not arguing about that. Will you sit, man? You're making me dizzy."

Meekelorr sat down in the chair opposite Pohl and stared coolly at him. It was a stubborn look, one that Pohl knew well. But men who were easily swayed were not good leaders. And Meekelorr was a good leader. The best. And much depended on him.

Unperturbed, Pohl tried again. "You returned only two nights ago, then spent both those nights in the boy's room. Gods and stars, Meekelorr, give us—and the remedy—a little time. Do you intend now to sit night after night staring at him, willing the moonleaf to take effect?"

"The boy saved my life, Pohl, and because of it nearly lost his own."

Pohl looked directly at Meekelorr. "It's more than that. You think this boy is the boy of your dream."

"What?"

"Meekelorr, don't obfuscate. You know exactly what I'm talking about."

"He could be. Yes, that thought has come to me."

"So that's it," Pohl said. "You think, by a stroke of fate, that we suddenly have our wild card in our midst. Now that's something to ponder. Yes, yes, indeed."

Meekelorr gave no answer. Instead he said, "Well, is the moonleaf potent? Will it take effect?"

"It will heal the burns. We apply it every few hours. There will be no scars, but you know the beast's breath is poison. I've also made a tea with some of the moonleaf and it is fed him every hour. It's the best we can do. The boy wanders somewhere in the land between death and life, or so his dreams say."

"I've heard them." Meekelorr's gray eyes were thoughtful. "It is just this that makes me think that he. . .he is the one. Yet another sign that the events humanity has long awaited will happen in our lifetime." Meekelorr rose up in one fluid movement, walked over to the tall windows, and stared out, down the long, snow-covered hill in the direction of the Valley of the Agavi.

"All the more reason for you to take care of yourself," Pohl said, and returned to his lecturing. "You drive yourself too hard, Meekelorr. You push your body past its limits. You barely arrive in Agavia with your troops from the Easternlands—a long and dangerous journey, I might add, and with too many skirmishes along the way. . ."

". . .that you made, too, that you fought, too."

". . .and within days you are off to that infernal cave where you engage in a battle with that beast. . ."

". . .which grows larger and larger, Pohl. Now it has scales of metal and its fire breath reaches over fifty feet." He turned to face Pohl, leaned back on the window frame, and crossed his arms over his chest.

". . .which grows larger and larger and for the first time you almost lose the battle. If the boy and his friends had not been there, you would be dead now."

"But I am *not* dead. And the boy and his friends *were* there.

If these are indeed the awaited days, the time of the incarnation of the Nethergod, then it is important that this other—the beast of the cave, this nemesis of mine, as you like to call him—is kept in his place. We would not want him joining forces with the Nethergod."

"No, no, indeed not. But if you die, my weary friend, careless in battle or from overtaxing your heart, who will lead us in the Last Battle, which we now know will come in our lifetime?"

"Some other," Meekelorr said, with a dismissive wave of his hand.

"Name him." Pohl would not let him off so easily.

Meekelorr was tall but not loose-boned the way so many tall men are. Broad of chest and wide of shoulder, he was well co-ordinated—even regal in his bearing. It was this, Pohl was sure, that caused many of the soldiers he led to call him *Prince*—and because he was consort to the leader of the Agavians. His dark chestnut-colored hair, almost to his shoulders, was tied loosely at the neck. It was a style much emulated by Meekelorr's soldiers, the Companions of the Way. His features were strong and handsome. But most remarkable of all were his gray eyes, which seemed charcoal black by firelight. They reminded Pohl of rushing rivers or storm clouds, so turbulent could they appear. Yet for all Meekelorr's restlessness, there was no nervousness in him, only a sense of urgency, of purpose.

Meekelorr once again began to pace about the room, picking up objects and looking at them, but Pohl knew his mind was elsewhere.

"It is an appalling arrogance to think one is indispensable," Meekelorr finally said, returning a jeweled silver candlestick to its table. "Some other would lead."

"Name him, my friend," Pohl went on. "We are too few."

"Yes, far too few. . .and who knows how many the enemy will enlist, has already enlisted, on his side."

"True, indeed," Pohl said. "Yes, he will draw many to him.

But these are not the days of old when human beings were tribal and therefore easily led. Human beings have changed over the centuries, as was foreordained. I hang on to that thought. I hang on to the thought that humans have become less tribal and more self-conscious."

"Oh yes, they have certainly become that, become more and more separated each from the other—as well as more selfish," Meekelorr said. "And they have forgotten the Gods."

"Why such pessimism, my friend? Why not rejoice in the fact that because of that separation, one human being out of free choice—no longer out of the determination of the Gods—can change the destiny of the world? One human being! Therein lies all our hope, not in numbers but in this possibility."

"Oh yes, why else have a wild card? This young man—if he is indeed the one—could change the future of the world. . .for good or for ill."

"And so could you, my friend. If this young man goes down the wrong road, who will be there to oppose him, if not you? Therefore you need to rest, to sleep, to restore the forces you spend so freely."

Meekelorr returned to the chair opposite Pohl and sat down. He looked directly at Pohl. "Pohl, stop clucking your tongue at me like an old hen. I know my role in all this. Each man counts, when have I denied that? To deny that would mean denying our whole past history, as well as our future. I don't underestimate what I have to do. This evening I go down to Claregole's mansion. Tomorrow when I return, I will begin training my men for mountain fighting. You know how little experience Easterners have of mountains. We have barely time to ready ourselves before we leave in early spring for the Westernlands."

"You're incorrigible!"

"We're going to make our headquarters in the Sorren Heights, and you know how rugged the mountains there are. For that reason, we all need training in mountain fighting if we are to be of use to the Companions there in the search for the Nethergod."

"Let others train them."

"No." He spoke it quietly, but in that one word was the voice of the commander. Meekelorr leaned across Pohl's desk. "There's no time, Pohl. You know it as well as I. You want me to spare myself and yet you do not spare yourself. You too have just arrived from the east and I know that you've been with the sick night and day since then. Shall I do less than you?" Pohl started to protest, but Meekelorr wagged a finger at him and continued, "I drive the Companions hard, how can I not drive myself?"

With that he rose again and moved to the fireplace. He took the tongs and poked at the fire. When he straightened up he looked thoughtfully at Pohl. "The long-awaited days will soon be upon us, Pohl. Not this year or the next—there may be several years yet—but it will be in our lifetime."

And suddenly Meekelorr smiled, which, Pohl observed, was a remarkable sight, so rare was it and so bright. No pessimism in that smile.

"Yes, yes, all the signs are there. I agree, my friend," Pohl said, and returned his smile. Pohl looked at the thoughtful man staring at the flames. It was clear now that they would be part of that generation chosen to find—and then do battle with—the Nethergod, the Adversary God incarnate. Thank the stars for Meekelorr, he thought, thank the stars that he is willing to lead in war.

Pohl too had his work. As a doctor, he had been able to travel about the Easternlands as an itinerant healer gathering information, listening, and observing. He had done that for years, looking for signs that the one who might be the Nethergod had, indeed, incarnated. Meekelorr, the Lady Claregole, her people the Agavi, the small army called the Companions of the Way, and a few others of their generation knew that if *all* humanity slept through the coming of the Nethergod, its future would be forfeit. Humanity would begin a rapid descent into greater and greater decadence and eventually into soulless bestiality. Should that happen, humanity and its home, the Deep Earth, would be forever lost to the Creative World, the world of the great Gods. Some had to be awake, watching and waiting. And so Pohl had traveled and observed and had looked for the signs. And he had found them. Yes, yes, indeed, the Nethergod was now on the earth, somewhere on the Grand Continent—either in the Easternlands, the Gandlese Mountains, or the Westernlands.

Meekelorr too had listened and observed as he had moved about the Easternlands with his troop of Companions of the Way, trying to right injustices, to defend people from the ever-present heavy oppression, from the cruelty of harsh, arrogant leaders. But in these last difficult years the people in the east had turned against the Companions. Lies and rumors had made the Companions feared. Therefore they were hunted down like animals. So the decision had been made. The Companions were to begin their departure from the east and make their way to the west.

And Pohl had come with the advance guard, the one led by Meekelorr.

"I must bathe and dress. Claregole is expecting me." Meekelorr interrupted Pohl's thoughts.

"There is a sadness in her now that she can't conceal."

"She has, as you well know, my friend, the most to lose." And Meekelorr walked to the door.

Pohl watched him go. How few Companions there were left, probably less than five or six thousand in the entire Grand Continent. Most were now in the Westernlands. Meekelorr had brought only thirty-three with him from the Easternlands. It was expected that the others from the east would begin arriving here in the spring—some to help with the work here, and some to march west with Meekelorr. Pohl wondered how many that would be. Not enough, he thought. The Nethergod had not yet shown his hand and already the toll they had paid was too high.

We are too few, Pohl thought. The Companions were too few. And how many students and teachers are at the Last School? Little more than a hundred. Pohl sighed audibly.

"...*One human being out of free choice—no longer out of the determination of the Gods—can change the destiny of the world...*"

Think about your own words, he chided himself, and not about numbers.

A moment after Meekelorr had gone, a messenger came to tell Pohl that Auragole had awoken. He hurried to the Healing Tower.

chapter eleven

POHL ENTERED THE chamber at the top of the Healing Tower in the wing that adjoined the school proper. Like all else that the Agavians had made, the Healing Tower and everything in it were the result of the fine craftsmanship so beloved of this ancient people. The round room where young Auragole lay was reserved for the gravely ill. His bed was underneath a skylight that could let in the shine of the sun or of the stars—as the doctors or healers saw fit. An ingenious structure of blinds could close or open the skylight as much as was thought necessary for the health of the patient.

On the round marble walls hung many tapestries depicting the legends of the Agavi and of their Gods. On pedestals and on tables were carefully crafted statues of Nature Beings. Each sculpture was chosen to promote health in the one who was sick. These were regularly changed, as were the dangling sheets of colored glass that were hung about the room to catch the light. Depending on the ailment, colors were chosen, tapestries hung, and sculptures placed. Art, that great educator and healer, had almost been forgotten in the Easternlands, but not in Agavia, where it was central to life.

In the middle of the room stood the large, high, carved wooden bed with its down comforters and woolen sheets. As Pohl entered the room from the door behind the bed, he recognized the voice and harp-strumming of Aza. She was greatest of the Agavian Healing-singers and could True-sing health into another if the sick one was willing—or the Gods. Of course, the greatest True-singer alive at that time was Lorenwile, now that Aiku was dead, but Pohl had no idea where Lorenwile was. Pohl stopped near the door, stood in the shadows, and listened to her song.

> *Warmth was thy mother.*
> *Life was thy father.*
> *From light thou hast come*
> *in the days before time*
> *in the days before time.*

> *A song was thy mother.*
> *A word was thy father.*
> *From sound thou hast come*
> *in the days before time*
> *in the days before time.*

> *Crystallized and formed thou art*
> *to tread the pathways of the earth*
> *to grasp with love thine egohood*
> *and return to the givers thine own true worth*
> *in the days after time*
> *in the days after time.*

A dream was thy mother.
A thought was thy father.
From their will thou hast come
in the days before time.
Remember
canst thou remember
the days before time?

Aza was sitting near the foot of the bed, her long black hair falling past her shoulders, hiding her delicate features. She looked up and smiled at Pohl as he came quietly around the bed.

The Agavi, Pohl was certain, were the most beautiful people in the world, with their black hair, high cheekbones and deep-sunken, black almond-shaped eyes, and pale, near-blue skin. There was a lucency about them that was almost otherworldly. *Agavi* meant God's people—and so they seemed, the few thousand who had survived the long isolation in this hidden, remote Gandlesean valley. Though the Agavi were an exquisite-looking people, what was most interesting to Pohl was their similarity, each to each.

The group soul still works actively in them, Pohl once again observed as he looked upon the lovely singer, making the community more important than the individual. And yet Aza had sung of egohood to the young Easterner who lay ailing in the bed. But then a Healing-singer can find what is true in each human—that is the power of a healing song. As Pohl smiled at Aza, he once again felt pain for the Agavi. They were a doomed race, an anachronism in these world days.

When Pohl arrived at the side of the bed, he could see that Auragole was indeed awake, but lying motionless, his pillows piled high so he could see the Healing-singer. His face registered little except listening.

Aza stood up and smiled at Auragole. Auragole's face began to take on expression. His dark eyes questioned. He smiled at her and tried to speak. The sounds coming from his throat were guttural and hoarse. Aza raised her fingers to her lips, smiled again, and moved toward the door and out.

Pohl warned Auragole, "Don't try to speak. You've been badly injured."

The young man turned his head to look at Pohl. "Am I dead?" he whispered.

Pohl smiled. "No, no, indeed no, not dead, not yet, not so soon."

"Where. . .where then?"

"You're on a hill, in the Healing Tower overlooking the Valley of the Agavi. The man whose life you saved in the cave brought you here, brought you all here. You were injured by the beast, whose fire breath is poison. But you are safe now."

"No, not here," Auragole said. His words were a whisper and there was a puzzled look on his face.

"Where then, child?"

"I don't know," and his eyes filled with both bewilderment and despair.

"Don't worry. Don't think about anything for the time being, son. Don't strain to recall anything. When it is necessary, you will remember." Pohl wiped the young man's feverish forehead, then picked up the glass with the moonleaf remedy in it and encouraged Auragole to take a few sips.

"The man. . ." Auragole struggled to get his words out. "The man on the horse, is he all right?"

"He's fine, uninjured. He brought you here. You did a brave thing, young man."

Auragole moved his head from side to side as if to deny that he had done anything out of the ordinary. And then his mouth opened and a look of awe infused his face. "Transparent," he whispered. "Everything around me became transparent, before I. . .before I. . ." He couldn't finish the sentence and he plunged instead into the next one. "We were in a cave, yet I saw stars and the sun." He brushed his hand across his forehead. "But that's

128

impossible," he finally said.

"Don't try to talk now," Pohl said, patting his shoulder and straightening his covers.

"But my friends. . .?"

"All safe. They're down in the Valley of the Agavi. They're staying with the leader of the Agavians, the Lady Claregole, at her Great Mansion. No doubt you will also stay there when we have you on your feet."

"Safe," Auragole repeated with obvious relief. "And the man. . ." he croaked again. "What happened after. . .?"

"You diverted the beast long enough for Meekelorr to rearm and remount. The beast nearly killed you but Meekelorr got to him in time. You didn't get the full force of his fire breath. No, no, no, indeed not. You wouldn't be here if you had. You've been unconscious for almost ten days."

"Ten days!" The words tore out of him, and Auragole began coughing painfully.

"Yes, it's now past the midpoint of October. Speak carefully, son. You're weak—not only from your injuries, but also from the beast's poison. It took a powerful remedy to save you. The moonleaf. Do you know it?"

Auragole shook his head.

"One small grove in the Gandlese is the only known place where it grows. Meekelorr rode two days and two nights looking for it. He found it. The poison from the beast's fire breath is so powerful that without it you surely would have died."

"Ah. . ."

There was little concern, Pohl noted, for living or dying in that word. "The moonleaf's potency doesn't last. A week or two and then it's as ordinary as grass."

"And the beast? Is it dead?"

"Now that is a difficult beast to kill. Many times Meekelorr has killed it only to find it risen again." Auragole's mouth fell open, but before he could ask about so strange a beast, Pohl went on. "Because of the moonleaf you'll have no scars. Your bones will mend—your ribs and your arm—and the burns will leave no scars. Your body will be whole in a few weeks. Nothing to worry about. Rest now. I'll send word to your friends, and tomorrow, no doubt, you will have some visitors." He pulled the blankets up around Auragole. He was asleep before Pohl left his side.

Pohl went to look in on his other patients—some students from the school and some Companions of the Way. The Companions were an exhausted lot and a full third of them were here in the Healing Tower—and many, many others would be coming in the spring. There would be a lot of patching up to do to make the men ready for the march west and the battles ahead. Well, Pohl thought, we do what we can.

POHL ENTERED AURAGOLE'S room the next day and walked to the side of his bed just as Aza had finished her Healing-singing. This time Auragole was alert and watchful and his eyes were filled with questions. As she rose and prepared to leave, Auragole asked her in a voice much improved since yesterday, "Who are you?"

> "I am a singer," she answered,
> "and I sang thee a song.
> I sing both for pleasure
> and to help thee grow strong."

> "Look around, feast thine eyes
> there is much thou should'st see.
> If thy glance falls on beauty
> it will help to cure thee."

And with a sweet smile and a light tread she left the room, nodding to Pohl before she passed under the ornate lintel.

Pohl greeted the boy.

"Hello," Auragole said, with a smile of recognition. "You're
. . .you're the man I talked to . . . when was it?"

"Yesterday. My name is Pohl and I'm a doctor. You're in the
Healing Tower above the Valley of the Agavi," Pohl reminded
Auragole as he plumped up his pillows.

"I don't understand. Where is this Valley of the Agavi?"

"In the Gandlese."

"The Gandlese? But I thought there were no other people in
the. . ." Auragole began to cough.

"Truly? But the Agavians have been here for centuries. Yes,
yes, indeed. Drink this." Pohl took the glass with the moonleaf
remedy and offered it to him.

"It's so bitter."

"It's saved your life," Pohl said. "A good man rode four days
and nights without sleep to find it for you."

Auragole took it and drank it without further complaint.
"The man who found the moonleaf, you said his name is
Meekelorr?"

"That's correct."

"Is he the man from the cave?"

"He is."

"Where is he now?"

"He's down in the valley at the Lady Claregole's mansion."

"Where my friends are staying?"

"Yes. He'll be back today. He'll most likely look in on you.
Yes, yes, indeed, I'm sure he'll look in on you."

"Meekelorr." The young man said the word as if he were tasting
it. "What was he doing in that cave where all the books are?"

"He goes into the cave to fight the beast."

"Why?"

"Well, he's a soldier, commander of the Companions of the
Way."

"Who. . .who are the Companions of the Way?"

"Soldiers who come to the aid of those who cannot aid themselves. In the wars that have torn the Grand Continent asunder for over five hundred years, the ones who suffer most are people who have neither wealth nor power. The Companions of the Way go out in small troops into both the Easternlands and the Westernlands to help those beset by the tyranny of those who call themselves leaders. The Companions are not political. They don't seize power. They simply redress wrongs wherever they can."

"Heroes—like in the old stories. . ."

"Well, yes, something like those in the old stories."

About the other task of the Companions of the Way, their search for the Nethergod, Pohl said nothing. One could not speak of Gods to most people in these world days.

"I've never heard of the Companions of the Way," Auragole said, and there was an apology in his voice, "but I was brought up in the Gandlese far away from either the Easternlands or the Westernlands."

"So you are not from the east like your friends. Tell me about your upbringing," Pohl said, as he began his careful examination of Auragole's wounds.

In halting tones, as if it were of little consequence, Auragole told Pohl about his life in his small, safe community.

"Then after your mother died, you decided to leave. Where did you intend to go?"

From the young man's silence, Pohl knew Auragole was wondering just how much he should tell him. Interesting, he thought.

Finally, "I was going east to search for my only known relative, an uncle of my mother's."

"I see. Then how did you come to be traveling with the Easterners?"

After a few moments' hesitation, Auragole told Pohl how he had met Sylvane and the twins and of his subsequent decision to join them in their journey west. "I'll go east after I see them all safely into Mattelmead. I. . .I promised my mother."

Then a look of pain crossed the young man's face.

"What troubles you, son?"

Auragole swallowed hard, coughed. His fingertips stroked his forehead. "I almost caused the death of everyone." Auragole then told Pohl how they had met Donnadorr. "Waiting for Don caused us to leave too late to make it to the Northern Valley. We were caught in the snows only days before we were to reach our destination. That's why we took shelter in the cave that eventually led us to the Cave of the Beast."

"You're the leader of the group?"

Auragole seemed embarrassed by Pohl's question. "The others don't know much about woods or mountains. And they don't know how to find direction from growing things or from the stars. I have some small skill there."

"You made a human choice," Pohl said. "I would not fault you for that."

"Glenorr blames me."

"Well, you are all safe now. And you will recover. How is it that your friends were traveling by themselves and not in a caravan?"

"I. . .I cannot answer your question," he said after some hesitation. "This much I will say, they began their journey with a caravan but were asked to leave. You must ask *them* why."

At that moment the door opened and a young woman hurried in. She was dressed in a rose-colored, long-sleeved woolen gown that fitted closely at the waist and dropped in pleats to the floor. At the waist and on the hem small mountain flowers were embroidered in delicate pastel colors. The dress was Agavian; the young woman was not.

"Come in, come in." Pohl beckoned to her with a broad gesture. "He's awake and much better. The fever is nearly gone. Yes, yes, indeed."

The woman came around the bed. Her scrubbed face glowed with happiness and her light-brown eyes shone. Her short hair was neatly combed and jewels sparkled from dozens of her curls in the Agavian fashion. By now Pohl knew her well.

"Sylvane?" The word ripped out of Auragole as he finally recognized her, and he began to cough in pain.

"Aurie, don't speak, it's all right. Everything is all right. There's some sort of community up here and another one down in the valley where we are staying. Help was near and we had no idea." She looked down at him with concern and caring.

Pohl had recognized from the first that Sylvane was in love with Auragole. It was only she who had trudged the two miles up a winding, snow-covered path from the Lady's mansion each morning and who had sat for hours calling to him, willing him back into the world of the living. Each afternoon Pohl had sent her away promising that he would send for her as soon as Auragole's condition showed improvement. Yet the next morning, message or not, Sylvane returned.

"You're a hero, Aurie." Her face shone with pride. "You jumped out from behind the boulder where we were hiding and threw a rock at the beast. It diverted the beast's attention long enough for Meekelorr to pick up his sword and remount. Your chest and left arm were burned by the beast, but you didn't get the full power of his fire breath, thanks to Meekelorr. Your right arm is broken and some ribs."

"They are healing nicely," Pohl said.

"You almost died." Her words came out in a rush. "You were unconscious for a long time. I was afraid you wanted to die. Meekelorr and Pohl saved you." She pointed toward Pohl. "Pohl has been taking care of you. He's a doctor and he just arrived from the east with Meekelorr and his soldiers. Everyone says he is an excellent doctor. He knows everything there is to know about broken bones, about burns, and healing herbs."

Pohl chuckled at this. "My kind young lady, no one knows

everything there is to know about anything. No, no, indeed not."

"The others have come. May I bring them in?" She turned to Pohl. "They are all anxious to see Aurie."

"Well. . .yes, but only for a minute. The boy needs rest and treatment. Go along then, fetch them in."

Sylvane squeezed Auragole's hand and hurried out of the room. She returned with her friends and Pohl was amazed at their transformation. He had seen them when they had first arrived a week ago. They had been a motley crew—half starved, dirty, and completely exhausted.

The generous Agavians had attired them splendidly. Wool trousers and linen shirts on the men, embroidered with birds or animals. After they entered, the two young men stood awkwardly just inside the door. But the young lady called Glenelle rushed to Auragole's side and grabbed his hand and held it to her cheek. She was lovely to look on. Her dress was of wool, a rich green, with a scene of running deer woven into its hem. Her long blond hair was curled, and threaded through the curls were ribbons and jewels.

"Oh, Aurie, we were so worried. Whatever would we do without you? Thank the stars you're alive."

Pohl saw the rush of joy that spread first across Auragole's face and then quiver down his whole body. Pohl exhaled sadly. If Sylvane loved Auragole, it was unreciprocated. Auragole was completely enthralled by Glenelle. Well, why not? She was indeed a charmer. Still, Pohl's heart ached for the sweet if plainer Sylvane.

Then the young men hurried over and there was a flood of talk, the friends trying to explain—all of them at once—how they had arrived in these hills and what it was like in the Lady's mansion and in the valley.

After a few minutes of this, Pohl escorted them to the door, telling them to come back the next day and to let the poor boy rest.

Moments later Pohl also left.

N

chapter twelve

WHEN POHL RETURNED after lunch, Auragole was gazing intently at the tapestry opposite his bed. In it, a tall man dressed in gray sat astride a horse that was also gray. He was leaning over, his hand on a sword that was plunged into a green monster. The monster was small with a sleek, oily-smooth body. The tapestry was an excellent piece, made with great skill. You could see and even feel the tension in the man's body and the sorrow on the man's face. The dying beast seemed not so filled with the pain of his death, though that was there also, as with hatred of the man. Behind man and beast were great jars of books and scrolls sitting on rock shelves.

All that are missing from the tapestry, Pohl thought, watching the intense stare of the young man on the bed, are Auragole and his companions. No, Pohl corrected, the beast in that picture would have to be much larger and have metal scales.

"Glorious piece of work, is it not?" Pohl said.

Auragole merely nodded, not taking his eyes away.

"The Agavi are all great artisans. There is little that you will see in their valley or up here on the hill that has not been made more beautiful by their work. That wall hanging was done by the Lady Claregole herself. You shall meet her when you are well."

"All my life I've lived in the Gandlese. . ." Auragole said.

"Yes?"

". . .and was told that we were the only humans in the entire mountain range, except for the caravans that crossed the Gandlese two or three times a year. Yet here you all are only a few weeks' journey. . ."

Pohl knew no answer was needed, and said instead, "Now young Auragole, you must be up and moving or your legs will soon seem like they belong to another."

He turned down the quilts, lifted Auragole up in his strong arms, and deposited him as gently as he could on the rug near his bed. A muffled cry escaped from Auragole's lips.

"Pain is a friend," Pohl told him, "or how else know where the illness lies?" Supporting Auragole, Pohl helped him move twice around the room. Then he helped him back to his bed. "The body is coming along nicely." Pohl tucked the covers about him.

"Why do you speak of my body as if it were separate from me?" Auragole asked, his face pale from his exertions.

"Oh, are you and your body the same? Rest now, for sleep is also a friend. In not too many days you'll be able to move freely about the tower." And Pohl left him staring at the tapestry.

POHL DIDN'T SEE Meekelorr all that day, but he knew that he had returned from the Lady's Great Mansion and had gone immediately to train with his men.

Before retiring that night, Pohl walked down the corridors of the school and up the stairs to the Healing Tower, first to look in on the soldiers who were his patients, and then for a final night check on Auragole. He slipped into Auragole's room quietly. If Auragole was asleep, Pohl would have to wake him for the moonleaf remedy. Upon entering, Pohl sensed, though there was no sound, that someone else was in the room. He was about to investigate but stopped abruptly and retreated into the shadows near the entrance. The stars were bright, their shine pouring through the unshuttered skylight. Pohl recognized the figure standing erect at the foot of Auragole's bed.

"Who's there?" That was Auragole speaking. From the slight slur of his speech, Pohl knew Auragole had just awoken.

"Greetings to you, young friend," a rich male voice said. That voice so often heard by Pohl in the dark countryside, where they had frequently camped without fire, reminded him again of cool rivers, of trees, of the rugged mountains themselves.

Meekelorr lit a candle, then came to the side of Auragole's bed. He was out of uniform, dressed all in gray—his trousers were wool, his shirt silk, and over it a short velvet tunic. Gray to connote seriousness, Pohl thought, as befits our times, as befits our task. Pohl's own garments were brown, better suited to one who needed to blend into crowds, who knew not to stand out, whose purpose as he traveled had to be shrouded in secrecy. Here in Agavia, Pohl would wear the occasional gold silk shirt or even a red one, but mostly he dressed in the familiar and comfortable brown.

"Are you Meekelorr?" Auragole asked.

"Yes, and you are called Auragole." It was a statement.

But Auragole answered it. "Yes."

The two were silent then, no doubt looking at each other—the older with strong, deeply carved features and solemn gray eyes, dark now in the candlelight, the younger with hollow cheeks and thin skin around his still-forming bones, but with vivid black eyes. Each in his own way, Pohl thought, was handsome.

Meekelorr broke the silence. "I've come to thank you. You saved my life."

"And you saved mine, so I thank you."

Silence.

Then, "I understand you and your companions are attempting to get to Mattelmead."

"Yes, but we were caught in a snowstorm."

"It's a long journey from the Easternlands. Why do you go there?"

"To help my friends. . .they are unfamiliar with mountain travel. But also I want to see the great king. I've heard it said that Ormahn will put an end to the battles in the west and unite it under his banner, then move on and do the same in the east. They say Ormahn brings peace wherever he goes. Some call him the King of Peace. I should like to see such a king." It was a simple, straightforward answer.

"Peace is a noble gift to bring. What price does Ormahn ask for his peace?"

"Price!" Auragole's voice was hoarse. "I've heard no mention of price. But even if there were a price, would it not be worth almost anything one could give to live in peace?" There was heat in his words, but only in part from the fever.

"Almost anything."

There was another silence, then a question from Auragole. "Tell me about the cave we were in—with all those scrolls and books."

"It's a place where the earthly thoughts of humanity are stored."

"Then why are the books left there in the dust to mildew and rot?"

"Because true wisdom resides elsewhere—and yet there is nothing greater in humans, as they are presently constituted, than their capacity for thought."

Pohl could not see Auragole, but the silence made him think that Auragole was confused by such an enigmatic answer.

"Then why is the beast there?" Auragole finally asked.

"The books belong to him."

"Then why. . .?"

"Why do I battle him? Because he no longer contents himself with the earthly thoughts of humans. He now wants all of the human being. If I don't battle him, someday he might leave the cave and threaten these mountains and the valley below. Many times I have battled him and each time I have killed him."

"Then how is it. . .how is it he rises again?"

"That is the nature of the beast. He must be battled and killed, but each time he rises again, larger and stronger."

"So you must fight the horrible monster again and again with no chance for a final victory? What a terrible task!"

"Even the beast has his lawful role in the world scheme."

"And what is that? Guarding the books?"

"Guarding the earthly thoughts humans have fashioned. When human beings become separated from their knowledge, the knowledge becomes the property of the beast."

"Is the beast some strange creature that was fashioned in the Golden Century?"

"No, it is far older than that, older than the world itself, but the Golden Century nourished him."

Once again there was a pause, as if Auragole were struggling to understand. "Does no one fight but you?"

"There are a few others. Perhaps in the future, if it becomes necessary, there will be more. It grows more difficult to battle him. The beast grows larger, denser, filled with the substance of the earth, craving the substance of the earth. The next time he may become rocklike, with the strength of a mountain. And, too, he is becoming cleverer. I think he eats the books. When he rises again I will battle him again—though the outcome is no longer certain."

"But if it is nearly hopeless, why do you do it?" Auragole's words were almost a cry.

Meekelorr reached out and touched the boy's cheek. "Why

did you step out from behind that boulder and throw that rock?"

Auragole didn't reply.

"We shall meet again, young friend," and Meekelorr strode toward the door. Pohl shrank back into the shadows.

"Good night, Pohl," Meekelorr said, as he passed him.

Pohl chuckled. "Good night, my catlike friend."

Meekelorr left, and Pohl went to attend his patient.

POHL WAS IN Auragole's room the next day when Auragole's friends came to visit. If the young man had been a bit stronger, Pohl would have left him and them to their reunion. But Pohl was afraid they might tire Auragole, so he stayed. At first the discussion was about the valley and the Lady's mansion and the Lady Claregole herself. Listening, Auragole looked from one face to the other. But mostly Auragole's eyes strayed to Glenelle.

She is like food for him, Pohl observed, a healing even the moonleaf could not impart. She accepted Auragole's adoration with equanimity, as if it were natural that the men around her should love her and admire her. It was not vanity—no, no, Pohl didn't think it was vanity. It was simply an acceptance of something that had always been hers.

Pohl watched the interplay, trying to understand the relationships between the individuals in the little band of travelers. But that was difficult in Agavia and the hills around it, because of the innate peace in the region. It permeated everything and everyone, causing a harmony to exist between individuals that might not otherwise exist—at least for as long as they were in the Valley of the Agavi or its surrounding hills.

"Can you tell us about it, Pohl?" He was pulled out of his musings by Glenelle, who, with a dazzling smile, had directed a question to him.

"Can I tell you about what, my child?"

"About the community up here, the other buildings, and about this Healing Tower?"

The visitors looked at him with friendly and expectant eyes.

"Yes, do tell us, Pohl," Sylvane said. "No one will say much about them down in the valley—only that it took the Agavi twenty years to build these structures and that they have been occupied by Easterners for fifteen."

"I'd like to hear about it too, Pohl," Auragole said.

Pohl looked at the group and made a quick decision. Too soon to tell these young strangers about the Last School. But should the Last Battle, against all odds, go well, he knew, it could become the First School. For the sake of the earth he prayed it was so.

"Oh, there's not much to tell," Pohl said. "The Agavi are a generous but rather reticent people, as I'm sure you have experienced. Thirty-five years ago, a man, a kind of a leader. . ."

"Like a settlement leader?" Sylvane interrupted.

"Well, yes, something like that," Pohl said. "Yes, yes, indeed, something like the leader of a settlement."

Out of the hundred and thirty students who had come here fifteen years ago, there were now only one hundred and twelve. And out of the dozen teachers who had come, there were only seven left. Even with the Companions now occupying some of the rooms, the school, never full, still remained half empty.

"This man came here," he went on, "and asked the Agavi if he could, in time, bring a small. . .well, a small community of men and women to live here. The Agavi, who have occupied the valley below for centuries without number, in their kindness, agreed. They built this tower and its adjacent structure."

Fifty years ago there had been seven such schools in the Easternlands. But not one of those schools was still standing. Perhaps this school, hidden here in the Gandlese, was the only one left in the world. The location and what was taught here were secrets best guarded—at least for a time. For the Adversary to fall upon the valley, upon the Companions, and the school before the time was ripe, could prove disastrous for the future of the Grand Continent. No, no, indeed, best not to say too much. These were, after all, strangers who had, by some quirk of destiny, been brought into their midst. Since the purpose was still hidden, best to say little. No doubt, come the spring, they would resume their journey to Mattelmead.

"The leader who brought his settlement here," Glenelle asked, "is he still alive?"

"No." Pohl's face clouded for a moment. "He set out from here seven years ago and was never seen alive again."

Donnadorr interjected in a strangely tight voice. "But that doesn't mean that he's dead—just because he disappeared."

"No, no, indeed not." Pohl looked at Donnadorr with interest. "That alone would not be sufficient evidence in these world days to believe he was dead. However, some friends found his body and the pack he was carrying. They buried him and brought his pack to us." He stood up. "Enough. Auragole must rest now. Come back tomorrow if you like."

Pohl escorted them down the stairs of the Healing Tower. He was about to bid them good-bye in the outer court when they were startled by a sudden and very loud noise—a roaring, thunderlike sound. It was coming from the skies. But it was not thunder—no, it was more terrible than thunder. And it was not the dreaded sound of an avalanche descending upon them. No, it was something else, something unfamiliar.

"What is it?" Glenelle asked, her voice shaking.

"I don't know." Pohl said. "I've never heard its like, but it sounds as if it's coming from the clouds." He looked up, but there was nothing to be seen.

The two girls huddled in the doorway of the Healing Tower, but the young men followed Pohl across the stone courtyard toward the grassy field beyond the school for a clearer view of the skies. Still, nothing that Pohl observed could account for the noise.

Then he saw Meekelorr standing on the grassy slope, dressed only in his gray trousers, white shirt, and his boots, as if he had been called unexpectedly from his desk. He held a sword loosely in his hand and he too was gazing upward.

"What can it be?" Glenorr asked.

Pohl, scanning the heavens, finally saw it.

The two young men following the line of Pohl's pointing finger saw it too. Circling high, high above the Healing Tower and the school was a green something—too big to be a bird, at least any that Pohl had ever seen before. It screeched, then laughed, and the laughter was a taunt so human in sound that Pohl's blood ran cold. Pohl knew then what it was, *who* it was.

"Stars in the heavens!" Pohl said. "It's out of the cave!"

Meekelorr knew too. He raised his sword and began to walk down the grassy slope away from the school and tower.

"I thought it was dead!" Glenorr said.

"It was dead," Donnadorr said. "I saw it dead. This must be another—the stars protect us."

Meekelorr can't fight the damned thing alone, Pohl thought. He started running toward Meekelorr, but realized he was unarmed. He turned to hurry back to the tower to fetch his bow and quiver.

"Stand still!" Meekelorr called in a voice loud enough for all of them to hear.

Pohl froze. So did Glenorr and Donnadorr several yards above him.

The beast was descending, spiraling ever lower.

Swords, he was big!

"Return to the tower!" Meekelorr commanded them, his voice low and tense. "But move slowly!"

Pohl would have disobeyed him had he his sword. His one hope was to get to the tower, arm himself, and find help. He began slowly to inch his way backward until he stood on the stone pavement of the courtyard next to the two young men.

As he reached the two Easterners, a dozen soldiers, armed with swords and bows, came running out of the building next to the tower. As they glanced up at the beast circling ever downward, shock registered on their faces. They quickly recovered. Their attitude changed. They began to strut insolently down the hill.

"Carefully and slowly," Pohl warned them as they moved past him, "but get to Meekelorr."

The Companions headed toward their leader, dressed in their gray uniforms and white tunics, their gray capes flying in the wind.

Pohl heard a sharp intake of breath behind him.

"Ho, Fire Starter!" Meekelorr called loudly to the flying beast. "Come into my territory, have you? To what avail? Go back to your foul cave. You have little power here."

The words were brave, but Pohl doubted, as he stood watching in fear for his friend, that they were true. He glanced at the two Easterners at his side and noted the look of shock on Glenorr's face as his eyes followed the movements of the Companions. Well, well, he thought, but no time for that now. He looked back at the scene down the hill.

The Companions had reached Meekelorr. They stood leaning contemptuously on their swords, staring up, as if fighting flying fire beasts was something they did every day. It was all bravado, Pohl knew.

The beast screamed and screamed, moving ever lower. The Companions of the Way stood their ground. A few laughed. One or two called it names. Pohl thought for sure they were all dead men. One blast of its fire breath and it would be over. But no fire came from its huge mouth, only small puffs of smoke. Still, it made a great noise and the ground beneath their feet began to shake.

"Look," Donnadorr said to Pohl. "I think it's going away."

Indeed, the beast had begun to ascend again. Perhaps

Meekelorr was right, the Gods be praised, and it did not have the same power so far from the cave. Not in Agavia and the hills surrounding it.

At least not yet.

"It isn't going to land," Donnadorr said, from the comparative safety of the outer court. "Pohl, I know it looks like the beast from the cave, but Meekelorr killed that one. Is this another?"

Glenelle, huddling in the doorway to the Healing Tower, moaned behind them. "Guttlubbers!"

"It's all right," Sylvane said, putting her arm around her foster sister's shoulder. "It's going away."

"They're Guttlubbers!" Glenelle insisted.

"I hope it's not a different beast," Pohl said to Donnadorr, expelling the breath he hadn't known he was holding. He had turned to watch Glenelle and Sylvane. "Yes, yes, I'm sure it's the same one!"

"They can't be Guttlubbers," Sylvane said, but she didn't sound convinced.

Pohl watched with relief as the beast flew higher and away toward the west. So, Pohl observed with foreboding, the beast leaves the cave and comes into Agavia. Indeed the times were changing. Another sign that the difficult days, long awaited, were drawing near.

But no time to contemplate that now. He had a more immediate task to handle. Guttlubbers, indeed!

"Why are there Guttlubbers here?" Glenorr demanded of Pohl, now that the beast was leaving.

Pohl turned to meet Glenorr's accusing eyes.

"I assume the soldiers you are referring to are those we call the Companions of the Way," he said. "Meekelorr's soldiers."

"They *are* Guttlubbers, then."

"Wait a minute, Glen." Donnadorr caught him by the arm. "Just because they wear gray-and-white uniforms doesn't mean they are Guttlubbers. You heard the doctor. They're Companions of the Way and Meekelorr is their leader. You know that Meekelorr is good. He saved our lives and brought us to safety."

"Don's right, isn't he?" Sylvane asked.

"What have you heard about these so-called Guttlubbers, Glen?" Pohl asked.

"What everyone in the east knows to be true. Guttlubbers are killers who try to destroy whatever government they find, that they are cruel and merciless, that they kill wherever they go simply for the pleasure of it. They are the ones responsible for the chaos in the Easternlands."

"I see." Pohl led the group to a circle of benches in a corner of the courtyard. "Sit down, please. Have any of you been in battle with these Guttlubbers? You, Glen?"

"No, but my father has. . .I'm sure of that." Glenorr fidgeted in his seat. "Or at least he knew someone who had battled them."

"And you, Glenelle?"

"No, not personally, but. . ."

"That doesn't mean that what we have heard is wrong," Glen said.

"And you, Sylvane?"

"No."

Pohl turned to Donnadorr, who was looking off in the distance, a troubled look in his eyes.

"Don?"

Donnadorr first shook his head, then said, "I think I saw them once—when I was very young."

"Were they killing?"

"Talking. They were talking. That's all I remember."

"So it's all hearsay, what you know about these Guttlubbers."

"It is them then!" Glenorr rose to his feet. "Meekelorr's soldiers are Guttlubbers. They dress in gray and white, and wear that insignia, a square on a triangle."

At that moment, the Companions who had confronted the

beast streamed into the courtyard with Meekelorr in their midst. They were laughing and joking and slapping Meekelorr and each other on the back. They were in high spirits. The group around Pohl was silent until the soldiers had entered the school. The elated soldiers had not noticed the little band of Easterners.

"I'm not going to deny it, no, indeed not," Pohl said, rising to his feet, and facing Glenorr. "You are in a place that not only trains your so-called Guttlubbers but also honors them highly."

"What?" Sylvane jumped up and began twisting her hands.

"Have you been treated badly here, Sylvane?"

"No, on the contrary. . ."

"Is Auragole being restored to health? Did Meekelorr ride day and night for the moonleaf?"

"Yes," Sylvane said, "then how is it. . .?"

Pohl turned to the stricken Glenelle. "Do you know what the word *Guttlubbers* means, or meant originally, before it was corrupted by ill-use?"

Glenelle shook her head.

"It comes from two words, *God lovers.*"

"God lovers?" Glenelle's face was blank with incomprehension.

This is not going to be easy, Pohl thought. But he was going to try. "It was once known in the east that these soldiers believed in the Gods of the Creative World, the Gods whom most in the east have forgotten."

"Soldiers who believe in Gods?" There was a note of sarcasm in Glenorr's voice.

Was there any among these Easterners who believed in the Gods? Pohl wondered. Well, perhaps they could understand this other task of the Companions. "It was also once known that these soldiers would help anyone who was injured or treated badly by cruel leaders or roving bands of thieves and killers. There was a time when the Companions were sought after, wished for. Wherever they went, they were greeted and revered like the friends they were. Now they are hunted down as if they were evil beasts out of the Golden Century."

He observed the faces of the Easterners. Glenorr looked skeptical. Glenelle seemed troubled. But Sylvane and Donnadorr were leaning toward him, each with an expression of great intensity.

Pohl went on, "It began as only a little lie, spread by cruel men who do not wish to see help given to anyone in need. And this lie is now believed by many. It has turned good men into fearful men who hunt down those who would aid them. A lie can be a potent force, a very potent force."

With that Pohl left them sitting there. Without looking back, he entered the tower.

chapter thirteen

IT WAS TWO nights later and Pohl had just visited his last patient. He had turned down the corridor heading to the wing of the school where he was housed when he saw Meekelorr striding toward him.

"Pohl," Meekelorr said, without any preamble, "I've been looking for you. We need to talk. Let's get some tea." And not waiting for a reply, he turned and led Pohl back through several corridors until they came to the kitchen of the school. Pohl, used to Meekelorr's abrupt ways, followed without a word.

No one was in the kitchen at that hour. The long wooden worktable was well scrubbed, and the stone floor glistened from its recent washing. Above the table, large pots that were used for preparing the meals hung on an oblong wooden rack. A low fire glimmered in the fireplace. Meekelorr removed two mugs from the large cupboard and with a dipper that had been hanging nearby ladled the tea that always simmered in a pot above the fire.

The two men stood across the table from each other holding their hot mugs in their hands. Pohl watched his friend with mounting curiosity.

Meekelorr was deep in thought. Finally he said, "Do you know who Auragole is?"

"What do you mean?"

"Who his parents are. . .were? Where he comes from?"

"Father, Goloss. Mother. . .I forgot. Wait! Itina. Auragole—didn't I tell you?—was raised in an isolated valley in the Gandlese somewhere."

"Well?"

"Rare, I'll admit, considering how terrified most Easterners are of the Gandlese or any mountains." Pohl sipped his tea and waited.

"Think, old friend, think." And Meekelorr began to pace the length of the table, watching Pohl as he did.

"What on earth has you so fired up? Tell me. I'm very sleepy and not up to playing guessing games all night."

Meekelorr stopped at the end of the table and looked down its length at Pohl. "Auragole is the great-nephew of Eagalorr."

"What?" Pohl sloshed tea on himself. Eagalorr was the teacher who had founded the Last School, the one the Agavi called Amarori.

"Auragole is the great-nephew. . ."

"I heard what you said. How do you know?"

"He told me only half an hour ago when I looked in on him. His parents are from my own country, Stahlowill. His father is Goloss, from the village of Pahtahl in the lowlands, two days' journey from Eagalorr's first school. Surely you remember Goloss, and Auragole's mother, Itina, the niece Eagalorr raised after her parents died?"

"Stars and nights!" Pohl had known the Master's niece as a child—sweet, dark-haired and dark-eyed, tall. But Pohl had been away when Itina married. When Pohl returned to the school in Stahlowill, she had already left with her husband—that much he had heard. Eagalorr didn't speak of it nor had Pohl asked him about it. There had been so many losses and so many separations. One simply accepted them. Pohl never knew her husband nor did he know his name.

"Did you know Goloss well?" Pohl asked.

"Oh yes, very well. Very well." And Meekelorr began pacing up and down the length of table, but his eyes never left Pohl's face. "My family's farm was an hour's walk from Pahtahl. Goloss was eight or ten years older than I. I was seventeen when he left for the Gandlese. That was twenty-two years ago when I was still in the school in Stahlowill. Goloss tried to convince me and other students to leave it, to leave our foolish pursuits and come with him. Did I never tell you this story?"

Pohl shook his head.

"Needless to say, Goloss was not successful—none of the students or teachers followed him, though others in the surrounding villages did. He fought with the teachers and argued with the students. After the death of his first child in a raid on his village, he turned his fury on the Gods."

"People want the Gods to storm out of the heavens and save them."

"Goloss became fed up, enraged at the constant raids on his village. It's a town broken and deserted now—like so many others."

"Is that where Elarr comes from?" Pohl asked.

"No, what happened to Elarr and his family happened the year the school was destroyed. That was about seven years later. Elarr's village was closer to the school, higher up in the hills, and at first more protected. But Goloss's village, just above the plains, had come under attack again and again. He got sick of it—who could blame him?—so he gathered a small band of people together and filled their heads with dreams of peace and a new community somewhere in the uninhabited Gandlese. He was fearless in his anger and eloquent in his fury. He shouted down any talk of terrible beasts that lived in the Gandlese and would brandish first his sword and then his bow.

"I can still hear him," Meekelorr continued. "He preached to anyone who would listen. 'We will live without Gods and without wars. We will raise up a generation of free individuals who will rely on themselves and on the good earth.' I'm not at all surprised to hear he made it deep into the Gandlese. More than thirty people went with him as far as the foothills, but only one other couple followed Goloss and his wife farther into the mountains, according to Auragole. Well, Goloss always did have a will of iron. What was so heartbreaking to me at that time, Pohl, was that Goloss had been a priest of the King God—in the old tradition, of course—who had lost his faith."

"A priest of. . .? Did Auragole tell you that?"

"No. Has he mentioned it to you?"

Pohl shook his head, still amazed at this turn of events, at the human connections that crossed and crisscrossed.

"I have a feeling that little fact was something his father kept from him. That would have been like Goloss."

"Not mention it? And what about you, Meekelorr? Did you mention it?"

"No."

"Or that you knew Goloss?"

"No. Nor did I tell Auragole that I knew his uncle. What about you? Did you tell him that it was Eagalorr who founded this school?"

"No. I only said there was a community up here that was founded by a man from the east. I didn't mention that the community was a school, and I deliberately didn't mention Eagalorr by name."

"Ah, that's good. Then please don't. And don't mention, as of yet, that we knew his father—or that his father had been a priest."

"Why all this holding back, Meekelorr?"

"I'm not sure." Meekelorr moved closer to Pohl. "Probably for the same reason you held back—these times call for caution." His voice was thoughtful. "We suddenly have strangers in our midst. . . And perhaps our wild card. There is much here to ponder before we speak so openly."

"I agree. Yes, yes, indeed. All these odd bits and pieces." Pohl scratched his head. "Yes, one needs to give this much thought."

"They say Goloss put the torch to his temple himself, but I doubt that. Once it burned down, however, he never put on vestments again. Though my own father was not interested in the Gods, I found my way to Goloss's temple as a youth. It served as a beginning for me. Goloss, you might say, was my first teacher."

"So our possible wild card is the son of your first teacher and the nephew of your second. One has to marvel at the machinations of destiny."

Meekelorr walked over to the kettle of tea steaming in the fireplace and ladled himself another mugful of the hot brew. "Eagalorr argued with Goloss only once. Then, seeing that he was determined to go, the Master drew maps for him and sat with him day after day poring over them, helping Goloss to choose the safest path to travel and even a valley for his new home—closer to the Westernlands than the Easternlands. Eagalorr was, after all, familiar with the Gandlese from his frequent travels here. Most of our maps of the Gandlese are from Eagalorr—did you know that?"

Pohl nodded.

"Do you want more tea?"

Pohl declined but joined him at the fireplace. He stared at the tiny leaves settling in odd patterns at the bottom of his mug. "I knew Auragole had an uncle in the east that he wanted to search for, but he never gave him a name and I never thought to ask him."

"He too is cautious, it would seem."

"Did you know that Auragole has postponed going east?"

"Yes," Meekelorr said. "He wants to accompany his friends to Mattelmead."

"Because he's in love with Glenelle, or so he imagines."

"Ah, the pretty blond one."

"Yes, the female twin."

"You don't approve?" Meekelorr raised his eyebrows.

"It would be better for him if he were in love with Sylvane. She is far better suited to him."

Meekelorr laughed. "Spoken like an old man, practical in every way."

And Pohl grinned.

"Now," Meekelorr said, "tell me all you know about these Easterners who are now in our midst."

Pohl told him what he had been told. "The twins and their foster sister are from the south, from Mape. Do you know that country?"

"Only by reputation."

"I was there years ago. It's a bad place, as bad as it gets. No wonder they fear the so-called Guttlubbers. Yes, yes, indeed. It is quite understandable."

"We sent some Companions there once. We never heard from them again." Meekelorr's tone was matter-of-fact. "Are they still a bit wary of me, of my men?"

"I read Glenorr this way—that it is hard for him to give up on something he has once believed to be true. But the others are more willing to trust the evidence of their experience." Pohl walked over to the sink and put his cup into the large pot of water there.

"And Donnadorr? Where is he from?"

"It seems he has roamed all over the east since he was a child. He can't remember any other life."

"Like so many abandoned or orphaned children. But at least he survived," Meekelorr said.

"So now Auragole is the only one left of Goloss's small community. So much for his father's dreams." Pohl shook his head. "If we don't tell Auragole that we knew his uncle and that he is dead, Auragole will eventually head east, looking for a man who no longer exists on the Deep Earth."

"I'm not saying that we won't tell him. But there is a jumble of fragments here, Pohl. We need to sort them out. And also Claregole needs to be consulted. And Galavi."

"Why?"

"Kinship, my friend. Claregole and Galavi, after all, are children of Eagalorr."

"Of course," Pohl struck his head with the flat of his hand. "Meekelorr, I'm getting old. I can't keep up with events."

"Destiny, Pohl, is weaving its web. One must really stand in awe."

A FEW DAYS later, Pohl received a note from the Lady Claregole asking if he would come down to the mansion that day for a short visit—at his convenience. Pohl told the messenger that he would come at once. He was more than a little curious about this request. He rode the two miles to the Lady's mansion with her messenger in one of the narrow wagons that the Agavi had built to transport goods and people up and down the mountains. The day was crystal clear, not too cold, but crisp. Pohl dozed as the wagon rocked its steady way down the hill.

The Lady Claregole greeted him in the Great Mansion's large, round reception hall. "Pohl, good of you to come so quickly, old friend." She grasped both his hands. "Will you ride with me in my carriage? I have a need to drive through a portion of my valley."

Her smile was beautiful, if sad, and Pohl thought he saw her lips tremble slightly. "It will be a delight for me to revisit your valley and see its memory signs again."

Pohl helped her into her long, deep-blue cloak.

Moments later they were in a covered carriage pulled by two

horses. The Lady Claregole was silent as they pulled out of the courtyard and drove through her beautiful gardens with its their sculpted bushes and evergreen trees. Pohl watched Claregole out of the corner of his eye, more than a little curious about this sudden invitation. Agavians did not often act spontaneously. Theirs was a life of ceremony and traditions, of courtesy and planning. But then Claregole was only half Agavian. She shared the dark hair and pale skin of the Agavi, but not their eyes. Hers were beautiful in a different way, green like her father's.

"Thank you for coming, Pohl," she finally said. "Tomorrow when we meet—you, Meekelorr, Galavi, and myself—I shall ask you about the east, but not today. Are you rested, soul-friend?"

"Yes, indeed. Thank you." Pohl had, of course, met with the Lady Claregole after he had arrived with Meekelorr, but they had spoken little at that time about the chaos enveloping the east. With great consideration, Claregole had permitted both Pohl and Meekelorr time to settle into their new regimen, and to rest and regain their strength before they spoke together of the task looming ahead.

They were traveling down a narrow, winding road through farmland. Trees rolled away from them like green and gray ribbons. They passed an Agavian sign, three large stones sitting one upon the other. The carriage stopped and the Lady looked out the window at it and closed her eyes. Pohl watched her with interest. This was one of the memory signs that stood all over the valley and nearby hills. Agavians could stand before such a sign and remembrances of their ancestors and of their history would appear to them in their minds' eye.

After a moment, the Lady opened her eyes and signaled to the driver to go on. They again drove in silence and again stopped in front of a wooden pillar with two crossbeams and some unusual carvings. Again the Lady closed her eyes.

What is she seeing? Pohl wondered. What is she seeking?

In a few minutes they were on their way again.

In Agavia, each man and woman was valued for what he or she did to contribute to the welfare of the whole community. Each worked for the good of all, be it as farmer or sheepherder or carpenter. But all were artists too—singers, musicians, sculptors, weavers, actors. Art, in all its sundry expressions, was the passion of the Agavi and each man, woman, and child participated. Still, the Lady was their acknowledged leader, as her mother had been before her, and her mother's mother before that, and back on into the long past. It gave Claregole few privileges, but at all celebrations, either religious or secular, she officiated. In addition to these tasks, she was a fine weaver.

Twice more the carriage stopped in front of signs. Finally, the Lady turned to Pohl. "I cannot find what I seek in these signs. Perhaps my brother will do better here. Galavi is more gifted than I at reading the memory signs."

"What is it you are seeking, soul-friend?"

"Meekelorr sent me a note yesterday. It seems the young man who lies ill in the Healing Tower is father-kin to Galavi and me." Her green eyes, always so expressive, looked thoughtful. "Meekelorr has asked that I and my brother not mention this kinship to any of the Easterners."

"I know—at least not until the four of us have had time to talk. Tomorrow, when we meet together, we can decide how to handle this new and most curious situation."

"So Meekelorr requests." Claregole then told Pohl of Binta's far-seeing at the end of the summer just past.

Pohl could only shake his head in wonder.

"I'm not surprised that one or the other of the travelers is the one of Binta's far-seeing," she said. "Strangers seldom come across our valley, guarded as it is by high mountains. And when they do, they come by the design of destiny. It is this design I seek in the memory signs. If there is something to be revealed, I cannot find it. Perhaps my brother will have more success."

"Auragole is mother-nephew to Amarori, as your people call

him, and so not Agavian. Perhaps that is why you cannot find it in the signs."

"Perhaps," and now she smiled a true smile. "Meekelorr wrote that he would tell all that he knows about this situation, as you call it, when we meet tomorrow. I decided not to wait." And she smiled again, this time a little mischievously. Then she sighed and once more her expression held a hint of sadness.

They were heading across the valley now, past farms preparing for the deep winter that would soon be upon them. Darkness was beginning to fall. Music could be heard from many cottages, from manor houses, and from the other mansions. As they rode, the two were silent, drinking in the unearthly peace. The Valley of the Agavi was indeed, Pohl noted with satisfaction, God-touched.

Finally the Lady spoke. "Will you tell me now about this father-kin whom you are healing in the tower?"

And so Pohl related first what Meekelorr had told him and then what the youth himself had told about his background, about his life in the Gandlese, the journey from his valley, and his encounter with the Easterners. The manner of Meekelorr's encounter with the five, she already knew. She listened thoughtfully to Pohl's tale. If any of it surprised her, Pohl could not see it. But then the Agavians seemed to meet most things with an enviable equanimity.

After he finished, Claregole asked, "Why were the Easterners not traveling with a caravan?"

"All I was told was that they had left the caravan. The *why* has not been told to me."

"How is it that the five of them were traveling these mountains so late? Surely there is snow in the Northern Valley by now."

"That I *can* tell you. This story was told to me by both Auragole and by Donnadorr." And he told her of how Auragole, Sylvane, and the twins had met an injured Donnadorr and had, at Auragole's insistence, waited for him.

When Pohl finished, the Lady said, "May I ask why you and Meekelorr have not told Auragole that he is father-kin to Galavi and me?"

"These strange events call for caution. But most important, as this involves you and through you the Agavi people, we thought it only right that we wait until we had spoken with you and Galavi."

"I see," Claregole said, her eyes thoughtful. "There are new strands here, Pohl. I have spoken of them to Galavi. But we do not know as yet where to place them in the tapestry—these odd-colored threads. They belong in the whole. But where? Ah well, there is always that in destiny that cannot be foretold. Perhaps we will have some thoughts for you tomorrow when we four meet. But I promise you, we shall ponder it."

"As will Meekelorr and I."

N

chapter fourteen

THE NEXT EVENING, Pohl and Meekelorr were in the Lady Claregole's rooms for the long-awaited meeting with her and her brother.

The four had just finished their supper, and were now sitting on chairs made plush by thick down pillows in front of a marble fireplace that was opulently carved. They were drinking the strong, flavorful Agavian tea blend.

There is no place more perfect in all the known world, Pohl thought, than the Lady's Great Mansion. To create an environment that is beautiful was, for the Agavians, a religious act. They must complete, they said, what had been given to them unfinished by the Gods. Their crafting was delicate, intricate, and ornate. Attention was paid to each element of furniture, rug, pillow, vase, or wall hanging that adorned any room. Detail was what they loved, and pattern and color. Compared to the rest of the mansion, however, the furniture in the Lady's apartment was less ornate. There were fewer hangings on the walls and fewer rugs on the floor. Indeed, Pohl thought with admiration, the Lady Claregole is so lovely herself that her own beauty fills a room and it is enough.

He looked at her sitting erect in her chair—tall, slender, regal, but also soft and womanly. Her long black hair, which she wore up for state occasions, hung down this evening in billowy waves. Pohl had watched her with pleasure as she served the tea.

Galavi, the Lady Claregole's brother, sat upright and motionless in the chair next to her. Pohl could see that he was troubled. He had not spoken throughout the long ceremonial meal, had not participated in the polite conversation that was part of the Agavian meal ritual.

The tea-drinking was finally at an end. The Lady Claregole put her cup carefully down on the table in front of her, folded her hands lightly in her lap, and said, "Tell me now, if you will, what the situation is in the Easternlands."

With that request she turned the conversation to the heart of their meeting.

"Chaos, total anarchy." Meekelorr stood up and began to pace about the room. "Even the settlements do not hold. They fight within, brother against brother. . ."

Galavi gasped.

Meekelorr waited, but as Galavi did not comment he went on. "The Companions of the Way, who used to be a welcome sight for most people, have been betrayed time and again—attacked, murdered by those very individuals they had previously helped. Guttlubbers, they are called, and it is a term of derision and hatred. They have become the scapegoat for all the evil that men fear. Therefore, for the present, there is no more that we can do in the east."

"Will you find the Westernlands more hospitable?" the Lady asked.

As Meekelorr watched her from near the fireplace, his eyes in the light of the flames betrayed his feelings. Usually restless, he gazed on her face with an openness and a delicacy that spoke of his love. Then he turned away and in a passionless voice said, "Claregole, I say to you what you too believe; the Nethergod has already incarnated. Pohl and I believe he is in the west and that he will begin his work soon—not yet the Last Battle, but the preparations for it."

The Lady looked up at him with calm eyes. "Yes, there have been many signs, heart-friend. But why do you believe it will be in the west and not in the east?"

Pohl picked up the narrative. As he spoke he watched Galavi's reactions. Galavi's face was like a lake in summer with a hard wind whipping across its surface, so often did his expression change. "We think he is in the west," Pohl said, "because the Nethergod must have some form of government to work through. You know that it is predicted he will come as a savior. He will promise the people a world filled with peace. . ."

". . .which humanity desires above everything else," Meekelorr interjected.

". . .and along with peace," Pohl went on, "he will offer them protection and prosperity. Then the Nethergod—their great savior—will take from them, bit by bit, the little freedom they have, until he has enslaved them all. . ."

". . .and has torn away our Deep Earth from the Creative World and its rightful Gods." The Lady intoned what they all knew. "Then the earth would become lost—a hard speck among the stars, and those on it chained forever to the Nethergod."

She breathed deeply and exhaled a terrible sadness. "Come, sit, Meekelorr." She gestured to the chair next to hers. "It is no more than I have suspected, given these past trying years. We too have seen the signs."

Meekelorr came and sat down next to her, a look of bald sympathy on his face.

She shook her head. "Do not sorrow for my sorrows, heart-friend. We each have our task—you both yours, and the Agavi theirs. We have prepared for these times for untold generations. We cannot now regret personal sacrifices. The future of the Deep Earth is at stake. Be at ease about me." She smiled at Meekelorr. "For these times, Galavi and I were born." And then she turned to Pohl. "You have your own difficult duties. I would not lay the weight of mine upon your hearts."

Pohl glanced over at her brother. Galavi's body was taut, his Agavian eyes dark with sorrow. Shorter and stockier than the Agavi, Galavi also had the auburn hair of his father. Half past, half future, Pohl thought, watching the tree shepherd. The Agavi trees that grew in the hills around this valley were Galavi's passion. He tended them with love and gratitude. Agavi trees were revered by the valley dwellers. Much of their furniture, utensils, houses, and outbuildings were made of this wood. And it grew only in this one area on all the Grand Continent. Galavi was also a fine woodcarver. The low table on which the tea utensils sat was Galavi's handiwork. And it was a fine piece, indeed.

Will he be able to fulfill the task set for him by us and by his destiny as an Agavian? Pohl wondered. Will any of us be able to fulfill the tasks set for us by our destinies? he amended.

Meekelorr leaned forward, arms resting on his knees. "I say this to you, my friends—for I cannot say this to any other—I am uneasy. The Companions of the Way were nearly wiped out in the east. I cannot say for a certainty, but perhaps there are only a thousand left to come here out of the east in the spring. And some of them are newly recruited. Though I have tried to speak to them of our goals, many, in truth, don't understand them."

"Then why do they join you?" Galavi asked him, speaking for the first time.

"For adventure," Meekelorr said, looking at the young man. "For food. And because life offers them little else except battles for survival. We offer them something youth needs—community and ideals. Freedom and love, we cry. And they repeat, freedom and love. But are they more than words to them?"

Pohl murmured, "Perhaps the full belly is enough for now."

Meekelorr turned to him. "But I ask you, for how long enough?" Then he looked at Claregole. "My men ask me over and over again, why don't the Creative Gods drive the Nethergod and his hordes out of our suffering earth? And I explain time and again that humankind would lose the whole meaning of the earth if the Creative Gods took away what humans have descended to the Deep Earth to develop: true freedom—even the freedom to choose evil—and genuine love. But freedom is just a word to most, a slogan. Every leader who wants to rally men around him yells, 'freedom, freedom.' And, of course, we know what love means to them—after all, they are young."

Galavi cleared his throat. Haltingly, he began to speak. "I do not understand much of what you say—neither about freedom nor about love—which seems such a mystery to you *outsiders*. Love is easy for the Agavi. An Agavian is born loving the other. It is given us. And freedom is not a dream for the Agavi. We do not long for it. We do not think about it. Each Agavian mercifully has his place in the scheme of things. He is born into his place. He longs for nothing else. The Agavi belong together, each to each, and it is good. If one Agavian suffers, all Agavians weep. It is the way we have always been.

"If we say 'I,' we mean something different than when you say 'I,' Meekelorr." Galavi looked at him with melancholy dark eyes. "We mean the whole community. We mean all our ancestors. Yet," he added, "it is for these times that all our people have waited, even as humanity has grown beyond us. You have told me what my part in it must be. I have trained myself to be a soldier, learned what you told me I needed to learn. Now we also make weapons of war in the craft shops that were created for the making of beautiful objects. It is an alien thing to us, this making of weapons of war. I say to you, soul-friends, that the only war I know is the war inside my soul. The Easternlander in me longs to break free into something new, something that has never been in Agavia. But the Agavian in me is in despair because it abhors change and feels not only that it cannot, but that it must not change. Yet come the spring, with the help of the Companions, I will begin to teach my fellow Agavi how to build fences and walls around their homes and mansions, instruct them in the fighting of war and the defense against war."

For a moment he paused and many emotions played across his face. Finally Galavi went on, turning now to look directly at the Lady Claregole. Locks of his auburn hair, curling on his forehead, glistened with sweat. "My sister, I go from memory sign to memory sign trying to awaken in myself the memories of our ancestors. I have remembered much—all our history plays before my sight. But nowhere. . .nowhere can I find in our collective memories any remembrance of war or battle."

Pohl's heart ached for Galavi.

"Yours is indeed a hard road, my brother," Claregole answered with all compassion. "In this you must be your father's son. I too have sought solace in the memory signs. But I tell you that Agavian memories will not serve you here— except, perhaps, to remind you that our ancestors too awaited these world days. We must not fail them or the Gods who have given us this task. It is we, you and I, Galavi, and all the Agavians of our generation who must fulfill the task laid upon our people so many centuries ago."

And Galavi sat with bowed head.

Claregole rose gracefully and walked over to the glass doors that led to her rose garden, sleeping under the blanket of snow that had fallen in the night, wrapped in the certainty that it would bloom again come spring. How many more springs? Pohl wondered, and knew she wondered too. Claregole stared into the night. Pohl knew she was looking at the dark, naked shapes of trees that waited patiently where they had been planted, as they had from time immemorial, for the waking season.

When Claregole spoke, she didn't turn around. "My people have known of the coming of the Nethergod, the Dark Breather, for thousands of years. It is in our tradition as well as in your mystery knowledge. When my father first came here with a request that my mother build for him a school, she understood the purpose. She understood that the Nethergod would come in a few generations. And that in our valley and in the surrounding hills and valleys the Last Battle would be fought. In our childhood, Galavi and I were taught this." She turned to look at them.

Pohl saw the weight of the thought of what would happen in her reign almost crush her. Meekelorr saw it too. But a look from Claregole kept him from rushing to her side.

"I shall be the last leader of the Agavi. May the Gods receive us and our deeds well."

The four were quiet then, not offering one another comfort, but sharing the grief of these hard world days.

And then they spoke about Auragole.

"Shall you tell him that he is cousin to you and Galavi?" Meekelorr asked her.

"What would you advise?" She looked first at Meekelorr and then at Pohl.

"I have been pondering this, and I think we should wait—at least for a time," Meekelorr said. "Who are these Easterners? For what purpose have they been brought among us? It is best we not connect Amarori with Eagalorr, and best that either name not be mentioned to Auragole or to the Easterners. We need to contemplate this a while longer. Do you agree, Claregole?"

"I do—at least for a time."

Meekelorr turned to Galavi. "And you?"

"Agavians do not keep secrets from one another. But neither do they gossip. In this I will take your counsel."

And so it was decided.

Soon after, around ten, Pohl took leave of the Lady. Meekelorr stayed on. Pohl too had been invited to spend the night in the mansion, but because he had patients to look in on before he retired, he declined her invitation.

LEAVING THE WAGON for Meekelorr to use the next day, Pohl decided to walk the two miles back up to the school. He wanted to breathe in the cool air and to digest all that had been said. He left the mansion by a side entrance and began his hike across the part of the valley that would take him to the narrow hill path that led to the Last School. It was a moonless night. The stars shone in all their magnificence. The snow-covered ground reflected enough light to keep him on a sure path. He inhaled the peace that was woven into the air of Agavia, into its ground, and into its trees sleeping gracefully under their white cloaks. Peace was in the wind that circulated gently over house and mansion, barn and stable, shop and craft room. Part of him noted all this with gratitude, part of him was lost in thought, taking in only the landmarks necessary to find his way, as he recollected the conversation that had just passed.

"I shall be the last leader of the Agavi. May the Gods receive us and our deeds well."

The last leader of the Agavi. That meant that Claregole would not have children. And that also meant that Claregole and Meekelorr would never marry. For the custom among the Agavians was to live as lovers for a time. If their union were blessed by a pregnancy, then the couple would marry at the spring celebration of Demeda, the Goddess of Fertility. That couple would stay married until their last child was twenty-one. If they chose to separate at that time, they could. Those whose union was not blessed by the begetting of offspring were free to choose other partners, or stay together. But they were not able to marry. According to what Pohl had been told by the teachers at the school, fewer and fewer children were being born to the Agavians. That was one of the signs for the Agavians that the Last Battle would be in their lifetime. That was the personal sacrifice that the Lady had to make—never to bear a child and consequently a successor. There would be no successors.

But if the Lady would never be a mother, if she were to be the last leader of the Agavians, then Meekelorr would never be a father. Pohl exhaled sadly. Meekelorr would not leave Claregole—no matter that they could never marry.

Pohl had been walking no more than ten minutes when something caught his attention and broke into his musings. Off to his right, moving very slowly, was an apparition in white. It startled him, for he knew Agavians seldom came out at night—except on feast nights—being a diligent people who rose early to work.

He stopped, uneasy in his tracks, and peered through the dim starlight at what seemed to be a figure floating over the snow. For a moment he thought he was seeing a ghost or a wraith, so ethereal were its movements. It had not the forceful tread of a man or a woman about on some business. Pohl was not a man without fear, but his curiosity often overrode his fear, as it did then. He turned and left the path he was on and walked ever so quietly toward the apparition.

He almost exclaimed out loud when he saw that it was a woman dressed only in her nightclothes. A sleepwalker, he thought, and he moved more slowly, concerned he might shock her awake.

At that moment, as if sensing he was there, she turned and came directly toward him. For a reason he couldn't explain, he stopped some twenty feet from her and waited. But she continued to advance. When she had come closer, Pohl realized with a start that it was Glenelle. But her gestures and the expression on her face in the star-shine kept him from speaking. She finally halted a half-dozen feet from him and looked at him with icy hatred out of a pinched face. She raised her arms and gesticulated angrily at him.

"You will not win against me and mine, not if you call down all the armies of heaven. I will have this place!" The voice was guttural and filled with venom. Pohl's blood ran cold. "I will have the whole earth. You plan, you build. . .all for nothing!"

Then a small horrified voice exploded in a wail from the same throat. "No!" it shrieked. And Glenelle fell in a heap on the snow.

Pohl reached her in seconds. Her breath was rapid and shallow and her pulse was racing. He quickly removed his cloak, wrapped her in it, picked her up, and carried her, not without effort, back to the Great Mansion. She did not regain consciousness.

In those days there were no guards at this or at the other mansions. No one remained awake in the valley watching the comings and goings of its inhabitants. No one looked up into the hills in fear of either thieves or invaders. There were no thieves in the Valley of the Agavi, nor had there been any invaders in the thousands of years of their history.

Pohl entered the front door, which had no lock, and went up the curved marble staircase to the second floor and headed toward the west wing where he had been told the small band of travelers was staying. He pounded on several doors along the hall with his foot and in a few moments all of the Easterners were gathered around him.

"Here, let me take her," Donnadorr said, without question. And Pohl gladly put the unconscious girl in his arms. "I'll take her to her room."

Pohl and the others followed Donnadorr with Sylvane walking alongside him, trying to uncover Glenelle's face. "Oh, my poor baby, what has happened to you? Did you have another spell?"

"Sylvane!" Glenorr's tone was harsh, his face red with anger. Pohl turned to Donnadorr, but Donnadorr had eyes only for Glenelle.

"Where did you find her?" Glenorr asked Pohl.

As they entered her room, he said, "She was wandering in the snow. Is she given to sleepwalking?"

"No, not really," Sylvane said.

"Nonsense. She has done it before." This from Glenorr. "Surely you remember, Sylvie. Yes, she sleepwalks. Not often, but yes, she is a sleepwalker."

Pohl looked at Glenorr's taut face. Glenorr was lying—not easy to do in Agavia. Pohl looked over at the unconscious figure that Donnadorr had placed gently on her bed. This depth of unconsciousness is not the reaction of a sleepwalker, he thought, but said instead, "Glen, rekindle the fire. Sylvie, go down to the kitchen and bring up some tea. Don, let's get her under these feather comforters. She needs warmth."

"Did she. . .did she say anything?" Donnadorr whispered from across the bed.

"Does she usually?"

"No," Glenorr called from the fireplace. "Hardly ever."

Pohl rubbed Glenelle's arms and feet under the blankets and finally, to Pohl's relief, she was moaning and then crying.

Just as Sylvane returned with the tea, Glenelle opened her eyes. For a moment nothing registered, but when Glenelle saw them all standing around her bed, her eyes widened. "Why are you all here?" she whispered.

"I found you wandering outside in the snow," Pohl said, before the others could answer.

"What?" She looked both terrified and confused.

"You don't remember?"

"No!" She shook her head, but the look of terror remained.

"You were just sleepwalking again," her brother said, in measured tones.

Glenelle didn't answer but looked from face to face, then bit her lip. Sylvane's face was flaming. Donnadorr did not meet Pohl's eyes or anyone else's. But Glenorr was watching Pohl defiantly.

"She needs rest," Pohl said. "Sylvane, can you spend the night here?"

"Yes, of course."

"I'll bring some remedies over in the morning to strengthen her," he told them. "Give her the tea now and keep her warm."

Pohl left them hovering about her bed and hurried to the other part of the mansion, to the room where Binta slept—not far from Claregole's chambers. He knocked hard on her door and in a few moments a lady with long white hair and the thin, smooth skin of the elderly of Agavia opened the door. She had thrown a wrap around her shoulders and greeted him with a startled expression on her sleepy face.

"My Lord Doctor!" she exclaimed in surprise. Then her eyes opened wide. "Is it my Lady? Does she ail?"

"No, no, indeed not." Pohl took her by the arm to keep her from fainting with alarm. "Your lady is well, Binta. Forgive me for waking you at such an hour, but I must leave a message for the Lady and for Meekelorr, to be delivered first thing in the morning."

The relief in her face was like sunshine.

"Forgive me for frightening you and for disturbing your sleep," Pohl said. "It is most important."

"Yes, yes, anything, Lord Pohl." Binta cocked her head to the side as if to listen better.

"Tell them that I will join them tomorrow morning—around nine, I think. As soon as I make the morning rounds of my patients."

She nodded, and waited.

"Tell Meekelorr that he is not to return to the school in the morning, but that he is to wait for me here."

"I will," she said.

"Thank you, Binta."

"The Gods strengthen you, Lord Doctor. The disturbing days have come. I feel it. May all of Agavia serve the need to which we were born." And with these words she closed the door.

As Pohl trudged across the valley and up the long hill, he thought hard, and not without dread, about what he had heard from Glenelle's mouth as she had confronted him on that snowy field. A message from the Adversaries, he told himself. He shivered in his warm cloak. He now understood why the group had been traveling alone through the Gandlese. Glenelle must have had these "sleepwalking" episodes before. She probably had frightened the travelers on the caravan. The peace of Agavia, which had settled on the valley and the adjacent valleys and hills thousands of years ago, seemed threaded through suddenly with an intolerable and unfamiliar cold. In his cozy room, after he had made his rounds, even with the welcome warmth of his fire and the thick feather comforters on the bed, Pohl could not dispel the chill he felt.

chapter fifteen

"THESE ARE INDEED the times for which we have been waiting," Claregole said, her lovely green eyes showing her concern.

The Lady, Meekelorr, and Pohl were seated in the breakfast room adjoining her bedroom, which overlooked her garden.

"Not since the First Days have the Adversaries penetrated into Agavia," she continued.

"To say that they've penetrated into Agavia is not quite accurate, my soul-friend." Pohl reached for her hand across the table.

"But how else to look at it, Pohl?"

"It is Glenelle they have access to, not the valley." It was Meekelorr who answered her. "The Adversaries pose no threat to the valley as yet."

"But Glenelle is here," she said.

"Yes, and when Glenelle leaves, those who gain access to her must leave with her," Pohl said.

"I understand, my friends, what you are saying. But she is here now."

"Yes," Meekelorr said, his gray eyes dark and thoughtful.

"My concern," Pohl said, "is that through Glenelle the Adversaries might find a way to return to us and bring the army of the Nethergod to the valley prematurely."

"Oh," Claregole said, with a sharp intake of breath. She then stared abstractedly at her barely touched breakfast.

Meekelorr got up and began to pace about the room. "We shall not make it easy for them to return to us. I have agreed to lead the band of travelers into the Westernlands after the spring thaw—when the Companions and I leave here. It's a long journey, but I will make it longer and more circuitous." He stopped and lightly touched Claregole's black hair. "She will lead no one here."

"As you know, Claregole," Pohl said, helping himself to another biscuit and some biddleberry jam, "the Nethergod must use humans, must corrupt humans. Everything must be done through the instrument of willing men or women."

"Well, they have it in Glenelle, it seems," Claregole said, with a sorrowful shake of her head.

"No," Pohl said.

"No?"

"What do you mean?" Meekelorr sat down again. "You heard it or them yourself, Pohl."

"Oh, I heard it all right," Pohl said. "But Glenelle doesn't cooperate willingly. She fights them. That I heard too."

"Oh, the poor child," the Lady said.

"Perhaps she doesn't cooperate on a conscious level, but on some level she has given them access," Meekelorr said.

"There's a weakness in her, of course," Pohl said, "but something in her also fights them."

"Then we must help her," the Lady said.

"Ah, perhaps not," Pohl said.

"We are not able?" the Lady asked.

"Oh, I think we are able—if she were to agree, if we were to take her to the Healing Tower and to the school for the winter, and if we were to work with her, give her remedies, and an education, and a training, but. . ."

"But what, Pohl?" the Lady asked.

"If we drive the Being out of her. . ." He left his words dangling.

Meekelorr finished them, ". . .where does it go?"

"Into another, perhaps?" Pohl asked.

"Surely not in the valley or in the school!" the Lady said.

"Are we all as strong as we would like to think ourselves?" Pohl said. "We are not all Agavian, dear Lady. Meekelorr, the teachers, the students at the school, the Companions, and I are Easternlanders. We possess all the frailties of the human race living in these times. Perhaps there are some among us with greater weaknesses than Glenelle. . ."

Meekelorr looked preoccupied, and Pohl knew he was thinking about his soldiers, those still new to the discipline.

Finally Meekelorr asked Pohl, "What can you do for her then, my friend?"

"Give her warming teas and keep an eye on her. I suspect that these strange spells of Glenelle's are the reason they are traveling alone. I suspect it is why they were put off their caravan."

"Poor child. They wouldn't help her and now we will not." The Lady stood. "Never in all our long history have we refused help to one who is ill."

"No." Pohl looked her squarely in the eye. "But never have the times been as grave as they are now nor as crucial. We must act with great caution. Much depends on this valley."

"But it is ordained that the Nethergod and his hordes will find their way here."

Meekelorr crouched by the Lady's chair and took her hand. "It is also ordained, Claregole . . . no, incumbent upon us that we protect ourselves and this valley until the time is right. It is too soon to meet the Adversaries. They must not come upon us prematurely. Much depends on timing. Too late and we lose, but too soon and we also lose. It is not yet the hour to draw down upon ourselves the forces of the Nethergod."

"Must the Dark Breather come when he is stronger?"

"Yes." Meekelorr held her with his eyes. "Yes, Claregole, when he is strong and when we are strong. His defeat then will either be decisive or his victory great."

She stared at him for a long time, then turned to Pohl. "Do what you must, but inform the council at the school."

Pohl felt both despondent and apprehensive as he left them. He walked the corridors to the western wing to look in on Glenelle. She was still sleeping deeply, but normally. Sylvane sat near her bed as if she were guarding her. When Sylvane saw Pohl, she greeted him perfunctorily, then lowered her head and did not meet his eyes. She said only that Glenelle had slept through the night. Pohl left her some warming herbs for tea, uttered a few words of encouragement, then met Meekelorr and rode back up to the school with him.

When they were almost at the school, Pohl said, "There is something I didn't want to say in front of Claregole, Meekelorr."

Meekelorr clucked encouragement to the horse and waited for Pohl to go on.

"The anti-Being that has hold of Glenelle, I think, is trying to kill her. . ."

"Kill her!"

"If I hadn't come along when I did, she could have died from exposure. If it succeeds while she is in this valley, it will be loose to find another host."

"What is the solution then? We cannot send her and the others out into the mountains in the snow to perish, Pohl. The Northern Valley is closed now. And I would not give them directions through the caves."

"No, we can't do that."

"Then we shall have to see that she is well guarded."

"Yes, that's a necessity. I shall ask the Council of Teachers to convene as soon as possible."

"Good," Meekelorr said.

They were silent as they drove into the courtyard of the Last School, where they turned over their wagon and horse to a groom. They were about to enter the building when Pohl saw Meekelorr look up. He followed the direction of his gaze and his stomach knotted. Meekelorr moved out into the courtyard for a better view and Pohl followed him.

The beast from the cave—it couldn't be anything else, for it was huge—was flying high, high in the sky. The two men stood there for a long time watching its flight. The beast did not come close to the ground. It emitted no sound. It merely circled around and around the Valley of the Agavi and the surrounding hills. Finally it moved off to the west and no doubt to its cave.

"Something will have to be done about that," Meekelorr said, as he entered the school.

"Don't be precipitous, Meekelorr. He may tire of this soon."

"We shall see."

AURAGOLE'S TREATMENT CONTINUED and he steadily improved. Pohl, in the meantime, arranged for the council to meet.

One day, in the Healing Tower, after Pohl had given Auragole his remedies, a young man came through the door. He had the pale skin, the tall build, the deep-set, almond-shaped eyes, and the dark hair of the Agavi. His smile was hesitant, as if a smile might have intruded on whatever was passing between the two of them. This awareness of the other, Pohl knew, which was a characteristic of the Agavi, had disappeared from the rest of humankind. Well, so be it. Humanity had to lose certain faculties in order that it might gain others.

The Agavian came forward carrying a tray with a large mound of clay. When he spoke it was in the melodic voice and in the rhyme that the Agavi often used.

> "I have brought thee clay
> as work for thy fingers.
> It will help to transform
> any illness that lingers."

"But my right arm is broken," Auragole said.

> "Then thy left hand must do
> the work of two."

He put the tray of clay on Auragole's lap.

> "Close thine eyes,
> think of spring
> and the thoughts
> spring can bring.

> "Ask the force that once
> formed the tree
> to work through thy fingers
> and help thee."

The Healing-sculptor nodded, bowed slightly, and left the room. Pohl followed. When he returned, perhaps an hour later, Auragole was lying back on his pillows, eyes closed—the thing he had created at the foot of his bed. The boy looked spent and there were streaks of tears on his cheeks. He didn't look up as Pohl came in. A few moments later, the Healing-sculptor entered and Auragole opened his eyes and watched the Agavian. He halted at the foot of the bed and contemplated Auragole's sculpture. Pohl looked at it too. It was only a form of angles and curves, but in it was a young lifetime full of the pain of loss. Pohl felt nearly moved to tears. The Healing-sculptor's eyes were brimming.

"Much sorrow is there.
'Twas heavy to bear.
To transform such pain
is to be as the rain
that penetrates deep
in the heart's soil.
Now sleep."

He took Auragole's sculpture and placed it on a pedestal not far from his bed. Then with a shy nod he left. Auragole closed his eyes again and in moments was sleeping, breathing deeply and easily. Pohl left him then, content with Auragole's progress.

ON THE THIRD day of the fourth week after the band of travelers had arrived in Agavia, the Council of Teachers met. All classes and all battle training had been canceled that day. The Lady Claregole rode up to the meeting astride Agate, her black horse. As she arrived in the courtyard, there were students and Companions at every window of the school, anxious to get a look at the beautiful woman who was leader of the Agavi and the beloved of Meekelorr. If Claregole knew she was being scrutinized, it was not apparent in her behavior. She dismounted, and Biehmar, the elected head of the school and teacher of the esoteric sciences, walked to meet her.

"Greetings and a sincere welcome to you, Lady Claregole, soul-friend to all in this school."

Claregole took both of his hands and thanked him for his welcome.

As part of the reception committee, Meekelorr and Pohl were

also present, but it was Biehmar who took Claregole's arm and led her through the school's halls and corridors, up stairs and down passageways, until they arrived at the small but cheerful council room. Meekelorr and Pohl followed behind the two. When they arrived at the carved double doors, Biehmar held them open for the Lady and she entered first. Pohl and Meekelorr followed with Biehmar last, closing the door ceremoniously behind him.

The other six members of the council—all the teachers at the school—were sitting expectantly around the massive table carved out of the black Agavi wood. They rose as the Lady entered. After the door was closed, Biehmar took the Lady's arm and led her to the foot of the table. Then he took his own place at its head. Meekelorr moved to Biehmar's left and Pohl to Biehmar's right.

Biehmar then introduced Claregole formally to the members of the council, though of course she knew them all. "Lady Claregole, you know Sandrofil, who teaches the natural sciences; Gewdril, our expert on history and evolution; Fllordon, who guides our pupils in the fine arts; Stor, who teaches the performing arts; Alumbra, at present our only female teacher. She instructs the students in their human and spiritual nature. And last but not least, the oldest amongst us, Mondrief, who teaches to the few who qualify, the new star wisdom."

Since the seven lived together and saw each other daily, the council, as council, met infrequently, usually only to handle a crisis. They had not met formally since Pohl and Meekelorr arrived from the Easternlands, though Pohl had spoken to each privately.

"Greetings to each and every one. It is good to see you, my soul-friends." The Lady smiled and seated herself.

The others then sat and the meeting commenced.

Meekelorr told of the retreat of the Companions of the Way from all of the Easternlands. Pohl picked up the narrative, describing the plans for the Companions to head west in the spring, enumerating all their reasons, and asking for the council's approval. Although there was no disputing the judgment of the battle leaders, there were many questions. The two answered as best they could. The Lady sat upright and attentive as she once again heard the familiar narrative.

"So you say the Nethergod *has already* incarnated? And in the west?" Gewdril asked Meekelorr. Pohl heard the shock in his tone.

"That is what we believe. But he is not yet working openly. He only prepares his work." Meekelorr's tone was matter-of-fact. "We still have several years before he falls upon us at the Last Battle—but, my soul-friends, I have no doubt that ours will be the generation to meet him."

"In what way does he prepare?" Alumbra, who was short, stocky, and motherly, asked.

Pohl answered her. "It's only a surmise, of course. But you know as well as I it has been foretold that the Nethergod will find his way to a center of power. There he will either become a leader, someone in the forefront of that government, or someone who stands close to a leader, working perhaps quietly behind the scenes. We know too that to prevail in his task, he must pervert humans. He must find men and women willing to do his evil work. Without that, he fails—for that is the point—this corrupting of humanity, this pulling humanity away from its rightful goals. So we look to the various countries whose leaders are strong or are becoming strong. Glovale, Thorensphere, Mattelmead are highest on our list."

"Not Isofed?" the Lady Claregole queried.

"We don't rule out Isofed," Meekelorr said, "but the people there are insular. Their culture is perhaps the oldest in the west. The Nethergod needs flexibility, a regime that is searching for something new out of what has failed. The Isofedians are content with their old traditions. They guard them zealously.

They would hardly be open to anyone who came touting change and a new way of life."

"You exclude the Sorren Heights, Wildenfarr-low-desert, and Noonbarr?" Biehmar asked. He took a great interest in all that happened in both the west and the east, though he had not been away from Agavia for many years.

It was Pohl who answered him. "The Sorren Heights is sparsely settled. To the north and west, along the borders with Thorensphere and Glovale, are little duchies whose leaders come into power like comets and go quickly out again. A mountainous land, it is not easily controlled under a central rule. Meekelorr will base himself in the Sorren Heights, in its high hills known as the Woefuls, as do the Companions now in the west under the direction of Cleege. . ."

"A good man, Cleege," Biehmar said.

"The best," Meekelorr affirmed.

"Meekelorr will rendezvous with Cleege this summer to plan the future work in the west," Pohl said, then returned to his survey of the Westernlands. "Wildenfarr is a desert with two warring tribes that dispute each other over land and old religious beliefs. Noonbarr, mostly farms, bears only a little watching because it has about ten major leaders with great estates on large tracts of land, many miles one from the other. It could be added to the list, but ease and noninterference seem more to their leaders' liking than conquest and ambition—so our reports from the Companions who keep a watch there tell us. Hameshall in the east of Noonbarr is probably the strongest leader there. But he leaves his neighbors alone."

"I would read the stars that way, also." It was the thin but certain voice of Mondrief, the eldest. He rose and stood with straight back, a tall, lanky man with a full head of white hair, a fine, thin, prominent nose, and merry eyes.

Everyone turned to him respectfully.

"I have not spoken of this to you before, my coworkers,

because you know that the stars no longer compel, but only show you possibilities, only offer you tools. And one can read their language in many different ways. I could not have said earlier with any certainty whether the Nethergod would come in the east or west. But after what has been told us today—which is similar to what Lorenwile told us—I too think it will be in the west."

"Lorenwile here? When?" Meekelorr leapt out of his seat.

"Three years—no, almost four years ago—Lorenwile was here." Mondrief sat again.

Meekelorr turned to look questioningly at the Lady.

"I would have told you sooner or later, my heart-friend," Claregole said. "But with the arrival of the Easterners. . . Had I known the news was of such importance, I would have mentioned it upon your arrival."

"Where is he now? What news did he bring?" Meekelorr's voice softened and he returned to his seat.

Biehmar answered. "Lorenwile resides in Mattelmead City and should be back there now—if all has gone according to his plans. As you know, at present Mattelmead has a strong and popular king whose ambition is to unite all of the lands of the west under his rule. Lorenwile has traveled throughout the Westernlands and thinks many countries will be ripe for a move by Ormahn in the near future. However, Ormahn's first task is to unify his own country, particularly the unruly southern provinces. But our news is old. No doubt he has done that by now—or has failed."

"Then if the Nethergod is indeed incarnated, it must be this Ormahn," Fllordon said, standing, his eyes hawklike in their intensity. He was small, wiry, animated, but fearless too.

"Too easy. Too obvious," Stor said. "The Nethergod would not be so obvious."

"Why not?" Fllordon asked.

No one answered.

At this point, the meeting was interrupted by students who brought tea and cakes. As the students served the tea, the conversation turned to the workings of the school and to the Feast of Ordavi, the Defender God, which had taken place before Meekelorr and Pohl arrived and was one of the four cornerstone feasts of the Agavian year.

After the tea utensils were removed, Biehmar reconvened the meeting. Claregole rose to speak. She spoke of the presence in the valley of the band of travelers. She told them of Meekelorr's battle with the beast in the cave, how Auragole had helped him, and how Meekelorr had brought them all back to the valley. These were facts that they had heard. But that they should be spoken of officially at a meeting of the council was important. It was the Agavian way.

However, what brought astonished gasps from all the council members was the information that Auragole was the great-nephew of Eagalorr.

"Pohl and I feel he has some role to play in the Last Battle," Meekelorr said. "But it is not only my own surmising, there is the lore also of the Agavians. Someone, a stranger yet not a stranger, will come in the days before the Last Battle. . ."

"Yes, that is one of the legends of the Agavi," the Lady Claregole confirmed.

That pronouncement was followed by many questions and by many suggestions. Gewdril, his gray-and-black short-cropped head bobbing up and down, his round face red with excitement, his eyes twinkling, rose to say that Auragole had been brought there by destiny, so he must be offered a place at the school, must be trained for whatever his role in the Last Battle might be. Alumbra rose to agree with Gewdril and to offer her services in the guidance of Auragole. And so did the youngest teacher, Sandrofil. There was a heated discussion about what the young man would need to learn in the few years that might be available before the Last Battle.

Meekelorr and Pohl listened without interruption.

Finally, after the discussion had gone on a while, Biehmar interjected. "Wait, my comrades, why are we in dispute? We don't know what Auragole's task is in the Last Battle, therefore we don't know what he needs to learn."

They argued about this in their friendly, lively manner.

After most had offered their opinions as to Auragole's task, Mondrief again rose and waited till all were silent.

"What has not been asked," he finally said, "are two questions."

"What are they?" Fllordon asked, leaning toward him.

"First, what is it that young Auragole wants? And, second, will his part in the Last Battle be for the good of humankind or for its ill?"

The silence that met his questions was like a peal of thunder, so loud did it seem to Pohl.

"We teach wisdom and we are fools—too many years away from the world," Biehmar finally spoke.

Meekelorr rose then and said, "While we take the time to ponder all that has been spoken today, I request that for now none of you mention the name Eagalorr to the Easterners or to Auragole—should your paths happen to cross—or tell him. . . them that what exists here is a school. All he and the Easterners know is that there is a community up here, similar to the settlements in the east."

"He and they are bound to hear that there is a school up here," Fllordon said.

"When they do, they do," Meekelorr answered. "But even if they know there's a school here, I request that none of you connect its founder with the father of the Lady Claregole and Galavi."

"What about the Agavians? Are they not likely to mention it?" Fllordon asked.

"Our guests will not connect Amarori with Eagalorr," Claregole said quietly. "Agavians do not chatter idly or answer questions of curiosity. We seldom need to speak words to reveal ourselves one to the other."

"Will you or Galavi tell them?" Again it was Fllordon who asked.

"It has not yet been decided."

Pohl rose. "Members of the council and my dear friends, let me add one more picture to your deliberations." And he proceeded to tell them about Glenelle and her spells. Now, for the first time, the Lady heard that Pohl suspected that the anti-Being that lived in her wanted to kill Glenelle. Claregole's intake of breath was audible.

"They must be sent away from the valley as quickly as possible," Fllordon said.

"But the child is ill. We must bring her here and attempt to heal her," Alumbra said. "Sending them out into the snows is tantamount to murder."

"Shall we become like the Adversaries, using any means to gain our ends?" Stor asked, obviously shocked by Fllordon's suggestion. "If we do, we have no future, not any of us."

"The boy Auragole is not one of them." Sandrofil rose quickly. "He only met them in the mountains by chance. Therefore we need to make two separate plans."

"Chance?" Fllordon said, his voice high. "You suddenly believe in chance?"

"All I am saying is that his destiny and theirs may no longer coincide. It is because of them, because he was attempting to lead them to the west, that he found his way to the cave and the meeting with Meekelorr. Perhaps his destiny with them is over."

"Perhaps, perhaps, perhaps," Mondrief said, softly. "Pohl, you've had time to think this through—you, the Lady, and Meekelorr. What do you think should be done?"

Pohl looked over at Meekelorr, but his friend gave no indication that he wanted to speak, so once more Pohl rose to his feet. He looked directly at Fllordon. "We have much to face in the future. If we allow fear or sentimentality to dictate how we act now, we give into the Adversaries. The Nethergod wins even before the Last Battle takes place."

There was a murmur of assent around the table. Fllordon continued to look at Pohl with a challenge in his eyes. But he was not angry. He often took an opposing position during meetings, merely to voice what many others seemed unwilling to voice.

Pohl continued, "We cannot send them out into the snow with no guide. That is out of the question. But I must also tell you that even though we might have the means, we must not heal the girl." He looked from one shocked face to the other. "If we do, we will drive the anti-Being out of her into these hills or into the Valley of the Agavi where it will look for another host."

"Good stars!" Alumbra said for all of them.

The council members stirred uncomfortably

"This is a fine line you walk, my brother." Mondrief smiled sadly at Pohl.

"Do you know a better way, Mondrief?" Pohl asked in all sincerity.

"I do not," Mondrief answered with no equivocation.

So Pohl went on. "But because we are refusing her the best help we can give her, we must guard her well, must watch over her, must finally see her safely to the borders of Mattelmead and to the medical help her brother seeks for her."

"You know the kind of medicine they are practicing there," Alumbra broke in. "There is nothing of the Creative World in their remedies."

"I know, but it is what Glenorr wants and, I think, Glenelle too. Even if we had decided that we should try to cure her here with remedies and an education, we do not know if she would agree. She is from the southeast and belief in the Gods died out there centuries ago."

"So we must keep this possible plague in our midst until spring?" Fllordon looked at them all with sardonic amusement.

"Yes," Pohl said.

"But what about the boy, Auragole?" Sandrofil asked. "Is he to leave in the spring? Surely not!"

"Why not ask the boy?" Mondrief said, with half-closed eyes.

"Yes," Pohl agreed. "Let us wait and ask the boy."

Stor, agile and small, but with a most sonorous voice, made a suggestion to which they all agreed. "Your guests, Lady, now that they have rested, should be given work. It is not good for anyone to be idle for long periods. Place them with others. Surely if they are with others, they can do no mischief. And conversely no harm can come to them."

The Lady thanked Stor for his suggestion and said that she had been planning to do just that.

They talked then about other matters and finally the meeting was adjourned. The Lady Claregole stayed for dinner, as had been planned, with all the teachers and students at the school, and returned home accompanied by Meekelorr later that evening.

N

chapter sixteen

AFTER NEARLY THREE weeks in the Healing Tower, Auragole was able to leave his room. Using a walking stick to steady himself, he managed to exercise by walking up and down the flights of stairs that led to his room. After he had conquered the stairs, he began walking out of doors and around the gardens and courtyards of the school. Occasionally, he visited Pohl in his rooms and sat, comfortably quiet, watching Pohl write in his medical journal.

One day he said to Pohl, "I have heard that the people who live up here participate in some sort of school."

Pohl looked up from his writing. So he had found out. Well, that was hardly surprising now that he was able to move about.

"I asked one of the Companions, whom I met as he was returning from training, about the buildings adjacent to the Healing Tower. He told me it was a school."

"Yes," Pohl said.

"What is taught in this school?"

"Well, Meekelorr and his captains are training the Companions of the Way for mountain fighting."

"But what about the others who are here who are not soldiers? Those who study and teach at the school."

"Ah," Pohl said, "those others." How much should he tell the boy? "The students here learn about our Deep Earth and its long history." After a brief hesitation, he added, "They also learn about the Gods and about the Creative World from which we descend at birth and to which we return after death."

After a moment, Auragole said, "But I understood all true knowledge of the Gods had disappeared in the wars, that only stories remained."

"No, all knowledge of the Gods has not disappeared, for how else would they teach what is taught in this school?"

As Auragole did not answer, Pohl did not elaborate.

LATER, POHL SAID to Meekelorr, "Auragole has finally heard that there is a school here, and asked me what is taught in the school. So I told him, but only a little."

"Did you tell him that knowledge about the Gods is taught here?"

"I did—but not in any detail. He seemed surprised, since he had heard that all knowledge of the Gods had disappeared. No doubt he will tell the others when he goes down to the Great Mansion."

"Well, there seems little point in secrecy any longer, Pohl. I take it you feel the same?"

Pohl nodded.

"The Last Battle will happen when it happens. What is important is that we make it impossible for the Easterners to find their way back to Agavia once we have guided them west."

"My thinking also," Pohl said. "I was curious to see Auragole's reaction."

"Which was?"

"Silence."

ONE DAY, DRESSED in his traveling cloak and boots, Auragole left the Healing Tower, crossed the stone courtyard, and went some small distance down the hill to watch the Companions of the Way train on the snow-covered slope north of the school. Pohl saw him from his window. Auragole stood there, his cloak flapping in the wind, silently observing for perhaps an hour. Then he turned and slowly limped back up the path and into the tower. Pohl wondered what thoughts had occupied his mind as he stood there.

"The Companions of the Way are quite skillful, are they not?" Pohl said to Auragole later that day when he came to give Auragole his remedies. "Yes, yes, indeed, quite skillful. Meekelorr is a great commander."

Auragole merely nodded.

"Something troubling you?"

"I'm not sure," Auragole said, taking the cup of medicine from Pohl. He stared at it for a few minutes. "You see everything is new to me. I have heard about armies, or warrior bands, from my father. He despised them all, hated war of any sort, could not condone battles for any cause, and yet. . ."

Pohl waited for a time for Auragole to resume speaking, but he didn't. Finally Pohl asked, "And yet?"

Auragole smiled uncomfortably. "How can I say this? Perhaps these words will make me seem a disrespectful son. But the more Goloss spoke against war—armies, battles, soldiers— the more curious about it I became. Does this seem terrible to you? Do I seem an unnatural son?"

The question was a serious one, so Pohl answered it seriously. "You told me that what your father wanted was for you to become a truly free human being. Correct?"

Auragole nodded solemnly.

"Then how can you be free if you assimilate your father's beliefs and make them your own without attempting to prove to yourself whether his beliefs are false or true, or at the least, right for you or wrong for you? Wouldn't he want you, expect you—now that you are grown—to make up your own mind based on your own experiences?"

"Yes, yes," Auragole's face lit up, "that's it exactly. You see, all my life I have heard about the horrors of war and of soldiering, but I don't know about it from my own doing or seeing. No one, not even Spehn, ever spoke about soldiers who go to the aid of those who cannot fight for themselves. I thought that was only in story. I loved the stories that my mother insisted I learn—for the virtues they represented and for their grace of language. But I was told that story and life were not the same. This is something that is quite new to me—what your Companions do. I was never taught that in battle one could find one's courage—just as one can find it hunting large game." He paused and rubbed his forehead. "There is much to learn in the world."

"Yes, but not all today," Pohl said. "You've been out and about too long. Time for you to rest. But drink that remedy first."

NOT MANY DAYS after the council meeting, Pohl heard that the travelers had been offered work, which they had gladly accepted. The work had been carefully selected to suit each one.

Sylvane went to work in the kitchen of the Lady's mansion, and she also learned sewing and how to do the intricate embroidery on the lovely clothes the Agavi wore.

It had taken much thought to decide what to offer Glenelle. After long consideration, Claregole sent Glenelle to one of the many nursery schools that looked after the children while members of their families worked. This, Claregole told Pohl, would be good for Glenelle. It put her in the midst of developing life. "If it were spring, I would have sent her to help in the gardens." Glenelle also was learning to weave with the Lady. Pohl was relieved, knowing Claregole would keep a good eye on her.

Donnadorr was assigned to Galavi and those who tended the great Agavi trees. These trees grew only in the mountains around the Valley of the Agavi and there were many rituals and ceremonies connected with their planting, care, and cutting. Donnadorr also learned woodcarving under the tutelage of Galavi.

Glenorr's assignment was to the great mines honeycombing the hills above the valley. There he helped extricate the rare and beautiful precious stones that were so much a part of the decorations of the Agavi. For the Agavi, stones held no value other than their ability to make things beautiful. Glenorr learned also polishing and stone-setting and the artistic working of metals. This satisfied his interest in all things of the earth, organic or inorganic.

A FEW DAYS after their first discussion about soldiering, when Pohl came with his medicines, Auragole once again returned to his question about the nature of armies.

"I've thought about what you said, Pohl, and there is something here that I could not abide." His eyes narrowed and he looked thoughtful.

"Where, young Auragole?" Pohl asked, putting the cup of medicine on the table next to the boy and drawing up a chair.

"I'm speaking about the Companions."

"What is it you could not abide?"

Auragole swung his legs over the edge of the bed where he had been lying and sat there staring at Pohl. "Something my father despised—hierarchy. And I think in this he was right. I could not abide being obedient to the will of another now that I am past childhood."

"Ah," Pohl said. "You don't like the fact that some lead and some follow."

"No, no. That's not quite it." Auragole got to his feet and walked to where a new sculpture had been placed. "It's that some must follow blindly, that the leader's word is law, that if one doesn't agree and refuses to follow, then one is punished."

"Yes, that is the way of armies."

"Where is freedom in that?"

"Freedom comes—at least for the Companions—in choosing to join or refusing to join. No one is forced to become a Companion of the Way, no one is brought in against his will as happens with other armies. But once someone joins, he agrees to give up, for the time he serves, his personal freedom. He agrees to follow orders. Without such an agreement, no army could function."

"But what if the leaders are foolish or ill-advised?" Auragole asked. He turned back to Pohl, his words heated.

"Then it is an ill day for all who follow or who lead."

"I was taught that a grown man's freedom is his most precious possession, that his own judgment is a thing to be valued, and that he should never give himself over to another's rule."

"It's a good teaching, Auragole. But sometimes for the sake of others, one gives up one's personal freedom for a time, gives it up without coercion—as a sacrifice for the greater good."

Auragole returned to his bed, sat down on its edge, and rubbed his forehead. Pohl watched him with interest. The boy was struggling and that was good. One could only wait and wonder in what direction the struggles would take him.

"I cannot follow you there, Pohl," Auragole finally said. "Either a man values freedom and guards it, or he does not and he gives it away. They seem two irreconcilable paths to me."

"Then follow your own heart, Auragole."

IN MID-NOVEMBER, Pohl drove Auragole down to the Great Mansion in one of the school's narrow wagons. It was a clear, crisp day. A moderately heavy snow had fallen toward dawn, but the wagon had snow runners. Their ride, though smooth, was slow. Auragole was flushed with excitement. His arm had been freed from its sling only hours before, and he still held it close to his chest. He had healed remarkably well. There were no scars, thanks to the moonleaf. He peered down into the valley as it came again and again into sight around each curve in the road. He pointed at this building, at that mansion, asking question after question. Pohl answered as best he could, delighting in Auragole's delight.

"You understand, Pohl," he said almost apologetically, "I have seen no buildings other than those we built in my own valley—and, of course, the school and Healing Tower. Do I seem too foolish, too backward?"

"Not at all. You are as you should be. But I must warn you, my enthusiastic friend, the Valley of the Agavi is like no other place in the world. I have seen all the great wonders of the Easternlands, and many of its great ruins, and I tell you nowhere is there, or has there been, a place as beautiful or as remarkable as what you will see in the Valley of the Agavi."

Suddenly Auragole's mood shifted. He looked at Pohl thoughtfully. "What about Mattelmead? What about its great city? I have heard that the king there has made it the most beautiful place in the world and that he has built for himself a palace that is unparalleled for size and grandeur."

Pohl answered truthfully. "I don't know Mattelmead. I cannot speak for the Westernlands. But there has been war in the west almost as long as in the east. It is difficult to imagine a city of beauty arising in so much devastation." Pohl glanced at him sideways, then clucked at the horse. "However, you shall find out come spring—summer at the latest."

"Yes," Auragole said, and there was little enthusiasm in his voice, "yes, I shall probably find it all out in the summer." And Auragole peered with greater intensity at the valley, as if he meant to take hold of something precious that he would have to lose all too soon.

As they were crossing the valley, they passed some of the

memory signs of the Agavi—large stone monoliths, heavily carved with odd figures and designs, also tall handcrafted marble sculptures scattered here and there, or others that were made of wood, or that were simple piles of unworked stones. Auragole asked about them.

"They contain the memories of the Agavi."

"Their history is written on them?" he asked, looking at two rocks one on top of the other.

"No, something quite different indeed." Pohl chuckled. "Indeed, yes, quite different. Agavians can stand in front of a memory stone or sculpture and in their mind's eye will arise particular memories from their shared history. Some individuals are especially adept at this. Galavi, the Lady Claregole's brother, is known to be the best at *seeing* the ancestral memories."

Auragole looked very puzzled. "I don't understand. How is that possible?"

"The Agavi are like no other people on this earth, young Auragole. The kind of memory that you and I have is of little importance to them because it is a personal memory, cut off at one end by birth and at the other end by death. That is not true for the Agavi. Their memory reaches back through the long line of their ancestors. The collective remembrances of the people are very important to the Agavi. They go to these ancestral stones or sculptures to recall what was done in a specific situation in the past, so that they will know what to do in a present situation. The Agavi rely on tradition. For them the old ways are always the best ways."

"How wondrous," was all Auragole said.

Perhaps he will choose to stay here, Pohl thought. Then he brushed the thought aside. There must be no pressure. No undue manipulating of events. Where was freedom if those who knew about it abused it?

The Lady greeted them in the reception hall of the mansion, and Pohl saw Auragole blush with pleasure. To Pohl's amusement,

Auragole could barely speak to her and turned red whenever she turned her attention on him.

As Pohl accompanied Auragole to his new quarters, following Binta, Auragole begged Pohl for information about Claregole.

"She doesn't look like an Agavian—not exactly. I mean, she has green eyes!"

"That's because her father was an Easterner—a teacher at the school." That much at least is true, Pohl thought.

"What happened to him?"

"Alas, he died."

And then all questions stopped because Auragole's companions came rushing down the hall to meet him with hugs and greetings and slaps on the back.

Pohl left soon afterward with the promise that he would visit Auragole frequently. He noticed that Glenelle had regained her strength and clung to Auragole, and Auragole responded in a way that made him look less like a young man and more like a puppy. She looked well enough, except for her eyes, which seemed a bit feverish—as if something smoldered barely below the surface.

Pohl tried to put that worry aside. But be vigilant, he warned himself.

AFTER AURAGOLE ARRIVED in the valley, he was given the task of working with the horses in the Lady's stables. He couldn't have been happier. He told Pohl that he and his father had caught one of the wild horses that roamed the hills near their own valley, and he had taught himself to ride. In addition to the care of horses, Auragole learned to make musical instruments out of the rich Agavi wood.

In the evenings, along with all the Agavians, the travelers learned that which many call the art of performing. Sylvane learned to dance, Auragole and Donnadorr to play the many-stringed harp of the Agavi. Glenelle and Glenorr practiced the art of acting.

And so for the rest of autumn and into winter, they toiled and learned and were contentedly occupied. At first, Pohl came down to the valley nearly every day to look in on both Auragole and Glenelle, but as the days passed without any incident, as both seemed to be healing well, he came less frequently. When Pohl did come down to the mansion, he observed that Auragole was growing in health. It's from the sheer joy of all his occupations, he thought. Perhaps Auragole will stay here in Agavia.

Unobtrusively, he observed Glenelle whenever he came. She seemed as normal as any other. The fever had left her eyes. She looked somewhat frail and ethereal, but was a hard and willing worker. She loved the babies she worked with, and she became, under Claregole's tutelage, a competent weaver. But most of all she loved acting and was very good at it.

Pohl noticed that the love Sylvane felt for Auragole never lessened, but she seemed accepting of the fact that he had eyes only for Glenelle. Glenelle, on the other hand, took Auragole's love as her due, as she did Donnadorr's, but did nothing to encourage either. Each of the two young men seemed content to leave their feelings as they were and not to pursue them. For all the time they stayed in Agavia nothing changed in them, no movement was made toward the fulfilling of any of their desires. But, Pohl knew, it was the Valley of the Agavi that kept them content and at peace. Had the school been down in the valley, it would not have been able to survive, to stride forward into learning and into research, both physical and spiritual.

So Sylvane loved Auragole, and he and Donnadorr, Glenelle. Glenorr poured what intensity lived in him into his work, and all was tranquil—until Glenelle had another spell. It caused such a crisis that it sent the travelers out of the valley in the dead of winter.

N

chapter seventeen

IT WAS NEARLY the end of December, almost six weeks after Auragole had gone down to the valley. Pohl had just finished his evening meal and was sitting in front of the fire warming his stocking feet, when there was a loud knock on his door.

"Come in!" he called, and was surprised to see Donnadorr standing there, cap in hand. "What is it, man? Come in, come in."

Donnadorr came into the room, gave Pohl his cloak, and took the seat near the fire that Pohl indicated. First he apologized to Pohl for having disturbed him, and then said, "The lad seems to have gone missing."

"Which lad?"

"Auragole."

"What do you mean *missing*?"

"I mean the lad's not been seen since morning." Donnadorr absently stroked his trim red beard. "He took a horse out of the Lady's stable to exercise it as he has done each morning these past weeks, but he didn't return for lunch. And for the first time since we began them, he missed our harp lesson. He wouldn't have done that willfully. I tell you, Ellie and Sylvie are frantic. They think something terrible has befallen the lad, an accident or wild animals or something more gruesome."

"Surely if he had had an accident, the horse would have found its way back to the stable. Has it?"

Donnadorr shook his head. "Perhaps the horse wasn't able." He drew his chair closer to the fire.

"Hmmm."

Pohl decided to inform Meekelorr and sent his help-soldier, Ulf, to fetch him. And now they would have to wait. He watched Don as the young man pulled at his red beard and stared into the fire, obviously too worried to speak.

"Don, can I ask you something while we wait for Meekelorr?"

"What?" He turned a distracted face toward Pohl. "Well yes, certainly."

"Tell me when and where you first saw the so-called Guttlubbers you once mentioned."

Donnadorr's usually open face suddenly closed. "I hardly remember it. I was very young, nine or ten. I. . .I didn't know that they were Companions of the Way."

"Tell me what you do remember."

It was a few moments before Donnadorr answered, and when he did his voice was tight, as if it held back some old grief. "Years ago, when I was a child, orphaned and wandering the Easternlands, there was this man who took care of me. I don't remember how he found me or how it came about that we were traveling together. But we did for several years. He taught me to sing, bless him for that. He taught me most of the tales I know, and for that I thank him also, for those tales have saved my hide on more than one occasion. . ." He paused and his brows drew together.

"But. . ."

"But I don't thank him for taking off one day, promising to come back for me and never showing up again." There was anger in Donnadorr's tone. It surprised Pohl. He had observed that Donnadorr could, without hesitation, feel sadness for another, but he had never displayed self-pity.

"The time I saw the Guttlubbers—the Companions of the Way—was during those years when we were still together. My friend used to go off by himself sometimes, telling me to wait, that he would be back in a day or two. And he always came back. . .except that last time." Donnadorr's cheeks flushed slightly, and his hands, resting on his knees, turned to fists. "Once I followed him. He never found out. I don't know where it was, don't remember what country we were in at the time—we moved about so much, and I was young. But I followed him to a small camp and there they were, a dozen or twenty men in gray-and-white uniforms. He talked with them for several hours. I watched from the trees. I don't know what they talked about, that I couldn't hear. But afterward he sang for them, and that I could hear."

Donnadorr's face was suddenly filled with wonder. "I can't describe it, Pohl, but the way he sang never left me. He had sung for me and others often—and we had sung together—but that night, the way he sang for the soldiers was a kind of singing that, glory be, I can't even begin to describe."

Pohl's eyes widened and he breathed in sharply. But Donnadorr was caught up in his narration and didn't notice.

"It was as if the woods, the rocks, everything broke open, showed their insides. Oh, not really, mind you, but it was like I saw into the heart of everything, felt the essence of all things. Maybe I'm misremembering—I was very young—but it has never left me, that singing. I wanted to ask him about it later, but I didn't dare. I was afraid that he would leave me if he knew I hadn't trusted him and had followed him when I was asked to wait."

A shiver of excitement went up Pohl's spine. "What was the name of the man who cared for you, Don?"

"His name was Aiku."

Aiku! But Pohl didn't repeat the name out loud. Aiku was a great True-singer, teacher to Lorenwile. But Aiku was dead now, so it had been reported—how long was it?—eight or nine years ago? Destiny was indeed strange. Here was a protégé of Aiku. . .but maybe not. He had taken Donnadorr under his wing, but he had not taught him True-singing. Had he intended to teach him? Had Aiku been killed before Donnadorr was of age?

Donnadorr looked directly at Pohl, and there was no child in him now. "I think he must be dead, for one day he went off and never came back. I wished that I had followed him *that* day. Perhaps I would have been able to save him."

"And perhaps you would have been killed with him, my young friend—if indeed he is dead."

"I shall never know. It's a secret sorrow of mine, for he was the only family I ever had—though not true kin. Heart-parent, as the Agavi would say." Then his face brightened and he smiled again. "We were together seven years."

At that moment Ulf came back with the news that Meekelorr had taken Sunflight and a week's worth of supplies and had gone off. He didn't know to where.

Meekelorr gone? And without leaving him word? And Auragole gone? What could that mean? And where was Meekelorr heading? Pohl's stomach knotted. Not the cave again! For a moment he felt anger. Was the man mad? Must he risk himself now when the need was so great?

Pohl decided to go immediately down to the valley with Donnadorr. They rode down in one of the school's wagons.

When they arrived at the Lady Claregole's mansion, Pohl hurried to the wing where the band of travelers was, and spoke first with them. No, they told him, Auragole had not returned.

Sylvane was pale with anxiety. They assured Pohl that Auragole had not told them of a plan to go off anywhere. Pohl calmed them, then went in search of Binta. He wanted to speak to the Lady Claregole.

A few moments later, Claregole received Pohl in her rooms. She had heard only a few hours ago that Auragole was missing and had immediately initiated a search for the young man.

"Ahhh, ahhh," came a small sound from Binta, who was standing near the door.

"What is it, Binta?" the Lady asked, rushing to her.

Binta's eyes were closed and she held her hands in front of her, drawing strange figures in the air. Pohl watched her in fascination.

"I see him, my Lady."

"Where, Binta?" Claregole urged gently.

"I see them both," was Binta's reply. "They are together—but not together."

"Who?" Pohl asked.

Binta's eyes flew open. "Why the young man and Meekelorr, good Doctor, dear Lady. They are both sleeping in the snow. . . but apart. They are safe and about some important business."

"What business?"

Binta looked crestfallen. "I. . .I don't know, Doctor. My gift is small. I can see far, far into the mountains, but I cannot see into the hearts of those who are not Agavian. I did not know I could find young Auragole or Prince Meekelorr with my sight or I should have tried sooner. This seeing came of its own."

"You have done well, my dear friend. You are the best far-seer in Agavia." Claregole put her arms around the old woman and hugged her close. "Your gift comes ever and again to our aid. Send Darrie to play the bells and draw home those who are searching. Tell them when they return that Auragole is well, that he is with Meekelorr."

Pohl hesitated for a moment, and then decided not to ask

Claregole if she knew where Meekelorr was heading. He had no right to ask about what passed between them. If she wanted to tell him, she would have spoken. However, he was much relieved. He returned to the travelers and told them the news. Sylvane and Glenelle hugged each other in relief and then Pohl, too. When he explained that it was Binta who had found them and how, they were astonished. Pohl spent an hour, late as it was, explaining the various gifts that were spread out among the Agavi. When all were calm, Pohl returned to the school. He was tired, anxious, and curious. But there was nothing he could do but await the return of the two from their enigmatic mission.

It was past midnight when he arrived at his quarters. He was relieved to know that Auragole was with, or at least near, Meekelorr. But had Meekelorr indeed gone to the cave? The beast had been seen several times circling the skies above the valley and its surrounding hills, but it had not made another attempt to come close, nor had it made any noise in an effort to frighten the Agavi and those at the school. His flights caused a stir among the Agavi, for nothing like them had ever happened before and there was nothing in their memory signs to tell them what to do. The Lady had told her people that it was another indication that theirs was the generation that would fulfill the goals the Gods had long ago set for them.

Pohl undressed and washed in the now cold basin of water.

Another battle with the beast could prove disastrous. It was growing larger. No one man could battle it, not on his own. Is that why Meekelorr had taken Auragole with him? But if he had taken Auragole, why had no one been informed? And if he had taken Auragole, why were they not really together? The only answer was that he had not taken Auragole. And what did that mean?

Pohl spent a restless night, the little that was left of it.

MIDAFTERNOON FIVE DAYS later, Auragole and Meekelorr came riding into the courtyard of the school. Without halting,

Auragole left the school grounds and rode down to the valley alone. This news was brought to Pohl by Meekelorr's help-soldier, Tor. But Meekelorr himself did not come. Pohl knew he would in his own good time. Though relieved, Pohl was not content with waiting. As Auragole was his patient, Pohl decided to pay him a visit after dinner.

In the early evening, he rode down in a wagon to the Lady's mansion and made his way to the wing where the travelers were housed. The Easterners had gone to various practices in preparation for the deep winter Feast of Aa that was to be held in a few weeks. But Pohl found Auragole in his room, tired from his journey, and resting before the fire. He invited Pohl in and placed a chair near the hearth for him. Pohl asked after the young man's health. Auragole assured him he was fine.

"I've apologized to the Lady for going off with her horse without permission and without letting anyone know. It was unplanned. I've asked the forgiveness of my friends for causing them such anxiety and now I ask also your forgiveness. I understand that you too were drawn into this business. I'm not used to having so many concerned about me. It was inconsiderate, but you see, this journey happened without forethought."

Though this told Pohl little, he accepted Auragole's apology and waited.

Formalities over, Auragole plunged in, "Tell me about my uncle, Eagalorr."

So Meekelorr had finally told him!

"Tell me first about your trip with Meekelorr."

"Yes," Auragole said, but then lapsed into silence.

Pohl watched him curiously. What is he thinking, so oblivious of me? He couldn't help but admire Auragole's ability to puzzle over something, lost to his surroundings, rubbing his forehead or temples, focused on some inner thought or picture. He'd make a good student of the Mysteries of the Creative World, Pohl thought.

At last Auragole said, "I had been out riding—you know that a part of my responsibilities is the exercising of the Lady's horses?" He lifted his dark eyes to Pohl, who nodded. For a moment they were shiny with pleasure. "I like that. I like riding out into the hills. I. . . I like being off by myself now and then. I'm not used to being so much with others." His tone was apologetic.

"Well, five days ago, I was on the horse they call Agate, just walking through the hills and the nearby valleys. It was a clear day. New snow had fallen the previous night, so the ground was as smooth and clean as the bedsheets in the Healing Tower, and the air was so clear one could see beyond these high mountains to the higher peaks farther north. I was about to head back when I saw Meekelorr on Sunflight crossing a not-too-distant ridge. I don't know why I followed him. I didn't think." He shrugged. "I just followed. I stayed out of sight but easily tracked him in the snow."

He paused. Pohl sat without comment, waiting for him to go on at his own pace. Auragole's face looked altered, almost trans-figured, as if what he was telling Pohl was playing out before his mind's eye.

"All that day Meekelorr traveled up the gentle slopes of mountains, through narrow, winding ravines or across valleys—and I followed behind him. It never occurred to me to turn back, though I had no provisions for a journey of any kind, neither for myself nor for my horse.

"Night fell. Meekelorr made camp and lit a fire, had a hot meal. I stopped not too far away, hidden by an outcropping of rock. I made no fire, had no meal, and slept fitfully, wrapped only in my cloak on the cold, wet ground."

Pohl had to admire how well the young man was telling his tale. Indeed, he had learned much at his mother's knee.

"In the morning, after Meekelorr had left, and after my horse had grazed on the little grass that could be found under the snow, I once again followed Meekelorr's trail. I was hungry, but did not turn back. Agate, no doubt, was hungry too. But he's a docile and well-trained gelding and obediently did as he was bidden. All that second day, I trailed after Meekelorr. I don't remember thinking about anything, don't remember asking myself what I was doing or why. I was following Meekelorr— that was enough. If there was a purpose, I felt it would be clear to me in the end, as things often are.

"Night fell once again. It grew colder. Down a steep incline, in a narrow cut of land, I could see Meekelorr's fire. It didn't occur to me to go toward it and tell Meekelorr that I was there. Once again I wrapped myself in my cloak and tried to sleep. But, as you know, when you are shivering it takes a long time before you are able to drop off. Eventually, I did.

"'Wake up.'

"I was being shaken by the shoulder. I rolled over, leapt quickly to my feet, knife in hand, crouching, ready. In the bright moonlight I saw Meekelorr standing there.

"'Come down to the fire or you will freeze to death in this cold,' Meekelorr said, and he took hold of Agate by his halter and led the horse down the incline to where the fire smoldered. Meekelorr didn't look back, but of course I followed him.

"When we got to the fire, Meekelorr built it up until it blazed brightly, gave Agate grain, and then handed me some welcome travel biscuits and a bowl of warm soup from the pot on the hot coals. We didn't talk that night but went to sleep close to the fire.

"In the morning Meekelorr prepared breakfast. We ate in silence, then we saddled and mounted our horses. I still followed Meekelorr, but now only a few yards behind. By late afternoon we had come to the mountain that contained the cave of books, not the cave entrance my friends and I had entered, but the one Meekelorr and my friends had taken me from, unconscious.

"'This is where the beast lives,' Meekelorr said, as if he were telling me something very ordinary. Then he said, 'Wait for me here.'

"I started to protest.

"'Wait!' Meekelorr commanded. 'I'm not going to fight. I intend only to talk with the beast.'

"'But will the beast talk and not try to kill you?' I tell you, Pohl, I was more than a little alarmed.

"'He will,' Meekelorr told me with certainty.

"And he entered the cave and I waited for a few moments outside. But I was uneasy and so I didn't obey Meekelorr." Auragole lifted his eyes to Pohl then. "After all, I'm not one of his soldiers."

Pohl merely nodded.

"I mounted Agate and started down the long tunnel that led to the cavern. It stank of the beast. There were his droppings everywhere. The walls were blackened by his fire breath and they gave off a barely tolerable reek. I wondered if the smell was as poisonous as his breath and if breathing it could kill, but I went on. Finally, I came to the opening that led to the cavern of books and the home of the beast. I dismounted just outside the entryway, tied my horse to a rocky protrusion, and entered the cave as quietly as I could. All I had on me was a knife, and I drew that. If either the beast or Meekelorr saw me, they didn't indicate it. The beast was sprawled out, stretched yards long on the cavern floor, jars and books scattered under him and about him. Swords, he was big! His large face was resting on his paws and he was staring at Meekelorr with cold but intelligent eyes. There was no hatred there, only listening, as if a truce had been called.

"'It will not bode well for you, old serpent,' Meekelorr said, from Sunflight's back.

"The beast only raised a ridgelike eyebrow. His expression was quizzical, almost human.

"'You know as well as I,' Meekelorr went on, 'that there is a special destiny laid on that valley and its inhabitants. It would be viewed with great vexation should you interfere either in the lives of its inhabitants or in the mission of the valley.'

"The beast made no sound, but raised his other eyebrow.

"'You have been seen more than once flying over the valley. . .'

"The beast lifted his head then and I was sure he was about to spew forth fire at Meekelorr. But instead, a shockingly small, barely discernible high, shaky, and rather whiney voice came out of his huge mouth. 'I have done nothing but fly high over that valley. It harms no one.'

"'It frightens many,' Meekelorr said. 'This cave and the nearby mountains are yours to roam over and to watch over. Your time has passed, Old Nemesis. Content yourself with the books yet awhile. In time you will be permitted to go home.'

"At these words the beast drew himself up on all of his four thick, scaly legs with such rapidity that I think I cried out. Neither Meekelorr nor the beast took notice of me. But Sunflight, startled by the beast's sudden movement, reared up. Meekelorr quickly quieted him.

"'Passed? Passed?' the beast hissed, and a trail of sulphurous smoke followed his words. Then he quieted down and in his small, tinny voice said, 'I do not choose to go home.'

"Sunflight was calm now and Meekelorr turned to face the beast again. I marveled at his fearlessness. 'Then content yourself with the books and grow fat,' he said.

"For a moment, a look of sorrow came over the beast's long green face. It touched me strangely. 'I'm bored. Besides, who back home will welcome me?'

"'You know.'

"The beast stood there staring at Meekelorr, looking as if he were trying to decide whether to wipe him off the earth or not. I held my breath. Meekelorr stood his ground. Minutes dragged by.

"'So be it then,' the green creature finally said. 'I will stay away from your valley.' He let out a long, smoke-filled sigh.

"'Do I have your word?' Meekelorr said.

"'Would you place value on *my* word?' the beast asked, with a chuckle.

"There was no laughter in Meekelorr's response when he said, 'Yes.'

"'Then you have it,' the beast said, trying to sound indifferent.

"'Thank you,' Meekelorr said.

"I know I let out a sigh of relief.

"As Meekelorr turned his horse, the creature said, 'Tell me, will we fight again?'

"Meekelorr turned toward him, and answered thoughtfully, 'I think not. My sword now has another goal.'

"'You will find him less accommodating than I,' the beast said. 'I think your sword will be of little help to you. More likely, look for a knife in the back. Be warned, he is a trickster who would give you his word and break it.'

"'But not you, Old Adversary?'

"'This path was chosen for me, Old Adversary, by one you care about. And I have done it well, I think. And yet. . .' his eyes closed slightly, '. . . I still have honor.'

"'I count on that,' Meekelorr said, and turned his horse and headed toward where I was standing. If he was surprised to see me there, he said nothing. He slowed down while I retrieved and mounted my horse. Then I followed him out of the tunnel and into the darkness. We rode a couple of hours before camping for the night."

Auragole shifted in his chair so that he could look directly at Pohl as he was talking. He was telling his story very well, Pohl thought again. He watched the mirror of Auragole's face as he spoke, trying to see past its reflective quality. But if Auragole sometimes showed all that he thought, he had also learned at times to school his face. At present, Pohl could only read the sound of his voice.

"Meekelorr and I did not speak that night, or the following day. It was much like those hunting trips that I used to take with my father, when for days my father and I would travel with little need to talk. Then a night would come when I would ask questions and my father would share stories out of his boyhood in Stahlowill. He was a grand talker, my father was—when he chose to speak."

You're a grand talker too, Pohl thought, when you choose to speak.

"I didn't ask Meekelorr about the beast then. It didn't seem the right time. It was Meekelorr who finally broke the silence— on our last night out. But it wasn't about the beast that he spoke. We had just finished our supper and were drinking hot tea when he said, 'I knew your uncle, Auragole.'

"His words startled me. I had not thought to meet anyone who knew my uncle until I had made my way to Stahlowill. I didn't think the world so small, and I was not certain, when I first set out, that even in Stahlowill he would be remembered. He was, after all, extremely old and likely dead. Still, I owed it to my mother to find him, or word of him. It was my promise to her on her deathbed."

"What did Meekelorr tell you about him?"

"He said he had been a great teacher, his teacher and yours." Auragole looked at Pohl through narrowed eyes. 'A Master,' he called him. He said he had been Master here at the school— called the Last School by its teachers and pupils—before that Master in the school in Stahlowill." Auragole swallowed. "Meekelorr told me my uncle was dead, that he had gone off several years ago to the east and had been murdered. He told me that his body had been found and buried and his pack brought back to the school."

"Yes, that's the essence of the story."

"You never told me."

"No," was all Pohl said.

"Did you think me too ill to hear that the uncle I sought was dead?"

"I did have some concern as to how you would respond to the news."

Auragole nodded. "I admit the news saddened me. Though I had little hope of finding my uncle, it would have been nice to have kin. I am, it seems, all alone now in the world." He looked solemn and very young staring into the fire.

So Meekelorr had not told him of his kinship to the Lady and Galavi. "It seems, since my uncle is dead, that I have no reason to go east."

"No," Pohl said, "no reason."

"I should like to see that pack and its contents some day."

"I'm sure that can be arranged."

"That would be good. Meekelorr said that since you knew my uncle quite well, I should ask you about him. Can you tell me about him, Pohl? Can you tell me about what he taught, tell me more about his school?"

"I can."

Auragole stood up. "I have a pot of tea left over from my dinner. Can I offer you some?"

"Thank you, yes."

Auragole headed for the table where a tray with empty dishes and a teapot waited to be returned to the kitchen.

Pohl watched him as he moved. He has a natural grace, Pohl observed with pleasure. A young man who is, by and large, comfortable in his own body.

Auragole picked up the lone cup and walked over to the stand where a basin and pitcher stood. He rinsed out the cup and returned to the table. He lifted the lid off the teapot. "I'm afraid it's not too warm."

"It will do just fine, indeed, yes," Pohl assured him. A handsome youth, Pohl thought. Still growing into his fine looks. Some day he will be very attractive to the ladies. And then he thought of Sylvane and sighed inwardly.

Auragole returned to the hearth and handed Pohl the cup of tea. He poked at the wood in the fireplace and then sat down in his chair. He looked at Pohl with large, intelligent eyes. Pohl liked him very much then. But be careful, he warned himself as he sipped the cool but tasty Agavian tea.

"Tell me about this Last School, Pohl. No one here in Agavia seems willing to say much about what is taught there. You know the Agavians. They are friendly and very kind—really very kind. But they seldom answer questions. Mysteries of the Creative World, wisdom of the Gods they say, and nod—as if that says it all. You said as much to me one day. But you didn't elaborate. The Agavians say that the building of the school was part of some great mission. Why is it called the Last School and why is it hidden in the Gandlese? Why is it near the Valley of the Agavi? And why are the teachings called Mysteries?"

What should he tell the youth? Indeed, how much was safe to tell him? Well, all he could do was trust his own intuition. He had to give the boy something. "This is a long tale, and the hour is late, but I will tell some piece of it now. There will be time for more later—should you be interested."

"Thank you."

"Lest all knowledge of the human being's true nature, and of his origin in the Creative World, die out in the turbulent years of war that followed the Golden Century, those individuals who could still directly experience the Creative World established seven schools throughout the Easternlands. They taught, not secretly, but openly as befitted the times, teachings that at one time had been hidden from human beings. That is why they are called Mysteries. These teachers instructed any who wished to know about the Creative World. This they did amidst terrible hostility and persecution in order that all true knowledge of humanity's origins not be lost forever.

"The destruction brought about by the chaotic wars was terrible indeed and eventually—mostly in this last century— much hate became focused on these schools. One by one they were destroyed. All this we, who belonged to the schools, knew was in preparation for the coming of the Nethergod—the Dark

Breather the Agavi call him."

"The Dark Breather?" Auragole suddenly sat bolt upright. "What do you mean? On earth? The Dark Breather, of whom the Agavians speak, will truly come to earth? I thought that was only in tales."

Pohl purposely ignored the question and the comment and went on. "The students and teachers, along with the villagers who had supported the eastern schools, were sought out and killed—for many people fell under the sway of the Nethergod's influence, willingly or unwillingly. Finally, only the school in Stahlowill, of the seven that had been founded, remained. That school, your uncle's, had survived the longest because it was situated in high mountains. And, as you know, Easterners fear hills and mountains. Then, about sixteen years ago, that fear was overcome. It too was destroyed and along with it the five villages surrounding it. It was a horrifying sight, battles as bloody as any I have ever seen. Our school there was finally engulfed in the madness that the rest of the east had been prey to for five hundred years.

"But long before the end of the only surviving school in the east, your uncle, knowing that the days of the school in Stahlowill were numbered, traveled here. He made his first journey to the Valley of the Agavi thirty-five years ago, guided here, no doubt, by the Gods who inspired him. And the Agavi, out of their own very old traditions, were waiting for him. He asked the Agavians to begin the building of what is now called the Last School.

"The Master, your mother's uncle, Auragole, came many times during the time of construction and was much revered here as well as in Stahlowill. The Last School was built out of love for him during those years."

"Did the Lady Claregole's father accompany him—Amarori? He must have."

Ah, so that much Auragole knew—that Claregole's father

was a teacher at the school and that his name was Amarori.

"Well, yes, I think it would be correct to say that Amarori came with Eagalorr on more than one occasion. Did I not tell you and your friends that it took the Agavi twenty years to complete the building of the school?"

"Yes."

"Well, as soon as it was finished—just fifteen years ago—the Master arrived with the students and their teachers, those few who had survived the slaughter when the school in Stahlowill was finally and irrevocably destroyed."

Pohl stopped his narrative at this point. There was a terrible look on Auragole's face. Was it anger or sadness or disbelief? Pohl wasn't certain. But he knew that he had said enough. He set down his cup, rose, and headed for the door. Auragole didn't try to stop him.

N

chapter eighteen

ONE MORNING, NOT long after Meekelorr and Auragole had returned from the Cave of the Beast, Donnadorr once again sought out Pohl. He was waiting in Pohl's room when Pohl returned from the Healing Tower. The moment Pohl entered the room he saw that the young man was agitated.

"Donnadorr, what, trouble again? Has anything happened in the valley?"

Was Glenelle ill again?

"No, no, not in the valley. It's. . .it's Galavi." The young man turned a concerned face toward Pohl.

"What ails Galavi?" The Agavi were a healthy lot, seldom troubled by the illnesses that plagued the rest of humanity. "Has there been an accident?" Pohl began putting on his cloak.

"No, the lad sits in front of the hut on one of the northern slopes, not far from here—do you know the one I mean?"

"I don't."

"He sits there moaning and weeping, hugging his knees and

rocking back and forth in some sort of misery. I tell you this, Pohl, I've not seen its like before."

Pohl picked up the pack with his remedies and tools and said, "Show me the way. We can talk as we go."

They were hiking through the mountains along a narrow, snow-covered trail made passable by the use of the many shasha goats that lived in these mountains, when Pohl finally said, "Tell me what happened."

"I'm uncertain if I can explain such a strangeness."

"As best you can, then."

"As you know, there isn't much work to do on the trees in winter, but each morning I go with Galavi and occasionally one or two others to walk through the Agavi groves." He looked over at Pohl. "He talks to the trees, you know—Galavi. Sings really—a kind of chant. Have you heard it?"

Pohl shook his head.

"They all sing—all the tree shepherds—and, oh, what a glory it is to hear. We leave food for the animals at various stations. He told me that the animals are essential to the health of the trees as the trees are essential to the life of the animals."

"Yes, yes, indeed."

"Well, every now and then during our circuit of the forest, the lad stops and ever so gently makes a small cut into the bark. There's a whole ritual to it—song, prayer, movements. I tell you this, Pohl, it's a marvel just to watch them. What a grand people they are."

Pohl listened without interrupting.

"Galavi told me that the cutting doesn't hurt the tree. The true purpose of the tree, he told me, is to be cut down when it is mature so that it can be used to serve the Agavi. Odd, isn't it, thinking of trees that way?—that they have, well, a kind of task. Agavians see all of life as an offering, as sacrifice, as service to others. It is for them the way the world had been ordered by Aa and it is the way it has always been. How remarkable they are—

and how rare." Donnadorr stopped speaking, no doubt pondering the uniqueness of the Agavi.

Pohl trudged along after him, curious, but waiting for him to continue.

Finally, "Today, it was just the two of us on the northern slopes. We had been out about two hours, by my reckoning, and had left the food for the animals in four different places. When we got near the northern end of the Agavi grove—not far from the hut I mentioned—Galavi began the cutting ritual.

"'No, by the Mothers, no!' he cried suddenly. 'It cannot be.'

"'What is it?' I asked, but I don't think he heard me. The lad was upset, I tell you that. Three times more, at three different trees, he did the cutting ceremony. And three times more he cried out, 'No!' When we came to the hut, he sat down in front of it and began to moan and cry.

"I tried to get him to come inside, where it was warm. I wanted to build a fire and make him some tea, but he paid no attention to me—answered none of my questions. I didn't know what to do, so, as you were closer than the valley, I came to get you."

"Good man," Pohl said.

They were climbing higher now along the wider lane kept clear by the tree shepherds so that the trees could be rolled down to the valley. The snow was hard and crusty and their boots, breaking through the surface, made a harsh, unpleasant noise. Pohl felt grim. He looked around at the dark, tall Agavi trees with their branches lifted high off the ground in a gesture of awe. They grew nowhere else except on these hills surrounding the Valley of the Agavi, nowhere else on all the vast Deep Earth. These trees belonged to the Agavi in the same way that the shasha mountain goats and the weswill sheep belonged to them. And the Agavi in turn belonged to all the nature around them.

At last they arrived at the small round hut with its thatched roof and walls made of the Agavi wood. It was here that the tree shepherds kept logs, food, and cots. There was an enormous hearth inside to provide heat when the mountains became suddenly stormy. Galavi was nowhere to be seen. They looked inside the hut, but it was empty and had not been disturbed. They stood outside, perplexed.

"Galavi!" Donnadorr called, and his voice echoed off the mountains. He waited, but there was no response. He called again and again, but no answering call came from the woods. "Perhaps he's gone back down to the valley."

"Perhaps." Pohl looked around. There was nothing wrong as far as he could tell. The winter birds sang. He heard the scurrying of small animals, the howl of a coyote some miles away. Suddenly something occurred to him. He turned to Donnadorr. "Do you know if one of the Grandtrees is near here?"

Scattered throughout the Agavi forests were very large trees, never cut down, older than all the other trees. In them resided, according to the Agavi, the essential spirit of the Agavi trees. These exceptional trees were never used for the ritual cutting. And somehow the Agavi always knew which tree would become a Grandtree. Tree shepherds had that sense.

Donnadorr looked around and pulled at his short beard thoughtfully. "This way," he finally said, and plunged into the trees.

It must have been about a mile from the hut where they finally saw both Galavi and the Grandtree. The tree was enormous. Around it was a sizable clearing, for the reach of its branches was great, and little grew under it except what the Agavi had planted—the small gali flowers. These tiny flowers loved the shade and the mulch of the Agavi leaves and one another, for they formed a kind of blanket that kept the undergrowth from springing up. In the springtime, they would be a sight to see with their tiny yellow blossoms that fluttered on the ground like thousands of butterflies. Now they were sleeping snugly under the snow.

Galavi stood in front of the Grandtree, his forehead and arms touching the dark, rough trunk. There was no sound coming from him.

"Come," Donnadorr said, and started to enter the clearing.

"Wait!" Pohl grabbed Donnadorr's arm. "Wait."

The two men stood there for over half an hour until Galavi raised his head and stepped back. He began to sing in a keening voice and to move about the tree in a graceful dance.

"What's he singing?" Donnadorr whispered.

"It's a song of mourning in the First Language. I only know a few words."

"What's this all about, Doctor? I understand nothing and fear the worst. What can ail the lad?"

"Let's wait. Perhaps he will tell us."

They waited and watched and shed their own tears, for the song was so melancholy, it hurt just to hear it. Was it Pohl's imagination or did the tree seem to sway to the music, its branches reaching up, up to the sky and then falling ever so gently back?

Finally, Galavi stopped, performed a few ritual signs in front of it, said a prayer of thanks in the common language, and then turned and walked toward them. He was not surprised to find Pohl and Donnadorr there.

But then Galavi was Agavi, Pohl thought, and therefore uncanny.

Galavi's face was white with sorrow and exhaustion, and streaked with tears. His Agavian eyes were unreadable.

"It is all true," he said softly, "all true."

"What is true, soul-friend?" Pohl asked.

"That these are the last of days." Galavi shook his head and looked from one to the other. "The time is near at hand. The Dark Breather prepares. Oh, my lovely trees," he cried out in anguish, and threw his arms up in a wide but futile gesture.

"What ails them?" Pohl asked.

"Dying."

"What?" Both Pohl and Donnadorr exclaimed as one.

"The Agavi trees are dying. Slowly, slowly dying. The Grandtree told me that in a hundred years there will be no more Agavi trees."

The two men couldn't respond. Donnadorr began to turn slowly around to look at the trees—thousands upon thousands of them—as if he couldn't believe it was possible that they would be no more.

"I made the ritual cut to look into the health of the trees, as I have done ever since I was a boy of twelve. Two showed little life and two none at all. I could smell death in them. After Donnadorr left, I moved into the forest and made other ritual cuts. Those trees closest to the edge of the grove show signs of dying. The ones deepest in the woods or farthest down the slope are the healthiest." He shook his head and began to move away. "I must go down to the valley and inform my people," he said. "This is the greatest sadness I have ever known." And he started down the hill.

"Wait," Pohl called after him. "Speak first with Claregole. Perhaps it's best to wait before this. . .this tragedy is made known."

Galavi stopped and turned to look back. "This is no matter for council. This is the heart of the people, these trees. This cannot be kept secret, for others will see it soon. We do not keep secrets from one another, Doctor. We are not able." He smiled a sad smile and continued on his way.

"Go after him, son," Pohl said to Donnadorr.

Donnadorr nodded and trudged off, following Galavi. Pohl took the upper path and returned to the school.

All that night, the valley and the mountains were filled with the pealing bells of mourning.

THE FOLLOWING DAY, Pohl rode down to the Great Mansion and sought out Galavi. He was pale but dry-eyed. The two walked together in the Lady's sculpted evergreen garden, down paths where the snow had been swept away. Everything was white around them—clean, pure.

Even in the lifelessness of winter, there is peace here, Pohl thought, but for how long?

Galavi's eyes were cast down as the two men walked in silence.

"I visit you in your mourning as is the custom among your people."

"Yes, thank you."

"Nowhere on the Deep Earth is there a people like your people, Galavi. Everything they are, they have as a gift of the Creative Gods."

"Is it so terrible to be Agavian?" Galavi's question came out harsh and filled with pain.

It was believed by the Agavi that they, unlike other peoples of the earth, had returned again and again as Agavians. In doing so, they had sacrificed the development toward individuality that was the common fate of other peoples. They had a task. And until that task could be accomplished they had forsworn the new faculties that other peoples had gained. Therefore, the Creative World was alive in them and for them in ways that were as beautiful to see as they were incomprehensible to one who was not Agavi.

"Try to understand what others in humanity struggle with now, Galavi. A·non-Agavian can be driven to madness or to destruction because he is unprotected from what pours through the inner portal that now stands open in his soul, unprotected from what pours out of the abyss that lives within each human being. Only strong individuals, awake to the dangers, can withstand the dark and dangerous onslaught rushing through that soul fissure. But even wakefulness is not enough against the temptations that beset humankind and that will continue to plague humans in these coming days, the days of the Dark Breather. But in an Agavian the abyss is hidden, is guarded.

There is no tear in their souls."

Galavi shook his head as if he couldn't grasp Pohl's words.

Pohl tried again. "Where you, Galavi, as an Agavian, find deep within yourself fellow love, where you find certainty, and the nearness of the Gods, the rest of humanity find only hate and the desire to destroy—unless they themselves have built the love there by winning past selfishness to true freedom. Where you look out into nature, into sign and symbol in the outer world, and find the memories of your ancestors, most of present humanity find only silence.

"For the sake of this new freedom, the Creative Gods—that is, the good Gods—have stepped back from this humanity, have renounced any inner coercion. This has been true for centuries now—long before the centuries of war, long even before the Golden Century. But while the wars have raged on, changing the face of the Deep Earth, soul conditions have also changed. With the modicum of freedom humanity has thus far acquired, it can find the Gods again. Therein lies all our hope. But for that to happen, each human must will it, must with great strength of heart will it."

"But this longing for freedom, for separateness, does not live in me, does not live in an Agavian," Galavi said quietly.

"No, my friend, not in an Agavian. As an Agavian you are cared for by the Gods, for you are children of the Gods. Yet you, Galavi, are also an Easterner."

"I know, Pohl, that I am also my father's son. No Agavian denies his birth parents."

"It is this Easterner in you that you must call upon now." Pohl knew that much depended on Galavi. "Your destiny, soul-friend, is a destiny of sacrifice. The time draws near when you must make it. You must give up what you have been as an Agavian, as must all your people, so that the humanity you have vowed to serve can cast off its youth and become mature and responsible." Pohl held Galavi's eyes for a moment.

"And yet, what you have been as an Agavian will also be needed in the end. For are these not the world days your people have long awaited? This the Gods have asked of you. I only tell you now what you and your people have always known."

"So be it, Pohl, for this goal of individual freedom and selfless love is what the Gods themselves want for humanity." Galavi's eyes welled up. "But, I tell you this, if one day I stand before one of the memory signs of my people and there is nothing there, I am not sure I could go on living."

IT WAS REMARKABLE to see how the Agavi mourned and then accepted their fate. They would do what they had always done. They would go on living their lives of duty, art, instinctive love until they met the Nethergod, the Dark Breather, and his hordes in battle. If each day had a little more poignancy to it, Pohl could not detect it. Perhaps it was because Agavi were so connected one to the other, because they were not so isolated in their individual souls, that they could support one another. This was the beginning of the days they had lived for and waited for, century after century. They went forward toward their destiny, living each day fully as they had always done.

AFTER RETURNING FROM the cave with Meekelorr, Auragole took to visiting Pohl frequently. Often when he was out exercising the Lady's horses, if he was in the mountains nearby, Auragole would stop in to see if Pohl was in his room. If he found Pohl there, he would sit quietly for a time and watch Pohl at his desk, writing in his medical journal. But sometimes Auragole had questions.

One day as Pohl invited him into his room, he surmised from the expression on Auragole's face that there was something troubling him. So he took Auragole's cloak, and ordered tea. The two then sat in front of the fire and Pohl waited patiently for Auragole to speak.

After staring at the flames for a time, Auragole asked, "Is Meekelorr a prince?"

"Ah, you've heard those stories, have you? From whom?"

"I overheard some of the Companions speak about it while I was still living in the Healing Tower. I used to come out and watch them practice in the field below. One day as they were returning to the school, I heard them arguing about whether Meekelorr was a prince or not. And then the Agavians always refer to him as Prince Meekelorr. They regard him with great respect, even with awe."

"Well," Pohl said, "he is the Lady Claregole's consort."

"Yes, I know that."

"Is it important whether he is a prince or not? What do you know about princes and kings?"

"Only what I've heard in story and song. That is what I wanted to ask you about. There is this song my mother taught me when I was very young. It's a riddle song, and I understand. . .that is, I've heard that all riddle songs have answers."

"Ah."

"Do you know the 'Prince Riddle Song'?"

"I'm not sure. Can you sing it?"

Auragole nodded, and then, without any accompaniment, began to sing.

> *There is a riddle*
> *here in my song.*
> *The tale is short*
> *but the melody long.*
>
> *I sing of a prince*
> *not born of a king.*
> *He wears neither crown*
> *nor does he wear ring.*

He has no silk cape.
He has no silk shirt.
Will this prince heal
or will this prince hurt?

Who is his father?
Who is his mother?
Some say he has
neither one nor the other.

Is he one cursed
or is he one blessed?
Will he bring strife
or will he bring rest?

Will he bring peace
or will he bring war?
Seek you the answer?
Then search for the door.

Some call him wise.
Some call him fool.
Where is his kingdom?
Whom does he rule?

Where is the door?
Where is the gate?
Where is the young prince?
Why does he wait?

So here is my riddle.
One you can ponder
whether at home
or whether you wander.

Will he bring love
or will he bring hate?
Would you an answer?
Look for the gate.

Yet where is the door?
And where is the gate?
And where is the young prince
for whom we all wait?

So here is my riddle
and here is my song.
The tale has been short
but the melody's long.

I sing of a prince
not born of a king
who wears neither crown
nor does he wear ring.

"I've never heard that song before," Pohl said, when Auragole finished his singing. "You want to know if the prince in the song is Meekelorr."

"Yes."

"And if he is?"

"If he is. . ." Auragole repeated. "I don't know. I guess. . . I merely wondered. Well, the prince in the song is someone for whom people are waiting, someone who will do great things."

"But whether they will be for good or for evil, the song doesn't tell us."

"No." Auragole rose. "I don't know why I suddenly thought of the song as I was out riding. . . It's probably just a song—not real. Likely my mother was wrong and there is no such person. It was foolish of me to ask you." And he looked embarrassed.

"No, not at all." Pohl stood up. "It's an interesting song. Not born of a king. Well, that would certainly fit Meekelorr. His father was a farmer. But he is a leader and he can have a regal air about him. I suggest, young Auragole, that you watch Meekelorr and decide for yourself whether he is the prince of your song."

"Yes, yes, I will. I had better return to my work." And Auragole fairly flew out of the room.

ANOTHER TIME WHEN Auragole came to visit Pohl, he again seemed perturbed. It was the Agavian day of rest, and Auragole had walked the two miles to the school.

"What is it, young friend? Is something troubling you?" He led Auragole to a chair near the fire and sat down opposite him.

"No…yes… You believe in the Gods, Pohl." It was a statement.

"Yes."

"How can you believe in something you cannot see?" Auragole's voice had a note of despair in it as well as of anger, which both surprised and interested Pohl.

"Yes, yes, indeed, yes, an important question. Well, Auragole, do you believe only in what you see?" Pohl waited for him to answer. But Auragole was silent, rubbing his forehead and staring fixedly at the fire. So Pohl went on. "Can you see courage or friendship, or pleasure, or love? Can you see any of what we call qualities, or any of the virtues some try to live by, the virtues you told me your mother tried to instill in you? Can you see any of them? Yet don't we accept them as reality?"

Auragole looked thoughtful, but he didn't speak.

"Tell me about your father, Auragole, and why he hated the Gods."

Auragole raised his eyes and looked into Pohl's. "My father said it was this belief in the Gods that had caused all the troubles for mankind, all the wars. What have you to say about that?"

Pohl ignored the question. He rose and added more wood to

the fire. "Tell me about your mother," he said without looking at him. "Did she never speak to you about the Gods?"

"Once," Auragole sighed, "when I was very young. And once before she died."

"Tell me about the first time." Pohl returned to his seat.

"One summer, my father and my mother had a terrible argument. It was because she had told me that it was Gods who had created our world, the Deep Earth."

"She told you that?"

He nodded. "And then she said the Gods had turned their backs on our world, that they had gone back into the Creative World and had left us to fend for ourselves."

"And your father became angry with her for telling you this?"

"They fought about it one night and I overheard them. I was only seven years old. Oh, it was not the first time they had fought. They seemed never to agree on how I was to be raised. But this fight was more fierce than others."

And Auragole proceeded, the way a storyteller would, to recount that summer night when he had overheard the quarrel. Pohl once again admired the way he told his tale.

"So it took you years before you could ask your father about the Gods?" Pohl said when Auragole finished his telling.

"I was eleven." And he told Pohl about that time.

"And you got hit for your temerity."

"Not just hit. It was certainly not the first time I had taken a beating from my father. I was. . .could be a very willful child. But this was the first time he had ever struck me across the face. And for what? For asking a question?" There was a note of bitterness in the boy's voice.

"It came as a shock to you."

"Yes. But if Goloss thought that blow would drive away all thoughts of the Gods from my mind, he was sadly mistaken. I certainly didn't forget them, but I never approached my father about them again. After the night they had that quarrel, my mother—no matter how much I pleaded with her—was silent on the subject. She simply said, 'Ask your father.' But I knew better.

"When I turned to Spehn, he laughed and said that tales about Gods were made up by leaders to explain things people didn't understand. I begged him more than once to tell me some of those tales. But he always claimed he had forgotten them. He told me to learn from nature since she was the best teacher. But after the time when I finally spoke to my father, the word *Gods* was never uttered in my community again—until the night my mother died."

Auragole exhaled. The sound was ragged with emotion.

"Yet you did not take your father's advice."

"What?"

"You said that blow kept the thought about the Gods alive in your soul."

"But buried, I think." Auragole shrugged in response. "It was my mother telling me my uncle taught about the old Gods that made me think about them again. And then Ellie's stories and Don's stories, and the arguments between Glen and Sylvie."

"I see. Tell me, Auragole, what did your father do before he came into the Gandlese? What was his work in Stahlowill?"

Auragole looked at Pohl, puzzled. "I thought I told you. He was a farmer."

So Meekelorr was right. Goloss had never told his son he had also been a priest.

"And do you still want to know something about the Gods?" Pohl asked Auragole, breaking into the silence that had now settled over them again.

"To know is not enough," Auragole answered, with temper. He rose and began pacing about the room. "Not at all enough. If there *are* Gods I would want to experience them myself. I have heard many stories on my travels. Some are very charming, and some are rather silly and make little sense. I assumed that what my uncle taught in Stahlowill were stories, fables, folktales. For how could he have real knowledge? Then down in the valley I've heard many different stories of the Gods." He stopped and stared unblinkingly at Pohl. "Can any of them be true? Am I to take story or song for reality? I never did as a child—was never allowed to." Auragole was angry. In it Pohl read a longing that, he was sure, Auragole didn't know he had. "And yet the Lady Claregole, Galavi, and the Agavians believe in the existence of the Gods—as do you and Meekelorr and the Companions of the Way. How? How did you come to such a belief?"

"Stories are often images of the truth," Pohl said. "It is what stands behind the images that is important."

"But if there is a reality that is true—that stands behind images and stories—I would need to experience that reality for myself, not just hear about it." He sat down on the edge of his chair and leaned toward Pohl.

"If I said that there is a path of training that could lead you to an experience of the Gods, would that be of interest to you?"

"Is such a thing possible?"

Pohl nodded.

"Where? Where is this taught?"

"For one, here. Remember I told you that they taught about the Gods here in the school—as they had in the schools in the east before they were destroyed? Well, they also teach how to tread a path that could bring one to an experience of those Gods."

At first a look of excitement flashed across Auragole's face, but it was quickly followed by a look of disappointment. "Here in the school? Away from the world?"

"Yes, here. But not only here, child. It is possible to go this path in life if one longs for answers. However, here lies a problem; without the concepts, without the knowledge, it is difficult to understand the meaning of the trials and obstacles that come to one. It is possible to come to a door, not see it, and therefore not open it. Or to have an experience, but without a context based in reality of the Creative World, misinterpret that experience."

He watched as Auragole brushed his lined forehead, obviously perplexed.

"Still, such a worldly path is possible and can be a safe one—if you could find someone who would teach you even as you both lived your lives in the world." Should he tell him that Meekelorr is such a teacher—that some of the Companions tread that path, even as they do their soldiering?

"It's all so confusing." Auragole said. "I don't know why I came today. Curiosity, I guess. I'm not sure I want to bother about the Gods. If there are good Gods, there seems to be little evidence of them. And I have heard from stories and tales, both in the travels with my friends and from the Agavian tale-tellers, that there are also evil Gods—not just the Nethergod. Do you believe in other evil Gods?"

"I do."

Auragole gave a small laugh. "Well, they would be easier to believe in than good Gods." He was silent again. When he finally spoke, he said, "I don't think it is so necessary to know about the Gods, at least not for me. What I really want to know about is our own world, our Deep Earth. That's what interests me now. I've seen so little of this world and have known so few people. . . There seems enough on this earth for a lifetime of learning. I don't know why I bother about the Gods. It only brings me confusion. Best if I leave them alone." He said these last words with a decided firmness. Too much firmness, Pohl thought. There's more than just a little Goloss in him.

And after a few moments of polite conversation, Auragole left.

chapter nineteen

IN LATE JANUARY, the Agavi celebrated the Feast of Aa, one of four major holy days, as they had always celebrated it. Aa, the most important of their Gods, was honored in the winter. In spring, it was Demeda who was celebrated. She was the Goddess of new life. In summer, it was Oahla, the Goddess of Wisdom, and in fall, Ordavi the Defender God. These were major Gods and Goddesses in the large Agavian pantheon.

There was much activity in the Great Mansion during the weeks that preceded the festival. The four holy festivals were events calling forth great anticipation and great reverence. The Agavi lived comfortably with their many Gods and Goddesses—and the greatest and most powerful among them was Aa, the Father of all existence.

When Pohl came down to the mansion to visit the travelers, it was all they could talk about. Donnadorr once again seemed his old self. After all, a hundred years is an eternity when you are young. Auragole too was caught up in the excitement, though something seemed subtly altered in him since both his adventure with Meekelorr and his subsequent conversations with Pohl.

The Great Hall, which was used only for feast days, was being prepared. Pohl purposely passed its open doors on his way to visit the travelers. It grew in beauty like a lily unfolding, and he looked forward to the night when the entire school would celebrate with the Agavi. Along with the traditional foods, there would be performances of all kinds between the food courses. Dancers and singers and players rehearsed. And among them, the newcomers. Music and voices came nightly from many of the rooms of the mansion. Everyone prepared to celebrate the deeds of Aa, the First God. On the appointed day, there would be over three hundred guests at the feast celebrated in the Lady's mansion.

The feast was to be observed in every mansion and manor house in the valley. Each morning during the week that preceded it, Claregole rode out or walked to one of them to perform the rites due Aa in the days before his feast. Pohl wondered about these old rites, but they were closed to all but Agavi. Claregole saw no one during that time but the twelve women and seven men who, as members of the priesthood, assisted in the rites and were with her day and night during that holy week. Pohl knew there were also rituals performed in her mansion afternoons and evenings, but these were carried out in the large chapel in the eastern wing and were conducted in the presence of the priesthood only, for these rituals were the most holy.

One day during that week, as he was on his way out of the Great Mansion after a visit to the travelers, Pohl saw Claregole and her entourage in stately procession, dressed in their purple robes and strange, many-peaked hats, moving toward another manor house or mansion. Everyone, in reverence, stepped off the road to let them pass. Pohl moved into the shadows of the trees and watched as they went by. The Lady was gowned in white under a long and trailing purple cape. To Pohl she looked radiant, even translucent, a vessel for her God in the upcoming ritual.

How grand and capable this Lady is, this last leader of the Agavian people, he thought. They will finish their task in dignity.

No matter what the outcome.

AT LAST THE evening of the Feast of Aa arrived. The procession from the school wound slowly down the hill, carrying lanterns and singing. Each individual was dressed in his or her best garment, each was wearing a small head-wreath made of evergreen and decorated with ribbons and jewels. As Pohl, the members of the school, and the Companions of the Way entered the valley, many Agavians joined them. They circled first through a portion of the valley. Some accompanied them for a time, then wound their way to other mansions and manor houses. Finally, those from the school arrived at the Lady's mansion and were greeted on the steps by the Lady Claregole herself. After words of welcome, in the rhyme that is often the speech of the Agavi, she turned and guided her guests inside.

They were led into a large reception room where they joined other guests. The Lady then retreated to a waiting room. When it was time to go into the Great Hall, she would come out in formal procession, first to greet once more her guests, then to lead them into the feast.

Pohl located the Easterners, who were handsomely dressed. He came to them and squeezed their hands in delight. They too were flushed with excitement. As was the Agavian custom for the Feast of Aa, they were clothed in white silk garments, flawlessly embroidered in bands of blue and silver, and made, with Sylvane's help, especially for this occasion.

After half an hour had passed, a hush came over the crowd. First there was heard the gentle strum of a hand harp. At the sound, the guests parted, leaving a path the length of the reception room. A young man playing the harp came walking down it, an expansive smile on his face. For a moment Pohl thought it was Lorenwile himself. But of course it wasn't.

Pohl gazed with pleasure at the Lady Claregole. There were so many ways one could describe her. She was beautiful. She was courageous. She was wise. Some would say all of that was true because she was Agavian and it was in her blood. But Pohl knew that didn't explain who and what Claregole truly was, for she was also the daughter of Eagalorr and therefore one of Pohl's own race. Yet Claregole transcended race. In the Lady Claregole, the outer facade and the inner secret were one—as was true of all the Agavians. However, in the Lady Claregole there was a rarity not seen among the Agavians, a uniqueness that came from her extraordinary individuality. Where others held back, she came forward. Her soul is in each gesture, Pohl thought, in each movement, in the brightness of her large, compassionate green eyes, in a face so open and so changeable that one is transfixed watching it.

The Lady walked—no—she floated down the aisle. Her black hair was coiled high above her head. Her gown, which seemed to flow about her as she moved, was of white silk and girded about the waist with a gold sash. Her feet were sandaled in twisted gold rope and on her head was a thin gold crown with twelve stars circling it. At her neck hung a small silver moon cradling a golden sun in its arms.

She paused to greet friends. As she spoke to each, it was as if the rest of the room had disappeared, so intense was her interest.

Meekelorr, bareheaded, dressed in white and gold, walked behind her. Stars, Pohl remarked to himself, he does look royal. He *could* be a prince, and wondered what Auragole was thinking at this moment.

The Lady halted before each of the travelers as she passed them. She offered each one her hand and said, in a melodious voice, "Welcome." Not one could answer her, but each nodded his or her greeting, and Pohl could see the awe in their eyes. It was as if they were looking upon a royal daughter of Aa, which in a sense they were.

Nowhere on the earth could there be a Great Hall as beautiful as the one in the Lady's mansion, Pohl thought, as they entered it. It was an immense room with twelve elaborately carved Agavi pillars holding up the arched ceiling. Two huge fireplaces dominated the west and east sides of the hall. These were made of carved marble. The floor was made of Agavi wood and inlaid with intricate patterns. Up above, on either side of the fireplaces, were great windows of colored glass—each piece cut and placed so as to form pictures. These depicted scenes from the creation of the Valley of the Agavi.

The mansion itself was very old. The Agavi believed that it was built before the Gods left the valley to return to the sun. That seemed hardly possible. Pohl did know, however, that if one stood in the center of the hall at noon on a midsummer day, the streaming sunlight was caught and cast down by the colored glass. Then one could see the Elementals, who live in air and light, dancing. That he had seen himself.

For the Feast of Aa, the hall had been transformed from merely exquisite to sublime—Pohl could not help but think in superlatives. If this people must pass away, perhaps even this mansion, then he wanted to remember that something extraordinary had been on the earth during all the great wars as an echo of the Creative World.

For the feast itself, twelve long tables were arranged like rays of the sun, leaving a large open circle in the center. Because it was winter, there were no flowers, but branches of evergreen decorated the tables, the pillars, and the walls. The lovely small pine trees that grew in large pots in the courtyard and on the terraces of the mansion had been brought inside. Nestled in their branches were jewels, ribbons, and ritual ornaments.

The Lady sat at the head of the table that included all the

travelers. It was quite an honor, but the Lady was ever gracious. Meekelorr was on her right and Pohl on her left. Next to Pohl sat Auragole, then Glenelle, then Donnadorr. On Meekelorr's right sat Sylvane, Glenorr, Galavi, and, of course, many others.

When all had been seated, the Lady rose. She held high a loaf of bread and a glass of wine and intoned in her clear, sweet voice:

"Wine and bread, grown in our land,
blessed by these words become God, become Man.
Heaven torn from earth's embrace
unite with each soul in this hopeful place.

"Holy the bread, holy the wine,
holy the guests who come to dine.
Be they of blood or be they of light,
welcome they are on this blessed night."

The guests in turn lifted their glasses of wine and the small loaves that had been placed on their plates. They rose from their chairs and echoed her words:

"Holy the bread, holy the wine,
holy the guests who come to dine.
Be they of blood or be they of light,
welcome they are on this blessed night."

Then all sat down and the feast began.

After each food course there was entertainment. During the meal the Lady led the conversation. She asked each of the travelers about his or her stay in Agavia. But out of the courtesy practiced by the Agavians, she asked nothing of their lives before they had arrived at her doorstep. Pohl listened and watched. They stammered their replies, even the loquacious Donnadorr. All except Glenelle, who was not flustered at all.

Indeed, she was like a rose blooming in these glorious surroundings. Auragole sat quietly, but his eyes were intensely observing, turning often to stare thoughtfully at Meekelorr, then at Claregole. He spoke to the Lady, haltingly, when she asked him questions, but for the most part he listened to the conversation around him and watched the Lady Claregole with a look bordering on worship. But Meekelorr he looked at with a questioning gaze. Pohl wondered how Auragole would feel if he knew it was his own cousin that he admired so—then wondered once again when, or if, they should tell him of that relationship.

Before the first of the food was brought in, five dancers, including Sylvane, gracefully depicted the birth of the earth. Sylvane was a pleasure to see. But no one could equal the Agavi when it came to movement, Pohl knew, for they could fill themselves with light and air and sail through space as if they were bodiless. Still, Sylvane looked filled with joy as she participated with all her heart.

Between the first course and the soup, an old storyteller, white-haired and tall and the greatest oral historian in the valley, told of how Agavia came into being. Pohl loved the story and listened attentively to the old man as he spoke.

"The Deep Earth was new. Lands rose from the all-embracing sea. Mountains poured out fire and earth. Mist covered the surface of the land and hid the heavens. And soon were sent down to the earth, the plants. And soon thereafter were sent down the animals. But humanity waited.

"Finally, waiting humanity, which had been gathered together from the seven wandering stars of the Creative World, was sent down to the Deep Earth, which had been formed for its use. But a small portion of humanity was held back, those who dwelled in the sphere of the sun, for as yet no earth home had been chosen for them. The Gods, those whose abode the sun was, looked far and wide over the vast stretches of the earth for a dwelling place for the last of the sun-humanity. Long and hard they searched, crossing and crisscrossing the whole world until they found the center of the earth in that part of the land we now call the Grand Continent—in the First Language, *Gahdahlooease.*

"Seeds were scattered on the warm wind and a lush green carpet soon covered the land, and on it grew every kind of fruit and grain, plant, flower, and tree. And the sun sent down its light and heat. The Sun Gods came and strode through the valley, fashioning it as a reflection of their own home, breathing their peace and their joy into the air, the earth, the streams."

Pohl watched the travelers as they listened. A look of delight was on Donnadorr's face. Glenelle seemed enthralled, Sylvane filled with wonder, Glenorr, in his detached way, mildly interested—as he was about most things. But Auragole was sitting upright, his body tense, as if he wanted to bore right through to the truth behind the words of the storyteller.

"But their work was to be challenged. The Dark Breather awoke, whether in the bowels of the earth or in the depths of the sky is not certain. And he came to the heart of Gahdahlooease, brought by his brother the Light Eater, and together they set about spoiling the piece of the sun that had been nurtured on the earth, for they hated humankind, hated Aa for loving humanity. They caused great craggy mountains to rise up around the chosen land and snow to fall and cover the valley. The mountains were called the Gandlese, or *Goondoolohanda,* meaning 'fear the power' in the First Language. The Dark Breather brought his own cold wind from out of the north to freeze the life out of the new land.

"When the Gods of the Sun saw what the Spoilers had done to their perfect home for sun-humanity, they sat in council and pondered.

"'We cannot undo the deeds of the Dark Breather or those of the Light Eater, for they are also sons of Aa, and he tolerates them for the sake of humanity's progress. But we can mitigate, soften, lighten, temper their cruelty.'

"So the tall mountains stood, but in them the Sun Gods placed marble and granite, crystal and jewels, and many metals. On their slopes they caused to grow the stately Agavi trees that yielded wood for furniture and carvings. And shasha goats and weswill sheep, like no other creatures on the Deep Earth, were set down in the high and low meadows surrounding the valley. The Gods could not end the snow, so it was given two seasons, fall and winter. But in the spring and in the summer the snows were melted by the warmth of the sun and by the friendly south wind. And for half the year the valley was as lush as it had been conceived of in the beginning, with many fruit trees and flowers.

"When the Gods finally took leave of the humans, they said to them, 'To our sorrow we are unable to give you a land as perfect as the land from which you descended. Therefore, two tasks we give you now. First, you yourselves must finish what we have begun. Love the land and all it gives you. Tend it in joy. Whatever you touch make beautiful to gladden the hearts of both humanity and Aa. Remain, however long it might take, in your valley, awaiting your second task. You, of all humanity, will stay much as you are now, losing little, gaining little. Near the end of the Dark Times, which will come in a future age, others will join you. Then you will fight the Dark Breather who will once more awaken and walk the earth. He will bring all his forces to bear against the Deep Earth so that he might enslave its inhabitants and win for himself the Deep Earth, win it away from the rule of Aa and the Creative Gods. This will be the Last Battle and it will mark your final days. For after the battle is fought, many will ascend to the Creative World, to live in the sun, in a home that we will prepare for you. Those who survive the Last Battle will go out into the Grand Continent and mingle there with others of humanity, for they too are the offspring of Aa. Be well, children. In the dark months and the cold, remember us.'

"Then the Gods flung their hands upward toward the heavens. The mist blew away and the first rainbow arched across the sky. The Gods returned to the sun and the sun-humanity named their new home Valley of the Agavi, Valley of the Children of Aa."

The storyteller finished the tale, tears running down his old face.

Something unexpected happened then. Auragole leapt to his feet, and in a voice filled with despair called to the old man, "Why do you weep?" Auragole immediately turned red and sat down, flustered and obviously embarrassed.

The old man dried his eyes, and as if Auragole's outburst were the most natural of occurrences, walked to the table where Auragole sat, then reached out to touch his face. He answered Auragole solemnly and softly, though all could hear, that he wept because even now, after years beyond reckoning, they had not made their small valley as gracious, as glorious as the Creative World where once they had dwelled. And now their days were coming to a close. The Dark Breather again roamed the earth. He was amassing an army that would come looking for the Valley of the Agavi, and soon, in perhaps only a few years, the Last Battle would begin.

Then he stroked Auragole's cheek and left, exiting from the hall slowly and with the humble dignity that an Agavian of great age possesses.

There was silence. All the Agavians wept.

Then the servers brought in the next course.

The evening moved majestically on through the meal and the entertainment. At one point, Donnadorr and Auragole played and sang together. Initially, Auragole seemed nervous, but as soon as he began to sing, all anxiety left him. He had a sweet, light baritone and Donnadorr a deep, rich one. Together their voices blended harmoniously as they played and sang. As Pohl listened, he knew that the Agavians, by teaching them to play the many-stringed harp, had given them a rich gift indeed.

The last entertainment of the evening was the performance of
a play. All that would remain after that would be the sweet
course with its special feast tea.

The Lady rose and the entire hall became silent.

"Respected friends, dear soul-companions, in honor of the
One God in whom all other Gods dwell, a group of actors has
prepared a small play in which is depicted an exploit of the
Defender God, Ordavi, sent by Aa to the earth."

And so everyone in the hall watched attentively while the
players, numbering twelve in all, including the twins, portrayed
a struggle of Ordavi against the Light Eater. The Light Eater, in
the shape of a fire-breathing beast, had come to earth to corrupt
its inhabitants and divert them from the goals of the Creative
Gods. Those good and innocent individuals whom it was not
able to corrupt, it carried away to its cave to devour. Glenelle
played one such incorruptible maiden and played her well. Her
brother, a bit stiff but willing, played another role, that of one
who was swayed by the beast. Of course, in the end, the maiden
was saved by Ordavi, who had been sent to the earth carrying
the great sun sword of Aa. The play was whimsical and naive,
and very old. Along with all the spectators, Pohl cheered as
finally Ordavi plunged the sword of Aa into the heart of the
beast and the maiden was set free.

"Was she not wonderful?" Auragole turned to Pohl, his eyes
glowing with pride.

"Whom do you mean?" Pohl asked, the corners of his mouth
twitching.

"Why Glenelle, of course," Auragole answered in all seriousness. "Could anyone have played it better? Could anyone be
more beautiful? Oh, look how well and health-filled she is."

Glenelle did indeed look well as she returned to the table, her
face glowing with pleasure. But to Pohl, her eyes looked unusually
bright, and he felt a bit uneasy when she turned to him with
cool, appraising eyes. Who are you, he thought? And then he

shook his head to clear it of such thoughts just as the servers came out with great trays of sweet cakes and the loka tea that is served only at feasts, because it comes from so rare a flower.

As the guests finished the last course, there was the sound of low-voiced and contented conversation buzzing throughout the room. The feast was coming to its end. At their table, the travelers were complimenting one another on their performances, and there was a feeling of contentment all around.

Suddenly the happy chattering was interrupted by a noisy disturbance outside the Great Hall doors. They were thrust open and four mud-spattered armed men almost fell through them.

Pohl and Meekelorr both leapt to their feet. There were no guards at any of the doors of the mansion. Nor did anyone yet watch over the passes into the valley. Was it now necessary? There had been no one to stop this motley band of intruders— for no one in centuries, save Eagalorr, had found his way to this valley without a map.

A wave of agitation at this most unusual occurrence rippled through the hall.

The leader of the group hesitated a moment. Then, seeing Meekelorr, the young leader, with his men, strode purposefully across the open circle toward Meekelorr's table. By the time they had nearly reached the table, everyone at it was standing and the rest of the hall had become stark still.

Meekelorr moved out to meet them, and Pohl and the Lady followed. When the group saw the Lady Claregole, they dropped to their knees in front of her, then rose quickly and bowed to Meekelorr.

Pohl was stunned when he realized that they were Companions of the Way.

"Forgive this terrible intrusion, Lady and friends of Agavia. I see it is one of your feast days," the young disheveled leader said, in a voice loud enough for all to hear, "and forgive us our appearance. But we have been on the way weeks now and our mission is urgent." He looked then at Meekelorr.

"By the description given us, you must be the commander we seek—Meekelorr."

"I am."

"Commander," he said, "my name is Peroll, and I bring you a message."

What dreadful event had happened, Pohl wondered fearfully, that this young Companion had been given directions to the Valley of the Agavi?

"My young friend," Meekelorr moved in front of him, his voice low, "what terrible mishap causes you to seek us out in the dead of winter?" He took hold of him by both shoulders and looked with troubled eyes into his. "What news do you bring?"

"Cleege is dead, captured by Boreen in Thorensphere, tortured and killed." His message out, Peroll would have collapsed had Meekelorr not been holding him.

"Dead!" Meekelorr looked shocked. He shook the young man.

"Meekelorr." The Lady's voice was gentle, but authoritative, as she put her hand on his. "These men are exhausted and starving." She motioned to a few of the servers, who rushed forward at her gesture. "Take them to our guest chambers. Let them be given warm baths, clean clothes, and food. Then when called, bring them to my rooms." To Meekelorr and Pohl she said, "We will meet there after the feast."

Meekelorr let go of Peroll. The four soldiers were led out of the hall. The Lady and Meekelorr returned to their seats. There was anguish in his face, but he turned with an act of will toward the Lady Claregole as she rose and spoke to the gathering.

"My soul-friends," she said in a voice that all could hear, "and respected guests, let us finish our feast with a toast and the prayer that is due Aa on his remembrance night." And she raised her cup of loka tea and said, "In the name of all the Agavi,

I drink to the honor of Aa." She took a sip of her tea, and then said, "In the name of Aa, I drink to the honor of all Agavi."

And all intoned, with great earnestness, "To the honor of Aa, to the honor of all Agavi."

Then the final prayer was recited and the Lady turned to Pohl. "Come to my rooms in an hour," she said in a low voice. She spoke a few words to the Easterners and then walked slowly and with calm grace from the room.

And the feast was over.

Meekelorr, his face composed but his eyes gray storm clouds, followed Claregole at the appropriate distance. Before he could leave the hall, the Council of Teachers gathered around him and Pohl. But Meekelorr had little to tell them, only that he would report to them all he knew, either when he returned to the school later that night or in the morning. The teachers accepted his words. They know how to wait, these teachers of the Last School, Pohl thought, and turned to his own circle of curious individuals.

"Who is Cleege?" The Easterners crowded around Pohl.

"He is. . .was commander of all the Companions of the Way in the Westernlands."

"Who is Boreen?" Sylvane asked.

"A rebel leader in Thorensphere who is challenging the old, unpopular king there."

"Then why did he attack the Companions of the Way?" Sylvane asked.

"That is a question," Pohl said. "Yes, yes, indeed. That is a question."

"Thorensphere. That's the land east of Mattelmead, isn't it?" Auragole asked.

"It is."

"Do you have maps of the west?"

"Yes, I do."

"May I see them someday? I'd like to compare them to the

maps given my friends—and maybe make some corrections to the ones I have."

"Yes, of course."

"Pohl, I'm sorry. . .for your loss. And for Meekelorr's."

Pohl reached up and stroked Auragole's cheek. "Thank you. I'll convey your sympathy to Meekelorr."

"Tell us, Pohl, what does the death of the commander in the west mean? Surely there is someone else who can take his place." This came from Glenorr.

"It means that the man who was second only to Meekelorr in the hierarchy of the Companions is gone. But more than that, Cleege was a close friend of Meekelorr's."

"Poor Meekelorr." Glenelle's mouth was turned down sadly, but her eyes were unusually shiny.

Pohl felt once again uneasy about Glenelle. "What are you going to do now?" he asked the group.

"We are all going to Don's room to talk about the feast, and have our own little celebration," Sylvane said. "Except for the ending, wasn't it an extraordinary evening?" Her gesticulating hands fairly danced with excitement.

Good, Pohl thought. Best if Glenelle isn't alone just yet. It was hard to worry about Glenelle when the news the soldiers had brought was so terrible. The death of Cleege—truly dreadful news. Pohl was anxious to know the details.

Pohl said goodnight to the travelers, and then went to the Lady's reading room hoping to find Meekelorr there. But he wasn't. Pohl had nearly an hour to while away and, frankly, he was restless. Cleege's death was a terrible blow for their work in the west. He sat and stared at the small cabinet where the precious sacred books given to the Lady by her father were kept, all written out by hand. The Agavi did not read or write. They had a method of picture writing, but its purpose had more to do with jogging the memory than with recording their history. And Agavians had memories that extended beyond their own personal lives to the lives of their ancestors. Therefore, all was recitation and word of mouth.

But the Lady read—as did Galavi.

Pohl began to pace about the room, and finally, in his restlessness, walked back to the Great Hall to watch those whose task it was to clean up. He could hear the quiet tones in which they discussed the strange event that had ended the Feast of Aa. All Agavians were aware that the return of Meekelorr to Agavia, that the unexpected coming of the travelers, and now the sudden appearance of these soldiers, were in preparation for their final mission, the Last Battle. How calmly they seemed to be taking the events that would lead to the end of the Agavi. Did they truly understand how dire the times were?

chapter twenty

AT THE APPROPRIATE moment, Pohl was at the Lady's door.

It was opened by Binta, who greeted him courteously and then went about setting a table in front of the fireplace with tea and cakes. Meekelorr was standing at the tall glass doors that led to the Lady's garden, staring out at the snow and at the valley dotted with lights from other homes and mansions. He acknowledged Pohl with a nod of his head as Pohl entered, but said nothing.

The Lady had changed into a simple green wool gown. A border of Agavi trees was embroidered around the bottom of it and along the sleeve cuffs. Her crown was gone, but she still wore the emblem of her office—a silver crescent moon cradling the golden sun—on a thin gold chain around her neck. Her dark hair, worn up for the feast, had been let down, and it curled around her shoulders. She looked both beautiful and vulnerable. The world that had left Agavia alone for centuries was once more knocking at her door, as it had done in her mother's time, when her father had first come to them from the Easternlands. Her brother, his face drawn, was kneeling near the fire feeding wood into it. The new visitors were not yet in the room, but eight chairs had been drawn around a low table next to the fire.

When the table was set, Binta bid them good night and left.

"Where are they?" Pohl inquired.

"They have bathed and been given dinner. They will join us shortly," the Lady said. "Come, Meekelorr, and sit with us."

She walked toward him, hands outstretched, and he turned from the window, moved toward her, took both her hands, and put each to his lips. Claregole led him to the chairs and Galavi and Pohl joined them.

"Whatever the details of Cleege's death, however it happened, it will not give us the solution to his replacement." Pohl opened the discussion.

"Who is second in command in the west?" the Lady asked.

"Elarr," Meekelorr answered.

As he didn't go on, Pohl added, "Cleege oversees. . .did oversee the Companions in Noonbarr and Thorensphere. Elarr oversees the Sorren Heights and Glovale."

"And Mattelmead?" she asked Pohl.

"I doubt that any of the Companions are in Mattelmead now," Meekelorr answered her. "Ormahn, when last I heard, was in control in the northern part of Mattelmead. By now, no doubt, he is also in control of the south—perhaps these young soldiers will know. If so, our people will have withdrawn from there."

"With the exception, perhaps, of Lorenwile," Pohl said.

"Yes," Meekelorr said, "Lorenwile is, I pray, still in Mattelmead. As the remarkable singer he is, he can travel and work almost anywhere."

"But not as a True-singer," Pohl said.

"No, that skill he must keep hidden. Over the years

Lorenwile has brought us much useful information. It heartens me to know that he was here not so many years ago."

"Are there Companions in the south of the Westernlands?" Galavi asked.

"There are only two countries there—and also the Southern Desolation, with the Deep Forest just above it. There is Isofed, which is a walled land," Meekelorr said. "It has not suffered the wars of the other countries. It is a land devoted exclusively to the worship of the King God and is still ruled by very ancient customs. Its council of rulers allows no one to pass through its gates. And only a few leave—highly trusted officials—to take care of trade. Their greatest fear is that their religion will be contaminated by others. They do not like change. There has been no possibility for the Companions of the Way to enter Isofed, nor has there been any need. Even Lorenwile would not be welcome there.

"The other is Wildenfarr-low-desert, to Isofed's west. It's an arid land with few people—two opposing tribes who fight each other over some obscure religious point. Therefore the Companions have not gone there. We have stationed ourselves where government has either broken down or where there is little stability—those are the northern countries I have mentioned. There are more lands in the south and in the north. But those are uninhabitable."

Pohl knew that what Meekelorr was telling them was not new to the Lady Claregole or to Galavi, but they were asking questions in the polite way Agavi have of easing into painful problems. And Meekelorr was passing the time as he waited for the newcomers.

Finally, there was a knock on the door. At the Lady's call, the four Companions were ushered in. The servers then retreated from the room. The four young men, bathed and shaven and richly attired in the clothes of the Agavi, stood awkwardly near the door. They were all young—barely twenty any of them—

and they seemed overawed by the Lady and the Lady's rooms. Despite their youthfulness, they had been in war a long time. Perhaps, like so many these days, it was all they knew of life. Perhaps, thought Pohl, all they would ever know.

At a gesture from Claregole, they came shyly to the table.

"Have you eaten?"

"Yes, Lady," Peroll spoke for them.

"Then you must sit and take tea with us." She smiled, and motioned them to chairs.

"Oh, Lady, it is not fitting that we sit. . ." the young leader blurted out.

"Do as you are bidden," Meekelorr said. His tone was mild, but it was a command and each sat down quickly and stiffly.

Wordlessly, the Lady served tea and each soldier took his cup and saucer and held them gingerly. After she served them, she asked, "How long have you been on the road, young friends?"

"Nearly eight weeks, I think. We were sent from the north of Thorensphere," the leader said.

"Eight weeks!" Meekelorr exclaimed.

The young man was immediately apologetic. "Well, you see it's winter with a lot of storms and the Valley of the Agavi is not easily found. I'm afraid we took some wrong turns. . ."

"It was not intended as a reprimand, Peroll. Forgive my tone. Who sent you?"

"Elarr," he answered.

"What message does he send?"

The young man swallowed. The other three looked down at the delicate cups and saucers held in their hands. "Elarr asks that you come as soon as you can. He asks that you not wait until spring to leave here." Peroll spoke as if he had memorized the words.

The Lady caught her breath.

Pohl turned to Meekelorr. He had not acted surprised at the message. No doubt, he had already suspected that it was for more reason than the announcement of Cleege's death that four young men had been sent out in the months of snow.

"Go on," Meekelorr said.

Peroll, his cheeks red from fatigue and strain, said, "There is no one to lead in Cleege's place, the west is too vast. Elarr has moved himself and his men to Cleege's territory, and another commander has been sent to take over Elarr's command in Glovale and the Sorren Heights. He begs that you come and assume leadership immediately or else send him other instructions."

"Is that true, Meekelorr, that there is no other to lead?" the Lady asked.

"So Elarr says. I'm not there. Elarr is." Meekelorr's words were clipped.

"Are there no other commanders in the west?" Galavi asked.

"There are."

Pohl found Elarr's message curious. There were many good commanders in the west. He knew some of them because they had been sent from the east in past years. Seasoned men. Yet it was Elarr who had been in the west the longest, who had been second to Cleege. Why hadn't Elarr wanted to be commander of the west in Cleege's place?

"How did Cleege die?" Meekelorr's eyes were penetrating as he looked from one Companion to the other.

For a moment Peroll's eyes sought the floor. Finally he mumbled, "A conference had been set up between Cleege and Elarr to be held in the foothills between the Sorren Heights and Thorensphere." Peroll's voice sounded hollow. "On his way south, Cleege and his soldiers—seven I think—were ambushed, as I said earlier, by Boreen's men. He's the rebel leader in Thorensphere."

"I know. Go on."

The young leader tried to meet Meekelorr's gaze. "Cleege's soldiers were all killed, but not Cleege. He was taken to a camp belonging to the rebels."

"Then how do you know he is dead? Perhaps he is still a captive."

"No, he's dead all right." That came from a freckled-face youngster who turned beet red at his own temerity.

"What is your name, soldier?" Meekelorr asked him.

"Sola, sir."

"How do you know that Cleege is dead, Sola?"

"I. . .I was with Elarr when he tried to rescue Cleege. We outnumbered the rebels and we killed most of them. But as soon as they knew we were in the camp, they killed Cleege and threw his body out of the tent where he had been kept prisoner. We fought and we revenged and then we left."

Meekelorr's face turned white. He stood up suddenly and then walked to the window. "The Gods help us," he said in a tight voice.

Before he could say more, Pohl stood up. "I think we have learned as much as we need to from these brave young men for the moment. They are exhausted. Let them rest, Meekelorr. You can continue with them tomorrow."

Claregole spoke then in a calm, soft voice. "In the morning I will see that they are driven up to the school, Meekelorr. Let us excuse them for now." Before Meekelorr could respond, the Lady called for the servers who were waiting outside her chambers. She then shepherded the young men to the door, without another word from Meekelorr.

When the door finally closed behind them, Meekelorr exploded. "The fool! To go after Cleege into an enemy camp! It's against strict orders and, the heavens know, common sense. We do not make rescue efforts. We lose more men in the attempt and we lose those we are trying to rescue."

"So Elarr made a bad decision," Pohl said, keeping his voice mild. "We all do in war, Meekelorr. Cleege was his commander. It was natural to want to go after him."

"He lost Cleege his life." Meekelorr would not be comforted.

"Which was probably forfeit the moment he was captured. Elarr probably saved him days of torture."

"And how many others died in that ineffectual battle? We don't have men to throw away in useless revenge."

Pohl's words were measured. "Meekelorr, Elarr is human. He is at war, has been at war for too many years. Revenge is a human response. Have you never responded so?"

"We become like our adversaries," Meekelorr answered, but his voice was calmer, "and then the Nethergod conquers us from within our own souls."

Claregole took his hand and drew him back to the chairs. "What will you do?"

"Go," he answered, keeping his voice neutral and not meeting her eyes, "in a week or ten days—as soon as we can prepare."

The Lady did not take her glance away from his face. She sat unmoving in her chair, her hands clenched tightly in her lap, but on her face there was an expression of resignation.

Meekelorr turned to Pohl. "In the spring, after the thaw, lead the group of travelers into the Westernlands. I ask that you and Galavi take them, not through the Northern Valley, and not through the other passes known to the Agavians, but through the caves—you know the ones I mean."

"But those caves will bring us far to the south, close to the hills between Noonbarr and Isofed."

"Yes. I don't want any of them leading an army back to the valley."

"Surely not?" the Lady said.

"How do we know not?" Meekelorr asked, meeting her eyes. There was no smile on his face. "The men of both the east and the west know only the Northern Valley, which the caravans use, and the Southern Pass, which no one dares use. I don't want them going through the Northern Valley. Why place our trust in them so completely? We must safeguard Agavia until. . . It is enough that some of the Companions now know the way to this valley. So it must be through the caves. Once in the west, point them in the right direction."

"Which is?"

"North, through the foothills of the Gandlese, until they reach the mountains that divide Thorensphere and Mattelmead from the Northern Desolation. Then turn west, keeping the hills to their right."

"But. . ."

At that moment, there was a loud, agitated knocking on the door. Then Binta rushed in, fear in her eyes.

"Come, oh, come!" she called. "There is a fire in the west wing."

"What?" Pohl said. That was the wing where the travelers were staying.

Immediately, they were out the door and hurrying down the hall.

"Which room?" Pohl asked.

"In the room where the twin girl sleeps."

Pohl almost stopped in his tracks. *I should have been more vigilant*, he berated himself. *I was too preoccupied.*

His suspicions grew, then were confirmed when Binta said, "She has set fire to her bedding and to some of her clothes. I don't understand how or why she would do such a thing."

No, Pohl thought, *it is not behavior an Agavian would understand.*

They were running through the corridors by then. As they neared the west wing, Donnadorr came rushing to meet them.

"The fire is out. There's been some damage to the bedding and the furniture, I'm afraid." He looked apologetically at Claregole.

"And Glenelle?" Pohl asked.

"She's safe. When we came back to our rooms after the feast, Ellie said she was tired, and so she didn't come to our little party. It looks like. . .she had another *sleepwalking* spell." Don almost tripped on the word sleepwalking. "But the fire, or rather the smoke, brought her out of it. She's heartbroken and sobbing inconsolably."

"Where is she?" Meekelorr asked.

"In Sylvane's room," Donnadorr answered.

The Lady and Meekelorr went first to Glenelle's room to see that the fire was under control, but Pohl hurried directly to Sylvane's room.

Glenelle was curled up in a chair, her body racked with sobs. She didn't look up as Pohl entered. Auragole, bending over her, was trying unsuccessfully to console her. Sylvane was nowhere in sight. Glenorr rushed over to Pohl as he came into the room.

"She's ill and there is no medicine here that helps her." He was wild with anger and worry. "What can you do for her?" he shouted at Pohl, but didn't wait for an answer. Gone was his attempt to play down his sister's illness. He turned back to Auragole and bellowed at him. "If you hadn't waited for Donnadorr to heal his blasted leg, we would have been in Mattelmead by now, and my sister would have gotten the help she needed. If anything happens to my sister, I swear I'll kill you."

Auragole straightened up then, his face stricken and white with blame. Pohl imagined that if Glenorr had lifted a finger against him at that moment, he would not have defended himself.

In time to witness this last outburst, Donnadorr, Meekelorr, and the Lady Claregole walked into the room, followed by Sylvane carrying a tray with tea for Glenelle. The Lady went immediately to Glenelle and drew her up into her arms and led her to Sylvane's bed, speaking to her softly.

Meekelorr stood just inside the room, his eyes dark and veiled. Abruptly, he spoke. "There has been a change in plans. In ten days, I and the Companions of the Way must leave for the Westernlands. You travelers will accompany us. I, or some of my men, will see to it that you get to Mattelmead, where no doubt you will get the help that Glenelle needs." This last he said to Glenorr.

There was stone silence in the room.

New plans, Pohl thought. It seems Galavi and I won't be needed after all.

Donnadorr was the first to speak. "Well, that's it then. If Meekelorr can travel in the winter, why so can we, lads and lassies." He tried to sound enthusiastic. "We shall miss this lovely land, but as Mattelmead is, and has always been, our destination, then we cannot refuse this offer of guidance to that other wondrous country."

Pohl looked at Auragole. There was a mixture of sorrow, worry, and excitement in his eyes. Pohl wondered then what he would do if he knew that he was cousin to the Lady Claregole. Would he want to stay?

Sylvane, helping the Lady get Glenelle into her bed, crooned to her. "It's all right, Ellie, everything will be all right. We will be leaving here soon for Mattelmead where there will be medicine and help for you. Don't cry, my love. You will be well and healthy soon, really you will." Good-hearted Sylvane. She was the most selfless of the lot, Pohl felt, ready to go wherever the road might take her for the sake of those she loved.

LATER, AS MEEKELORR and Pohl walked across the valley and up the dark hill to the school, Pohl said, "How quickly plans change."

Meekelorr didn't speculate on that. He had other concerns. "What do you think, Pohl, could it be Boreen? Why else attack the Companions?"

Pohl knew what he was asking. "I don't know. Ask Elarr's soldiers, when you speak to them tomorrow, what they know about Boreen. Our information is old."

Meekelorr changed the subject then. "What should we do about Auragole?"

"In what way?"

"If I see to it that the travelers get to Mattelmead, which was what Auragole intended to do, he could stay here."

Pohl thought about it for a while, looking down at the snow that had been trampled by many feet coming and going to the feasts. "He's been raised alone," Pohl said. "He longs to know the world that he has not yet seen, not yet experienced. That is understandable, is it not? Yes, yes, indeed, very understandable," Pohl answered his own question and then went on. "And for the first time he has friends. I'm not sure he would want to part with them so soon—particularly to part with the girl, Glenelle—even though I would say he seems very happy in Agavia."

"She would not be good for him."

"That is not for us to say."

"She will break his heart."

"Now who speaks like an old man?"

But Meekelorr paid no attention. "She's ill and cannot love selflessly."

"Then Auragole will find that out and suffer pain. Which one of us has not?"

They walked for a while and then Meekelorr let out a long breath, "I wish I could fathom his part in the Last Battle."

"How fathom something that even the Gods do not know, friend? Such is freedom in our times."

"For freedom's sake we must abide this uncertainty," Meekelorr said, "put so much in the hands of. . .of. . ."

". . .of a wild card?"

"We could offer him a studentship at the school."

"He *is* interested in the Creative World," Pohl said. "No, let me amend that. He is curious about the Creative World. But right now he longs to know more about the earth, and why shouldn't he? He's barely experienced the Deep Earth, why should he turn his interest to another world so soon?"

"We could keep him here, I think," Meekelorr said.

"How?"

"By telling him that he is cousin to the Lady Claregole."

"Don't attempt to manipulate the Gods, Meekelorr."

"Am I?" He laughed. The sound was brittle in the cold, dry air. "No doubt you are right."

"If the boy has a part to play in the battle with the Nethergod, then he will be here when it happens. Leave it to his own destiny."

"Then we are left with the same old question."

"Which is?"

"Will Auragole aid us or contribute to our downfall? If he studies here. . . If he helps us, it could turn the tide in our favor. If he opposes us, either out of willfulness or ignorance, we will have a hard, hard row to hoe."

"That is a heavy thought, my old friend, but not a new one."

"No."

Pohl, trudging through the new snow, suddenly felt the cold penetrate his heavy cape. "But all does not depend on him, or why bother to train ourselves or the Agavians?"

"No, all does not depend on him. Yet he will play no small part, mark my words, Pohl."

"So you prefer that he be here where one of us can watch him."

"Frankly, it would ease my mind. Yes, I would like it if he were where one of us could keep an eye on him."

"And away from Glenelle? Because of the Being that lives in her."

"That too." Meekelorr sighed deeply. "He is innocent in many ways. Is he also corruptible? His corruptibility is the hope of the Nethergod."

"I understand you. But let it be."

"This much I will let be, Pohl." Meekelorr kicked at the snow. "I will not tell him that the Lady Claregole is his cousin. But neither will I ask Claregole to remain silent any longer. Should she wish to speak to him, then destiny will follow that course. As for me, I will watch and wait."

"So be it," Pohl said. "Come, I see lights in the school. Some of the teachers await word from us and they will remain sleepless until we bring it to them."

N

chapter twenty-one

IN THE ENSUING days, Meekelorr met frequently with Elarr's men. Then, in conference with Pohl, the travel plans were changed once more. Meekelorr would leave Agavia first with his troop. Five days later, Pohl and Galavi would lead the Easterners through the caves and then meet Meekelorr at a rendezvous point in the foothills of the Westernlands, a few days north of the East Gate of Isofed.

"It's imperative I meet as soon as possible with Elarr—so much time has already been lost—and I don't want these Easterners or Auragole with me when I do," Meekelorr told Pohl. "Peroll says Elarr and I are to meet in the forested hills between Noonbarr and Isofed. After that meeting I'll head back to where you and the Easterners will be waiting. I have pledged to see the travelers to the borders of Mattelmead, and so I shall. But not north—that makes little sense now, and I don't have the time or the men to spend on that circuitous route. I'll guide them through the Sorren Heights, staying away from the

Woeful Peaks, where our main camp is. I don't want these Easterners to know where any of the gathering places of the Companions are. As I am in a great hurry, and because I don't want even my soldiers to know the way back here, I too shall lead my men through the caves."

Pohl sighed at the need, shook his head, but agreed to the new plans.

In the days that followed, Pohl gathered together and packed as many medicaments as he felt Meekelorr's troop could carry, and then did the same for his little band.

A FEW DAYS after the Feast of Aa, the council met—without the Lady, who still had duties to perform in this season of Aa—to hear from Meekelorr and Pohl the quickly formulated plans and to discuss what they called the *Auragole situation*. After a long and heated discussion, it was decided, albeit somewhat reluctantly, that none of them would tell Auragole of his relationship to Galavi and the Lady Claregole. But it was also agreed that if Claregole and her brother wanted to tell Auragole that they were cousins, then so be it. The council did, however, want to meet with Auragole. They wanted to share with him some reminiscences of his great-uncle, and they wanted to offer him a place in the school. Pohl was present at both meetings and listened and watched carefully.

The reminiscences were listened to and received with obvious gratitude by Auragole. He sat at the foot of the long council table listening gravely to all that was said. When it was over, Biehmar stood up at the head of the table and looked down its long expanse at the young man. "I understand that you have promised to lead your companions to Mattelmead?"

"Yes, that is so," he answered, clearing his throat as he began to speak. "Though they are each very good travelers, none has experience reading direction from plants or the stars, and none reads maps very well."

"You do know that Meekelorr, who is an excellent guide and who knows the west, will see them to the border of Mattelmead, and that Pohl and Galavi will see them to the meeting place with Meekelorr."

Auragole nodded, his eyes suddenly wary.

"I remind you of this," Biehmar said, "because I want you to be assured that you need no longer feel obligated to see them west. Should you be of a mind, you could stay here in Agavia, either continuing the work you are doing with the Lady's horses, or you could come up here to the school and become a student and learn what we are able to teach you about the Deep Earth and the Creative World, and of course, about the Nethergod and his coming activities on earth."

Biehmar sat down suddenly. There was a pregnant silence. No council member spoke. Neither did Auragole. He seemed, for a time, lost in thought and oblivious to the fact that all were waiting for some word.

Finally Biehmar rose to his feet again. "Auragole," he said gently, "do you have an answer for us?"

"No. . .no, sir," he said. "Must I answer you at once? May I not think about this. . .this offer?"

"Of course," Biehmar said, "of course. No one expects you to be able to answer immediately. But do you have any questions before we let you go?"

"No. . ." Auragole hesitated. "Well, yes," he finally said. "You say you teach about the Gods of the Creative World. I have heard that you also teach a way to find these Gods? Is that true?"

Fllordon spoke up. "That is precisely what we teach." He turned his hawk eyes in Auragole's direction.

Auragole nodded, his eyes downcast, his fingers rubbing his forehead. "How many days do I have before you must have my answer?"

"Will three be enough?" Biehmar asked.

"Yes, thank you."

At this, Biehmar rose and came around the table and, thanking Auragole, led him to the door.

When he returned to the table, Fllordon said, "He will not stay."

"We shall see," Biehmar said, and dismissed the meeting.

IT WAS DURING those three days that Auragole was called also to a meeting with the Lady Claregole. Pohl did not know all that was spoken of in that meeting, but he did know, for she told him herself, that she did not mention that Eagalorr was Amarori and consequently her father.

It surprised Pohl that he felt a sense of relief that Claregole had been silent about her relationship to Eagalorr. Perhaps deep in his soul he knew—as he assumed Claregole knew—that Auragole had to go out into the greater world before he played his part in that critical event called the Last Battle. Agavia was a land rich in beauty, smiled on, and still supported by the Gods. The Agavian sense of self merged into a sense of community. And that was not the way of humankind today. Humanity was painfully developing individuality. Only individuals could be free—and this was a great goal for humanity. Even the Creative Gods were not free. They were great and loving and capable of sacrifice and renunciation, but that was their nature, and Gods act according to their nature. Human beings would be free after a long evolution. Then they would join the ranks of Gods in the Creative World and participate in the making of worlds in some glorious far-distant future—if the Nethergod did not win the day. Here in Agavia, as a great renunciation, a people had stayed behind in their development, holding fast to the elder Gods, eschewing freedom for a time, in order that some light might still shine when the world fell into darkness.

And, of course, to give battle to the Nethergod with the few in humanity who understood his coming.

But Auragole, Pohl sensed, needed to experience the world, and neither in the school—since in these world days it had to be isolated—nor in the valley could he experience what had transpired in humankind's evolving.

Yes, Pohl was relieved to know that the Lady had not tied Auragole to her glorious valley with her pronouncement of kinship.

It was Pohl who took Auragole to look at the pack that had been found near Eagalorr's body. Auragole looked at the items very carefully—the clothes, boots, sword, and books. There was a medallion there on a chain that had been, Pohl knew, of great significance to Eagalorr. It was the last of three medallions that had been found there. One Galavi wore beneath his clothes. One Claregole had in a box with keepsakes from her mother. Pohl asked Auragole if he would like to have this one. The design on it was of a bird in full flight. Auragole fingered it lovingly, thanked Pohl, then put it on and tucked it inside his shirt.

ON THE THIRD day after the council meeting, Auragole showed up at Pohl's door and asked if he could speak with him. Pohl welcomed the young man in, took his cap and cloak, put his mittens near the fire, and called the student who served him to bring them some tea.

Auragole sat in the chair that Pohl had offered him, staring into the fire, and Pohl watched him. Once again Pohl was fascinated. The young man could sit with others as if he were alone, plumbing in silence the depths of his own thoughts. On that day Pohl simply waited. It wasn't until the tray of tea had been brought in, perhaps some twenty minutes later, that Auragole spoke.

"There is so much that is new for me, Pohl, since I left my own valley. There are decisions whose complexities my childhood and youth did not prepare me to make—in spite of all my mother's attempts. There were decisions, of course, as I was

267

growing up, but somehow, if one chose wrongly, life corrected one quickly. If one planted early and then the spring rains continued harsh and washed away the seeds, you knew that you had chosen wrongly, had not read the signs of nature correctly. If you were following an animal on the hunt, and took a wrong turn, misread a sign, you knew immediately that you had made a mistake, for you lost your prey."

He shifted in his chair and now turned his dark, serious eyes directly on Pohl. "But since I met my friends and since I became leader of the group, I have been forced to make decisions—decisions that life does not correct so easily. Was it wrong, for instance, to wait for Donnadorr? Would we have been in Mattelmead by now, if we hadn't? We might have been, but then we would have missed knowing, not only Don, but also coming to the Valley of the Agavi. That seems an intolerable thought. But would Ellie," and his voice cracked and his face softened as he said her name, "have been healed by now had we gone straight to Mattelmead? If we had left some supplies with Don, trusting he would find his own way, would he have managed to find his way to Mattelmead alone, or would he have become lost and perhaps died of starvation? These are all questions I have no answer to. If answers come so seldom, how can one make decisions?"

He stopped speaking and Pohl could see that his question was not rhetorical, that he wanted Pohl to answer.

Pohl cleared his throat and tried to explain something that was almost impossible to explain. "You are asking, young Auragole, if there are simple answers to life's questions, and I can only say there are no simple answers, since there is no one right way. Every choice has a cost, a price to pay. If you do one thing instead of the other, it is only perhaps years later—or not until you see your life from the Creative World—that you understand what your choices truly meant. For each decision, a fee. For instance, you say the thought that you might have missed Agavia is intolerable. And yet you see the cost has been perhaps in Ellie's health. If you had left Don and gone on to Mattelmead without him, you would have, perhaps, healed Ellie quickly, but you would have never known Donnadorr. And you would have never come to, or experienced, Agavia."

"Nor met you, nor Meekelorr, nor the Lady."

"Yes, all true. You would not then have been in the cave and Meekelorr might be dead now. And Donnadorr might have not made it through the pass alone, and perhaps have died of the weather or from an encounter with wild animals."

Auragole looked thoughtfully at the fire, taking in Pohl's words.

"Everything must be paid for in some way," Pohl continued. "But what makes it doubly difficult is. . ."

". . .that you don't know the cost from the beginning, from the time you make the decision. If we had gotten through the pass and gone on to Mattelmead, we wouldn't know we had missed Agavia, nor all of you." He shook his dark head as if it were all too confusing.

"To make it even more complicated," Pohl added, "you don't know, had you chosen not to wait for Don, if you would have arrived safely in Mattelmead as was your hope. Perhaps you would have been killed by an avalanche in the mountains, perhaps attacked by wild wolves, perhaps by callous soldiers."

Auragole thought about this for a while. "Glen blames me for his sister's continued illness."

"You must not take that blame upon yourself. Glen is not thinking clearly. You made the best decision you could at the time. You made a judgment. That is how we educate our capacity for freedom. We make a judgment. Glen says his sister would be healed by now. But he makes too many assumptions. One, that you would have made it safely to Mattelmead, and we know that there is much that could have happened on the way, and two, he assumes they have medicine there that will heal Glenelle."

"But surely they do!" Auragole looked at Pohl, startled, as if he had never even questioned whether or not such a cure existed.

"It is open, my young friend. Let us hope they can help her, but there is no guarantee."

Auragole slumped back into his chair and stared dolefully into the fire and was silent again. Pohl hoped it would not be another twenty minutes before he spoke. It wasn't.

"Pohl, I have come up here to tell you, and to ask you to convey this message to the rest of the council, that I will be leaving Agavia with my friends." He turned toward Pohl. "Part of me loathes leaving. I do so love the valley and I have been happier and more at peace here than at any other time in my life. But still I have decided to go. Why?"

After he didn't go on, Pohl realized that once again he was asking him for an answer. "Perhaps there are many reasons. We could list several. Perhaps if your uncle were still alive you might choose to stay."

Auragole nodded.

"But your uncle is dead. So perhaps you want to continue your relationship with your friends. You want to see more of the world." Auragole nodded after each of these. "You want to have adventures, to visit Mattelmead, to see this new king, to see Ellie healthy."

"Yes, yes, all correct. " He smiled for the first time. "But. . ."

"But there is something else?" Pohl prompted.

"Yes, but I can't name it."

"Perhaps then the greatest reason may still be hidden from you. But deep in the secret chamber of your heart, you sense it is your path, your destiny that you are following."

Auragole looked soberly at Pohl. "Somehow that feels right, but it is all beyond me. You believe I have a path and yet you believe I have freedom also."

"That seems contradictory?"

"Well, isn't it?"

"Not really. You feel your path, your destiny suggests to you that you should go with your friends."

He nodded.

"But despite that feeling, you are free to choose not to go."

"Yes, I could do that. But then what happens to my path?"

"It takes a different turn. The Gods are endlessly creative. They will help you achieve what lies deep within you as a task."

"Yes, yes, that's just it. I do feel I have a task. But if that is true, must it be so hidden? Shouldn't I know what it is? Must your Gods make it so difficult for humankind?"

"You will find it, my dear young friend. That is the way it has to be in this time of freedom. You must be allowed to find your task without coercion." Pohl stood up then. "Return to your friends and prepare for the journey. We leave in ten days, Meekelorr in five."

Auragole took both Pohl's hands in the way of the Agavi, thanked him, and left.

Later that day, Pohl told first Meekelorr and then Biehmar. Both took the news solemnly, but without surprise.

THE DAYS OF preparation were hectic. Meekelorr and Pohl went over their maps and their plans again and again. Each evening Meekelorr went down to the valley to be with the Lady Claregole. In the morning he returned to train with his men. In the afternoon he held council with Pohl and with others of his soldiers who were the most experienced. Meekelorr spoke frequently with the four young emissaries from Elarr—who were to remain at the school—going over again and again the maps they had brought with them, locating the rendezvous places of the Companions, getting as much information about the terrain of each as he could wrest from the four. He spoke also with Galavi about the caves as he intended to take his men through them.

Pohl found it a sobering thought. Meekelorr loved his men but did not fully trust them to keep secret the location of the

Valley of the Agavi. Well, in these world days one must take precautions and then trust in the help of the Creative Gods.

In the first days of February, Pohl stood on the roof of the Healing Tower and watched Meekelorr and the Companions of the Way wind their way down the long hill, first through the valley and then turn southwest. He felt cold both inside and out as he watched them leave.

The world was once more with them.

FIVE DAYS AFTER Meekelorr and his troop had taken their leave, Pohl, Galavi, and the band of travelers left the Valley of the Agavi. Pohl had been present when many fine gifts had been given to the Easterners by the Agavians to make the journey less burdensome. First, lightweight traveling clothes woven from the wool of the weswill sheep, which far surpassed their old clothes for warmth. Then, long cloaks woven from the hair of the unique shasha goats, in autumn colors, except for Glenelle's, which was worked in the brilliant blue she so loved. Also given to each were delicately balanced bows and arrows. This gift particularly delighted Donnadorr and Glenelle, who seemed fully recovered. All were given swords, lighter than the ones they had brought with them, with carved handles and scabbards of finely tooled leather, and fur-lined boots to make the walking in the snow warm and easy. Their backpacks were filled with biscuits, dried meat, dried fruit, nuts, and cheese.

And because beauty, rather than necessity, was the governing word in Agavia, Glenelle and Sylvane received jeweled silver combs for their hair, Glenorr received three elaborately carved Agavi boxes for his stones, which were strapped to the back of their donkey, and Donnadorr and Auragole were given hand harps hewed from Agavi wood and inlaid with silver and jewels. This last gift brought tears to Auragole's eyes, as it was put in his hands by the Lady Claregole herself. He impulsively kissed her cheek and then blushed.

There was one more gift given to each. A pouch filled with precious jewels that were for the Agavi decorative stones, but in the east and in the west they were worth a legendary king's ransom, Pohl was sure of that. They wore these on chains under their clothes, close to their hearts.

And so on a clear, winter day, one week into February, they left the Valley of the Agavi. They circled around the Lady's mansion—a final tribute and a final good-bye—before they headed toward the southern mountains that would take them to the entrance of the caves. Galavi led with Pohl beside him. Pohl could feel both the excitement and the sadness in the little troop as they looked down on the valley for the last time.

Around a bend, and Agavia was lost to their sight.

journey west

PART THREE OF AURAGOLE'S JOURNEY
AURAGOLE OF THE MOUNTAINS

N

preface

DURING HIS LAST night in the Valley of the Agavi, Auragole had a dream.

He stood at the edge of a blue lake. The water was still. It stretched before him like a silk shawl. Behind him stood the white Flaming One, watching. Auragole had come for something. For what? Ah, yes, yes, now he remembered. He had come to speak to the Beautiful One, the one who seemed to be made of light, whose feet left living rubies where they trod.

But the Beautiful One was not there. Only Auragole and the Flaming One stood near the radiant lake.

"Where are you?" Auragole called.

"I am where you are, child," a voice like music answered. "I am on the Deep Earth. You have come with a question."

"Yes."

"Then ask it, Auragole of the Mountains."

"Thank you, I shall. Once you told me to find you with what is most myself. What is most myself?"

"Ah. . . Listen and see if you can understand. All the great faculties the Gods gave you as gifts in past ages have been taken from you, from all of humankind. . ."

"But why?"

"So that you can acquire even greater gifts. You are no longer children living in the arms of the Gods."

"Greater gifts! What gifts? How acquire them?"

"In these difficult world days, you must reacquire, for yourself, everything you once had as a legacy from the Creative World, must make each gift no longer a gift but your own. And you must do it with that which is most truly yourself."

"But I don't know what that is. That is why I have come to you."

"You can know, Auragole. Only you must wake up."

"You must wake up, Auragole. We are leaving in a few hours."

Auragole opened his eyes. Donnadorr was peering down at him.

He sat up in bed. "Yes," he said. "I'll be ready."

By the time he stood on the floor next to his bed, the dream had faded from his mind.

chapter twenty-two

DONNADORR GLANCED BACK at the Valley of the Agavi only once; then in a full, cheerful voice he began to sing. His song echoed throughout the cold February mountains. It was satisfying to imagine that below them the Agavians could hear his song of tribute. But now was not the time to reminisce. He knew that if he indulged himself in too many thoughts about the land they had just left, he would become slobberingly sentimental. There might even be tears in his eyes. So he fought that part of himself in the usual way—with a song, or a story, or a joke. He was good at diverting himself, good also at hiding his feelings. It was, after all, a matter of survival. Don couldn't remember his natural parents. His memory didn't reach that far back. All his life he had been on the road, as others in the Easternlands had been. It had not seemed peculiar to be on his own. The road was a normal life for many. He wasn't bitter. It was just the way things were and had been for as long as anyone now alive could remember. And, of course, there had been those wonderful seven or eight years when Aiku had taken him under his old wing. Donnadorr couldn't recall exactly how they had been together. He had only been six or seven and on the road for a long time alone. Then he wasn't alone. He was with Aiku, an old man—or so he had seemed then. And Aiku had taken care of him, had taught him things—the use of the bow and of the sword, to sing and to make a flute out of reeds, to make songs of his own, to speak well and to tell stories, and, of course, how to think about the world, and how to survive in it.

"Watch and keep silent, Don. If any man demands you speak, tell him a story. If he does not like your story, sing. A song has healed more ailments than eldenmyrr. Take nothing from another that belongs to him, neither what he owns nor what he declares himself to be. For to each, his own self is his most precious possession.

"If you come to a group whose leader you do not like, do not challenge him, leave. You are free, born to wind and music. For that, thank the Gods. But if the man is cruel, and you see him wield his cruelty, fight him with all your skill. You have three gifts that you can give, so give them liberally: a story, a song, and most valuable of all, your love. No one can take these from you. Give these in abundance. It is medicine in an ailing world. But, my child, never show all that you know, neither your skills nor your knowledge. In a world gone mad, caution is also needed."

So Donnadorr sang as Agavia, moving behind the up-thrusting peaks, disappeared from sight. And the others joined in.

It was Galavi who set the pace, walking briskly through the dry February day, his eyes and ears tuned to things no one else saw or heard. Pohl walked beside him. Both were just ahead of Donnadorr. Donnadorr watched Galavi openly and with curiosity, as he had during the weeks he had worked with him. It was too bad they couldn't have stayed longer in the Valley of the Agavi. The Agavi were a remarkable people, different from any he had come across in all his years of wandering in the

Easternlands. But what was not to be was not to be, and he didn't dwell on it. He merely watched Galavi with interest and pleasure and hoped mightily that some day he might return to Galavi's valley.

The clear weather held. It took only three days traveling southwest to reach their destination—the first in a series of caves. They camped that night just inside the first cave, near its opening. Perhaps it was so they could see the stars, Donnadorr speculated. It would be their last view of them for many days.

Pohl called them together for a conference when their supper and the cleanup chores had been completed. They gathered in a circle, all except Galavi, who sat outside the cave's opening and stared at the stars. It's as if he's reading them, Donnadorr thought. What could they be saying to him? But that thought left him quickly as he turned his attention to Pohl.

Pohl's face was serious, and for the first time Donnadorr felt a little twinge of worry, which he quickly brushed aside. Never worry about that which has not yet happened, Aiku had taught him. Each day has its own worries. They are enough.

Pohl warned them that the caves they were about to enter were dangerous, that their courage would be tested, perhaps severely. But if they paid strict attention to his instructions and to the words of Galavi, they would come through safely. However, attentiveness was needed, alertness, no daydreaming. And each must be aware of the group at all times. Pohl reminded them that caves are not natural places for humans, that they would be in damp, cold darkness for days, their only light the dimness of the torches. Humans, he told them, needed sun as much as plants did. Being deprived of it for long sent their spirits diving. He warned them not to treat his words lightly. "And watch your footing," he said.

But the five of them had traveled through caves before, so Donnadorr was not concerned. He glanced over at Glenelle. Her face was pinched and pale, but she looked resolute. They were traveling in the winter for her sake. Everyone wanted to help Glenelle. She was the heart of their group, their center, their vital core, for everyone loved her. She needed to get to Mattelmead and to the doctors there. If to do so meant traveling in the depth of winter, meant going through these abominable caves, then so be it. They would do it and put up with whatever those dark places presented to them. Surely nothing could be as horrible as the beast that Meekelorr had fought.

Donnadorr glanced over at Auragole and once more saw a rival. He had not bothered about it for months. But here it was again. Auragole loved Glenelle. That was clear. But how did she feel about Auragole? That wasn't clear. And now once again he saw in his friend Auragole, the one who had saved his life, a competitor. Strange that he had hardly thought about it while they were in Agavia. He had merely loved Glenelle as she had deserved, loved them all, really—even Glenorr. He glanced over at Glenorr and then at Sylvane. On each of their faces was an expression of determination. When Pohl was finished with his admonitions, Donnadorr sang a song to help them sleep.

The next morning, the fourth since leaving Agavia, the group of travelers left the entrance and moved, in single file, into a narrow tunnel that led them into the depths of the cave. Pohl had tied them together with a rope. Galavi led the way with Pohl immediately behind him. Donnadorr sang a marching song in a defiant voice and Auragole joined him. Then everyone joined in. They marched all that day, halting only once for a quick lunch. When they finally stopped for what was supposedly the night, they were exhausted. They ate their dinner, slept for what felt like only a few hours, and awoke cramped and cold. They hoisted their gear to their backs and followed Pohl without speaking.

Almost as soon as they resumed their march, something uncanny happened—the atmosphere began to change perceptibly. Donnadorr's skin felt prickly. The air was becoming heavier and with it their breathing sounded labored.

Odd, Donnadorr thought, and ominous.

The pace slowed. They were descending now and as they moved into the depths of the mountain, Donnadorr heard strange sounds about them. Faint rumblings, cracking noises, sometimes whispers that sounded like human sighs. Donnadorr reached down to feel the knife he carried in his boot—good, it was there—then kept his hand on his sword. Whatever was out there, he was prepared for it. He no longer felt like singing, nor did anyone else attempt it. He reached for Glenelle's hand behind him and she grasped it tightly.

Pohl offered no explanation. He stopped Galavi once or twice and they conferred in low voices. Then they continued on, steadily down and forward. They halted finally for the midday meal on a large rocky protrusion overhanging a vast, dark cavern. In the dim light of the torches, Donnadorr couldn't see the bottom, but Pohl told them that the bottom was indeed their destination.

Stars, Donnadorr thought with a shudder, it's like entering the bowels of the earth. No human belongs here.

No one spoke as they ate until Glenelle cried out, "What's happening? Why has the air around us changed so? And what are those terrible sounds? Are they the dead?"

How frail she seemed to Donnadorr, how fragile. Perhaps she was not enough recovered from her last spell. But what a strange question she had just asked. Did Ellie believe in the survival of the dead? She had never said so, though she loved to tell ghost stories. She had never indicated more than a tale-teller's interest in unseen things. How many facets there were to her character! How hard she was to know.

Pohl took Glenelle's hand. "The dead? No, no, indeed, not, my child. What you feel is fear, is anger, is hatred."

"From what. . .or. . .from whom?" Glenelle shivered.

Pohl's face looked grim. "From the Elemental Beings. The ones who live in dark places, the ones who serve the Nethergods."

"Elemental Beings! Nethergods! We don't believe in Nethergods—in any Gods!" Glenorr tried to sound scornful, but his voice echoed eerily all around them.

Chastisement was what Donnadorr felt, and a chill crept up his spine.

Pohl gave Glen a calculating look, then turned to his sister. "This realm—the dark depths of the earth—belongs to one group of anti-Gods."

"One group! Is there more than one group?" Donnadorr asked.

"There are two groups, Don," Sylvane spoke up. "Haven't you been listening to any of the tales of the Agavi?"

"I thought those tales had only to do with the Agavians," he said, almost aplogetically, "and not with the rest of the world."

"There is only one world, Don," Pohl said. "The one the Agavi call the Dark Breather, and whom we call the Nethergod or the Adversary Being, is the leader of one group of anti-Gods. The one the Agavi call the Light Eater, is leader of the other group. Throughout humankind's history, there have been many names for these two Beings. There was even a long period in our history when the two anti-Beings were thought of as one, which caused much misunderstanding. And, of course, centuries where the belief in any Gods, good or bad, faded from the consciousness of most of humanity."

"That's our time, isn't it, Pohl?" Sylvane said.

"Yes, that's our time."

"Well, if any Elemental shows himself," Donnadorr said, rising to his feet and unsheathing his sword, "I'll make short work of him, make short work of all of them."

"Your sword would be useless, my brash young friend. It takes other kinds of weapons."

"Tell me what they are," Donnadorr said, "and I'll use them." Perhaps it was bravura, but he meant it. Action was better than sitting and waiting for someone or something to attack. He looked over at Auragole. He too had pulled his sword half out of its sheath.

Suddenly Glenelle was on her knees, swaying from side to side. "I can't go on. I must go back. This place is too horrible. They want me. They want me!"

Glenorr knelt beside her and tried to calm her, but when he told her that they must go on for her sake, she screamed and struck out at him.

Donnadorr watched in disbelief. Glenelle had never lacked courage before. Was this the beginning of another spell?

Then Sylvane bent over her and tried to comfort her, but Glenelle tried to hit her also. She even tried to strike Auragole, who had assured her that he would protect her from anything seen or unseen.

For a moment they watched her helplessly. When she started pounding on the ground with her fists, Pohl walked over to her, pulled her head up by her hair, and struck her a hard-ringing blow across the face. Sylvane gasped. Glenelle sank back to the ground, whimpering.

Glenorr, his face red with rage, his hands knotted into hard fists, leapt at Pohl.

"Are you mad, Glen?" Auragole shouted, as Donnadorr and he grabbed Glenorr from behind. "Do you want to go over the edge?"

And take Pohl with you, Donnadorr thought.

Glenorr struggled furiously. It took all of their strength to hang on to him. He shouted, "Let me go," and then some obscenities. With effort, Auragole and Donnadorr grappled him to the ground. Finally he gave up the struggle and his body went limp. When they let go of him, Glenorr rolled over, sat up, and covered his face with his hands. Auragole and Donnadorr dropped to the ground next to him, both trembling with exhaustion. Donnadorr was furious at Glenorr. Didn't the man have any control?

Auragole looked more shocked than angry.

Pohl crouched down beside Glenorr. "I know you love your sister, Glen, and want to protect her and help her. But Glenelle was hysterical, dissolved in uncontrollable feelings. Pain or shock brings one out of them quickly. I would have doused her with cold water had we any to spare."

Pohl sat down next to Glenelle then, who was sobbing quietly, and put his arm around her trembling shoulders. "I'm sorry, Ellie. You melted into fear. You must take hold of yourself. The Nethergods and their cohorts are formidable foes. They find your weaknesses and work through them. You can do nothing to protect yourself if you lose yourself in fear. Tell yourself, 'courage, courage,' as we go through these deep hidden places. When we get through this cave, and back into the light, the worst will be over. Repeat the word *courage* over and over, but not mindlessly. Put all the force of your will behind it. Can we go on now?"

Glenelle took a deep breath and got up. She looked white and very pale.

"Do you think she can make it?" Auragole whispered to Donnadorr.

"We'll help her," Donnadorr told Auragole, and they put her between them and held her hands as they once again began the slow descent to their destination far below and out of sight. Galavi led, holding his torch high. Glenorr, his jaw tight, brought up the rear, pulling the placid donkey. The path was narrow, and filled with fallen stones. They stumbled again and again. It was good the rope was tied each to each. There were times when Donnadorr almost panicked, thinking he could not breathe, times he felt he must be under water and drowning. He would suddenly gasp for air and know that he had nearly been asleep. He found himself mouthing silently, over and over, the word *courage*.

chapter twenty-three

AT LAST, AFTER what seemed like hours, they reached the bottom. Pohl said that they had done "very well, very well indeed." He told them to make camp, that they would spend the night there. They ate silently, then bedded down for the night. Auragole was certain that he wouldn't be able to sleep. However, he closed his eyes to shut out the oppressive darkness.

The next thing he remembered was Pohl shaking his shoulder gently. It was morning. Somewhere on earth, it was morning. He struggled to his feet. If I've slept, Auragole thought, it has done nothing for me. He could feel every weary bone in his body, and not one bone wanted to go on. He rubbed his forehead, then looked at the others. How exhausted they all seemed. Glenelle, in particular, looked pallid, ghostly, too frail to take another step. How would she manage? And they were only at the beginning of their journey. Weeks of travel lay ahead of them. Had they made the right decision—leaving in the middle of winter? But if they had waited till the spring, there would be no Meekelorr, no Companions of the Way to guide them to Mattelmead. It would all have been up to him, and he inwardly shuddered at the thought of taking on that responsibility again.

In the dim light of a single torch, his friends looked like colorless shadows. Sylvane was chewing nervously on her lip. Donnadorr sat, pulling at his red beard and watching Glenelle with open concern. Glenorr was feeding the donkey. Glen had never said anything about his behavior the day before, but he did avoid looking at anyone. Auragole couldn't stay angry with him. His sister was all in all to him. That love Auragole thought he understood.

"We are about to begin the most difficult part of our journey," Pohl said as they ate their breakfast. "We are going through that tunnel." He pointed to a dark hole. "Because of the difficulties ahead, not only will your waists be tied each to each, but also your hands—one hand to the one ahead, one to the one behind. After we enter the tunnel—hear me well!—we must not stop, not until we reach its end. You must gather all your inner resolve and concentrate on one thing, and one thing only, going on. No matter what you see or hear, no matter what feelings rise up in you, you must say to yourself, 'I must go on! I must go on!' Is that clear?"

They all nodded. But Glenelle's face was chalk-white and Sylvane's lips a thin line. Glen looked grim, and Galavi thoughtful. Auragole smiled fleetingly at Donnadorr, who looked back at him with unseeing eyes. Only the donkey seemed unperturbed as it munched on its breakfast.

After they had repacked, Pohl tied the rope about their waists and wrists. Then they started across the cavern, Galavi leading, holding the torch; then came Pohl grasping Sylvane's hand behind him. After Sylvane came Auragole, then Glenelle, Donnadorr, and finally, Glenorr, leading the docile donkey.

The tunnel they entered was narrow and low. They stooped uncomfortably. The ground they walked over was wet and slimy. The walls oozed a green, foul-smelling substance. Again they heard strange sounds—rumblings and sometimes a wailing that was all too human.

It is as if the earth herself is weeping and forlorn, Auragole thought uneasily.

Without warning, something spun about Auragole's head. There was no wind, no stirring at all of the air, not a hair on his head moved. But something terrible, albeit unseen, was spinning about him, and he was suddenly gripped by a great fear. The thing, whatever it was, flew at him, rained blows down on him. He felt his body attacked as if by knives of ice. He gasped and groaned. He could hear the others moaning and sighing. Someone screamed. Auragole wanted to run, wanted to get away from the horrible terror. He pulled at his bonds, but he was tied to Glenelle and Sylvane, and they too were pulling. They were all trying to get away from it, and from each other, but with every effort the rope only tightened. It happened suddenly. Auragole was unable to move. Where his bones had been, there was only liquid.

Dimly he heard a voice calling from miles away. No, it was from inside his watery head. "You must go on! You must go on!" Yes, yes, I must go on, he told himself. Suddenly there were feet beneath him. He directed his will toward them, poured thought into them as if the thought were light and light the source of movement. I must go on. And miraculously, his feet began to move. He concentrated on each step. He had never realized how difficult walking was. It seemed impossible that a human being should walk. After what must have been hours, the fear began to subside. Relief ran through him like a rapid river. He squeezed Sylvane's hand in front of him and Glenelle's hand behind.

Then dawning slowly, like a hot summer sun over the river of his relief, came anger. Really, what right had Pohl to take them through such a place? How dare he subject them, particularly poor Ellie, to the terrors of the Netherforces? Why did they have to come through these tunnels instead of waiting until spring and going through the Northern Valley? Because of Glen! Glen who insisted they not wait. Glen who was willing to risk all of them for the sake of his sister's health. And because of Meekelorr! If it was necessary for Meekelorr and his soldiers to go off in the dead of winter to play their little war games, what right did he have to insist they also go? And Pohl, what kind of a doctor was he? Why didn't he try to heal Ellie in Agavia or up at the school? His blood burned and his heart beat faster. And Sylvane! Auragole felt furious at Sylvane for always protecting Ellie, for constantly excusing Glen's bad behavior, for her sacrificial ways—as if she had no worth of her own. And Galavi! How irritating he was. . .no, really exasperating with his aloof manner, with his lofty and often archaic speech. Why was he never perturbed? Auragole devised a plan to kill Galavi. But first he would kill Donnadorr. How dare Don, who owed Auragole his life, interfere with Auragole's desire, Auragole's right, to have Ellie for himself. Yes, he would kill Donnadorr. He would get his hands loose and kill Donnadorr. Then he would kill them all, all these unworthy companions. He felt rage at the ropes that tied him to these hateful people. He opened his mouth and screamed at them. Then he realized that they were all screaming, "Kill! Kill!" Auragole pulled at his bonds. He would have bitten through the ropes with his teeth if others had not been pulling so hard in different directions. He saw spots of red and black all around his head. Then suddenly he was blind. He could see nothing!

He must have stopped moving, because again he heard a voice saying, "Go on! Go on!" And he remembered that Pohl had warned them not to stop. So once again Auragole poured all his will into his legs and moved on. Then the hate was gone as swiftly as it had come, but he was sweating and panting. He could hear the others gasping for breath.

Why had he come on this journey? Why hadn't he stayed in Agavia? It was so good there. What did he owe these others? Perhaps he should have taken the offer of a place in the school instead of coming on this ridiculous trip. And what if they became lost in these tunnels? Or, say they did get out, but Meekelorr never came back for them? Or what if Pohl and Galavi just abandoned them? His stomach began to knot up. What if that was really Pohl's plan, to lose them in the caves? How did any of them know that there really was a land called Mattelmead? What if everyone had been lying to them? The uncertainty crept into his chest and spread throughout his limbs. And what if there were no king there, no great leader who would save humanity? What if it were all a hoax, a lie? What use was there in going on? Why had he given up Agavia for a lie?

Auragole had stopped walking. They had all stopped walking. His body was rock. It was as heavy as the earth. Doubt paralyzed him. What was the point of going on if you didn't know what was story or what was real? He would stand there until he knew. But then a voice made his decision for him. "Go on," it said, "you must go on!" He concentrated with all his might, pouring his will into his marble legs. Finally he stepped forward, pushing Sylvane and pulling Glenelle. Little by little, the line began to move again.

How Auragole wished that Pohl would stop and let them rest. Ellie's hand was ice in his. Perhaps he could pour some of his own warmth into her. It was good to hold her hand. Was there anyone as lovely as she, as endearing, as frail, as in need of help as Ellie? And it would be he who would give it to her. He would take care of her, see her to Mattelmead despite Donnadorr's interference, despite Glenorr's possessiveness. He felt Ellie's hand grow warmer in his own. In his mind he listed all the things that he would do for her to make her happy. He would take her to the finest doctors in Mattelmead. Then with some of the jewels given him by the Agavi, he would build her a palace filled with beautiful things, filled with servants to care for her—just as in the stories he had learned at his mother's knee. He would sing to her, make love to her. She would be happy with him, be completely in love with him. His love alone would cure her. It became harder to breathe. He was gulping in air, then letting it go again in short gasps. He longed to hold Ellie in his arms, to touch her face, to kiss her eyes. He longed to whisper his feelings to her under the stars far away from the others. No, he had to have her now! At all costs he had to have her. His manhood rose up in fire. He felt the flames all around him, burning through his blood, pounding in his head, coursing through his limbs. All he could see everywhere was the conflagration of his own blazing desire.

"Go on!" the voice commanded, and he realized that he had stopped moving. He forced his legs of fire to move. He had to go on. As soon as they got out of that place he would tell Ellie, no, he would take Ellie. They moved forward for a long time before the flame died down and his resolve melted with shame into air.

The tunnel was wider and higher now. How long had that been so? The walls extruded slime, and the stench was still there, but it no longer bothered him. They still walked on the wet, slippery ground, but he ignored it and concentrated on moving forward. Then he wondered why he should go forward. They had to get through these tunnels was the answer. But why? Because they had to get to Mattelmead, he told himself. Wondrous things were happening there. But it all seemed far away, so very far away. Ellie needed the help of the Mattelmead doctors. But the truth was, he was bored with Ellie's spells. Of what importance in the larger scheme of things were Ellie's spells? He thought about Agavia. Would it be good to be back there? Yes. No. Yes. Frankly, it didn't make any difference where he was—here, there, anywhere. He wondered if the Gods of the Agavians cared about Ellie, or Pohl, or Ormahn. Who cares if there are Gods? He yawned. Who cares? Who cares about anything? He thought about his farm, about his life there. Would it be good to get back home? It didn't make any difference. It took too much thought to ponder places or people, even himself. People were all the same. Would they get out of these caves or get through the Westernlands to Mattelmead? He wasn't going to think about that. It wasn't very interesting. To think about whether the world finally achieved peace wasn't interesting either. That was his father's dream, not his. Anyway, peace or war, it was all the same, all boring. He turned his thoughts to himself. He felt cold, but so what? His wrists ached, but so did his back. He didn't care, didn't care about his fellow travelers— none of them was interesting, none of them mattered. Why was he moving? Auragole stopped. They all stopped. The thought of putting effort into another step was boring.

"Go on! Go on!" the voice begged, but so what? He was not interested in its entreaties. The sound of the voice bored him. He thought about sitting, but couldn't decide if that was less boring than standing.

Suddenly Auragole felt a tremendous jerk and he was pulled forward. He began to run because he found himself running, and that was no more boring than standing still or sitting down. How long they ran he didn't know, didn't care.

Finally, they tumbled out of the tunnel and at once the atmosphere changed, the air became lighter. Galavi held his torch high and the party moved into a large cavern, stumbling up against one another as they came to a halt. As soon as they had exited the tunnel everything changed. Auragole felt new, reborn. He shouted just for the pleasure of hearing his voice. He felt shame too. But never mind. His friends were laughing and talking loudly and exuberantly. They began to dance around one another, slapping one another on the back and hugging. In a few moments they were all tangled up in a heap on the ground because of the ropes. They were nearly hysterical with relief.

Donnadorr burst into song and the others joined in—all except Glenelle. Auragole's own voice faltered for a moment when he saw her face. It was as white as the snow they had left behind them when they entered the caves.

Galavi untied them, and Pohl told them to rest. They had been, to Auragole's astonishment, less than an hour in the tunnel.

WHILE THE OTHERS rested, Pohl was sitting near the torch he had wedged between two rocks, sewing the strap on his backpack. He looked up to see Auragole approach him.

"What was that place?" Auragole asked, squatting down next to him.

"It's called the Cave of Terrors."

"An apt name. Is it a trap set there by the Netherforces?"

"You could say that," Pohl said, watching Auragole curiously. "But if you think you were battling some alien force, you are mistaken."

"What then?" Auragole's fingertips brushed his temples and then shoved the hair away from his face.

"Each of you confronted what you carry inside you. What was inner became outer. That is the terror of the cave. That is its so-called secret. It was all your own dross that came to meet you. The Netherforces only made it possible."

Auragole shuddered. Then his face lit up. "But we came through. None of us failed. They didn't trap us."

"You endured, Auragole. You did not overcome. Overcoming does not happen so easily. It takes many trials."

"In these caves?"

"No, my child, not in these caves." Pohl chuckled, then asked Auragole, "What was your most dangerous encounter in the Cave of Terrors?"

Auragole sat down on the ground, arms hugging his knees, and stared at his boots. "I think. . .I think it was hate," he said finally. "I think it was hate." His voice dropped to a whisper, he was obviously appalled by the horror of what he was saying. "Because I wanted to kill!"

"As terrible as it is to know you are capable of such an act," Pohl said, "there was an encounter that was more dangerous for you than hate and the desire to kill—far more dangerous."

"What?" Auragole looked genuinely puzzled. "What can be more terrible than the desire to kill another?"

"The last, my young friend, indifference, boredom. That was the worst."

"Truly? That can't be so. It seemed rather mild compared to the other. . .to the other. . .terrors."

"But look carefully, Auragole. All the others you were able to confront, to endure, to rise above, if only long enough to move your legs. The last, indifference and boredom, you gave into. You didn't rise above them. Isn't that so?"

Auragole was obviously shocked. "But that seemed the least bothersome, the easiest to deal with."

"Did it?"

"But it wasn't."

"No."

Then Auragole noticed Pohl's hands. "Your wrists are rubbed raw, and your hands are bleeding. Is that from pulling us out of our indifference?"

Pohl looked at his hands in mild surprise. "Yes, I suppose it must be. Yes, yes, indeed, it must be. I grabbed the rope and yanked on it as hard as I could and with the help of Galavi's amazing Agavian strength, we were able to pull you out. But look at your own hands and at the hands and wrists of your companions."

To Auragole's surprise, his hands and wrists were rubbed raw.

Pohl searched in his knapsack and pulled out some ointment, which he began to rub into his hands and wrists, then handed the jar to Auragole, which Auragole took. He mechanically began applying the ointment.

Pohl caught the worried look in Auragole's eyes. "My young friend, it's always the subtle emotions that can bring us down. The larger ones announce themselves loudly and we know we must respond. The subtle ones can creep up on us and overwhelm us before we take notice of them."

AFTER THEIR REST, the travelers ate lunch, then sang song after song, accompanied by Donnadorr and Auragole on their Agavian harps. Though there was little light except from the torches, after the ordeal in the Cave of Terrors, Auragole felt as if he and his friends were in full sunshine. Only Glenelle did not sing. She smiled occasionally at one of Donnadorr's outrageous songs, but it was only an echo of a smile.

Finally, the singing stopped, and Pohl told them that though it was barely noon on the outside, they should sleep now as if it were night. Time, he said, mattered little inside these dark mountains. They would sleep eight hours and then continue on their way. The worst was behind them.

Auragole walked over to Glenelle then. "What's the matter, Ellie?" he asked looking down at her. "Why do you look so troubled?"

"I shan't get out of these caves, Aurie. I know it." In the shadowy light her blue eyes looked black and frightened.

His heart ached. "Of course you'll get out of here, Ellie." Auragole squatted next to her. "We all shall. The Cave of Terrors was the worst that we have to endure—Pohl just told me so. And see, we've all survived."

"They want me," she said, with a shudder. "They want me, Auragole."

"Who, Ellie?"

"The Netherforces."

"But we won't let them come near you. We'll protect you. I'll protect you. Ellie, don't worry so. Before we go to sleep, we'll tie our wrists together. They won't be able to take you without taking me. And they won't take me without a fight."

Glenelle didn't answer. She looked at him with large, sad eyes.

"I'll stay awake, Ellie. I'll watch over you, I promise." Auragole saw Donnadorr just beyond them. Had he heard him?

"Dear sweet Aurie," Glenelle said, with a hint of her old smile.

And his bones felt like liquid once again.

As they settled down to sleep, Auragole tied his wrist to hers and vowed once again that he would stay awake and keep a close watch on her. She squeezed his hand and closed her eyes. In a few minutes she was asleep and breathing deeply.

chapter twenty-four

SOMEONE WAS CALLING to him.

"Wake up, Don." It was Pohl.

"Is it time?" he asked, sleepily.

"It is time."

Donnadorr rolled over and began to pull on his boots. Suddenly, he saw Auragole in front of him, a rope dangling from his wrist.

"Where's Ellie?" Auragole's voice nearly choked on the words.

"What has happened?" Pohl asked.

Auragole wordlessly held up his wrist and showed him the rope hanging there.

"He was tied to Ellie," Donnadorr said. He could hardly keep the alarm from his voice.

The others gathered around the three men. Then when they heard that Glenelle was gone, torches were lit and the entire cavern searched.

"Ellie, Ellie," Glenorr called frantically, but to no avail.

It soon became clear that Glenelle was nowhere in the cavern.

"How did you let her get away, lad? How could you not stay awake when you promised her?" Donnadorr could not stop his words. "How could you be so careless? How could you fail her so?"

Auragole staggered away from Donnadorr as if Donnadorr had just hit him.

"Wait, Aurie. Wait," Donnadorr called after him, with sudden remorse.

"Over here," Galavi called to them. He was standing before the exit of the Cave of Terrors. "She's returned to the cave." He pointed to the blue cloak given to Glenelle by the Agavians that now lay crumpled and deserted at the mouth of that terrible tunnel.

"Oh, no!" Glenorr moaned.

They all froze as the horror hit them.

"I'm going in after her," Auragole said, and started toward the entrance.

A hand reached out and grabbed Auragole by the arm and jerked him to a halt. "Hold on, Auragole," Pohl said. "No one goes after Ellie until we first have spoken together."

"There's no time!"

"Wait!"

"You don't understand." Auragole tried to shake himself free. "It's my fault! I promised to stay awake, to watch over her."

"I'll kill you," Glenorr yelled, and went for Auragole.

Donnadorr grabbed Glen from behind.

"Quiet!" Pohl thundered.

And Glen went limp in Don's arms.

Pohl turned back to Auragole. "You may indeed be at fault, Auragole. But the decisions made now and the action taken now must be the right ones. Thought as well as feeling must play its role."

Leaving Glenorr red-faced but silent, Donnadorr walked up to Auragole and put his arm around his tense shoulders. "Let's listen to Pohl. He'll figure something out."

They sat in front of Pohl, who asked Auragole to repeat his conversation with Glenelle before they had gone to sleep. Auragole, with ragged breath, repeated what was said and what he had promised. At that point Glenorr started to bellow angrily again at Auragole until Pohl told Glen once more, in no uncertain terms, to be silent.

"I doubt that she has passed out of the Cave of Terrors. I don't think she could on her own. If she's still in there, then we'll find her," Pohl said. "More than likely she will need to be carried out of the cave. Therefore, three of us must go and fetch her. Two to carry Glenelle and one to bear the torch."

"I'll go." Auragole stood up.

"No." Pohl dismissed him with a wave of his hand. "It must be myself, Galavi, and Glenorr."

They were all on their feet now.

"The fault is mine! I have to go!" Auragole insisted, his voice rising. "Let Galavi stay. I must go!"

"There's no time to argue, Auragole. You will remain here. Come," he said to Galavi and Glenorr.

Auragole seized Pohl by the shoulder and Donnadorr grabbed Auragole.

"Auragole, abide now," Donnadorr said. "Leave this part to Pohl."

But Auragole pulled away from Donnadorr. "I have to go," he yelled.

Pohl turned on him and raised his torch so his face could be seen clearly. "Don't test your will against mine, Auragole." Pohl's expression looked as hard as carved granite. They stood glaring at each other for a few tense moments.

Then Auragole gave way.

"Pack up, so that we can continue our journey as soon as we

return with Glenelle." With that, Pohl handed the torch to Galavi, tied Glenorr between them, and moved at a trot into the tunnel.

Auragole stood watching them go, his face filled with fury.

Donnadorr spoke to him. "Lad, we are all to blame. Let's do now what is needed. We must prepare to leave."

Auragole worked in what Don could only describe as a smoldering silence. The three repacked the donkey and then the backpacks. When they finally sat down to wait, Donnadorr noticed Sylvane. She had not uttered a word throughout all that had happened. Now she was sitting opposite the Cave of Terrors. No sound came from her, but tears were streaming down her face. Donnadorr went over to her, took her hand, and sat down next to her, humming half under his breath, his eyes fixed on the entrance to the cave. And Auragole joined them.

It seemed hours before the rescuers returned. When they did, they burst through the entrance with loud shouts. Auragole, Sylvane, and Donnadorr rose quickly to their feet and ran to meet them. Galavi and Glenorr were carrying Glenelle, who was unconscious. Pohl held high the torch. A rope was wound around all four of them. Donnadorr and Auragole quickly untied them and Glenelle was placed on her abandoned cloak on the ground. Pohl and Glenorr sat down breathing wearily. Only Galavi looked untouched by a second encounter with the Cave of Terrors.

"Wrap her in her cloak," Pohl told Sylvane and Donnadorr. He turned to Auragole. "She got as far as Doubt. We found her unconscious."

They all stared at Glenelle, stricken. Her face was bruised and her clothes torn and streaked with slime. But worst of all, her breathing was quick and shallow.

"Listen to me, all of you!" Pohl's voice was incisive. "I have no medicines with me that can cure her. She's close to death. There's one small hope, however. If we can get her into the light, I may be able to help her."

Sylvane wept audibly and Glenorr moaned, "No, no!"

"It's still night. We might reach the end of this first cave before the end of the day tomorrow. We'll be in a ravine, however. Still, if the light is good. . ." He stopped. "It will mean a sixteen- to seventeen-hour march, carrying Glenelle the entire way. We have nothing with which to make a stretcher, nor do we have the time. Glenelle cannot support herself on the donkey over the narrow paths. We therefore must take turns carrying her, two by two." He didn't wait for a response. "Put on your packs. Auragole, you and Don will carry her first."

In a moment they were striding across the cavern into a tunnel that Galavi chose out of several. They walked rapidly. Donnadorr thought that if he had been leader, he would have made everyone run. It would have been foolish, no doubt, but still he would have done it. Glenelle was near death. She had foreseen the danger to herself, and out of politeness to a rival, he, Donnadorr, had done nothing to reassure her, to help her. He shifted her weight a bit, gritted his teeth, and went on. After an hour or so, Pohl made them halt for a five-minute rest. He said he and Sylvane would carry Glenelle the next shift. Auragole argued that he would take Sylvane's place, that Sylvane was not strong enough.

"You're making this your personal affair," Pohl said, his tone brusque. "You'll have a turn again soon enough."

With that he picked up Glenelle under her arms. Sylvane took her legs. It amazed Donnadorr that tiny Sylvane could call on a reservoir of strength when she needed it. Galavi led the way with his torch, choosing tunnel after tunnel in the many that presented themselves. They changed carriers often. Donnadorr couldn't imagine how Galavi knew which was the right one and anxiously wondered now and again if he might not be lost, and leading them deeper and deeper into the mountain.

Many hours later they reached a large cavern. They stopped to rest. Pohl carefully wiped Glenelle's feverish face with water.

He turned to Donnadorr, his expression one of obvious distress. "Her breathing is so shallow, I can barely hear it. We must hurry. Pick her up," he commanded Donnadorr and Auragole. He looked harshly at Auragole then. "You want to feel pain, boy? You'll feel it now. We're going straight up that wall." He pointed to the far side of the cavern. Donnadorr couldn't see the path that he knew must be there. Pohl tied them all together and, taking up his torch, led the way.

The path upward was narrow and perilous and they watched carefully for loose rocks and stones. They stumbled but no one fell, such was their determination to reach the top. The pain was near unbearable. They had been marching too many hours to count. Donnadorr's legs seemed in danger of giving out. His back ached and his arms felt on fire. When they had reached a wide spot in the path, Pohl stopped them. "I'll take your place," he said to Donnadorr. All he said to Auragole was, "Let's go," and taking Glenelle's legs he climbed upward.

Their climb ended abruptly. Donnadorr hadn't seen it coming, and he stumbled as the ground underneath them leveled out, and he nearly dropped the torch.

"Hurry!" Pohl shouted, running toward a spot of light. They all ran then, shouting encouragement to Auragole and Pohl. Then they were out. Donnadorr felt blinded by the sudden bright daylight.

"Up this way," Pohl called back to Auragole.

"I can't see," Auragole shouted, in alarm.

Donnadorr rushed to take Auragole's place and Auragole didn't argue.

"Squint and look at your feet," Pohl instructed Donnadorr. "We must get Glenelle to higher ground."

In a moment he and Pohl were climbing out of the ravine and up a goat path on the side of the mountain. Auragole was just behind them, his hand on the small of Donnadorr's back with as much a sense of urgency as of support. The others climbed behind Auragole. In only moments, they arrived at a small plateau about twenty feet above the ravine outside the cave. They were in dazzling sunlight.

"Let's lay her down," Pohl told Donnadorr. Then Pohl bent over her, as she lay limp and pale on her blue cloak in the snow. His ear was near her mouth. When Pohl lifted his head Donnadorr could see the anguish there. She was dead; Donnadorr was sure of it. He could feel the tightening in his throat, the stinging behind his eyes. He willed the tears away.

"All of you go back down to the ravine," Pohl ordered.

"Wait a minute," Glenorr began to argue.

"Go!" Pohl barked.

Immediately, they turned around and retraced their steps down the side of the mountain to the entrance of the cave. They stood in the painful light and squinted up at the tall figure of Pohl, a hundred feet above them. Donnadorr could not see Glenelle lying on the ground, but he could see Pohl. He was facing the sun, standing motionless, legs wide apart. His right hand held Glenelle's, his left arm was stretched out horizontally from his side, palm up.

Donnadorr found himself praying. Oh, dear Gods, he prayed, save Ellie, send her strength and peace and courage. Over and over he said it. He knew that Sylvane was praying, as was Galavi, his words barely audible, as he stood apart from the others. Don glanced over at Auragole, whose face was as white as the snow. His lips were tight. His eyes fastened unblinkingly on Pohl. And Glenorr was sitting up against a rock, his fists clenched, his eyes turned downward. Occasionally he raised them to stare up at Pohl.

Precious minutes passed. Still Pohl stood there motionless.

Glenorr rose to his feet and walked over to Donnadorr. "He's doing nothing." Glenorr's bitter voice cut through Don's prayers. "I'm going up there."

Auragole caught his arm. "Don't interfere. Pohl is very wise. If there's anything to be done, he'll do it."

"But I should be with her at the end." Glenorr's voice broke and his shoulders shook.

Donnadorr put his arm around him and they stood like that, Glenorr weeping and Donnadorr praying.

"Look!" Auragole called to the others moments later. "He's kneeling down."

Pohl had dropped to his knees and was partly out of view. Abruptly he stood. "Glen! Aurie! Come up! Sylvane, Don! Gather wood. We must have a fire."

"She's alive?" Donnadorr shouted, afraid to believe.

"She's alive but very weak. Come, come, you two," he called to Glenorr and Auragole. "Let's get her down to the cave entrance where she'll be protected from the wind."

Glenorr and Auragole hugged each other as they tripped and stumbled up the path to Pohl. They carefully lifted Glenelle and carried her down to the cave entrance. She was pale, but her breathing had returned to normal. Donnadorr soon had the fire going, and Sylvane put the dried eldenmyrr plants on to brew. When the tea was ready, Pohl spooned a little into Glenelle's mouth. She was not yet fully conscious, but she swallowed the health-filled liquid.

The fatigue of that sixteen-hour march finally took its toll, but no one wanted to go too deeply into the cave they had just left. They decided to sleep just inside it, to sleep where the sky was visible. To Don, the stars in all their remoteness were like welcome friends whom he had not seen for years.

First Sylvane dropped off to sleep, and then Glenorr. Donnadorr tried to sleep. He felt drowsy but happy looking out into the star-shine. He was so relieved that Glenelle was alive that he was loath to leave his thoughts. Was it love he felt for Ellie? He wasn't sure. What was love, anyhow? Donnadorr had taken his pleasure with many a lady he had met on the road, but had never called it love—well, once, and she had died. He turned his thoughts away from that.

Donnadorr watched Pohl from under his blanket. Pohl sat near the slumbering Glenelle, wiping her forehead and feeding her an occasional spoonful of eldenmyrr tea. Then suddenly Auragole was standing in front of Pohl.

"YES, AURAGOLE," POHL looked up at the silent figure hovering over him, "let us speak." He rose and moved out of the cave toward a group of rocks in the shadows not far from the cave entrance.

"Sit," he told Auragole, as he himself sat down.

But Auragole hovered over him like a bird of prey. "Why did you forbid me to come with you after Glenelle?"

"You think I refused you as a punishment?"

"Yes."

"No. You punish yourself. It is enough."

Auragole sat down.

"When you saw how fearful Glenelle was, you should have come to me or to the group. What was necessary at that moment was that help be given Glenelle, not that it be you who gave it. You were exhausted by the trials in the Cave of Terrors. There is no way that you could have stayed awake to keep watch over her. Had you told me of her fears, Galavi and I would have taken turns guarding her. We were the least affected by the cave. I too am to blame. I should have anticipated Ellie's fears. I am, after all, a doctor. I should have noticed that the cave still pulled on Ellie. The blame will live with me, also, Auragole, as a scar and a warning."

"You saved Ellie's life."

"No, not I." He shook his head. "Auragole?"

"Yes?" Auragole's voice was still strained.

"You could not have endured the Cave of Terrors so soon again. That is why I could not allow you to come."

"But Galavi could and Glenorr could?" Auragole's tone refused the explanation.

306

Pohl sighed. How hard it was to explain. "Galavi could because he is Agavian."

"And what about Glenorr?" Auragole bit hard on the name.

"Glenorr, ah well. Glenorr is. . .shall we say. . .asleep. Yes, yes, indeed, Glenorr is asleep." Pohl watched the emotions play across Auragole's face.

"What do you mean?"

"Glen lives mostly in his upper consciousness. Much goes on below that consciousness, yes, yes, indeed, but he is cut off from it. Once in a while something bubbles up from below and one sees a. . .shall we say, a different Glenorr. Not in control, no, no, indeed, hardly in control. But ordinarily much of his being is asleep."

"Is that bad?" Pohl could hear the puzzlement in Auragole's voice.

"Well, you watch and decide, son. There are miracles all around and Glenorr sees little of them. A bit like a blind man. You watch."

"My father said there were no such things as miracles."

"Ah, yes, your father. Anger too can create blindness."

Can one pass on one's anger to one's children? Hate, yes, oh, yes, yes, indeed, hate. But anger? Pohl looked at the youth who sat beside him. Or one's blindness? Ah, well, only time will tell.

"Go to sleep, son. You will need your strength in the morning."

N

chapter twenty-five

TO DONNADORR'S RELIEF, Glenelle opened her eyes briefly the next morning. Pohl fed her a broth he had made with his healing herbs. And then she slept. Everyone had sore limbs and backs from the hard march, so Pohl rubbed them all with an ointment. They rested and slept most of the day, content in the euphoria one feels after a crisis.

As evening approached, they moved once again inside the cave to protect themselves from the wind that raced now and then through the ravine. Though he must have known that it would make them late for their rendezvous with Meekelorr and the Companions of the Way, Pohl insisted they remain in the cave and ravine until Glenelle's strength returned—at the least, five days.

"Will Meekelorr wait?" Sylvane asked.

"He will wait," Pohl said.

Slowly Glenelle's strength returned. She never mentioned her experiences in the Cave of Terrors, nor why she had been drawn back into it. And no one questioned her. She was as thin as a fallen leaf and as fragile. Her eyes looked large and haunted in her pretty face, as if she had seen a horror she could not describe. She spoke only a little when one or the other addressed her. Donnadorr tried to tell her jokes and little stories to cheer her up, and she smiled sadly at him when he did. He looked at his companions, knowing that each one ached for Glenelle. Each would have given up a limb for her if it would have made the difference. He hoped that their loving concern might help mend her.

What is more difficult, Donnadorr wondered, than wanting to help another and not knowing how? Again Aiku's words came to mind. *"We cannot take another's pain upon ourselves or spare him his road of terror. But we can walk with him as long as he will allow it."* He vowed to try.

On their second day in the ravine, Auragole and Donnadorr caught a mountain goat. Auragole tracked it and Donnadorr brought it down with a single arrow. The fresh meat was a welcome addition to their diet during the respite in the ravine.

That afternoon, Pohl was sitting on a rock near the fire repairing a tear in his cloak. Sylvane was next to him sewing several rips in Glenelle's blue cloak. Galavi was whittling, his back up against the mountain rock, his bare feet in the light, immune, it seemed, to the cold. Auragole was lying near the fire dipping in and out of sleep. Donnadorr had just awoken from a nap after the morning's hunt and was strumming his harp across the fire from Pohl and Sylvane and a few feet from Auragole. Glenelle was sleeping inside the cave.

Pale clouds that would soon become gray and pink were drifting by. The sun was winter white, pure and perfect. Shadows, with long strides, were leaping across the mountains, but a stream of light like a comet's tail dove through the ravine and settled there. Donnadorr, strumming his Agavian harp, was trying to turn the scene into melody.

Glenorr, who had been gathering rocks in the mountains, climbed down the slope behind them, empty-handed. He walked up to the fire and squatted down in front of Pohl, a troubled expression on his face. Pohl looked up expectantly.

"I've walked around and around that place and I can't figure it out."

Donnadorr stopped playing and listened.

"What place is that, young Glen?"

"The place on the mountain where you cured Glenelle. I see nothing special about it." Glenorr turned to look up at that high ground, still lit by the sun.

Donnadorr saw Auragole sit up to listen to Glenorr and Pohl.

"There is nothing special about it," Pohl said, and continued to work on his cloak.

"How was it done, then? I don't understand it."

"The land was high up, you see, and still bathed in the light. So I used the sun's forces and the forces of those stars that move around it—the ones you can't see in the daylight."

"But that's impossible," Glenorr said. "What forces? A man cannot take hold of the sun's forces or the stars' forces and use them."

"Can't he?" Pohl said. "I thought he could. Then how was it done?"

"Pohl, don't play word games with me. I'm a scientist. . . going to be a scientist. What you say is impossible. There has to be another explanation."

"Glen!" Sylvane chided. "Mind your manners. Pohl saved your sister's life. Isn't that enough? Don't interrogate him so rudely."

Pohl chuckled. "It's all right, Sylvie. Glen is perturbed."

Here, once again, was the familiar Glenorr, Don thought. In Agavia, Glenorr had been content not to question and not to argue, but rather to observe, accept, even enjoy the different ways of the Agavians.

"How did you do it?" Glenorr's question was politer this time.

"There are cosmic healing forces in the sun and in those stars wandering close to it. With the help of the Gods, I used them."

"Without medicines or instruments? It's not possible," Glenorr insisted.

"Glen!" Sylvie was vexed again, but he paid no attention to her.

"It's a power the human being once had, though it wasn't so conscious in the past, no, no, indeed not. It was for them a natural power, one could say. We lost that power for this power," and Pohl tapped the side of his head. "More and more individuals will reacquire that older power in the future but keep also the thinking that you so rightly value."

Glenorr stood there glaring at Pohl. "How can you know that?"

"How was your sister healed then, Glenorr?" Pohl rose and put on his repaired cloak.

"I don't know. The fresh air. Perhaps she simply healed herself, as so often happens. But this much I know, a man cannot take hold of forces from the sun. Why should they heal anyway?"

"Oh, Glen, you are so pigheaded!" Sylvane said.

"Good then," Pohl said, "your sister cured herself. She's alive and for that we are all grateful, agreed?"

"Agreed," Glenorr said, a bit angrily. He kicked at the fire and walked away. He found a patch of sun several yards away, sat down, drew out his notebook, and began to write in his tiny hand. Soon he was completely absorbed and his face took on that quiet and concentrated look that had become so familiar to Donnadorr.

Auragole picked up his harp and began strumming it. Donnadorr responded with an answering melody. Soon the two of them were playing and singing the songs they had learned in the Valley of the Agavi. In the pleasure of the songs, Donnadorr quickly put aside the conversation that had just taken place. Life, he concluded, was a matter of doing what was there in front of you. Glenelle was recovering, that was the important thing. How it had come about was less important. He would leave speculation to the wind.

THE NEXT MORNING, their third in the ravine, the sun, only a pale winter glimmer, rose over the mountaintops. An early morning mist lay as heavy as a cold, wet cloak on the floor of the ravine. After a warm breakfast cooked over a fire within the cave, it was decided that some should go searching on the nearby slopes for firewood. By midmorning the mist had blown away, so Sylvane and Auragole set off in one direction, Donnadorr and Pohl in another. Galavi and Glenorr were left to tend Glenelle.

Donnadorr and Pohl marched up an easy incline. The snow cover was light and they quickly found the branches and twigs they were looking for, not so soaked through that they would not burn. They had tied the firewood with rope and net and were about to return to the campsite when suddenly Donnadorr spoke.

"Pohl, may I speak with you?" He stopped Pohl with a touch of his hand.

"My young friend, how can I help you?" Pohl asked, leading the way to a large fallen tree.

Donnadorr dusted off the snow, and the two of them sat down. Don stared at his hands. Pohl found it curious that Donnadorr, the loquacious one, was suddenly tongue-tied. He waited.

"This is hard for me to put into speech, Pohl, though that may come as a bit of a surprise to you. I am, as you know," he said immodestly but truthfully, "a good talker. Indeed it is words that have saved me from many a tight spot. But this is from so deep a place I hardly know how to give it voice."

"Indeed?"

"Do you remember that once I spoke to you about a man whom I had traveled with in my early years?"

"Aiku."

"You do remember."

Pohl saw relief light up Donnadorr's red-bearded face, and found that most interesting. So he said, "Oh, yes. I was acquainted with him."

"You were? Ah, Pohl, this is confirmation, indeed. I knew it. Somehow, I knew it." The young man began to talk faster. "This will sound crazy. . .but I think. . .I *feel* Aiku is alive somewhere. I know the evidence is against it—his disappearing like a stone in deep water—but there it is."

"I see."

"You know it's possible, don't you? Surely, you see that it's possible?"

"It is possible." Pohl's words came out slowly.

Donnadorr's mood suddenly shifted; it became angry. He leapt to his feet and walked about kicking at snow tufts. Then he faced Pohl, hands on his hips, and demanded, "How is it possible? If he is alive, why did he desert me?"

"That's the child in you speaking, Don. It's the child who feels deserted."

"*Was* deserted. I know, I know," Donnadorr's tone softened. "It's a shame in me, this anger. At first I believed he was dead, had been killed. When the weeks dragged on and he didn't return, I knew it was time to go, to leave our meeting place. Still I waited. When it became dangerous to remain, I left with great reluctance. But as I traveled, I began to have this feeling that he was not dead. Eventually I believed it with all my powers of belief. Then I began to worry that it was *I* who had deserted *him*, that I should have stayed longer where he had left me."

"You stayed as long as you could."

"I know. But maybe one more day. . .maybe that would have been the day he returned."

"And maybe not."

"I started to search for him, knowing that he was alive, depending on that feeling, that belief, thinking he was held prisoner somewhere. So as I journeyed I sang, wherever I could, for whoever would listen. Just for the trees if there was no one about. I was hoping that he would hear me and find me."

Donnadorr sat down again and looked thoughtfully at Pohl.

"That feeling is still in me—this knowing. Not finding him in the east made me wonder if he had answered the call to go west, to go to Mattelmead." His large blue eyes fastened on Pohl's. "Do you think it is only the child in me that wants Aiku to be alive, Pohl, or is there some hidden wisdom to this feeling, this knowing?"

Pohl picked up a stick and absentmindedly drew in the snow. Above, in the bare branches, winter birds twittered, then flew away. Others took their places. The sun, cleansed of the fog, drifted through the branches and finally slipped behind a jagged peak. How to answer Don's need? Pohl straightened up.

"Only you can say whether your feelings, or shall we call them your intuitions, have more the quality of truth or the quality of wish. You were heart-parented by Aiku—so the Agavians would say. He gave you the great free gift of his love. But because of it you have also suffered a great loss. If we have loved and were loved in return, the one who has crossed the threshold of death can stay close to us, can follow our life's progress." Pohl resumed his drawing in the snow. "The rumors came back to us that he was indeed dead. But as no one had actually seen the body, it was accepted as rumor. Still, he has not been heard from for these past ten years."

Donnadorr wiped his eyes with his sleeve. "But you say no one you've spoken to has seen his dead body?"

"No one."

"Then I shall continue to believe."

"Follow your heart-knowledge, young Donnadorr. Yes, yes, indeed, yes, there is little else that one can depend on today."

They returned to the camp, walking down the slope in silence.

BY THE FIFTH day in the ravine, Pohl asked Glenelle if she was up to continuing on their journey the following day. "We don't want to delay Meekelorr longer than is necessary."

"Will he wait?" Sylvane asked, once again.

"He'll wait. But he does have important duties in the west."

Glenelle answered that she was ready to go on. Her eyes were sunken, her face was thin and drawn, her shoulders tight, her whole frame looked fragile. But she was willing, almost anxious, to go on. Watching her nearly broke Auragole's heart. What choice did they have but to go on?

"There are three more caves to travel through," Pohl told them the night before they were to leave. "None is as difficult as the first, though there are places where the walking will be treacherous. It shouldn't take us more than a week, if all goes well. When we leave the caves, we will be beyond these high peaks and in the foothills of the Westernlands. A week's walk through the foothills and we will be at the rendezvous point where Meekelorr should be awaiting us. We're a bit behind schedule, but he will wait."

THE TRAVEL THROUGH the other caves was accomplished without further event. For Glenelle's sake, they rested frequently. Donnadorr and Auragole had divided up her pack and weapons. She carried nothing but the blue cloak on her back. She rarely spoke. Auragole watched her apprehensively—as did they all—wondering what kept her moving forward. Was she clinging desperately to the one bright hope called Mattelmead?

They came out of the last cave at noon, a week after they had left the ravine, and spent the afternoon walking through the still-high but rounder, snowless mountains that made up the western foothills. The weather was warmer, and when Auragole asked Pohl about it, Pohl told him that it was unnaturally so. Auragole took in this information with some concern. But he did not repeat it to the others.

Once they had left the cave, Pohl told them that it would take another seven or eight days to reach the agreed-upon meeting place. If all had gone according to plan, Meekelorr should have arrived at the meeting place a day or two before them. The more human scale of these foothills and the warmer weather seemed to cheer the group. Donnadorr often burst into song and the others joined him—all except Glenelle.

They had come quite a distance south from Agavia, Auragole realized, looking at the maps he still had from his first journey with the Easterners. From their rendezvous valley in the Gandlesean foothills, it was only three or four days' journey to the East Gate of Isofed. But that was not their destination. Once they met Meekelorr, he would guide them to the forested hills between Noonbarr and Isofed—a journey of four or five days—and through them into the Sorren Heights. Once in the Sorren Heights, Meekelorr would see that they were escorted as far as the border of Mattelmead.

It was just past noon when they finally arrived at the meeting place. To Auragole's dismay, Meekelorr and his men had not yet arrived. It was a desolate place. There was no sign that any humans had been there recently. There was a pond there and they set up camp near it.

"No one has lived here for centuries," Pohl said.

"Are you sure this is the right place?" Donnadorr asked.

"Yes," Pohl said.

After they had cleaned up the remains of their evening meal, Auragole took Pohl aside and asked if he was worried about Meekelorr's tardiness.

"No," the old man said. "It's difficult to be exact about arrivals when one is traveling such long distances. We will rest and wait."

Four days passed and still no Meekelorr. Glenorr was convinced that Galavi and Pohl were mistaken about the meeting place and told Auragole so. Auragole repeated what Pohl had told him, but Glen was not convinced. Auragole knew that the others were also troubled—as was he. Why was Meekelorr so late? Even Pohl seemed quieter than usual. Each morning Galavi went out to scout the terrain, to see if Meekelorr and the

Companions could be spotted, and each evening he came back and greeted them with merely a shake of his head. They ate meagerly of their dwindling supplies. There were some small fish in the pond, but the travelers were unable find anything edible in the barren hills that surrounded them.

AFTER WAITING ANOTHER three days, Pohl decided they should move on. Something obviously had delayed Meekelorr. Pohl was worried. He tried not to show the travelers how much.

"Tomorrow," Pohl told them, "Galavi and I will lead you back into the safety of the Gandlesean foothills." He told them that he and Galavi would accompany them north for about a week. After that they would have to make their own way. But he would give them maps. Everyone looked grim and uneasy.

"But, Pohl," Auragole said, looking at his own map, "the way Meekelorr was going to guide us is west, not north. See?" And he offered his map to Pohl.

"North is by far the safest way, my friend," Pohl said. "I can't send you west through the woods below Noonbarr and then through the Sorren Heights without an armed escort." Not, he thought, if something had befallen Meekelorr on that route. "Best to go north through the foothills of the Gandlese, then turn west, and follow along Noonbarr's northern hills. I have very good maps that will take you on a route even safer than the route the caravans take."

Auragole turned to the usually silent Galavi. "Do you also think that north is the safest route?"

Galavi looked at him solemnly, then turned a full circle and stared out at the landscape before answering Auragole. "I do," he said.

"We were promised an escort as far as Mattelmead," Glenorr said to Pohl in a querulous voice.

"Glen," Sylvane said, "the Agavians and Pohl have been good

to us. They owe us nothing. On the contrary."

"I'm sorry, Glen," Pohl said, "but Galavi and I can't accompany you all the way to Mattelmead. We are needed in Agavia."

Glenorr grimaced but made no other comment.

"Auragole," Pohl turned to him, "you must lead when Galavi and I depart."

Auragole bit his lip and was silent.

"Does anybody disagree with me?" Pohl looked from face to face.

Glenorr laughed.

"That's the best choice," Donnadorr said. "Auragole can track better than anyone I've ever met—other than an Agavian. He can tell direction from growing things and from the stars. That's important when we are trying to get through land none of us has ever laid eyes on before. And he can read maps." He clapped Auragole on the back. "Aurie's our man."

Everyone assented, everyone except Glen, whose eyes looked cold with anger. Let's hope he doesn't give Auragole trouble, Pohl thought with some fervor.

Out loud he said, "Good. I'll give you better maps, Auragole, and chart the course with you. Agreed?"

Auragole ran the back of his hand over his forehead and stared at his boots. Finally, he answered. "Agreed."

IN THE MORNING they broke camp, having abandoned hope of a rendezvous with Meekelorr, and set off first east, back into the safety of the foothills of the Gandlese, and then after a day turned north.

What has happened to Meekelorr? Auragole wondered as they walked. Was he still alive? Seeing Pohl's set face as they marched through the barren, snowless hills, Auragole decided to keep his questions to himself. By avoiding the route leading to and through the Sorren Heights, Pohl, he felt certain, feared something had happened to Meekelorr along that particular route.

They walked four days until the event happened that was to turn their plans upside down once again.

N

chapter twenty-six

DONNADORR WAS IN the middle of a lovely dream about Agavia, but someone was kicking him in the back. It made him angry.

"Stop it," he mumbled and rolled over on his face.

"Get up!" a strange voice said.

Donnadorr turned over on his back. There was a long knife six inches from his face. Before he could react he was pulled roughly to his feet by several pairs of hands. His own were tied behind his back and he was shoved up against the rocky side of the mountain that had sheltered them. As he looked around, trying to shake the heavy sleep from his eyes, he saw that all his companions had been captured in the same way. Strangely, they were silent, standing there, trying to take in what was happening as the attackers tied him and his friends to one another. They had kept no watch. These barren hills were presumed uninhabited.

There were perhaps thirty of the intruders—mostly men, but

also about half a dozen women. They were young, still in their teens or early twenties, dressed in an odd assortment of tattered and torn clothes. They all had long, scraggly hair that was tangled and neglected. The passive look on their faces chilled Donnadorr. There was something strange there, something he couldn't put his finger on. He watched and waited.

The leader stood in the center of what had been the campfire and looked on with cool enjoyment as his followers stuffed the belongings of the travelers into sacks. He was a large man with wild, brown hair and a full beard and mustache. They had not been searched, not as yet, and Don could feel the small bag of jewels given him by the Agavians against his chest. What provisions they had with them for the journey were strewn over the ground and the captors were stuffing the food into their mouths as if they were starving animals.

The leader finally came over to where they waited. He wore a proud expression on his face and stared at the captives with obvious pleasure.

"Who is leader here?" he bellowed.

Pohl spoke up immediately. "I am."

"You!" The leader spat contemptuously. "An old man? How stupid! Where were you and this pitiful group headed?"

"Mattelmead."

"Ah, Mattelmead. Everyone is hurrying to Mattelmead to meet the new king. Well, not I!" He threw back his head and laughed.

A young man hastened to his side. He was tall and thin. His blond curly hair framed his face like the aura of the sun. Donnadorr thought him beautiful.

"Lumoss!" the young man called breathlessly as he approached.

"Ah, Meridon, there you are." The leader clasped the blond man's shoulder.

"We retrieved the donkey, but it had nothing of value in its packs, only pretty boxes filled with rocks and plants we couldn't eat. We threw the rocks and plants out, but we have kept the donkey and the pretty boxes."

Donnadorr later wondered where the strength had come from, but with a cry of anguish, Glenorr tore his bonds loose and began running toward the donkey at the edge of the clearing. He had gone only a dozen steps when he was hurled to the ground by Meridon and a few others who had witnessed his escape. They kicked and punched him till he was nearly unconscious. Then they brought him back to the line of prisoners. Glenelle cried out in agony.

Meridon tied him between Glenelle and Pohl. Glenorr couldn't stand. Pohl spoke to him softly, instructing him to breathe deeply and rhythmically. Both girls wept. Donnadorr could hear Auragole's labored breathing and knew he too was struggling with rage.

Don't be foolish. Wait, Donnadorr told himself, and his eyes said the same to Auragole.

"The one who tied him to the others forfeits his share of the spoils because of his negligence and stupidity," Lumoss said coldly. He strolled up and down the line staring at his prisoners, his eyes calculating. Meridon followed him. Lumoss stopped and looked at the two girls. "What do you say, Meridon?"

"Very pretty." Meridon grinned.

"One for me and one for you, eh? I shall decide tonight. What shall we do with the men?"

"Kill them," Meridon said, his sunlike face serious and thoughtful.

A hard knot lodged in Donnadorr's stomach.

"That would be the simplest," Lumoss said.

Donnadorr looked over at Pohl, who was watching the two young men with seeming interest.

"On the other hand," Lumoss said, "they're from the east. It might bring pleasure to hear the news from there."

"We could take them back to the village and talk to them. You can kill them afterward." The innocent face sought his comrade's approving smile.

"Yes, that would be good." He slapped Meridon gently on the cheek. "You are my favorite, you know that, Meridon. That's why you are second only to me."

Meridon grinned proudly.

"See to it that they are tied and ready to move out quickly," Lumoss said as he started to leave.

"May we have our boots?" Donnadorr spoke up.

The leader turned back to stare at him. His look was ice. "You have no boots." He was about to move away again, when he turned to Meridon. "On second thought, Meridon, return their boots for the time being. We don't want them slowing us down. Bondill and his troop may be roaming about near here. I have no intention of sharing our prizes with him."

Their good Agavian boots were returned to them, but their cloaks, their weapons, the belongings they had carried, and what remained of their food were stuffed into large sacks.

But not our jewels, Donnadorr thought with wild hope. What good would they do their bedraggled captors anyway? They would probably throw them away as they had Glenorr's stones and plants. He shivered in the morning air. One by one they were allowed to put on their boots, and then immediately their hands were tied behind their backs. After everyone had put on his or her boots, they were tied to one another with a rope about the waist so that they could march single file. Donnadorr's shirt, tunic, and trousers were of wool, as were those of the others, but they were not warm enough to keep out the icy mountain wind. How would frail Glenelle survive such a cold march? He was about to speak up again when he heard Pohl.

"Would you spare cloaks for the ladies?" Pohl asked Meridon.

Meridon stared at him and then at the ladies.

"One has been ill," Pohl added.

"Which one?" Meridon asked.

"The golden-haired one."

Meridon went away and came back with a short, ragged blanket. He put it around Glenelle, who accepted it without speaking. Her body was shaking.

Then Meridon walked over to Sylvane. Smiling at her sweetly, he touched her curly hair. "You're very pretty," he said. "I hope you're given to me." Then he took off his own cloak and put it around Sylvane's shoulders. She looked at him contemptuously, but it was a poor show of defiance.

If Donnadorr had been loose, he would have killed him with his bare hands, but he held on to his rage. He knew it was best to bide his time, to wait for the right moment. He tested the ropes. They were secure. Be patient and pick your moment, he told himself, remembering Glenorr's beating.

A young man came up to Meridon and said softly, "Be careful, Meridon. He hasn't chosen yet."

"He loves me," Meridon said with a shrug, and moved away.

Soon captives and captors began the march north. They were heading, Lumoss told them, to his village. The walking was difficult, more because of the cold and their bonds than because of the terrain. They moved in a single line behind Lumoss and some of his cohorts; Auragole first, behind him Donnadorr, then Pohl, Glenorr, Glenelle, Sylvane, and last a silent but observant Galavi. Behind Galavi was the rest of Lumoss's band. Pohl had talked Glenorr to his feet, and he was marching bent over in obvious pain.

Once Lumoss dropped back to walk alongside Pohl. He looked at Pohl with open curiosity. "I don't understand why they allow you to be leader. You are old."

"Is there no value in age?" Pohl's voice was polite, filled with interest.

"Truly you are stupid. Can you compare your body to mine? Could you beat me in a race or in a wrestling match? Could you tackle a wild beast without a weapon? Are you as able with the women?"

"You would surpass me in all you mention."

"There, you see." Lumoss's tone was smug. "Why are so many from the east going now to Mattelmead?" he finally asked, trying to sound as if the answer held little interest for him.

"Because of the great king there. They say he will save the entire west from chaos and bring a lasting peace."

"It is nonsense!" Lumoss spat his words out. "A king is a king, which means he takes your freedom in the end."

"Is freedom then so important to you?" Pohl asked.

"You are stupid," Lumoss said, with a toss of his head. "Freedom is the only thing that is important. Why do you think we have all left the towns and countries of the Westernlands? To get away from their laws, their prisons, their armies, and their endless restrictions, to live as we want, in freedom. My people are the freest people on the earth." There was pride in his voice and pride in his walk.

Donnadorr listened in fascination, forgetting his bonds for the moment, and the danger.

"You're as free as the animals, eh?" Pohl asked.

"That's right," Lumoss said, "only smarter. We take from the land and we take from the animals and we take from people what we want. That's freedom."

"Is freedom more important than love?"

"You are truly an ignorant old man. Love is something you can always get. But freedom is something someone always wants to take from you. We all love each other in our village. I love my women, my children, my friends. Love is easy. You think the Mattelmead king will save the west and give you your freedom, but I know better. He'll conquer the west and then make laws and soon you will all be slaves—except for my people. We bow to no laws and no kings."

About two hours into their march, they halted, and Lumoss and Meridon conferred.

"Why should we go around?" Meridon asked.

"The territory is disputed."

"Bondill pays little heed to the agreement. Why should we run? We could take his band easily."

Donnadorr looked from one to the other. He saw Lumoss stare at Meridon hostilely for a moment, but then he smiled. Lumoss tapped Meridon lightly on the cheek. "Fool," he said, "why should we risk the booty we have found? We'll fight them another time, when our hands are free and our stomachs empty."

Meridon grinned his agreement.

They guided the captors and captives off the path they had been following and climbed into the hills. The way was rugged and they stumbled along. Donnadorr cursed under his breath and pondered their chances for escape. Seven against at least thirty, and who knew how many more at the village.

Four hours later, they arrived at the village. It was not yet noon. To call it a village was to give it airs. It was a clearing with several small caves carved by nature into the surrounding mountains. In the center of the clearing was a huge fire. Perhaps another twenty-five or thirty people greeted the captors as they entered the village. They were mostly women and small children. The children were as poorly clothed as the adults. Few wore shoes and none seemed to mind the cold. Seven against fifty, Don thought. They needed a plan.

There was excitement as they entered. The captives were stared at unabashedly. The children came over and touched them and laughed. How is it that the cold seems to bother them so little, Donnadorr wondered, as he and his friends were hustled into a cave and made to sit, hands tied to one another, against one dark wall. A small fire in the center of the cave cast a smoky light. Around it were eight people rolled up in dirty blankets. The smell was terrible. At first glance Donnadorr thought they were sleeping; then he heard the moaning.

"Other prisoners?" he whispered the question to Pohl.

"The ill, I think," Pohl whispered back. "This is likely the cave of the sick."

Outside they could hear the shouts of laughter and pleasure. Their captors were feasting on their supplies. Donnadorr's stomach began to rumble. It had been hours since they had eaten or had anything to drink.

Two guards sat near the cave entrance watching their comrades outside. They were soon brought food and drink. Donnadorr watched them hungrily. One shouted that he wanted a smoke. A voice from the outside answered that they could have no smokes while they were on duty.

"Pohl?" Donnadorr heard Auragole whisper.

"Yes?"

"We must try to escape."

"There may be a way," Pohl said. "Be patient, Auragole. Donnadorr, do nothing rash. It could mean death if we do not choose our moment wisely."

The time dragged by. Perhaps an hour had passed when finally Pohl called out. It had become eerily quiet outside.

"Guard!" Pohl shouted.

A young man jumped to his feet.

"Get your leader. Tell him I'm a doctor. Tell him I can cure these ill comrades of his." He motioned with his head toward the moaning group around the fire.

"He dreams. I cannot disturb him."

"When will his dreams end?"

The young guard said, "Who can tell?"

"When he wakes, tell him that I wish to speak to him."

The guard nodded, and went back to stare out of the cave.

"Pohl," Don heard Auragole whisper. "What does he mean by 'he dreams'?"

"They smoke, probably the uliluli plant. I can smell it in the air."

"I don't understand." Auragole said.

"It gives them potent dreams—strange fantasies that cause them more pleasure than their lives, little wonder. It grows everywhere. You probably know it as lime weed."

"Yes, my mother used it for a tea or for flavoring meat. They smoke it?"

"Yes. I thought by their eyes when I first saw them that they smoked. Pass these words down the line. Tell no one to lose hope. I have a plan. Be patient and try to rest."

Smoke that gave strange dreams. Donnadorr had heard about such plants and those who smoked them. But everyone knew it was a kind of suicide. In lands where survival was the aim of life, few used those substances. The most one did was drink wine on occasion—to celebrate. But the effects of that lasted only a little while. After all, even at night one had to be ready to defend oneself.

chapter twenty-seven

HOURS PASSED. AURAGOLE was too uncomfortable to sleep. He wondered how the others were faring. Pohl, he knew, was wide awake, watching the cave entrance. One of the young guards finally went out. When he returned, he told Pohl that Lumoss would come later.

As the sun was beginning to set, several men and women led by Meridon came into the cave. Auragole's heart beat fiercely, wondering if they had waited too long to make their move.

"Lumoss invites the men to eat with him," Meridon said. "The women will eat here," he grinned at them, "with me and our own women."

Auragole, in consternation, turned his head to see if he could catch Pohl's eye, but he could not.

The five men were taken out of the cave and made to sit around the campfire. There were about twenty of Lumoss's men there. The feet of the prisoners were securely tied but their hands were freed. Still, they were given no utensils. Auragole eyed the knives that their captors were using and wondered how he might get hold of one and if he could cut his bonds before he was overpowered.

Lumoss sat down next to Pohl. The prisoners were given a warm drink and a biscuit, which Auragole recognized as one of their own. They were not offered any of the meat the captors were eating.

"It is my desire that brings you to this meal," Lumoss said. "I wish to hear news of the Easternlands. Who will speak first?"

Auragole glanced over at Glenorr. His face was bruised and swollen, but there was a look on his face that made Auragole uneasy. Donnadorr must have seen it too, for suddenly he began to speak. Soon he was telling tales that were both poignant and humorous. Auragole thought that he spoke, not only for their captors, but also for his own pleasure and for the pleasure of his fellow travelers. Was it because he feared that this might be the last time they would sit together listening to his stories?

Lumoss listened attentively and with obvious gratification— as did the others. He laughed occasionally. "Fools! They are all stupid in the east," he commented once. "They don't know how to be free."

Donnadorr made no mention of the Valley of the Agavi. It was as if he knew that he should protect that valley from any- one who might bring harm to her. Auragole approved.

After nearly an hour had passed, a series of loud screams came from the cave of the sick. It stopped Donnadorr in midsentence. Was it Glenelle or Sylvane? Auragole's blood turned to ice. But Lumoss, his face clouding over, said, "It's my favorite woman. I think she is dying." There was a touch of regret in his voice.

"I'm a doctor," Pohl spoke up then. "Let me examine her. Perhaps I can heal her."

Lumoss looked at him blankly. "That's stupid. No one can heal another. When one becomes ill, either he dies or the illness goes."

"Did they not have healers where you come from in the west?" There was a hint of incredulity in Pohl's voice.

"I ran away before I was ten. Where I lived there were no healers, only fools and rules and endless work."

Auragole felt all hope ebb away. Had Pohl been given a chance to help the sick, he might have made a bargain for their lives.

"Listen to me, Lumoss," Pohl said. "When you smoke, you are changed, is that not so?"

"Yes," Lumoss smiled, "the weed brings the greatest freedom. It is a freedom only the wind knows."

"I too have weeds," Pohl went on. "My weeds can make the body well again."

Lumoss eyed Pohl with uncertainty and distrust. "There are no such weeds."

"There are."

"Let me see them."

"I will do something better, I will show you how the weeds work. Take me to your woman and let me cure her."

"It's a trick. I untie your bonds, and you escape."

"Now who is foolish? Can a man my age outrun a youth like you?"

For a moment, anger blazed in Lumoss's eyes, and Auragole thought all was lost. Then Lumoss laughed. "Let us see your weeds and your healing."

He instructed a youth to untie Pohl and the two of them stood up.

At that moment, as the two turned to leave, there was a clamor outside the circle. A young man ran up to Lumoss.

"Lumoss!" he said breathlessly. "Meridon has taken the curly-headed woman to his cave."

Auragole had never seen anything as cold as Lumoss's face.

"Fetch them here!"

Moments later, Meridon was dragged to the fire by half a

dozen men. They brought also an ashen-faced Sylvane, who tried to hold up the bodice of her dress, which was torn down the front. All the women who had been in the cave eating with Meridon came out to watch, and children seemed to appear from nowhere. Meridon tried to grin, but there was fear in his eyes. Then his beautiful face took on an expression of innocence, and Auragole had to admire the skill with which he hid his terror.

"I knew you liked the blond one better. You said one was mine. I've done no wrong."

"I said I would choose tonight."

"I only took what was promised. . ."

He never finished his words. Lumoss had whipped out a hunting dagger and plunged it into Meridon's chest. With a piercing screech Meridon fell to the ground.

Auragole shouted in horror. He could hear the shocked denials coming from his own companions, but only silence from the companions of Lumoss.

Lumoss wiped his knife on his cloak, looked down at the once-handsome face now distorted in death, and said, "He was my favorite." Then he looked up at the young man who had betrayed Meridon to him and said, "Now you are my favorite."

The other grinned and straightened his shoulders in a cocky gesture.

"Come." Lumoss beckoned to Pohl, whose face betrayed no emotion, other than a slight tightening of the jaw. "Let us see what your weeds can do for my woman." He took Pohl by the shoulder and started to leave, but first turned to his new favorite. "See that his body is thrown down the side of the mountain, but remove his clothes and boots. You there," he motioned to two of the young men watching. "Bring my woman from the cave of the sick to my cave."

Then he turned and led Pohl away.

Auragole watched as some of the men picked up the once-lithe body of Meridon. What disturbed him most was that the young people who stood around showed no sorrow, no regret. Even the children had drawn close to see the body of the former favorite. They displayed no shock, only a vague curiosity.

Donnadorr looked green and Auragole saw that he was willing himself not to be sick. Sylvane, however, could not control her retching. It didn't even bring a sympathetic glance from the women.

They were soon hustled back into the cave of the sick. Glenelle was there, her eyes wide with fear. "What happened? Was it Pohl?" she whispered. Donnadorr shook his head.

Their captors retied them and left, leaving two guards at the mouth of the cave. Galavi mumbled softly, and Auragole realized that he was reciting a prayer for the dead. What was Pohl doing? Perhaps the thieves had thrown away his bag of herbs. Perhaps Pohl too was dead.

They waited anxiously. Auragole tried to work his bonds free, and so did Donnadorr next to him. Neither had luck. They needed something sharp. Down the line Sylvane was weeping. What had happened to her?

Don't think about that. Think about a way to get out of here, he told himself.

AURAGOLE AWOKE ABRUPTLY and was surprised that he had been dozing. There were voices at the entrance to the cave. Pohl had returned.

"Why are you alone? Where is Lumoss?" a guard was asking. His dagger gleamed in the moonlight.

"He dreams," answered Pohl.

"Ah," the guard said.

"His dreams are deeper and freer than ever before," Pohl said. "I have given him a better weed. All the others in the camp now dream."

"It doesn't seem fair," the second guard said. "Twice today

the others have dreamed and we two have sat here awake with nothing to bring us comfort."

"It does seem a shame to punish you so." Pohl's voice was filled with concern. Auragole saw him hold a thin black object between his thumb and forefinger, rolling it gently. The guards watched him also.

"It smells different," the first said.

"It's powerful," Pohl said, and put it to his own lips. "It brings the freest dreams imaginable."

He walked to the fire and with a twig swept up a flame, put the weed to his mouth, and lit it. The guards watched him with longing.

"Soon I too will dream," Pohl said. He sat down near them, took another puff and was suddenly asleep. The weed fell from his mouth and went out.

The two guards looked at it and then at each other. "We share," shouted one and grabbed it. He went to the fire and returned with the lit weed.

"We will take only a few puffs each," the other said, "so we will awaken before Lumoss and the others."

They passed the weed back and forth and soon they were asleep, breathing deeply, strange expressions on their faces.

Auragole pulled at his bonds but they only cut into his flesh. Then to his relief and amazement, he saw Pohl rise to his feet, take a dagger from each of the sleeping guards, and then hurry over to him. He cut Auragole's bonds first, then gave him one of the daggers. Auragole cut Donnadorr's bonds, then Galavi's, while Pohl freed the women and Glenorr.

As soon as their numb legs could move, Pohl led them out of the cave. The sight that greeted them was astonishing. All around the dying fire and in front of the cave people were sleeping—their bodies strewn indifferently over the hard ground like so many fallen boulders. Auragole looked with regret and sadness at the children snoring softly.

Pohl, Auragole, and Donnadorr quickly entered Lumoss's cave. They found what was left of their belongings stuffed into two large sacks, waiting for Lumoss to distribute at his leisure. They took these, and the group hastily left the campsite and moved into the hills. There they retrieved from the sacks their own warm cloaks and their backpacks, armed themselves, divided the contents of the sacks quickly, and set out again as fast as they could. They needed to put as much ground between themselves and Lumoss's band as they were able.

Galavi suggested that they travel south, away from the territory of both Lumoss and Bondill. Pohl agreed, suggesting that they aim for the East Gate of Isofed.

Auragole didn't question them, nor did Donnadorr, even though they were heading away from their goal of northern Noonbarr. He was sure that Pohl had an alternate plan and he stopped thinking about anything other than putting as much distance as possible between themselves and Lumoss.

When they stopped for a short rest, Pohl told them what had happened. "Lumoss took me into his cave and they brought his woman. She was unconscious, lying on filthy blankets. I washed her thoroughly and examined her. She is dying of too much ulululi weed. No wonder there are no old people there. The weed will kill them all before they are thirty. I made a broth of healing herbs in which I put a strong narcotic called anos to ease her going. It occurred to me that anos smoked might perhaps do the same as the broth. So I rolled the leaves and gave it to Lumoss. I'm sure he didn't expect it to affect him so quickly or he would not have left me untied. I must say, the speed with which the drug took effect surprised me. This was our only hope, for I knew I couldn't heal the woman. Lumoss was asleep after only a few puffs. I rolled the rest of the leaves and passed them around to everyone with Lumoss's compliments. They were as eager as children are for sweets. The last one I kept for our guards."

"But why weren't you affected?" Donnadorr asked. "You smoked it."

"Because," he smiled, "I didn't breathe it in. Even so, it has made me less than fully awake."

THEY WALKED BRISKLY the rest of the night and all through the following day, backtracking south and putting many miles between themselves and Lumoss. If Lumoss hunted them, Donnadorr thought, he followed a wrong trail, thanks to Auragole, who knew how to obliterate signs of their tracks. But Pohl said that Lumoss and his men might not be following them at all. The anos weed might have left them ill, might have taken from them their desire to act. Whether they were followed or not, Pohl was taking no chances. He insisted that the band move with caution and haste.

chapter twenty-eight

THAT SECOND NIGHT, the group sat huddled close to one another for warmth—not daring to light a fire—making new plans.

"It is too risky to head north, now," Pohl said. "We know of two bands of outlaws roaming these foothills. There may be more. We must once again alter your travel plans. You are too few to battle any of these roving bands."

Sylvane asked, "What other way is there?"

She was shivering as much from exhaustion as from the cold. And. . .and from something else, Auragole thought with distress.

"We must try to get you entry through Isofed's East Gate, then across a portion of its land to its North Gate."

"But, Pohl, why Isofed?" Auragole stared at the map Pohl had given him. "Shouldn't we go through the hills between Isofed and Noonbarr?—the way Meekelorr was going to take us?"

"Yes, and that was the way Meekelorr and a troop of soldiers went—and they haven't returned." Pohl's face looked troubled.

"I think that could prove a very dangerous way, my friend."

"But the North Gate also takes us into the Sorren Heights, which you have told us is risky to cross without an escort."

"Don't head north after you leave the North Gate, but go west following the Noonbarr River all the way to Glovale. Then you can turn north toward Mattelmead."

"Isn't that also a dangerous route?" Don asked.

"All routes are dangerous. This one, I hope, less so."

"If only Meekelorr had come for us," Glenelle said.

Auragole looked at Pohl's unsmiling face. No question, he thinks something bad has befallen Meekelorr. Yet the idea of Isofed seemed not a very promising one. "Didn't you tell us that the Isofedians allow no one to cross their land?"

"Yes, but what other choice is there?" Pohl's words sounded curt, impatient. "You can't go north and you can't take Meekelorr's route. You can, of course, return to Agavia with us. Perhaps that's the best alternative." He looked at Glenelle. "However, I'm not sure Glenelle can make it back through the caves."

"Even if she could," Sylvane said, "you are unable to heal her in Agavia. And isn't that why we left in the middle of the winter—so that Glenelle could get to a country where there is medical help?" She turned to Glenorr.

But Glen was silent. And Pohl didn't answer her.

It was Donnadorr who spoke up. "Well, we can at least give Isofed a try."

"Yes," Pohl said, "let's give it a try. We shall ask the gate-keeper at the East Gate to allow your small band to cross Isofed and leave by the North Gate. What are your opinions?"

Donnadorr, Auragole, Glenelle, and Sylvane readily agreed. Only Glenorr was silent. Auragole eyed him uneasily. He had barely spoken since he was beaten by Lumoss's gang. Yet he couldn't have been badly injured, for he had kept up on two long marches. His eyes looked sometimes angry, sometimes vacant. Glenelle hovered over him solicitously. Sylvane told Auragole that Glen grieved for what he had lost. Gone were the things he cared about. All of his stones and dried plants were gone—even his donkey, for it had not been in the camp when they hurriedly left. Sylvane tried to explain Glenorr to Donnadorr and Auragole. Though he said nothing, Auragole dismissed her attempt to defend her foster brother. Glenorr had his life and the hills were filled with plants and stones. Let him be grateful, for once.

DONNADORR TRIED TO understand what Sylvane was saying about Glen. But it was difficult. He thought they had been very lucky. After all, they had retrieved everything except most of their food and the donkey. They had left Glenorr's beautiful Agavian boxes behind. Without the donkey, they had not been able to carry them. Thank the stars that Glen had not put up a fuss then. They would have to hunt and fish as they traveled and that would slow them down, but they had their lives. And right now, that seemed very precious, indeed. Donnadorr was relieved that their weapons had been rescued. Most of all he was thrilled that their harps were intact. And since they had not been searched, they still had their Agavian jewels. Donnadorr knew that these were their entry into a good life in Mattelmead. All they had to be concerned with at present was a viable route. They were in the west. Surely finding a route shouldn't be all that difficult.

Suddenly, and to Don's astonishment, Glenorr spoke. His words exploded into the air like a summer thunderstorm—all quick anger and roiling darkness. "Freedom!" He spat the word out. "You see what it does? What good is it? I would give up freedom for peace and a quiet place to work. A world filled with order seems infinitely more desirable than freedom. Order and peace. I would fight and give my life for that. For without it," he said bitterly, "life hardly seems worth it."

"Freedom does seem dangerous," Sylvane said, and she shuddered. "What do you think, Don?"

"I think I've always felt free. After all, I've been on the road all my life and no one to tell me which way to go, or when. Like Glen, if I've longed for anything it would be an end to these ceaseless wars."

"And what about you, Aurie?" Sylvane asked.

Auragole sat staring at his hands for a moment before he spoke. "It was my father's greatest goal. . .for me."

"But surely you of all of us were free, Auragole," Glenelle said. "I'm not so sure living in a settlement, always concerned for one's safety, allowed any of us in the east to think about being free. Not even you were really free, Don, when you had to be constantly on the move, never able to settle anywhere without causing upset to some individual or some group. Perhaps Aurie is the only one amongst us to experience freedom."

"What about the Agavians?" Auragole said.

They all turned to look at Galavi, who had been listening in that unobtrusive way of his.

"The Agavians follow an old tradition," Galavi said. "We don't long for freedom, nor do we concern ourselves with it. But ours is a different path than the rest of humanity. Freedom, I have been told," and now he looked at Pohl and his smile was sweet, "is a great goal of humanity's."

"Well, the Companions of the Way aren't free," Glen said. "After all, they are soldiers and soldiers take orders. I agree with Galavi, we need not concern ourselves with freedom. Freedom can be dangerous. You saw what it has done to Lumoss and his crowd. What we need is peace—how can anyone argue with that?—peace and order so that we can study and work without fear."

"What do you think about freedom?" Sylvane turned to Pohl.

"Freedom, as Galavi has just said, is one of humanity's greatest goals."

"But how can that be, Pohl?" Sylvane asked. "Look what freedom has done to Lumoss and his comrades."

"True freedom must be developed alongside love."

"Why?" Glenelle asked.

"So love doesn't become licentious, unprincipled, selfish."

"There, you see!" Glen said.

"Nevertheless, to acquire love and freedom is why we've been put on this Deep Earth," Pohl said.

Glenorr sniggered.

"Lumoss said he loved," Sylvane said.

"Do you believe it?" Pohl asked.

"Swords, no!" Donnadorr shook his head, and then stroked his red beard thoughtfully. "I've met many a person in my time and in my travels. I've seen cruelty and indifference, anger and hate, but never have I met a man as loveless as that Lumoss." He looked over at Auragole, who was rubbing his forehead and staring at his boots.

"Yet Lumoss said he loved," Pohl said.

"Just because he said he loved, doesn't mean he actually loved. People often say they love when they don't really mean it," Sylvane said, and then blushed.

"My point exactly. So just because he shouted 'freedom, freedom, freedom,' does that mean he is free? Is an animal free who must follow his instincts? Is the wind free when it has no consciousness? Lumoss and his comrades are none of them free. They are slaves to their passions. They follow them blindly. To be hungry means to feast until they are near bursting, but never to plan ahead. To be angry means to kill but never to forgive. They lie with each other only to dampen a fire but never for the tender moment freely given another. They live with fear and filth. Their instincts given wild rein are a greater taskmaster than any law that has ever governed them. With the world around them so unbearable, no wonder they turn to the uliluli weed. It will eventually kill them all. To Lumoss, perhaps death is the ultimate freedom. No, my dear young comrades, they know less of love and freedom than any I have met in all my years of travel. Does it matter that the word *freedom* is constantly on their lips?"

Freedom and love. How important are they to me? Donnadorr wondered as he sat, his back up against a rock, staring at the countless stars. If love is to be loyal to friends, then he wanted to love, and he knew he could. If freedom meant he could choose which leader to follow and which tyrant to leave, then he knew and wanted freedom. Neither seemed difficult to achieve.

But maybe that wasn't the kind of freedom and love Pohl was speaking about. He felt too foolish to ask.

Auragole had spoken little during their discussion of freedom, but Donnadorr saw something burning in his eyes. What is he thinking?

THEY TRAVELED SOUTH for six days through land that became increasingly colder, though it was now the spring equinox. The hills were barren and brown and there was little snow. Pohl had told them that the climate was unnatural and unpredictable in this part of the foothills. When the climatic changes had come to the Southern Desolation, the climate had also changed in these foothills. What was now called the Southern Desolation, legend said, had once been a land of great abundance and many people had lived there. Now it was a vast, uninhabited desert. People became ill if they tried to enter it. Though there were passes from the Gandlese into the south, no one used them, because they brought one down into the dreaded Southern Desolation. Pohl said that there had been no known inhabitants there for four or five hundred years.

Each day the travelers made camp early, and Auragole and Donnadorr were able to catch small game or fish. Galavi knew what roots were edible and he dug up many. Auragole watched

Galavi carefully. And because Auragole was willing to learn, Galavi taught him. Donnadorr often watched the two deep in conversation over what looked to him like a patch of weeds. Donnadorr too tried to discern what was edible from what was poisonous. But it was difficult because many of the plants were similar in appearance. Finally, he gave up and left it to Auragole, who seemed to have a good eye.

When they were a half-day's journey from the East Gate of Isofed, the band of travelers again made camp.

"Tomorrow morning, Auragole and I will make our way down to the gate," Pohl told them as they ate their meager meal. "I hope we can persuade the guards there to let you through. The rest of you wait here. If we don't return in two days, you must go back to Agavia with Galavi."

That was a sobering thought, Donnadorr noted. But no one said anything. They finished their meal and went to sleep. In the morning, the two left, carrying only some biscuits, water, and their weapons.

Sylvane and Donnadorr fished in a little tributary that flowed into the Isofed. Galavi collected his roots, never moving out of the sight of their camp. Glenelle and Glenorr, who were both somewhat weak, were instructed to rest. Standing at the edge of the narrow stream, pole in hand, Donnadorr observed the twins and Sylvane. It's a miracle that we have made it this far, he thought. Glenelle had walked as if all that lived in her was the will to move her legs. She was pale and thin, and though Sylvane constantly urged food on her, she ate little.

Sylvane herself had changed since the encounter with Lumoss. She battled within her own being in a way Donnadorr had never seen before. He had always thought that Sylvie was like him, not given to inner worrying, but to adjusting, to doing . . . But now? As they fished, Donnadorr saw a parade of emotions march across her face, as it had done so often since they had freed themselves from their captors. Her whole soul seemed reflected in her eyes, but he was not good at naming another's trials and he didn't try. He was about to sing her a silly ditty, when he looked over at Glenorr, and the words died in his throat. Glenorr's face looked hard as marble, cold as a winter wind. Even his walk had changed. The grace with which Glenorr had previously moved had changed to sharp, angular, erratic movements. His feet hammered the ground. Donnadorr wondered uneasily about what lay beneath his frigid stare. Would it surface, he wondered, and if so, how?

Before night had fallen, Pohl and Auragole returned. Both looked grim as they strode into the camp. The others quickly gathered around them.

"No good." Pohl shook his head.

"They won't let us pass?" Sylvane asked.

"We couldn't get near the gate," Auragole said.

"What?" Glenorr said.

"The Isofedian army is parked outside it." Auragole told them. "Thousands of them along the Isofed River, stretching both north and south of the gate as far as the eye can see."

"What does this mean, friend?" Galavi asked Pohl.

"The Isofedians are worried."

"About what?" Donnadorr asked.

"Invasion. The whole west must be astir with the news of Ormahn and his intentions to unite the Westernlands under his rule. They have a formidable army, the Isofedians. Ormahn will not have an easy time with them. They have been prepared for hundreds of years to protect their people and their God from possible attacks by others. They are a pious people, but also a people who honor their warriors."

"What now?" Glenelle asked.

"We must head north the way you originally intended to take us before we met Lumoss," Glenorr shouted.

They all turned to stare at him.

"Not a good idea, Glen," Pohl said. "If you go north through the foothills, you will likely encounter Lumoss again, or Bondill, or another savage band like his. If you try to move north by first staying close to the Isofedian wall or within some miles of it, you will no doubt encounter Isofedian soldiers. Indeed, yes. They are very edgy, it seems. And they would kill you without concern, for so they are trained. To an Isofedian, you are little more than an animal, hardly human at all. If you try to go the route Meekelorr took. . .well, we've already discussed that."

"Then what can we do?" Glenelle asked.

Auragole spoke up then. "Pohl and I have been speaking about this on our way back here. We must make for the South Gate of Isofed."

"The South Gate!" Sylvane said. "But isn't that in the Southern Desolation?"

"The Deep Forest," Auragole said.

"But aren't there likely to be Isofedian soldiers there too, dear lad?" Donnadorr asked.

"I doubt that they will have soldiers at the South Gate." It was Pohl who answered him.

Donnadorr noticed an odd look cross Pohl's face, then disappear. It made Don uneasy.

"Why not?" Glen asked, his tone bellicose.

"The Isofedian generals are great strategists." Pohl turned to Glen. "They wouldn't waste manpower where it was not needed."

"Why are soldiers not needed at the South Gate?" Sylvane asked.

"Who would attack from the south? There are no settled lands to the south of Isofed, only the Southern Desolation—and of course. . ." Pohl hesitated for a moment, ". . .the Deep Forest."

"What's the matter with the Deep Forest?" Donnadorr asked, with an attempt at a chuckle. "Queer animals, ghosts, and the like?"

"Possibly," Pohl answered. "But more likely those are only

stories. However," and now his voice regained some of its heartiness, "perhaps those stories can work for us. The Deep goes right up to the South Gate. It's a natural barrier between Isofed and the Southern Desolation. My guess is there are no soldiers there, at least not outside the gates."

"Your guess!" Glenorr spat out the words.

"We have to try it," Auragole said evenly. "Or we will have to turn back to Agavia," and he looked at Glenorr, whose only response was a smirk. "We are now in the Westernlands. Shall we turn back to Agavia, or give the South Gate a try?" It was to Donnadorr that Auragole now turned.

"Lead on to the South Gate, lad. I will follow Pohl and you wherever you go."

"Well, if that's the safest way," Sylvane said, "then that's the way we must go." She looked at her foster sister. "Because we must go on. What do you say, Ellie?"

"I can't go back." Ellie shuddered. "Yes, we must go on. As Auragole says, we are already in the Westernlands. It would be a shame to turn back now."

Auragole turned to Glenorr.

He merely shrugged and smirked.

"Then, my stalwart young companions," Pohl said, "Galavi and I must leave you in the morning." He stopped their protests with a firm gesture. "We are too long away from our duties in Agavia, and no doubt have caused a lot of worry by our long absence. Auragole must lead you the rest of the way. Trust him."

At the news that the band was finally breaking up, they all became silent.

"Now then, friends," Pohl said, "we must have our dinner and get to sleep early. Come now, for surely we will meet again. Yes, yes, we are bound to meet again."

N

chapter twenty-nine

LIKE IT OR not, Auragole was leader now.

We're a sad little group without Pohl and Galavi, Auragole thought, as they moved like shadows through the winter-bare foothills.

Pohl had warned Auragole to stay away from the Isofedian wall even when that wall turned west. Soldiers, Pohl said, might be stationed for some miles along the Isofed River, which was both its eastern and southern border. The plan was to head south to the Deep Forest, enter it, and continue south until they came to the Roaring River.

Auragole often consulted the maps Pohl had given him. Once they found the Roaring River, they would follow it due west until the river bent toward the south. There they would leave the Roaring River and head north to the South Gate of Isofed just across the Isofed River. If they made good time, it should take little more than two weeks to get to their destination, which according to the map was approximately 225 miles from where they left Pohl and Galavi.

Because they were close to Isofed, they moved cautiously and silently as they headed south. When they made camp at night, there were no songs and few stories—and no fire. All were tired, and long miles lay ahead of them. They ate frugally of the food they had caught or gathered since leaving Lumoss, and at night they slept close together. They set a guard, and each took his or her turn. Until they reached the Deep Forest, they intended to be extremely careful.

Four days later, they stood on the crest of a hill. Beneath them stretched a forest as far as their eyes could survey, and much of it was green. Well, in two days it will be April and it is warm here, Auragole noted. To everyone's relief, the mountains were finally behind them. They made camp there on the hill. Like animals too long caged, they began to talk, to laugh, to make jokes. After their dinner, Auragole and Donnadorr took out their harps and sang the songs they had been taught in Agavia. Glenelle's face brightened and softened. Soon Sylvane joined them in the singing. Even Glenorr, who had become quite taciturn after the loss of his treasures, smiled as they recalled Agavia in song.

The next morning they were loud and raucous as they made their final descent. It was a relief to see green, to see signs of life after weeks of barrenness. They cheered each new tree as they passed it with a loud hurrah. Auragole refrained from telling them to keep still. Pohl had said that he doubted people lived in the Deep Forest. When Auragole had asked why, Pohl had merely shrugged and said, "Old fears."

They had been in the woods five days, heading in a southerly direction, expecting soon to encounter the Roaring River. It had been an easy walk because the trees in the Deep Forest were large and there was little underbrush. They had seen no signs of human habitation; therefore they sang often. Their mood improved, all except Glenorr's. He spoke little and sat usually apart at night. They still kept guard while they slept, but no incident troubled them until that fifth day.

It was morning. They had been walking a few hours, laughing and chatting amiably. But gradually they fell silent. There was something odd here. Auragole could feel it in the air and puzzled over it until Sylvane came up beside him.

"Why aren't there birds singing? Why can't we hear any animals moving about?" she asked in hushed tones.

That was it. It was too quiet. And it had grown warmer, much warmer—almost like a hot summer day—even though it was barely April. Had the heat been gradually coming on them without their noticing it? Were they, perhaps, closer to the Southern Desolation than they had thought? They took off their cloaks and carried them, though it added to their burden.

And why did the air seem so heavy? It was still morning, but Auragole felt bone-weary, sleepy. Several times he tried to stifle a yawn, but the others were yawning also. Their footfalls made loud sounds in the too-quiet forest. Now unfamiliar trees appeared, larger than any they had seen before—green-leafed, but not like any Auragole was familiar with in the Gandlese. Because of their incredible size and the spread of their great branches, the light filtered sparingly down. The sun looked like a prisoner gripped in the giant arms of the strange trees.

"Do you know these trees?" Donnadorr asked Glenorr.

Auragole looked back to see Glen shake his head. Staring about him, Glenorr's interest in his surroundings seemed to revive him. His eyes lit up with interest—and then the light faded. Auragole once again moved ahead, leading his little troop deeper into the woods, but with some trepidation. After only a few moments, Donnadorr called to Auragole to wait up.

He was kneeling over Glenelle, holding her hand and slapping it anxiously. Auragole hurried back to Don and knelt beside him. Glenelle opened her eyes, yawned and said, "I'm so sleepy. Just let me rest for a few minutes." She closed her eyes again.

Sylvane, who had come over to see what was wrong, said, "That's a good idea," and she sank down to the ground, curled up, and went immediately to sleep.

"What's happening?" Auragole asked Donnadorr, with mounting trepidation. How could the women be so tired after only walking a few hours?

"Everyone's tired, dear lad," Donnadorr said. "Why don't we all rest a bit." He sat down, his back against a tree, his sword across his legs.

"But we've only walked a few hours today," Auragole almost shouted.

"You can see for yourself, Auragole," Donnadorr gestured with his arm, "everyone's sleepy."

And Auragole turned around and saw that Glenorr too had stretched out on the ground and was sound asleep.

"So let's all do it," Donnadorr said, and he closed his eyes. In moments he was breathing rhythmically.

Auragole shook Donnadorr violently. "Don! Don! Please wake up! You must wake up!"

With difficulty, Donnadorr got to his feet, sword weaving in his hand. He blinked and tried to focus. "Where is it, lad? Where's the danger?" His words came out thick.

"This fatigue is uncanny." Auragole spoke in a loud voice. "Look, Don, look around you," and he yanked Donnadorr over to some bushes. There at their feet was a strange sight. A deer and her fawn lay sleeping on the ground. Auragole yelled at them. They were breathing, but they did not wake up.

"This is very odd," Don said, struggling to pull himself into greater wakefulness.

"Look," Auragole pointed to the branch of a tree. Birds were sleeping, many birds. "It's morning and full daylight!"

"Strange. . ."

"Help wake up our friends," Auragole said. "If we can only get to the river. . . We've got to wake them up."

350

Auragole knelt next to Glenorr and shook him hard. "We have to go on," Auragole called loudly as he felt Glenorr stir. "You can rest when we get to the Roaring River. We're bound to come across it today! Let's go on!"

Glenorr retorted with a yawn. "What's a day or two longer? Let's sleep." A chill went up Auragole's spine.

But with shouts, cajoling, and a few slaps, Donnadorr and Auragole soon had the little troop on its feet. Auragole led the way with Donnadorr in the rear. Auragole glanced back often. His friends were moving as if their legs were made of lead, as if they had not closed their eyes for a week. Auragole was himself struggling to stay awake. He wasn't sure how long he could fight the intense desire to lie down and close his eyes. He felt sure that if he could only get them to water, they would be all right. He pulled out his map and stared at it again. They should be at the Roaring River. Keep them going, he thought. Keep them going.

They didn't find the river, but within the hour they came to a small creek. It was shallow but rushing rapidly over small stones. "We'll rest here," Auragole told them. The air seemed perceptibly lighter. Auragole suggested that they all swim. He stripped down to his trousers and jumped into the icy water. It came up to his waist. But it revived him.

Donnadorr jumped in after. "Come in," he called to the others. "The water is delicious. Come, dear lads and lassies, time to play."

The girls came to the stream's edge and laughed at the two young men romping about. Donnadorr and Auragole flung water first at each other and then pulled the two girls in. Even Glenorr, who had come to the stream's edge for a drink, was doused and pulled into the water. He protested, but not too angrily.

They finally came out of the water, lit a fire, and set their outer clothes near it to dry in the warm air. Glenorr and Auragole fished. Donnadorr played the harp and the women mended the latest tears in their garments. Auragole watched them from the bank. The fatigue was gone, but no one other than Don seemed to realize that it had come upon them in an unnatural way. He decided not to tell them—best not to alarm them unduly. After all, what choice did they have but to go on? He tried not to think of what might happen when they left this stream with its life-restoring waters.

The next day, as they moved farther and farther into the Deep Forest, it became increasingly colder. Once again they assumed their cloaks. Then, to Auragole's dismay, the fatigue took hold again. In desperation, he started to sing and urged the others to join him. Only Donnadorr responded. But even before the sun had moved above the trees, Glenelle, Glenorr, and Sylvane had dropped in their tracks. Donnadorr fell to his knees. But Auragole shook him hard and screamed at him to stay awake, or they would all die. Donnadorr pulled himself heavily to his feet.

"Look, Don, over there!"

Donnadorr followed the line of Auragole's arm. There was something glittering through the trees a few hundred feet away. Metal in sunlight. Auragole ran toward it, with Donnadorr loping heavily behind him. There must be help ahead. Surely there was help.

In a small clearing they found a cottage. Its thatched roof was partially blown off, but clinging tentatively to it and rotating wildly was a metal weather vane. It was this that had caught Auragole's eye. The yard around the house had been cleared at one time, but now it was overgrown. Bundles of twigs were stacked everywhere. Some had lost their bindings and the sticks were scattered about the yard.

"It must be deserted," Auragole said, feeling a terrible disappointment. But he walked up to the door. It was half off its hinges. Auragole knocked and the two men waited with little hope for an answer. The sound that came back was unexpected. Snoring! Auragole knocked again and then carefully pushed the broken door open. They stepped into the room. At a table in front of a reeking bowl of rotting fruit, a man was sitting in a wooden chair. He was sound asleep and snoring loudly. Near one wall his unmade bed waited. In the unlit fireplace, a kettle emitted the smell of old, sour soup. The room was cold, damp, and cloying, but the thin little man, his shaggy beard bobbing on his chest, looked comfortable and content.

Auragole walked over to him and shook him. The man made some gurgling noises but didn't wake up. Still, his breathing was normal.

"What is this strange sleeping ailment, lad?" Donnadorr asked. "You seem unaffected. I'm struggling to keep my eyes open."

"I am affected though," Auragole answered, stifling a yawn, "but not as much as the rest of you. I don't know why. Acute worry, I suspect."

Donnadorr came over and tried his hand at waking the little man. He shouted in his ear. "Wake up! You're going to freeze to death if you don't wake up, or else you'll starve. Wake up!"

To his surprise the man opened his eyes. "Tried it. Don't like it," he said clearly, and then closed his eyes and was soon snoring again.

"You've got to wake up and patch your roof and fix your door and keep your fire going or you'll die." Auragole shook him again.

"Can't get the hang of it," the man said to them, suddenly wide-eyed. "Can't get the hang of staying awake," and he dropped off again.

The two young men looked at each other, then burst into momentary laughter. Together they shook the man until his teeth rattled.

"Stop!" the man complained. "Can't you see that I'm sleeping?" But he didn't open his eyes.

Donnadorr grabbed the man's beard and gave it a hard yank.

"Ouch! Ouch! Ouch!" The man grabbed his face in pain and opened his eyes. He pointed at Donnadorr and said firmly, "You are a rude young man. You should let sleeping dogs lie," and he closed his eyes again.

"There's little we can do here, lad," Donnadorr said. "Let's get him to his bed and get a fire started."

So the two of them lifted the thin little man, put him in his bed, then covered him with a blanket. Soon he was snoring peacefully. A fire was quickly started. Then the two left to attend to their own friends. As they walked the short distance to where the other three were contentedly sleeping, Donnadorr dropped to his knees. "Lad," he yawned. "I don't know how long I can hold out."

"Stay with me, Don. Don't give in!" Auragole's voice was desperate.

"I don't think I can."

"Fight, damn you! Fight! Fight!"

But Donnadorr flung himself over on his back, and was asleep in seconds.

Auragole walked from one friend to the other, calling each by name, begging each to wake up. One or the other would open his or her eyes, smile at him, then close them again. Auragole was feeling desperate. He slapped Donnadorr as hard as he could.

Don opened his eyes and muttered, "You're too rough, dear lad," and then went back to sleep.

Auragole sat down and put his head in his hands. He fought against the tears of helplessness that threatened to well up in his eyes. Had they escaped the murderous hands of Lumoss only to die here in the woods without a battle?

And then he heard the sound. It was very faint. In an instant, Auragole was on his feet and running toward it.

He ran half a mile and there it was, a wide river careening furiously over the myriad rocks in her path. The Roaring River!

Just as at the stream, the air near the river felt lighter. Auragole breathed deeply. The waters with their life-giving forces would awaken his friends. He stood at the bank of the river taking in large gulps of the moisture-laden air. Then he turned and hurried back to the group of sleepers.

He carried Sylvane first—she was the smallest. He took her right down to the river's edge. In a matter of minutes she opened her eyes and smiled. "Oh, Aurie, I dreamt I was walking in a heavy mist. I couldn't find anyone, but it didn't seem to matter much."

"Sylvie, if you knew how good it is to hear you speak. . ." He hugged her and kissed her cheek.

She turned red and so did Auragole. He stood up quickly and explained, in a rush of words, about the strange ailment. Then he left and returned with Glenelle. By then Sylvane was up and moving about. She had gathered twigs and had lit a fire. Sylvane is like a mother bird, he thought, building a nest wherever she finds herself. He set down the sleeping Glenelle near the river's edge.

"Help her," Auragole called to Sylvane, and returned to bring first Don and then Glen to the riverbank. He could not lift either of them, but he managed to drag each slowly out of the ill woods and over to the Roaring River.

By then he was exhausted and his back and arms ached. They sat near the campfire talking about the strange events of the last couple of days. Suddenly Auragole jumped to his feet. "I've got to get the old man," he told Donnadorr. "He'll die of starvation if I don't." He headed back into the trees.

"Wait up, lad! I'll come with you." Donnadorr hurried after him.

Auragole turned. "Don, I'd be glad for your help, but I don't relish dragging you out of these sleeping woods another time."

"Sorry, lad. Right you are. But how come you are so unaffected?"

"Intense fear." And Auragole gave Don a tired smile. "Tell the others about the old man. And do see if you can get some fish out of that river."

Within the hour Auragole returned with the thin old man. Luckily he was small and light. But it took a long time to waken him. He lay between the river and the fire, and the girls spooned broth into his snoring mouth. He swallowed and slept.

"A most curious malady," Donnadorr said, shaking his head. He looked out at the forest whence they had come. "They're beautiful enough." He motioned at the trees. "Who would have thought they could bring slow death?"

"Pohl should have warned us about these woods!" Glenorr said fiercely.

"If he had known about this ailment, I'm sure he would have told us," Auragole said.

"He knew something!" Glenorr laughed his mirthless laugh.

"He knew legends, Glenorr, that's all!" Auragole said evenly. "And what other way was there, short of walking into danger or turning back to Agavia?"

"The man's a fool with his ridiculous preaching about freedom and love!" Glenorr's voice quivered with barely controlled fury.

"That man saved your life and your sister's. Where's your gratitude?" Auragole's words were both loud and cold. He turned his back on Glenorr and picked up his fishing net and pole and went to stand at the river away from the rest of them. He was fighting his anger, his fears, and his fatigue. Truth to tell, he wasn't sure if he was angry with Glenorr or with Pohl.

When the sleeper finally woke up, he panicked at the sight of the five travelers. He begged them, with trembling voice, not to harm him. It was Glenelle who finally calmed him down. The sleeper told them that he didn't know how long he had been asleep. He listened intently when Auragole tried to explain that some malady was affecting this part of the forest and all its living creatures.

The man shook his head in resignation. "Getting queerer all the time. Don't know what to make of this new trouble. Lived in these woods all my life. So have my folks and their folks back to the beginning of time. But they're getting queerer, these woods. That's the truth of it. Queerer and queerer."

Glenelle told him that they were on their way to the South Gate of Isofed and suggested he come with them. It was too dangerous, she said, for him to return to his cottage.

He dismissed their invitation with a wave of his hand. "People coming and going today, coming and going. Can't stay put. I was like that. Couldn't stay put when I was younger, so I got up one morning and left my home that very day and came out here. But the woods are getting queerer. I'll have to leave. Can't stay here if I can't stay awake. That's the truth of it."

"Where will you go, old father?" Donnadorr asked him.

"Back home, I guess. Got some relatives I ain't seen in twenty years by the sun's reckoning. Besides, it's time I took me a wife. Living alone can make you queerer than the woods."

"Where's home?" Auragole asked.

"Why back up the river, of course. Ten miles about, give or take a few yards."

"Ten miles!" Sylvane said. "And you haven't seen your relatives in twenty years?"

"I'm a roamer, I told you," he said, staring at her suspiciously. "I roamed all this way to be alone. Why would I go back?"

They merely nodded at his indignant reply.

Auragole tried to question him further. "You call the woods queer. How are they queer?"

"Well, it's not because of the wild beasts, I can tell you, though there's plenty of them. Some beasts came at the end of the Golden Century, so the folks say. But it's not them. Them you can see. It's what goes on that you can't see that makes the Deep queer." He shrugged. "Like this sleeping ailment. And strange weather, first cold then hot—and it doesn't matter what the season is."

"Maybe an evil God put a curse on this part of the forest," Sylvane said.

Glenorr snorted.

But the old man stared at Sylvane out of narrowed eyes, as if she herself were the essence of queerness. "What does he look like?" he finally asked her.

"Tell me," Donnadorr said, "do you see many travelers?"

"Yep, too many. Saw one not so long ago."

"When?"

"Oh," he looked ponderously at the sky, "about five years ago. Of course, I could be wrong. It could be six."

Sylvane could contain herself no longer, and she started to giggle behind hands clasped hard to her mouth. Her shoulders shook.

The old sleeper looked at her curiously. "She got a bellyache? She keeps making strange noises."

Over dinner, he told them about the village he had come from, though it could hardly be called that having only a dozen families in all. From what he said, travelers were few. Auragole was relieved. They needn't worry about any unfriendly meetings. Auragole felt sure they could deal with wild animals—he was less certain about unfriendly humans.

Their sleeper had never heard of Mattelmead. Armies and soldiers were in the tales his grandpa had told him, but those were happenings up north. He knew of the Southern Desolation and shook his head firmly. "That's a place queerer than the Deep Woods," he assured them.

The next morning they parted company. The old man headed east up the Roaring River, and the troop of travelers west along its bank.

N

chapter thirty

THE ROARING RIVER, as they marched along it, was deafening, rushing as it did over great protruding rocks. But the air was light and fresh, and Don reveled in it. They saw nothing unusual, no strange animals. Still, they remained alert. By the end of the second day the river quieted. The turbulent white water was behind them. It flowed smoothly. That night they slept soundly.

They had been marching for two hours on the third day when Auragole spotted something. "Stop!" he called out and walked closer to the river. There in the grass were two small boats.

"Well, looky here, lad." Donnadorr whistled softly as he came up beside Auragole. "Now isn't that a welcome sight. We can ride the river until it turns south. Then it's a few days' walk until we come to the gate at Isofed."

The others crowded around.

"Let's put them in the river and see if they're water worthy," Auragole said.

In a few moments the boats were in the river.

"They haven't been used in ages. All the paint is gone, but they're floating," Donnadorr said.

"Let's take them out, Don. You can swim, can't you?" he asked, with a grin. "Or are you afraid of the water like the rest of the Easterners?"

"Like a fish, lad, like a slippery fish."

They stripped down to trousers and shirts and pulled off their boots. It didn't register on Don then, but later he recalled it—Auragole had stuck his knife into the waist of his trousers. Later Auragole said it had been a sudden whim.

"If your boat sinks, Aurie, have no fear. I'll save you," Donnadorr quipped as he climbed into the larger boat.

"I'll be back on land before you can get over the side," Auragole laughed as he climbed into the smaller boat.

With a few hefty strokes, their boats were yards from the shore.

"Dry as the desert, lad. This boat could. . . Now will you look at that! The tide is rising right here at my feet. This one's no good." Donnadorr stood up. "It's over I go. See you on shore."

Donnadorr made a show-off dive, leaping off the stern of the boat into the cool water. Suddenly, to his shock, something powerful wrapped itself around his chest and dragged him down. He fought with all his might, first to free himself from the crushing grip and then to get to the surface, and to the air. He burst through the water, gulped air, but was pulled back under. He didn't see Auragole swimming swiftly toward him. He was struggling with the powerful snake, trying with all his might to pry its deathlike grip from off his chest.

Later he remembered that the girls on shore had screamed. He had lunged through the surface again. The next thing he recalled was the loosening of the snake's hold. And then he was free, but falling under the water. Pictures from his life flitted by. There was Aiku. And there. . . He became interested in all the

360

images and tried to breathe the water. An arm grabbed him around his neck, yanked hard, and pulled him above the surface.

"Easy now," Auragole called softly to him. "I'll pull you ashore. Don't fight me."

And that was the last thing Don remembered until he woke up, sprawled on his stomach on solid ground. Auragole was pressing hard on his back and water was pouring out of his mouth and nose. Coughing wracked his body and his chest. The pain was severe. He tried to roll over and sit up but a groan escaped from his lips and he lay still.

"What's wrong with him?" He heard the concern in Glenelle's voice.

"His ribs," Auragole answered. "They could be broken. That was a powerful snake."

"I'll start a fire, Aurie," Sylvane said. She handed Auragole his cloak and covered Donnadorr with his.

Donnadorr lay next to the fire, breathing painfully, coughing now and then. But he was alive, blessedly alive. He listened to the talk around him. He smiled as Glenelle tried to spoon some tea into his mouth, but he refused the liquid. He had had quite enough liquid to contend with. He heard Glenelle say to Auragole, "He's breathing normally, but he's hurting. Ah, Aurie, thank you for saving his life. What would we have done if we had lost Don?"

Warmth poured through Donnadorr. She does care, after all, he told himself, and turned his head in time to see an odd look cross Auragole's face. He closed his eyes with a sigh. Now what could be done? They both loved Glenelle. And he once again owed his life to Auragole, his rival.

He closed his eyes and was asleep in moments.

Don woke perhaps an hour later and, with difficulty, pulled himself into a sitting position. Glenorr watched him with curiosity but said nothing. Gingerly, he felt his ribs. "I don't think they're broken, just bruised. I won't hold up the journey again with my injuries."

"What nonsense you speak," Glenelle said. "Was it your fault that the boat leaked? Was it your fault that the snake was there? Take off your shirt and let me wind this bandage around your chest."

Donnadorr's chest was circled with thick, red lines where the serpent had squeezed him. By tomorrow, he knew, they would be black and blue.

"I owe you much, Auragole. And I'll repay you one day." Donnadorr sat with great care on the stone next to him as they ate their noon meal.

"You owe me nothing," Auragole said, his voice unusually cool. "I would have done it for any of you."

"I know you would have, lad. Still I owe you."

But Auragole had turned away.

THE NEXT MORNING, both boats gone, they started on their way again on foot. Auragole watched as Donnadorr picked up his heavy load, but he said nothing. He knew that Donnadorr was in pain. He knew that he should have taken some of Donnadorr's load. But he didn't. He felt cranky and short-tempered. He was worried because the trip in the woods had taken longer than he and Pohl had anticipated. And they weren't at the gate yet. And what if something else went wrong? Being leader of this group was a burden and at that moment he didn't want to carry it. Why couldn't Donnadorr lead, or Glenorr? No one seemed concerned about the journey. They had left all the worrying to him, and it irked him. And then there was that something that wove between Don and Glenelle. If Glenelle noticed his bad temper, she said nothing. She had brightened considerably in these last days. Often Auragole felt Sylvane's eyes on him, but he made himself inaccessible. He didn't want pity. Glenorr was still wrapped in his own sorrows and anger and noticed little. Donnadorr, Auragole thought—

because Don was unusually kind and careful with him—understood at least one cause of Auragole's irritability. It made him uncomfortable, but there was little he could do about it.

After three more days of marching along the Roaring River, it turned south. So, as previously planned, they left it and continued northwest. To Auragole's relief, the strange sleeping malady had not come this far.

Four days later, in mid-April, three weeks after they had parted from Galavi and Pohl, they arrived at their destination—the southern wall of Isofed and its gate. But between them and their destination was the now narrow but rapidly running Isofed River, flowing only yards from the gate. A drawbridge was the only way to approach it. As Pohl had assumed, there were no signs that soldiers had been there. However, the bridge was up.

"Now what?" Glenorr demanded of Auragole as they stood on the south shore of the Isofed.

Donnadorr spoke before Auragole could answer Glenorr with the caustic remark that was on the tip of his tongue. "There's probably a bell near the raised bridge, lad."

They found it on a post near the bridge. It was tied with a rope. Don pulled it. Its clappers made a large clanging sound, which could certainly be heard on the other side of the tall, closed gate. They waited. After a few minutes Don pulled it again. They took turns pulling the rope. After fifteen minutes of constant ringing, at Auragole's command, they stopped.

"This is your plan, Auragole, what do you suggest we do?" Blame was in Glenorr's blue eyes, making them like two frozen pools.

Auragole tried to return his stare with a coolness of his own, but it was a poor show. Finally he said, "I suggest we ring the bell every five minutes until someone answers it."

And that is what they did.

Just as the sun was beginning to set, the door opened slowly with a loud screeching noise. Rust and disuse were in that sound.

The travelers gathered eagerly at the shore. A tall, broad man with long white hair, clean-shaven and dressed in a heavy white robe, moved through the gate. He did not come down to the shore, but stood erect just outside the gate.

"What is it you wish?" he called out in a deep but shaky voice.

The others turned to Auragole. So Auragole answered loudly, "With your permission, sir, we would like to travel across your land to your North Gate. We're on our way to Mattelmead."

"Why?" the old man's question sailed across the river.

"Sir, it is by far the shortest route to Mattelmead from here."

"Why do you go to that wicked land?"

Auragole was momentarily taken aback. "Sir, all we ask is that you allow us to go as far as the gate that leads to the Sorren Heights."

"No outsider crosses our land."

"But we desperately need your help," Auragole said, "or we must add many weeks to our journey." He was pleading now.

The old man answered without emotion. "That is your own affair. You are not Isofedian and therefore no concern of mine."

"One among us is ill." Auragole said. "We must get to Mattelmead as speedily as possible. There are good doctors there."

"Which Gods do you serve? Do you worship the great King God or are you worshippers of the Prince who is a false God?"

Before Auragole could answer, Glenorr stepped forward. "We worship no Gods for they are myths for fools and tales for children!" His harsh words echoed across the river.

Auragole stared incredulously at Glenorr. Glenorr's eyes looked glazed—like frost on stone.

For a moment there was no answer from the large man near the gate. Then he gestured at them accusingly. "You shall, indeed, do well in Mattelmead, for there the King is all but forgotten and even the Prince is little considered. Strange Gods do they worship, or none at all. But through these lands you may not travel, for you would contaminate the very soil dedicated and consecrated to the King. Our people follow strict laws given to our ancestors by the King. We do not allow outsiders in, nor do any but a few of our own people go out. Three gates there are to our lands and three gatekeepers. We alone may speak to strangers."

With trembling voice, Auragole called to him, "We shall talk to no one, nor shall we take any food from your land, for we have plenty of our own. Will you not help us?"

"You may not step foot on our holy soil. You would defile it."

"You ignorant, superstitious ass!" Glenorr screamed. "When Ormahn marches through the west no mere ten-foot-high wall will stop him. How will your King God save you then?"

To Auragole's surprise, Glen was lying on the ground. It was the throbbing in his knuckles that made him realize he had struck him. Glenorr leapt up and lunged at Auragole. Before he could throw a punch, Don grabbed Glenorr from behind, pinning his arms to his sides.

"Stop it! Stop it, lads!" he said, as Glenorr struggled to break free. "No quarrel between us will change that man's mind."

Auragole stood stricken, staring down at his bruised knuckles and then at the furious Glenorr. Rage had taken a hold of him so suddenly that he had acted without thinking. Across the river, the gatekeeper was reentering the gate. Auragole's heart twisted as he saw it close behind him.

"Is there no honor left in you, Glen?" Glenelle moved between Glenorr and Auragole. "You owe your life to Auragole, as I do."

Auragole was stunned at what he had done. He believed himself more in command of his feelings than Glenorr. His loss of control shook him. But he couldn't rid himself of the anger he felt at Glenorr.

"I owe him nothing!" Glenorr said, between gasps for breath.

"Had we not waited for the thief we would have been in Mattelmead long ago."

Glen's words hit harder than any blow Glen could have inflicted with his fists. Auragole did not see the muscles on Donnadorr's face tighten.

"Oh, nonsense, Glen. We know nothing of the kind. Besides," Glenelle's voice was almost light, "if we hadn't waited for Don, we would have missed Agavia. And that would have been a terrible loss, don't you think?" Glenelle took Glenorr by the hand and moved away from the river's edge, talking quietly to him.

Auragole turned away and walked along the bank, picking up pebbles and hurling them into the water that was growing darker in the twilight. In an instant, Auragole had stripped down to his trousers and jumped into the icy water. He reveled in the ache it caused him. It stopped the anger from overflowing into more harsh words. It stopped his frustration at being thwarted on the road to Mattelmead. It didn't stop the shame he felt at his own violence or at the knowledge that what Glen had said was true. What was most terrible was that part of him wished he had left Don where they had found him. Part of him would have gladly missed all of Agavia to have Ellie to himself. Another part of him was appalled. He swam until he was numb.

Sylvane stood at the shore of the river as he came out. She handed Auragole his shirt and cloak. Her light-brown eyes looked as dark as the water he had just left.

"What is it, Aurie? What troubles you these days? You've been so unapproachable."

He rubbed himself vigorously with his cloak. "Nothing troubles me," he said, avoiding her eyes.

"I don't believe you." There was a note in her voice that Auragole had never heard before.

"It's difficult guiding this group to Mattelmead, as you can well see, Sylvane."

"It's more, Aurie," her voice became soft-edged. "Won't you

let me help you?"

"I'm fine!" he said, unable to bear her kindness. He started to move away, all the good the swim had done, evaporating. Auragole walked past Donnadorr, who had been watching his exchange with Sylvane, to where Glenorr and Glenelle sat talking. "We camp here tonight," he said.

DONNADORR WAS THE first to awaken the next morning. He rekindled the fire and put tea on for the breakfast. Auragole rose next, grunted a good morning to Donnadorr, then sat down on a rock near the fire to study the map of the Westernlands that Pohl had given him.

After the others were up and were huddled around the fire sipping the morning tea, Auragole announced in a grim, somewhat unsteady voice, "We must follow the Isofed River west until we come to Wildenfarr-low-desert, and then head north to Glovale and then north through Glovale to the border of Mattelmead. It's a longer route than we had anticipated, but we have no choice."

Glenorr gave a mirthless little laugh.

"The Isofed River meanders," Don said, looking at the map over Auragole's shoulder. "If we follow it, we will lose even more time. Is that not so, lad?"

"True, following the river closely could mean almost doubling our travel time in these woods. We'll try to cut through the Deep Forest in a more or less straight line toward the hills on the border between Isofed and Wildenfarr."

Glenorr made a grunting noise, but everyone ignored him.

"But Aurie, what about the sleeping illness?" Glenelle asked.

"It didn't bother us when we left the Roaring River to head north. I'm hoping it has not come this far west. We'll go a short distance and see. If we must, then we will follow the river, no matter how much it winds."

All but Glenorr murmured their agreement. He spoke then

and his voice was tight as he pressed words out through his clenched teeth. "If I speak, will I be heard?"

"Of course you will, lad," Donnadorr said, with little enthusiasm.

Glenorr didn't answer him, but looked directly at Auragole. There was insolence in his stare.

Auragole coldly met his eyes. "We are all willing to hear your thoughts, Glen."

The sun drifted through the trees spilling light and shadow on the river in a lovely pattern. Donnadorr noted it—one moment of pleasure—then turned his attention to Glenorr.

"Your plan is foolish." Glenorr sneered. "It leads us into lands and dangers we know nothing about, and miles out of our way. I say, let's cross the country of Isofed as originally planned."

"But, Glen," Sylvane spoke for the first time that morning. "We haven't been given permission."

"We don't need their permission," he answered angrily.

There was silence from the travelers. Above them birds twittered noisily, immune to the worries of humans.

"What are you suggesting?" Auragole asked.

"I'm suggesting we build a ladder—there's plenty of wood in this forest. That wall can be scaled easily. All we need do is go a few miles away from gate. We build a raft—the river is narrow—and then go over the wall at night. During the day we hide. We travel when it's dark. We could be at the North Gate in a couple of weeks." He stared at them defiantly.

It was Sylvane who responded first. "But we would contaminate their land if we did that."

Glenorr's laugh was a dismissive bark. "Superstitions! You give credence to ignorant superstitions!"

"No, I don't Glen." Sylvane bit her lip. "I honor their beliefs." She turned to Auragole for help, but he glanced away.

Glenorr pointed at Donnadorr. "You've lived a life of adventure and necessity. Does the thought of crossing Isofed without permission offend your precious soul?" His grin mocked Donnadorr.

"I could do it, should it be the best choice, lad. But I don't see it necessarily as the wisest choice. Isofed is a populated land. Its people are a warrior people, well trained to defend themselves. They have a large army, part of which may be on the other side of that wall." He gestured across the river with his head. "I don't think they would deal too kindly with us should we be captured. They're a fanatical lot, as we have heard and seen. We're little more than animals to them."

Glenelle spoke up before Glenorr could retort. "Can you tell direction by the stars, Glen?"

"You know I can't."

"Nor can any of us, save Aurie. For good reason has he been chosen leader. He's given up much to guide us to Mattelmead. It's his judgment we must follow, not yours nor any of ours."

Donnadorr saw Auragole redden. He loves her, he sighed. Well, why shouldn't he?

"We go around," Auragole said, in a low voice. He turned then and started to repack his belongings.

Donnadorr heard Glenorr chuckle, but he ignored it. To dwell too much on Glenorr meant wanting to respond to him just as Auragole had the previous night, and that would lead to no good. They packed quickly. In only a matter of minutes, they had left the river and reentered the forest.

chapter thirty-one

AFTER HALF AN hour's walking, Auragole called a halt. Donnadorr heard the singing in the trees, the movements of small animals. Auragole questioned the travelers, but no one was sleepy. They went on, stopping now and again to monitor their reactions, but all seemed well. After a few hours, they ate a meager lunch and then continued on their way.

The woods offered few difficulties. The land was flat. There were tall, familiar evergreens keeping the smaller plants and trees from growing toward the sun. Auragole marched ahead, talking to no one. Donnadorr sang and the girls joined in, but not Glenorr, or Auragole, who looked grim and preoccupied.

At the campfire that night Auragole sat apart studying his map. Glenorr kept to himself writing in his notebook. Donnadorr, on the other hand, told stories, and the air rang with the laughter of the two girls. Now and then he caught Auragole staring coolly at him and he was troubled. He would have to do something about that.

They had been moving through the woods about four days and had made camp near the Isofed River, to which they had returned two days earlier. Donnadorr and Auragole had gone half a mile upstream to fish. They had caught enough for both dinner and breakfast, but had spoken little. This is the time, Donnadorr thought. As Auragole was about to head back for the campsite, Donnadorr caught his arm.

"Aurie, can we speak?"

Auragole stared at him calculatingly, then sat down on the bank. Donnadorr joined him. The hurrying water seemed to be whispering as it passed over the rocks. Auragole threw a pebble into the sound.

"It's about Glenelle," Donnadorr said, pulling grass absent-mindedly from the ground.

Auragole's face paled.

"She's very dear to me," Donnadorr rushed on. "I've known many a pretty lassie in my time, but Glenelle is special. She's beautiful and wise and laughs easily. She's brave and clever. . ."

Auragole leapt up. "Why must you speak to me, Donnadorr? I see that you care." He started to move away.

But Donnadorr rose quickly and blocked Auragole's way. "Aurie, I see that you care also." Auragole's face flooded with color, but Donnadorr stood fast.

Auragole waited.

"It stands like a wall between us. It troubles me, lad, for I owe you my life three times over." He put his hand on Auragole's shoulder. It was tense and rigid under Donnadorr's touch.

"I'm not used to speaking of such things."

"Yet we must. Sit, please, Aurie."

Once again they sat on the hard ground. Auragole began throwing fists of grass into the river.

"Say the word, Aurie, and I'll back off. If you want her, she's yours."

Auragole looked at him curiously. "Why would you give her

up? Because you feel a debt is owed me?"

"Do you think I value my life so little? Or take your deeds for granted?" Don laughed. "Perhaps there is little honor left in the east, but I still honor the man who has three times returned to me my life."

They sat staring at the shallow stream for several minutes. Then Auragole stood up. Donnadorr rose to face him.

"Let me think about it," Auragole said. He headed back up the stream, but after a few steps he turned around and offered Donnadorr his hand.

Donnadorr took it, sober-eyed, but smiling.

As they were walking Auragole spoke. "Don, can I ask you a question?" His voice sounded strained.

"Ask away, lad?"

"Do you. . .do you believe that you have a task—I mean a life task?"

"A task. . .? Well, yes, to survive. But," Don added, "to survive with honor. And to help others survive." He felt happy with his answer.

"But what I mean," Auragole brushed a lock of hair off his forehead, "is something that you have to do. . .to accomplish in the future. I mean. . .do you feel as if something out there is waiting for you?"

"Like what?"

"I don't know. . .just. . .something."

"Well, lad, I don't worry too much about tomorrow or the day after. Do what each day asks of you, that's my motto. Why, Aurie? Do you feel you have a. . .what did you call it, a life task? If so, given by whom?"

Auragole stared for a time at his boots, then finally said, "When I lived in my valley, my life followed a predictable routine. This may sound like someone who isn't grateful for the peaceful childhood he's been given. But I always wanted to leave my valley, couldn't wait till I was old enough. It's as if I felt *something* was waiting for me out there, something that I must do."

"What, lad?"

Auragole shook his head, "That's just it. . .I don't know. It hovers near my mind, but I can't quite reach it."

"Well, Aurie," Donnadorr shrugged, "then you'll just have to wait. If your feeling is true, your task will show itself to you sooner or later, don't you think?"

"Yes, I suppose it will." But Auragole didn't look very comforted.

THEY HAD BEEN traveling about a week after his conversation with Donnadorr when Auragole noticed that the forest was again changing—starting to feel queer. It happened gradually. The tall evergreens gave way to shorter, leafless trees, without the buds that should have appeared as April drew to a close. Luckily, there was still little undergrowth, so they walked with ease, but something in the air had altered.

It isn't that it's heavier or lighter, colder or warmer, Auragole thought, but it feels odd, as if it has senses, as if it has eyes and ears—a little like that time in the cave with Pohl.

As the forest began to transform, Glenelle became increasingly anxious and their pace slowed. She spoke little, had difficulty walking, and stumbled frequently. Often she would moan and sigh. More than once one or the other tried to help her, but she would motion him or her aside with an impatient gesture of her hand.

It was after they had been in this odd part of the Deep for four days, now away from the river, that Glenelle had another spell.

They had come across a creek, barely a cut in the ground, but it ran freely and the water was sweet. Since entering this strange part of the Deep, they had seen few ponds or streams, so they were relieved to have come across water. Their supplies were low, but for them to go back to the Isofed would have meant adding days to their already long journey. Hovering over the creek was a large, gnarled tree—larger than most they had seen these past days. Spehn had called these peculiar-shaped trees *rope trees*, and it seemed an apt name. Its sprawling branches reached out, twisting in all directions. That night they camped under it.

Auragole had been sleeping soundly when something dropped onto his chest. He woke with a start, grabbed his sword, rolled over, and was on his feet instantly.

Then he heard her—from high in the rope tree.

"How did she get up there?" Donnadorr asked as he came alongside.

Auragole, who was standing close to the trunk and staring straight up, felt his body grow rigid and alert. Glenelle was sitting on a branch, halfway up the tall tree, first moaning, then cursing, all the while throwing small twigs down at the sleeping figures. Auragole stood paralyzed as Glenelle reached up and began to shake the branch above her.

"Swords, she will fall," Donnadorr said.

"Oh no, oh sweet sky!" Sylvane wrestled free from her blankets and came up to the two of them. "Oh no!"

A torrent of vile words issued from Glenelle in an ugly, deep, unfamiliar voice. Sylvane grabbed Donnadorr. He put his arm around her shoulders and held her. Suddenly Glenelle let out a series of piercing screams. Sylvane buried her head in Donnadorr's shoulder. In a moment Glenorr was standing next to them.

"Glenelle! Stop it!" Glenorr shouted. "Stop it!"

Auragole's hand clasped his mouth. "Don't startle her!" he whispered. "She'll fall."

Glenorr quieted immediately, and Auragole took his hand from Glen's mouth.

"We must bring her down, lad," Donnadorr whispered to Auragole. "Stars, how did she get up there?"

The tree began shaking violently again, and branches came tumbling down upon them. They moved quickly back. Then curses began to flow out of Glenelle's mouth in a deep, ugly voice.

Donnadorr shuddered. "I've only heard words like those from the lowest, vilest men. Where could she have learned them?"

"It isn't her speaking, Don," Auragole answered.

"She'll fall and kill herself." Anguish was in Glenorr's voice.

"I'll get her down," Auragole said, and started to move.

"I'll do it," Donnadorr said, and grabbed Auragole's arm.

"No," Auragole insisted. "I'm lighter than you and I've spent many childhood days climbing." He ran to their supplies and got a rope. "Don," he said, as he began his climb, "Stand below her. If she falls. . ."

"Right you are."

His ascent was a difficult one. Glenelle shook the tree frequently. Every time she did, Auragole caught his breath and waited to hear her fall through the branches. Miraculously, she didn't. How had she been able to climb so high? Auragole finally reached the twisted branch that she was sitting on. She was a few feet out from the trunk and he would have to slide out on it very carefully if he was to reach her. Would the branch hold their weight? If he slid out on the branch and grabbed her, would she struggle with him? If she did, they would both come tumbling down. Auragole first tied the rope securely around his waist, measured carefully, and then tied it around the trunk. He tied a second rope to the trunk and made a large loop, hoping to put it around Glenelle. Then straddling the branch, Auragole put the rope over his shoulder and began to slide toward Glenelle as silently as he could.

The moonlight on her hair made it look like liquid gold. To Auragole, moving slowly toward her, Glenelle appeared unreal, undefined. Fortunately she was looking away from him. He moved as quickly as caution and silence would allow. He reached her and tried unsuccessfully to put the rope around her before she turned to face him. Her face looked wild. When she saw him, she cursed in an ugly, harsh voice and began striking out at him. Just before they toppled over, he grabbed her around the waist with both hands. Auragole hung on to her with all his might as they plunged through the layers of prickly branches. Suddenly, the rope that was tied around Auragole jerked. He was slammed against the trunk. And Glenelle fell out of his arms.

Stars in the heavens, he had dropped her!

"It's all right, lad," Donnadorr called in a low, breathless voice. "I've caught her. We're both fine. Just got the breath knocked out of me. Wait, I'll come for you in a moment."

Auragole didn't know how long he dangled there, trying to catch his breath and to clear his head. Then he heard Don's voice a little above him.

"Lad, are you all right?"

"Yes, winded, that's all. Glenelle?"

"She's all right, some minor scratches. Glen and Sylvie are taking care of her. Now grab my hand."

With Don's help Auragole pulled himself up onto a thick branch. Don cut the rope holding Auragole and carefully guided him down the last several feet. Auragole stepped painfully onto the ground.

"Nothing broken, I trust."

Auragole shook his head, but he knew that his back would be black and blue in a day or two, and that his face and hands were covered with scratches. And there were new rips in his clothing. He and Don walked to the fire where Sylvane was sitting with Glenelle's head in her lap. Glenelle was sleeping.

"The fall brought her to herself," Sylvane said, her tear-streaked face shiny in the firelight.

"You see! You see!" Glenorr came out of the shadows, his fists clenched. He thrust his face, red with anger, close to Auragole's.

"She should be in Mattelmead. Because of you and your cursed scruples we are weeks from there. If anything happens to Ellie before we get there, I'll kill you. By the earth and all its rocks, I'll kill you!" And he stormed away.

Auragole stood there stunned. The rage began to rise up hot from Auragole's chest into his face. His breath came in large gulps. He started to rock back and forth. He was about to go after Glenorr when he felt a powerful arm across his chest.

"Pay no attention to him, lad," Donnadorr said. "Glenorr's not himself. He hasn't been since Lumoss took us captive, as you well know." Donnadorr held Auragole until the tension went out of Auragole's body.

"I tell you this, Don," Auragole said, as Donnadorr let go of him, "if he makes any more trouble on this journey, I'll kill him myself— and without an ounce of remorse." The anger he felt was hard to let go of and hard to bear because in it was woven a thread of fear. He was leader and guide, the stars help him, and Mattelmead seemed farther away than ever. They were walking in uncharted land—the maps telling him little, their calculations often wrong—and four people were depending on his decisions and his judgment. That knowledge was as unbearable as were Glenorr's rages.

The travelers stayed near that sliver of a stream for three days. Glenelle recovered slowly. They had little eldenmyrr and though they looked, could find none. There were strange plants there and no one was willing to try them. Without Galavi's uncanny earth and plant sense, they would do without.

Donnadorr fished. Glenelle slept and Sylvane sat near her, keeping watch over her. Glenorr stayed away from the group, sitting upstream writing in his notebook. Auragole, feeling bruised, moved stiffly about the woods on short walks or sat near the fire studying and correcting his maps.

Finally, Glenelle, pale and silent, was able to walk and they again resumed their journey, moving slowly—too slowly, Auragole feared.

chapter thirty-two

THEY HAD STOPPED for the noonday meal a week later. Donnadorr sat observing Auragole, who was once again staring at the map Pohl had given him. He was making marks on it with a stub of a pencil, then rubbing the back of his hand across his forehead. Donnadorr knew what the trouble was. They should have been out of the Deep Forest, and they weren't. They should have come to hills on their way to Wildenfarr-low-desert, but they hadn't. Well, maps were only paper, Donnadorr thought. These endless woods are the reality.

The other three were napping when the mysterious attack came. First, the wind picked up, blowing gently through the campsite. The fire went out in an instant, as if smothered by an unseen blanket. Then the map was plucked from Auragole's hand by a swoosh of air. He chased all over the campsite after it. It finally dropped at his feet. Donnadorr stood up. There came a sound that to his ears seemed like humming, or perhaps it was laughter. Donnadorr stood there listening, fascinated, until his legs were knocked out from under him. As he lay on the ground he heard the calls of his friends.

"What's going on?"

"Stop it!"

"Get off my chest!"

Auragole pulled out his sword and yelled to the group to get their weapons. They were under attack. They tried to get up, but invisible pushes and punches and blows were raining down on them. They could not see their adversaries. Donnadorr crawled to his sword, which was lying near his pack, got to his feet, and lunged at the air, only to get swatted by an unseen sword across his rear, again accompanied by the ripple of something like laughter. "What is this?" Donnadorr hollered at Auragole, as he once more lunged at nothing at all.

"I don't know!" Auragole said, then stumbled and fell on his face.

Over and over they were pounded, pushed, and tripped. Around them, floating in among them like invisible birds, were strange rumblings—almost speech, almost anger, almost laughter.

Finally Donnadorr lay sprawled on the ground on his stomach just a few inches from Auragole.

"Don," Auragole whispered, "I have an idea. Drop your sword! Get your harp and play!"

"What?"

"Play!" Auragole said, desperation in his voice. "And sing something about beautiful forests. You know a dozen songs about forests."

"Right, lad. It sounds mad, but it's madness we're in."

Donnadorr got a few swift kicks before he made it back to where his harp lay. Auragole was pushed and pulled by unseen hands while attempting to pluck his harp. Donnadorr picked up his own harp and began to play. He too was attacked, but he managed to open his mouth and sing as if his life depended on it.

In an instant, the blows stopped. The erratic wind died away.

Donnadorr sang in a rich, bold voice that belonged as easily to the woods as did a tree or a stream. And Auragole's light baritone was a wonderful complement to Donnadorr's. The uncanny sounds began to subside.

As the two young men sang, the sun brightened and the air became so translucent that Donnadorr thought that with just a little effort, he would be able to see right through it. To what, he wondered? Some hidden world that men's eyes were too veiled to see—Pohl's Elementals, perhaps? Birds landed quietly on the branches above them and listened. The girls joined them for the choruses and soon the forest around them was filled with the songs of humans—their love for tree and stream, grass and flower—songs from long ago, written by those who had cared about and lived with all the earth as with a mother.

Then Donnadorr and Auragole sang a song they had learned in Agavia.

> *Through stately trees*
> *and golden grass I roam*
> *in a shadowed wood*
> *far away from home.*
>
> *Silence like sorrow*
> *sits in the leaves*
> *and the wood is a widow*
> *who waits and grieves.*
>
> *Gone, gone away*
> *are the Small Ones who cared*
> *for brook, flower, tree*
> *and the life that they shared.*

Donnadorr knew that he had never sung better, and Auragole added quiet vocal harmonies and supporting chords on his harp.

He thought they listened, those hidden creatures—quietly weaving their essence into the sound. He knew that Auragole, and maybe the others, felt it. Perhaps these creatures were remembering a better time for the Deep Earth.

Gone, too, the dancing
in palest moonlight
and the joyous noise
of a woodland night.

Gone, now, the chorus
of lion and deer
singing together
before birth of fear.

Gone, too, the love
that fell with the sun.
The woodland is empty,
the forest undone.

Now silence and sorrow
sit in the leaves
and the wood is a widow
who waits and grieves.

Through stately trees
and golden grass I roam
in a shadowed wood
far away from home.

Without pause, Auragole began another song and then another. And now it was Donnadorr who supported him with harmonies, and the girls sang with them. When they stopped, the travelers looked at one another with wonder. The air was no longer agitated. Peace, like the warmth of a hen on her nest, settled over the woods. The troop laughed and hugged one another—all except Glenorr, who sat silently watching and brooding. Had he neither seen nor sensed anything? Donnadorr wondered. Has he so closed himself off?

They had been fiercely pushed, punched, and pounded, yet no one had any bruises. Donnadorr felt no lingering pain, nor did anyone else complain of any. They didn't speak. What was there to say? But they stayed there, in that tranquil oasis, the rest of the day and through the night. Again and again, Donnadorr and Auragole picked up their harps and played and sang. Music wove calmness like a protective net around them. Not since Agavia had there been such a feeling of harmony in the atmosphere around them.

By midmorning of the following day, it was memory. They were again inching their way toward Mattelmead.

EIGHT DAYS LATER they came to a shallow, narrow stream coming from the north. Here the woods ended. "This, I think, is the Isofed," Auragole said, looking at his map.

"You joke, lad," Don said. "This paltry thing? There's certainly no fish in it, not even any minnows," he said, staring at the shallow water they could almost leap over.

"According to Pohl's map," Auragole said, "the Isofed makes a turn and heads south—going I don't know where. Certainly not where we're going. Look!" He pointed west. "That's our goal."

Donnadorr squinted and stared across the flat, sparse, grass-covered land toward the horizon. There were ghostly shapes that Don realized were not clouds, but hills.

"We'd better refill our water canteens," Auragole said.

"The water looks awfully brackish," Sylvane said.

"This might be the last water we come across before we get to those hills," Auragole told her. "So it's best if we fill the canteens."

Two days later they came to the hills that divided the Deep from Wildenfarr. As Donnadorr surveyed the hills ahead of them, his heart sank. Their food supply was dwindling. There had been few streams for many days now, and the narrowing Isofed had held no fish. And there had been little game. Their progress had been achingly slow, and now before them were hills so barren that all hope of food taken from the land was gone. Donnadorr knew that they had about a week's supply—that is, if they were careful. He looked over at Auragole, who was staring at the hills stoically. What was he thinking? Probably Auragole's thoughts were as gloomy as Don's own. Too soon to lose hope, he chided himself. Perhaps something better would be found on the other side of the hills.

Three days later, in the afternoon, they stood on the crest of the last hill and looked out at the land below them. Donnadorr's breath nearly failed him. He could hear the others groaning behind him, and an ugly chuckle from Glenorr. As far as the eye could see there was sand—nothing but an undulating sea of sand. It was both awesome and terrible to behold.

Donnadorr walked over to Auragole, who stood, his body rigid, gazing out over the vast wilderness. "What do we do, lad?"

"You tell me," Auragole answered. "You make a decision."

"We have to go back, idiot!" Glenorr shouted at him.

"We can't." Auragole smiled, grimly. "We don't have enough water to get us back."

With a growl, Glenorr lunged at him, pulling him down to the ground. "You knew. You knew. . ."

They rolled over and over, striking and cursing at each other. Had their strength been greater, perhaps they would have hurt each other, but they were weak from lack of food and little water. Donnadorr and the women finally managed to pull them apart. Auragole's lips were bleeding and Glenorr's cheek and eye were bruised.

"Let him lead," Auragole said between breaths, jerking his head toward Glenorr. "He's such a fine thinker, let him take on the burden of this group. I'm finished."

"You should have listened when I said to cut through Isofed," Glenorr shot back at him.

"Since when do you know anything about direction? You completely lost your way crossing the Gandlese. That's as much as you know!"

"Stop it!" Sylvane was suddenly between them. "Men! When things get hard they want to solve it with fists or weapons. Must men become children when we need them most? You want to stay here and hurl curses and blame at each other? Then do it. I will lead." And with that she picked up her pack, swung it on her back, and started down the slope.

Auragole stood up. "Sylvane," he shouted. "Come back!"

But she paid no heed. Then Glenelle, without a word, started down after her.

Donnadorr grabbed his pack. "Come along, lads. We have no choice but to go on. Perhaps we'll find help up ahead, or water." And he too strode downhill after the women.

Donnadorr could hear, to his relief, the other two men following him. Auragole quickly overtook him and moved ahead. Donnadorr could feel rather than hear Glenorr behind him, moving, no doubt, with that pounding step of his, the sound lost now in the sand. He could see the anger leave Auragole's shoulders. Auragole finally caught up with Sylvane.

"We need to go in a more northerly direction, Sylvie," he said. "Keep the afternoon sun to your left."

Sylvane turned without a word. Donnadorr caught up with them both and saw the tears sliding down her cheeks. He knew Auragole had seen them too.

When they reached the flatlands, Auragole moved out in front and once again took the lead. They headed due north, treading with laborious steps over the heat-shimmering sand until there was no more light. They camped that evening out on the desert. There was no brook, no tree, no shelter of any kind, only the desert stretching wide and wild around them.

We're going to die, Donnadorr thought. We're going to die, either of thirst or the sun's parching heat. He looked up at the indifferent desert stars and thought that it was not death that was so sad a thought. It was that life seemed so incomplete, still barely begun. Perhaps that was the way death always came— no matter how old one was—with a sense of how much there was still to finish on this earth. He shrugged away the thoughts. Too late, he thought with some amusement, to begin to wax philosophic. He fell asleep.

"Don, wake up!"

Donnadorr sat up instantly and grabbed for his sword.

"It's Auragole," the voice reassured him.

"What's the matter?" Donnadorr asked him, shivering in the cool desert night.

"Did you call out to me?"

"No."

"Strange, I heard a voice that distinctly said to me, 'Travel by night.'"

"Well, it wasn't me," Donnadorr yawned. "Maybe it was Glen."

"No, no, not Glen, but a male voice."

"Well, maybe you dreamt it. Anyway, it's a good idea, lad. It's brutal walking in that sun."

They woke up the group, told them the new plans, and in moments they were on their way. They traveled through the few dark hours that were left, and then well into the morning. When it became hot, they made shelters against the sun with their cloaks and blankets and slept.

They did this for two days and two nights. They met no one, saw no living thing, nor did they come across water. They were eating one small meal a day and drinking one cup of brackish water. On the third day, Donnadorr could not sleep. One day, he thought. Two days at the most and it will all be over. The chance of finding water now was remote. He didn't much care. Why does Auragole insist we keep going? Why should we push our bodies beyond their strength? Why not stay put, close our eyes, and wait for death?

Another day passed. Perhaps it was two. They walked and walked, but the land never changed. That final night there was no moon. Don fixed his sight, as Auragole had taught him, on the North Star and willed his body to go forward. Finally he could go on no longer. He dropped to his knees, turned to seek his friends, and saw no one behind him or in front of him. Had they all fallen?

No good-byes, was his last thought, no good-byes.

N

chapter thirty-three

AURAGOLE WAS ASLEEP and dreaming when he heard hoofbeats. It sounded like hundreds of horses. He looked out over the desert waste and saw on the horizon to his left an army attired in raiments of black, seated on horses whose gear was also black. On the horizon to his right, he saw an army in red garments with horses also geared in red. The two legions were charging full speed at each other behind two leaders. Their spears were ready and in a moment there would be a terrible, bloody battle. But when they were a hundred yards apart, the armies stopped and the two leaders rode out to meet each other. They spoke for a long while. Then they rode off side by side between the two armies, and the soldiers turned and followed their leaders over the horizon and out of sight. I'm dreaming, Auragole thought. Soon it will all be a dream.

AURAGOLE WAS PICKED up by many hands, then placed on a horse in front of one dressed in white robes that concealed everything except pale blue eyes. A moist rag was pressed against his cracked lips. Auragole sucked at it eagerly, but it was quickly taken from him. He fell into unconsciousness again, partially waking to feel the wet cloth at his mouth. He heard voices but thought little of it, longing only for the moisture of the cloth. It seemed to him that they slept on the ground at least one time. He recalled the smell of roasting meat and unfamiliar herbs. Perhaps he only dreamt it. They rode on, and again and again the rag was given him to suck, fuller and fuller, until finally he was allowed to drink from a flask. On and on they traveled. He was sometimes awake, but no thoughts formed themselves in his mind. He never wondered who his rescuers or captors were—or whether his friends had also been taken.

Then one morning Auragole awoke fully. Underneath his body were soft, thick furs. He was in a large tent. He sat up and saw, to his great relief, all his friends on furs like his own. They were still asleep.

"Thank the stars!" Auragole exclaimed. "We are safe."

"Wake you now?" a light voice behind and to his right asked.

He turned his head and saw a small female figure in voluminous robes of brown. Only her light-blue eyes were visible.

"Yes," he nodded.

"I go to the chief then." She bobbed her head and quickly left the tent.

When the man strode in, the others were awake and they were greeting each other weakly. Auragole, knowing that all his friends were safe, turned to observe the stranger who had entered. He was very tall, and he wore white robes that were trimmed with silver threads. His bearded face was uncovered. His eyes were the lightest blue Auragole ever recalled seeing and his hair was almost white. He was handsome, strong-jawed, with a look of authority. He was, Auragole estimated, about forty.

"Who speaks for all?" the man asked in a voice of command.

Auragole struggled shakily to his feet and faced him. "I do," he whispered.

The man looked him over, carefully and soberly. "It is the territory of Chief And-ul-farr and his tribe that you are in. I am And-ul-farr. It is guests you are. Or have you some other purpose?" His eyes narrowed as he waited for an answer.

"No harmful purpose, sir," Auragole told him. "We only wish to cross your lands."

A look of incredulity crossed And-ul-farr's face. But then, as if he had caught himself in an unseemly gesture, the solemn noncommittal look returned.

"Prepared for you soon will be the baths and then the food. After, we will hear your talk as is our custom and our right." And-ul-farr turned and abruptly strode out of the tent.

Auragole sank back to the ground, hoping he had satisfactorily met the chief's interrogation. He lay there half dozing, too exhausted to worry. Not much time elapsed before some women came to escort them to the baths, first the men, and after, they were told, the women.

The men walked out into almost blinding sunlight. They were in what was a tent city by a small but clear blue lake. All around there was grass growing a deep lush green. Odd trees laden with fruit Auragole had never seen before swayed gently in the constant breeze. There were sheep and goats moving through the tent city. He couldn't tell for certain, but from the number of tents, he guessed there were perhaps two hundred souls here. Beyond the green, and stretching unimpeded toward the horizon, the desert sparkled brightly in the sun, as if waiting.

The men were taken to a tent at the edge of the lake where large tubs of hot, steaming water awaited them. They were stripped and scrubbed thoroughly by young women. When the women started to undress Auragole, he began to protest. If the fully covered ladies noticed his embarrassment, they said nothing, nor did they stop their activity. Donnadorr called to him cheerfully from his tub. "It's the custom, lad, do not offend. Water is a most precious commodity here. We are being given an honor. Enjoy it," and he grinned happily as two ladies scrubbed his now lean body.

Auragole smiled with effort and stopped his protests.

After they had been bathed, the men were given clean white robes. Later, when Sylvane and Glenelle returned from their baths, they were robed in brown. When they were all together again, they were led outside to dinner. Men and women sat cross-legged on the ground at long, separate tables.

Auragole, Donnadorr, and Glenorr were given places opposite And-ul-farr. Behind them were Glenelle and Sylvane, seated with the women. And-ul-farr, the chief, was flanked on either side by several men whom he introduced as his brothers. While they ate, there was total silence. At the beginning of the meal, And-ul-farr held up his dish of food and gave thanks to the Prince. Here is something familiar, Auragole thought, from story. These strange desert people worship the fabled Prince God.

The food was simple fare—flat breads, cheeses, curdled milk, and the tasty purple fruit they had seen growing on the trees. After the meal, when all was cleared away except the hot drink, And-ul-farr looked at Auragole. The look was neither friendly nor unfriendly. It was, Auragole imagined, correct as custom demanded.

"Speak," And-ul-farr said to Auragole, "now is the time."

Auragole swallowed hard. What was expected of him? Some words, obviously. So he thanked the chief for rescuing them and then for the courtesy bestowed on them in his tent city. Then he told their hosts that they were trying to make their way to Mattelmead.

There was just a hint of change in And-ul-farr's light eyes. "Of the king in Mattelmead we have heard strange tales," he finally said, and again that covering veil passed over his eyes.

Auragole waited, fearing to speak a word that might cause danger to his companions and to himself. Was And-ul-farr an enemy of Ormahn's?

The chief went on. "The ways of death it is said he will bring again with his probing into nature's ways."

"That's nonsense!" Glenorr broke in testily. "Progress is what. . ."

Auragole pinched him hard, hoping no one saw. Glenorr stopped speaking with a grunt.

The chief did not even glance at him.

Auragole went on quickly. "Many are leaving the Easternlands, for there is only war there, and in Mattelmead they are welcome."

And-ul-farr looked at Auragole gravely. It was a tense moment, utterly still. Even the mild breeze seemed to hover expectantly in the trees, quiet, lest it disturb.

"Unprepared have you come to cross Wildenfarr-low-desert. She would have claimed you. But I am lord here in the south. Wildenfarr is like a woman. One must serve her but also tame her. My mistress she is, but I am her master. I have bested her this time. Your lives were not forfeit, for I would not have it." And there was a shadow of a grin on his handsome face.

"Then we are grateful, indeed," Auragole said, and waited.

Again And-ul-farr spoke, "Strange artifacts I have seen in your belongings."

Auragole was puzzled, wondering what they carried that was unfamiliar to him. "Harps!" he suddenly answered.

There was no recognition in And-ul-farr's eyes.

"To play music," Auragole said.

"Ah!" The chief's face lit up, and then he waited expectantly.

"Would it offend if we played for you and your tribe as thanks for saving our lives and for your generous hospitality?"

This time And-ul-farr's smile was broad. "We cannot ask, but as you have offered out of your own desire, then yes, yes!"

A young boy was sent to fetch their harps. The pitchers and cups were hastily removed. Somehow word was carried swiftly through the village oasis, and Auragole was convinced that every inhabitant was soon gathered about them, including babies in their mothers' arms.

First, Donnadorr played melodies and Auragole harmonies. Then they sang songs about battles, about romance, about animals. They knew no desert songs. They must have played two hours and could think of little else to sing. But no one moved. It was dark. The cool night breezes had begun and still the people of the desert sat there waiting.

Auragole turned to Donnadorr, and said in a low voice, "They worship the Prince here. Do you remember the song you taught me about the Prince while we were in Agavia?"

Donnadorr nodded.

Auragole announced loudly to the waiting gathering. "For our final song, we will sing to you about the Prince God."

There were "ahs" and "oohs" of approval.

They sang then of the God known as the Prince—a many-versed song about his deeds when he walked the earth in human form. When they finished there was silence. But it was a charged silence, as if a storm was about to break forth. Something was wrong!

The chief stood up, followed by the entire tribe.

Auragole rose to his feet and beckoned his companions to rise also. He looked at And-ul-farr. And-ul-farr's light-blue eyes were as cold as the winter sky he had never seen.

"Heretics! You are heretics!"

"How have we offended?" Auragole asked in alarm.

"You sing of a Prince who has walked the earth when such tales are lies and deceits whispered to men by the great Illusorer!"

"It is only a song," Auragole said. His voice shook.

"Only a song! Falsely to sing of the Prince! Distort his Being do you, and perpetuate falsehoods! This tribe reveres the true Prince who dwells on the sun. His essence no God of goodness would soil in the corrupt body of a man. It is the task of a man to rise to the God, not the task of the God to descend to a man. Heresy you speak! Offend the God do you with your song."

There were murmurs of agreement. Auragole saw hands clasping swords and he was afraid.

"My lord," Donnadorr spoke up, "let me explain. . ."

"Silence!" And-ul-farr roared, and Donnadorr stopped mid-sentence. "Only one speaks here to me," and he turned again to Auragole.

It was up to him. What should he do? And-ul-farr was staring at him icily. Auragole saw death there. Because of their Gods men were ready to die or to kill. He didn't understand it. The desert brothers, their swords out, moved to flank their chief. What could he do?

He would tell them the truth.

Auragole began to speak. He spoke of the east and how in the battles that had lasted centuries, most of the Gods had been forgotten, how only fragments and stories remained. He spoke the truth as he understood it. He told them also of his own rearing, free of knowledge of the Gods.

And-ul-farr listened intently, as did all those who were near. At last Auragole stopped his narrative. He held his breath and waited.

"Strange has the world become," And-ul-farr said. "Blame be on the fathers and not on the children. I have saved you once from Wildenfarr. It was my choice and my choosing stands. She shall not have you. Tomorrow to the end of our territory we will take you. How Wildenfarr will treat you then is for her to decide and for others."

With a curt nod he turned and strode away. The brothers followed according to rank. The travelers were taken back to their tent.

"Well spoken, lad." Donnadorr cuffed Auragole's shoulder in affection.

"Well spoken, lad!" Glenorr mimicked Donnadorr's voice.

"Glen, quiet!" Glenelle said. How thin and strained Auragole thought she looked. "Once more Auragole has saved our lives. Have you no gratitude left?"

"Saved us for what?" He spat out the words. "And who risked our lives with their stupid songs?" He gestured at Donnadorr with the back of his hand. "Don here is like a fawning dog. I expect him at any moment to lick Aurie's feet."

Auragole saw the color rise in Donnadorr's cheeks. It was alarming, for Don was slow to anger, but when it came Auragole knew it would come like a howling tempest.

"Lad," Donnadorr said to Glenorr, almost under his breath, "I have heard you and listened to you and turned aside, lo, these many months. I am a peaceful man but no coward. For your sister's sake and the others I have held my tongue and my temper. But enough! You want to fight? I will fight you any way you want—fists, knives, swords. . ."

Instantly, Glenorr pulled out his knife and crouched low, stalking Donnadorr. Donnadorr pulled out his own knife and began to circle Glenorr.

"No!" Auragole growled, and leapt on Glenorr's back, knocking him to the ground. Glenorr's knife spun away and landed at Sylvane's feet. She grabbed it.

Glenelle rushed over to Donnadorr and threw herself into his arms. "Don, no, please, for my sake! Please!"

Donnadorr dropped the knife and held her, but he was trembling with anger.

"Hear me!" Auragole's voice was a harsh whisper. He was sitting astride Glenorr's back and holding his arms pinned behind him. "You jeopardize us all. Our lives will be worth nothing here amid these desert people if we quarrel amongst ourselves."

"We need each other more than ever!" Sylvane's words were intense. "Put off your anger if you cannot forget it. It serves no one. Let's pour our strength into getting to Mattelmead and not spend it fighting each other. Who else have we to rely on but each other?"

Finally Auragole let go of Glenorr and stood up. "Let's get some sleep—tomorrow we travel again."

THEY RODE ON horseback for nearly two days through the endless sameness of Wildenfarr. It was early June and the desert was hot, but they were dressed in the robes of the tribe, and it surprised Auragole how cool he felt inside them. Auragole loved that ride. To feel one's body move to the rhythm of the small, spotted desert horses was to feel at one with the wind and with time. When we walk, the earth seems to possess us, he thought. But on a horse we belong to the movement of air and light and weightlessness.

Two men accompanied them, guiding them steadily north-ward. It was near evening on the second day that they stopped.

"Farther we cannot go," the leader said.

Auragole looked around bewildered. There was nothing but sand.

"Are you going to leave us in this cursed desert to die?" Glenorr called to him, his tone irate. "Your chief promised us help."

The man pointed to a bright star easily seen in the twilight. "A few hours' walk toward that star and you will come to water and shelter. Farther we cannot go, for our territory ends here."

"It's a trick!" shouted Glenorr.

"Quiet!" Auragole told him angrily, but he too wondered if And-ul-farr had decided, after all, to turn them over to Wildenfarr.

The two guides stared at Glenorr in the veiled way of their tribe. Ignoring his outburst, the leader went on, "Your robes you must return, for dressed so you would not be welcome. You are now entering the land of Tul-farr and his tribe. He is heretic. His whole tribe is heretic and, therefore, our enemy for generations. Yet the same blood flows in our veins as in his, for back when the earth was kinder we were one people. Avoid we must meeting and confronting, for then blood will flow and it disturbs our ancestors."

"Does Tul-farr not believe in the Prince?" Sylvane asked.

"He believes," the leader said, "but his beliefs are false, for he believes the Prince walked the earth in the body of a man."

Silently, they changed back into their old, but washed and repaired, clothes. They were each given a packet of food, and their flasks were filled with water. They were instructed then to wait at the oasis for some of the tribe of Tul-farr to come, then to ask of them help in reaching the hills between the desert and Glovale. The travelers watched as the two men of And-ul-farr's tribe left, leading the horses the five had ridden. It was with a feeling of trepidation that Auragole and the others began their walk in the direction of the oasis on legs that after the ride on horseback felt heavy and reluctant.

N

chapter thirty-four

BY THE TIME they reached the oasis it was dark. Stars enveloped them, providing a cloak of comfort. Their nearness had intrigued Donnadorr since entering the desert. Sometimes, while walking, he tried to discern their patterns, but nothing up there made sense. Perhaps the stars were like life on the earth, no discernible pattern.

The oasis was small, a water hole only, a few patches of grass, and some trees. They approached it in silence, except Glenorr, who laughed as if the tribe of And-ul-farr had played a bad joke on them. The thought also occurred to Donnadorr. Wildenfarr was there, stretched out all around them like a patient woman. It amused him to think of the desert as And-ul-farr did. The desert was a beautiful, cruel, and capricious lady and she was playing with them. They could do nothing but wait.

That very night, half a dozen men in green robes woke them from their sleep.

"How come you here?" the leader asked. He stood tall in

front of them, young, pale-eyed, hair almost white, neither friendly nor unfriendly.

It was Auragole who rose to face him. Briefly he told him, first where they were headed, and then, without mentioning the Valley of the Agavi, how they had crossed the Gandlese, told him of the bands of thieves in the foothills, which had driven them farther south than they had planned on going, of their travels through the Deep Forest, and of meeting And-ul-farr in the desert.

"Fortune is indeed with you," the leader said, and gestured for all to sit, "if And-ul-farr did not kill you. His tribe is barbaric and clings to primitive beliefs."

One of his men lit a fire, and another prepared a kind of tea, which they were offered.

"We were treated well," Auragole answered with more veracity than Donnadorr thought was necessary.

The leader's eyes flickered with solemnity, and Donnadorr held his breath. But the man chose not to speak of And-ul-farr. He spoke instead of Ormahn and Mattelmead. "We follow with interest Ormahn's deeds and words. Should he acknowledge the Prince Who Walked, then we might consider an alliance."

He looked at Sylvane and Glenelle with veiled interest. "The fatigue of many weeks' march lies heavily on your women. Should you choose it, we will take you to our city for rest. Or if hurry you must, we shall escort you to the hills that lead to Glovale, five days' journey from here with two to a horse."

His kindness made Donnadorr light-headed. He saw his own relief mirrored in the faces of his companions.

"I am In-tul-farr, son of Tul-farr, chief of these lands," the leader went on, "and since you come in peace, seeking peace, we welcome you."

Auragole requested leave to speak in private to his companions to ascertain what their wishes might be. In-tul-farr nodded solemnly and withdrew with his men to tend the horses.

Though the thought of rest was tempting, the closeness of their destination was even more so. With this unexpected help they would soon be in Glovale. In a few weeks they could be at the borders of Mattelmead. The goal suddenly seemed attainable. Donnadorr hadn't felt so happy since he had left Agavia. With little need for discussion, all agreed to go on. Auragole told their decision to In-tul-farr, who nodded in understanding.

"Tomorrow we begin our journey. Slow we shall move for there will be two to a horse, but safely we shall bring you through our lands."

They rode with little difficulty for the next five days. Sometimes, as they were riding along, the men of Wildenfarr would suddenly break into a gallop, and cry out like flocks of birds calling—back and forth, back and forth—one group calling to the other. It was thrilling to be in the middle of that sound.

In the evenings, they learned much of the life of In-tul-farr and of his beliefs. Donnadorr and Auragole played for them on their harps and all the companions sang, even Glenorr. Though the desert men had never seen harps, they had their own instruments, delicately carved flutes, which they played for the travelers. To everyone's delight, the two groups were able to make music together—flutes, harps, voices. Song can soothe and bind, Donnadorr observed with satisfaction. The music must also have pleased Wildenfarr, for she did not hamper them on their journey.

One night, with the stars arched around them like a well-lit dome, Auragole asked In-tul-farr an odd question, but Donnadorr listened raptly for his answer, wondering a little at Auragole's boldness. Auragole wanted to know if In-tul-farr and his people believed in repeated earth lives as some who worshipped the Gods did. It was an Agavian belief, but nowhere else had Don heard it mentioned—except from Aiku.

He leaned closer to hear the desert-man's answer.

"It is heresy," In-tul-farr answered, but his tone was mild. "I have pondered the thought, and do not like it. Look out at this desert," he said, his arm making a sweeping gesture. "It is a land of rare loveliness, but not a place of ease in which to live, a burden to those who must do so. But accept do we this burden, for in accepting what has been given us, a place of beauty and fullness we are assured on the other side of death."

Auragole asked, "Why did your Prince come to walk the earth?"

"Our wise men tell us it was to share the burdens of humanity came he to our earth, to assure humans that here among the stars they are not alone, that understood they are, that loved they are. To the earth he came to teach us how to be one with the other, as was he with those who followed him all those ages ago—so story tells us." In-tul-farr was a thoughtful speaker and his companions listened reverently to his words.

"It is said," In-tul-farr went on, "before the centuries of death, books there were, perhaps written by the Prince even— but destroyed were they in the terrible catastrophes. Now we pass on what was known and remembered from father to son, mother to daughter. It is in Wildenfarr before she became barren, for so tell us our elders, that the Prince walked. Killed he was, though it is not remembered how, and after that Wildenfarr refused to bloom. It is her way of mourning, believe all our tribe, that which was so cruelly lost."

On the fourth day of their journey with In-tul-farr, the land began to change, gradually becoming undulating. The earth, though still dry, was firmer beneath the horses' feet. There were plants now, curious spiked things with thick, shiny leaves. And here and there were trees, unfamiliar to Donnadorr—stunted, ugly, but alive.

On their last night together, the two groups made camp near the first water they had seen since leaving the oasis. In-tul-farr told them, "A great distance this stream comes, from the tree-

and snow-covered hills overlooking Glovale. Follow you it, but keep you to its northern side. Into the hills will it lead you. Out of the Noonbarr River to the great sea southwest flows this stream. Northeast do you follow it, then you will be assured of water and fish. Six or seven days and to the Noonbarr you will come. Follow then the Noonbarr northwest two or three days. Down to Glovale will it guide you before again it returns to the hills."

The next day they parted company. In-tul-farr and his companions mounted their horses. "Perhaps we shall meet again should Ormahn prove true. With the blessing of the Prince Who Walked, go now, and seek your new destination."

The travelers thanked them for the help they had received, and then Donnadorr watched them go with regret, a graceful group of men and horses moving back into the fiery demands of Wildenfarr to assume their burdens for the sake of the far side of death.

The stream was shallow, in places a mere trickle. They walked right in it for part of that first day, exalting in the feel and smell and sound of that great giver of life. But after a while, the rocks and stones on the bed of the stream got the best of them, and they returned to its bank. It was not easy to follow in the coming days, for sometimes it cascaded over sheer cliffs. So now and then they turned aside to climb the hills on more hospitable paths. But always they returned to the stream and stayed as close as the way allowed.

Donnadorr told them jokes as they walked. They had heard them all before, but they laughed as if they were new. He did imitations of various people they had met, even of Lumoss, and they were able to laugh at it all.

Glenorr had lost the wild look that had been in his eyes since their encounter with Lumoss. He didn't speak much, but he chuckled at Donnadorr's imitations. Donnadorr noticed that the antipathies between him and Glenorr seemed to dissipate in the fresh, moist air and that they seemed gone between

Auragole and Glenorr, also. Well, he thought with goodwill, it had been a difficult journey. We've been tested severely, but look, we've come through.

The women, Donnadorr noted with satisfaction, were frail but in good spirits. Glenelle seemed her old self and bantered with Donnadorr, much to his delight. If Auragole felt jealousy, he hid it. He has learned to veil his expression, Donnadorr thought, almost as well as the men of Wildenfarr. What would be Auragole's decision, he wondered? Will he take Glenelle from him? Now is not the time to think about that, he told himself severely. When we are safely in Mattelmead, we shall have it out once and for all.

Sylvane, Donnadorr observed with affection, drew strength from Glenelle's recovery and from Glenorr's release from anger. As always, her joy came from those she loved. Why could not Auragole see her value? She is the right one for him. She will make him a fine wife. She's what he needs, not Glenelle.

Fortunately, the supplies In-tul-farr had provided them lasted until they were able to fish their stream, which had widened after a few days. Now the mountains they were crossing became thick with trees. Once again they were in hills, and though it was mid-June, there was frost on the ground in the morning.

A week after they had left In-tul-farr, they saw from a hilltop the widest river any of them had ever seen, obviously the Noonbarr, rushing all the way from the Gandlese to the Western Sea and cutting the Westernlands in half. It ran through a meandering valley that, according to In-tul-farr, would eventually open up into the broad farming land of Glovale.

That night, they camped in the hills about a mile from the river and sat together to discuss their next step. Auragole suggested that they move west parallel to the river and look for a way across. If they had no luck in a few days, they would build a raft—a somewhat shaky proposition, since the river was wide and rapid—and row themselves across.

It was just after noon the next day that they saw something that alarmed them. On the other side of the river, below them, was what looked like a soldiers' camp, and next to it a small settlement. There were boats in the river, but they too were on the other side of the river.

"It's not safe here," Auragole told them.

So they continued on in a westerly direction, all their senses keen. For a while the sounds from the camp accompanied them, echoing strangely through the hills. But to Donnadorr's relief they encountered no one. They saw a few scattered cottages, smoke coming from their chimneys almost invitingly, and the smell of cooking. They once encountered a dog so friendly that he followed them the rest of the day with no encouragement.

A day beyond the soldiers' camp brought them again into an area where there were no houses. They spotted a road along the river, but kept away from it.

For two days more they marched west, keeping the river to their right, a half mile to a mile distant. The next day, Auragole called a halt to their march. He pointed to where there was smoke rising along the river.

"It's likely another settlement," he said, and Donnadorr agreed.

They kept to the south side of the hills as they moved west and closer to the apparent village. Donnadorr was sure that there would be boats also in that village, but would they be able to steal one? How large was the village? Did it have soldiers? When they had come parallel to the village, Auragole took Donnadorr and went to scout it. Donnadorr carried his bow in readiness and Auragole his sword. Half an hour later, they were looking down on a small settlement of about a dozen cottages on this side of the river. There was little activity in the road below—some children playing, a boy pulling a cow along, but nothing else. There were, as they had hoped, small boats bobbing in the water. But how could they get hold of them?

Auragole motioned Donnadorr to follow him. Only a few miles farther west, around a bend in the river, they saw their way across. Tied to a small dock were two boats and a large raft. A man sat on the dock, dozing.

"It's a ferry," Donnadorr whispered to Auragole. Auragole looked puzzled, so Donnadorr explained. "The man's a ferryman and he'll take people across for a price. There might be another village across the river."

"I don't see one," Auragole answered in a low voice.

"No, but maybe there's a road leading to a town or village."

Auragole grinned at Donnadorr and they hurried back to the others to tell them what they had seen.

By the time the sun was setting, the entire group was overlooking the dock and boats. Before they could descend, the ferryman got up, dusted off his cloak, put something into his pocket, picked up a pack, shouldered it, and headed toward the village.

"What do we do now, Aurie?" Glenelle asked.

Auragole hesitated, though the answer seemed obvious to Donnadorr. They take the boat and cross under cover of darkness.

"We can leave a jewel, Aurie," Sylvane said, and Donnadorr knew she sensed some concern in Auragole for a boat taken from a man who earned his keep by it. Auragole does not know the ways of people, Donnadorr sighed inwardly, and was about to insist that they be wise and self-concerned. But Auragole abruptly agreed and they headed cautiously down the slope to the deserted dock.

There was a large raft—good for ferrying livestock—and two sturdy rowboats, one large enough for them all, but not for their belongings. Auragole decided to put their packs and their weapons into the small boat and tie it to the stern of the larger one. Donnadorr insisted he carry his harp with him. "I'd lose anything but this, dear lad." Auragole shrugged. When everything was ready, Sylvane carefully wrapped a small jewel in a handkerchief and tied it to a post.

The sun had set by the time they pushed off and there were many gray clouds gathering, which made Donnadorr uneasy. They would have to hurry. The girls sat together in the bow. Glenorr and Donnadorr sat in the middle in order to row, and Auragole sat in the stern directing the rowing from there. He gave the count as Glenorr and Donnadorr rowed hard. They were only three-quarters of the way across when it became dark.

Suddenly there was a snapping, banging noise. It startled them.

"What's that, lad?" Donnadorr called to Auragole.

"It's the boat with our belongings. It's broken away. I'll get it." And removing his boots, Auragole dove into the black water.

"Wait, Aurie," Donnadorr called. "Don't be a fool."

Glenelle screamed, "Auragole, don't leave us!"

"Don't worry," a voice called out in the night. "I'm safe. I've found the boat, and I'm in it. There's a small paddle here. I'll meet you on shore."

It was pitch black now, all stars hidden by shapeless dark clouds. The shore they were paddling toward was only a darker line in the blackness about them. Donnadorr kept looking back over his shoulder to keep the boat going in the right direction. Auragole called to his friends frequently and they answered, but from the sound of his voice the distance between them was increasing. Auragole had, after all, only the one paddle. And Glenorr and Donnadorr were rowing together.

Fifty feet or so from their goal, they encountered a strong current. Donnadorr called out to Auragole to warn him.

"I hear you." Auragole's voice was a long way off.

Donnadorr and Glenorr were able to hold their own against the current. They maneuvered their boat to the pilings of the old wooden dock they had seen from across the river. They climbed up the few stairs to the dock surface, pulled in their boat, and tied it to a post. The women climbed out and followed them up the steps.

It was then that Don heard it, the sounds of horses' hooves in the trees only yards from the shore.

"Who's there?" he called out. "Who are you? Grab your weapons. We've got visitors, friends. Swords!" he groaned. Their weapons were in the other boat. "Auragole, beware!" he shouted into the night. Then something pierced his leg. A woman screamed. "Oh Gods, they've killed Glenelle," his voice rang out across the water, then a blow caught him on the back of his head. Oh, my poor Ellie, he thought.

And then he thought no more.

DONNADORR HOLLERED, "AURAGOLE, beware!"

"What?" Auragole called out in panic.

Then a woman shrieked in pain. Or was it a death cry? It sounded like Glenelle. "Oh Gods, they've killed Glenelle!" That too came from Donnadorr.

From the small boat with all their supplies, Auragole shouted into the night, "No!"—one loud, panicky denial. He tried to see over his shoulder, but the darkness mocked his effort. He could hear the sounds of scuffling, of battle. He could hear guttural shouts, and the anxious neighing of horses.

Sylvane called out, desperately, "Aurie, turn back, turn. . ." then silence.

Auragole, filled with both fear and frustration, doubled his effort to get to the shore with his tiny paddle when suddenly it was ripped out of his hands by the powerful current Don had warned him about. The boat spun quickly around, then tore downstream away from the beach where Auragole's friends were fighting some unknown enemy. He grabbed hold of his seat while he urgently tried to find something he could use for a paddle, and decided his sword would have to do. He slid off his seat in the careening boat to search for it, but was violently thrown back. He hit his head on the hard wooden seat and blacked out.

N

chapter thirty-five

SOMETHING HARD WAS under his cheek, making him uncomfortable. Auragole raised his head. It was throbbing. He touched his face. His cheeks were bloody. He tried to sit up. His back, his arms, his legs, all ached. He attempted to stand but was too dizzy. He ran his hands over his body, probing it tentatively with numb fingers. Nothing seemed broken, but he was cold and shaking. His clothes were wet beneath his drenched cloak.

He moved his head slowly, trying to focus his eyes on the surroundings. Auragole was on a beach of stones. A few yards from him, half in the water, half out, the boat he had been in lay broken. Most of its contents were strewn over the rocky shore.

His harp! What had happened to his precious harp? Auragole looked desperately around until he located it. It lay on the unyielding stones still wrapped in his blanket. He crawled toward it and with shaking hands unwrapped it. It was whole and dry. He held the harp close to his chest and rocked back and forth with relief.

Then, as if a cold wind had swept away the dullness from his mind, he remembered that his friends had been under attack on a beach upstream. And he remembered the horrible death cry he had heard.

"Oh, my stars!" he cried out in a hoarse whisper. "Ellie! But she can't be dead!" He pulled off his dripping cloak, slung the harp on his back, and stood up. Too quickly. Dizziness and darkness almost overcame him. As he sank to his knees, he began to breathe rhythmically, intent on staying conscious. Then he stood up again. Through sheer will Auragole remained on his feet. He fought to bring his breathing to normal, counting one, two, three, one, two, three, over and over again until the faintness retreated. Auragole was feverish and shaking. He was freezing, never mind that it was late June. He was wet and had lain exposed to the cold mountain air all night.

He looked around until he found his pack. It was dry. With effort he changed into his other trousers, removed his wet socks, put on a clean pair and then his old boots. He put on a dry shirt and started on his way. How far downstream had he been carried? But the thoughts in his head seemed buried in thick, suffocating wool. He looked at the sun, now halfway up the eastern sky. Had he been unconscious all night and also half the morning? He had to find his friends, so he started walking along the shoreline. He hadn't gone more than a few yards when he nearly fell over his sword. That, like his harp, had been a gift from the Agavians. He picked it up, still in its beautiful sheath, strapped it on, then proceeded step by torturous step.

If Ellie was dead, he vowed to kill whoever was responsible. No, she couldn't be dead. No, no, no, his mind repeated. Wave after wave of alarm rolled over him even as the river sloshed over the wet, slippery stones and slapped against his boots. His legs and arms felt as if they might fly away at any moment, so foreign did they seem, so out of his control. Time and again, he fell—hard—bruising his already bruised body. But grim determination drove him toward his destination.

After an hour, he came to the dock where his companions had come ashore. The boat was still there, but not his friends, nor those who had attacked them. Auragole looked across at the pier from which they had departed. The ferryman was not there. Why, he wondered.

Then he saw it.

Lying near the edge of the dock was a crumpled blue cloak. It was Glenelle's. There was a pool of blood near it, drying brown in the sun.

"Oh, no, please, no," he moaned. Auragole knelt down on the ground and gathered up the cloak into his arms. He buried his hot face in its folds, still redolent of Glenelle's scent. "Oh, please, please, not Glenelle, not Glenelle!" he whispered. A hopeless rage rose up in him. It was unlike anything he had ever experienced before. But if she was dead, where was her body? Had they taken that too? Or thrown it in the water? For a moment he thought of diving into the river to look for her, but he remembered the swiftness of the current. He stood up and gazed about him. The grass beyond the small wooden dock had been trampled by horses and boots. Soldiers or thieves must have been waiting for them in the orchard that stood fifty feet away, no doubt watching as they had set off from the far shore. They had been too eager to get across the Noonbarr, and therefore reckless. Auragole should have known better, should have been aware of possible danger on this side of the river. He was the leader. Why had he been so careless?

Stumbling toward the orchard, he called out, "Ellie! Glen! Sylvie! Don!" Over and over he shouted their names. He came upon a footpath and followed it through old, gnarled apple trees, refusing to believe his companions were gone. On the other side of the orchard, there were roads running in three directions, east, west, and north. Of course! That was why the ferry came to this dock. He should have known! He was leader and he should have known.

Which way had his friends been taken? There were fresh footprints and hoof marks on all of the roads. He searched each road for some small sign. But found nothing. In which direction should he go to rescue them?

Auragole stood there, cold, sweating, and indecisive, unable to move, hugging Ellie's cloak to his breast.

"Earth and metal! How weak you are!"

Startled, Auragole whirled about, but he didn't see anyone on any of the roads.

"The one you love is dead—the woman Glenelle. And you are to blame," the voice taunted him. "Only she wasn't so loving toward you, was she? It was Donnadorr she loved."

The voice was coming from the orchard. Auragole ran back into the apple trees, but could find no one, could see nothing.

"In all your life, you've had one task to fulfill and you failed miserably. Failed, failed."

"Where have they taken them?" Auragole called to the branches.

The voice rippled through the sparse grass. "Why should I care? Why would I tell you?" It was coming nearer. "What would you do, try to rescue them and botch that up and lose more lives?"

The accusation was a wasp's sting.

Wait! There was someone moving in the shadows of the trees, a tall man enshrouded in a cloak as dark as a bat on a moonless night.

"I beg you, tell me where they took my friends." Auragole ran toward the man, but suddenly the man wasn't there.

"Why should I tell you?" The voice was behind him now.

Auragole whirled about and his breath exploded out of him. Facing him, only a few feet away now, was a man with features so distorted, so mangled and twisted, he seemed barely human. He looked like a creation spawned of destruction and madness.

The eyes, black and sunken, were like small mouths chewing up the light. The nose was long and sharp, a knife blade that injured the onlooker. The face, whose right side didn't match its left, was thin and angular—a face as white and as dead-looking as the barren hills overlooking Wildenfarr-low-desert. This creature, this man, was a distortion of everything human. He stood only a few feet away from Auragole, leering at him. Fear froze Auragole's limbs.

It spoke. "Why are you alive? It would have been better if Goloss had thrown you into the river the day you were born. But Goloss was a fool with his idea of freedom."

At the mention of his father, Auragole was suddenly galvanized into action. He moved toward the man threateningly. "Don't speak my father's name!" Auragole grabbed his sword but couldn't pull it out of its scabbard. He yanked and yanked but it stayed stuck.

The man laughed an ugly, grating laugh. "You ignorant, ridiculous boy! You can't destroy me!" His eyes shone now like wet stone.

Auragole leapt at him, his hands going for the man's throat, but a blow he hadn't seen coming sent him spinning back against a large tree.

"Fool! You can't touch me!" The man spat the words out. "What would Goloss think of his son now? His free child. What good is he? Can he think? Not too clearly. Can he feel? So many emotions war in him that they incapacitate him. Can he do anything? Sometimes—but when he acts, it is blindly and foolishly."

Again Auragole ran at him and again he was struck before he himself could land a blow—this time so hard that he crumpled, panting, to the ground.

"You are a useless man in a meaningless world. To want anything is foolish. To want for yourself, more foolishness, but to want for others, the greatest foolishness of all. You should have stayed on your farm in your valley, tilling the soil and living like a dumb animal among the other dumb animals."

"Go away!" Auragole's voice cracked with the strain of his cry.

"Never!" the man sneered.

Auragole raised himself unsteadily to his feet. He picked up Ellie's cloak and moved away—stumbling, falling, standing again, finally staggering out of the orchard, where he collapsed near the river. He peered across the water for the ferryman. Maybe he would help him. But still he had not come. Auragole held Ellie's cloak next to his face, felt the dried blood, dropped the cloak, then picked it up, examined it carefully, and saw the rip, saw the large brown stain around it. His stomach turned over and he was sick. He heaved until there was nothing left inside but gall. He lay then on the grass, trying to breathe deeply.

But grief was a whirlwind around him. He felt light and brittle, a dry autumn leaf, tossed, tumbled, dropped by an unconcerned wind. Here was a new kind of sorrow—a sorrow of dreams dashed and broken into a thousand cutting pieces. He had found friends, but had lost them. He had loved and his love had been taken from him, killed before that love could be consummated. And there was no one left with whom he could grieve. He was alone. Again alone. If his heart hurt any harder, it would burst. Friends and the beloved, all gone, swallowed up by this vast and intolerable Westernlands. The floodgates of his soul opened and he wept for the first time since leaving Agavia—great convulsive sobs—until he was too empty to weep more.

"Goloss was right," a voice said.

Auragole looked up. The grotesque old man was sitting on the ground a few yards from him.

"There's no such thing as love, never has been and never will be. What nonsense! If Glenelle had not been so fair to look on, would you have loved her? You should have heeded your father. He tried to warn you."

"Please go away," Auragole said. And when he looked up the man was gone. Auragole lay back on the grass, exhausted, and thought about his father, and his mother, and Spehn—all dead now. The memory of their loss mingled with Auragole's feeling of loss for Glenelle, for all of his friends. And he wept again, bitterly, then drifted into a shallow, agitated sleep.

He was awakened by the cool wind whipping across his face. At first he couldn't remember where he was, then he felt Ellie's cloak around him and a spasm of pain surged through his body. He had a fever that left him hot and cold in turn. He was now too spent for tears, too tired to think, too grieved to look for shelter. His body ached, but he didn't know whether it was from the ugly man's blows or from the boat wreck or from the fever. The man! Where was he?

Auragole looked around and saw the river drifting along quietly, doing what it always did, unconcerned with losses or love. He turned to look at the orchard, but there was no one there. He was alone. And for the first time there was a quality about it that he could not name. He had been raised with only a few others, had played alone, had roamed the woods and mountains around his home alone. But this. . .this was something he couldn't fathom. It was as if each loss left him less himself. And there had been so many losses. Everyone whom he had loved was gone. Who was he without others? And where was he? Hundreds of miles from Mattelmead, hundreds of miles from the Valley of the Agavi, hundreds of miles from home.

He walked back through the orchard to the three roads just as a light rain came down. Willing himself to search carefully, he moved down one road after another, hoping for some small clue that would show him in which direction his friends had been taken. But nothing. The rain continued until even the hoofprints were gone. Finally he gave up. He was tired from fever and tired from grief.

Auragole staggered out of the trees and stood gazing at the

Noonbarr River. And across it. Still no ferryman. What should he do? Where should he go? Where had they taken his friends? The emptiness he felt could have encompassed all of Wildenfarr. He couldn't make the idea of going on grow in his thoughts. But staying in this place was intolerable. He wanted to obliterate all feelings, all thoughts, all memory.

"Death is the only way," a voice behind him said.

Auragole didn't even turn to look at him.

"You will never be free from pain and suffering on this earth. You dream of something called peace, but peace doesn't exist. It is a meaningless dream. Ultimately a foolishness. All of life is a pursuit after meaningless dreams. Give up. End it all. Now. Stop the pain. Stop the absurdity."

"Go away." Auragole carefully folded Ellie's cape, took up his sword, and began to walk downriver.

"Free yourself. Walk into the river and end it all."

"I'm hungry," was his answer.

When Auragole came to where his boat had been washed ashore, he methodically gathered all their possessions together and piled them against a large rock away from the river. He sat down then and ate some of the food that had escaped the water. He had little appetite, but knew that he would become sicker if he didn't try to get some sustenance into his battered and feverish body. How long had it been since he had last eaten?

Finally, he slept.

The moment he awoke the grief slammed into him. He could take hold of nothing inside himself to keep it at bay. It came from everywhere, from the howling wind, from the cold stones, from the hurrying river. Even the warmth of the sun seemed like sorrow. The earth is conceived in pain, he thought, brings to birth its mantle of green in consummate suffering. He could not stop the misery and he was too ill to run from it.

For many days he slept in a fever and woke into grief, struggled, gave up the useless tears, ate, and little by little his body began to heal. But not his heart. Often the old man would come to talk to him about death. Then Auragole became afraid, because he felt tempted to close his eyes for the last time.

"From the moment you are born you have death in you," the man told Auragole that last night. "You want to find meaning and purpose so as to deny death. You want the Gods to exist so as to deny death. But all that is in you and all that is around you are death and its forces. And in the end, death wins. You become his, as the earth is his."

With every bit of strength left in him Auragole shouted, "Go away!" and the man disappeared, melting into the darkness.

That night from out of his dreams, Auragole heard, "You must leave this place, Auragole of the Mountains."

"No, no, I can't die. The Beautiful One will send me back." Auragole's own words woke him with a start. "You must leave this place," he told himself, and he staggered to his feet in a fog of pain. But where would he go? Where?

And then he knew. He would search all of the Westernlands for his lost companions. That would be his task now. What else was there?

"I'm going to find my friends," he announced in a loud voice to the man who was no longer there. "That is my reason for living."

Then, with great effort of will, Auragole began to pack his things.